Darkness for a time, and then:

Alive! Joy in the morning dew!

Table of Contents

+++

+++

Corvette Nightfire

Daniel Wetta

with

Robert Selfe

Published by Daniel Wetta Publishing

Second Edition

Please visit author website and blog at
http://www.danielwetta.com

Prologue

Rogelio Nightfire
Just Outside Bridgetown, Barbados

Rogelio wondered exactly how they were going to kill him. He had received a five-minute warning from a poker friend by pure chance. The phone call in the house hadn't awakened Madeline or his son. He had happened to be in the kitchen when the wall-phone rang. He got the news, didn't ask questions, and ran to the bedroom trying to be light on his feet and quiet. It took him forty-five seconds to do this and slip on the pants that he had left on the floor. His wallet and keys were in the pockets because he had simply dropped his pants earlier, playing with Madeline, who was teasing him from the bed. She had fallen asleep after their sex. Rogelio, as usual, lying beside his wife, had fallen into his recurring post-midnight state of anxiety and hunger. So he had gotten out of the bed to go to the kitchen to make a sandwich. Then the phone had rung.

He had always heard that your life passes before you in the instant before death, and he thought that he had about ten minutes before they would catch up with him. He wanted to spend this time reviewing where he had been, what he had done, and whom he had loved.

That should be ample time, he thought, *but, then again, I'm speeding on a motorcycle in the middle of the night on this goddamn island road to keep killers away from my family sleeping at the house. Yeah, a little distracting. I have to focus.*

Over the course of a lifetime, "whom he had loved" boiled down to a handful of people: the old Texas rancher couple who had raised him when his parents got deported to Mexico (never to be known again); a few friends through the years (all living back in San Antonio); Madeline, his long-legged wife whom he had worshiped since their first dance on the cruise ship; and Corvette.

1

Always Corvette.

Since the moment of his son's birth when the kid had snatched his heart and had made it his own, Rogelio lived for him. Rogelio could talk Madeline into anything when it came to giving to Corvette. Even more than Madeline, Rogelio liked the child to be dressed in style. That is to say, he shopped for his clothes to give the boy the flair of the father: little caps, ties, striped shirts and knee shorts, and wool scarves. To go with the clothes, Corvette had the smile and winning mannerisms all his own. He grew up tall like his British mum and Latino-looking like his Mexican padre. There were two things the boy could do:

He could dance.

That was a genetic no-brainer. Madeline and Rogelio stopped the show when they got on the dance floor, so smooth-stepping and rhythm came naturally to Corvette. In addition, Mum kept him in dance lessons until he was seventeen.

And he was one hell of a poker player.

God, forgive me. I did that to him, Rogelio thought, *in the backrooms of Texas and Barbados. Those led to my downfall. Corvette, though...he's just an eighteen-year-old kid, but Dios, what a head he has for probabilities! I'm sorry, Lord. It's just that he's always dying to play, and he can seduce anyone at the table into thinking what he wants them to think. Even I can never resist him! The thing is, he adores me. I know this. He thinks I'm something I'm not.*

Rogelio came up suddenly on a curve and downshifted two gears with his foot as he braked. Just before he rounded the bend, his side mirror caught the flash of headlights behind him. He gunned the throttle, and his engine thundered coming out of the curve. No one would be on this road at three a.m. unless he was there for him. He was ninety-eight percent certain that he knew who it was behind him. Probabilities again. A lifetime of those! These calculations told him that his pursuers were employees of El Gato, the capo in the Cartel of Sinaloa. Like Rogelio, they were a long way from Mexico. The cartel had global reach.

2

Well, I'll give them a run for the money.

The irony of that expression made him chuckle.

He had many regrets, but what now surfaced from a hurting place in his heart surprised him: He should have learned Spanish. He should have taught it to Corvette. That would have helped his son confront what certainly would come to his life: the necessity of reconciling the sins of the father and probably those of the grandfather. That wouldn't be possible unless Corvette knew who he was. Corvette would discover that the key to his redemption lay hidden in the canyons of Chihuahau. Somewhere in those places were either the footprints or the graves of Rogelio's parents. Corvette's grandparents.

Rogelio had failed to find them, and now he had run out of time.

The headlights behind him separated in his mirror, and he saw that these weren't from a car at all, but from motorcycles. Suddenly he understood how he was going to die.

He made a deal with God:

Give me eternity, Lord, in some limbo or some barren plot of heaven. Just not hell. I want to watch after my boy. I want to love him forever. I want to scream his name through the impossibilities of his hearing me from the faraway place that you put me. I want him to know that I'm always close. For this favor, I'll accept an infinity of penance for the wrongs I've committed. I'll guide him to you.

In the blinding flashes of light, Rogelio couldn't see. He wasn't sure what he had hit, but his last sensation was one of flight.

Chapter 1: Dangerous Impulses

Corvette Nightfire, Nine Years Later
Las Vegas, Nevada
Saturday Morning

Plodding weekend sheep, Corvette sighed impatiently.

Being stuck in the middle of them meant that he had to baby-step the inclined walkway to the casino entrance. The desert heat already was sucking the sweat from his skin into the stratosphere, making him feel salty and baked. The unusual October heat was why the people ahead of him were ambling listlessly.

Unbelievable, he thought petulantly, *it's only eight in the morning and these people aren't going to make it to the doors!* He could just see the headline: "Seventy-two Saturday Gamblers Succumb to Heat." Sub-headline: "Group Did Not Take Casino Transit." The story would then report that the tall lone survivor, Corvette Nightfire, stepped over the bodies and made it to the air-conditioned sanctity of the casino thanks to the undiminished adrenaline of the previous night's poker win.

He was anxious to get inside to play. He still felt happy. He noticed that he was bobbing up and down as he walked, which is what he always did when he was happy. He said his prayer to his father, St. Rogelio:

Gracias, Rogelio, for giving me my charmed life. I'll never take for granted my looks, my dancing, or the luck that snatches me again and again from the clutches of bankruptcy. I owe these things to your genetics and to your cleverness in naming me Corvette. He chuckled to himself.

Seventeen thousand dollars won the previous evening had put the bounce into his step. He had cashed in around midnight, had rushed the money to the safe in his hotel room, and then had strode joyfully along The Strip to his favorite club for dancing. It was at the top of the Magnifico, the newest mega-tower resort on Las Vegas Boulevard. He liked this club because on certain nights it hosted evenings of ballroom dancing with bands that favored Latin rhythms. Two nights previously there, he had invited to dance the most beautiful young woman he had seen in his life. She was Mexican and told him that she didn't speak English, but her smile said, "Sí, let's Merengue!" She wore a sleeveless light-blue floral dress that clung to her energetic bosom and revealed the dangerous curves of her body with every swing of her hips. Corvette envied that dress for its light landings on her skin when she moved: airy kisses of fabric that he wished were the brushes of his lips on her body. Perhaps it was the flush of her skin from dancing that brought the flowers of her dress to life. They looked like new blooms gliding on breezy satin. In her midnight-black pinned-up hair she wore a blue rose that matched the color of her dress and shoes. They danced lambadas and merengues and even managed a couple of tangos together reasonably well. Corvette was enthralled. He asked her name in English. She understood his question and told him that her name was Valentina.

Corvette didn't speak Spanish. He knew a few words and phrases because of his Mexican father, but at the time the only language that mattered to him from the girl was that of her smile. Hers expressed that she wanted to dance just with him that evening. His heart felt electrified and tender. They enjoyed every dance, but, to Corvette, the most thrilling were the slow ones. He held Valentina tighter in each successive dance, never wanting her to go; but, alas, the night ended when an older, powerfully-built man appeared in the club to take her home. With some sort of Spanish apology, Valentina took her leave from Corvette before he thought to ask how to see her again.

He hadn't been able to forget her. The next night Corvette had returned to the club in the hope that she might be there. His luck had been so good for two days that he was certain he would arrive to find the señorita awaiting him.

What a disappointment to find that Valentina wasn't there! But several women were eager to dance with him. He had energy to spend, and, hoping that the young woman might arrive, he danced while he waited. Valentina never came. Corvette spent his evening dancing with women who didn't move his heart. He said goodbye to the last one when an ellipse of rose-colored light heralded the coming dawn in the indigo eastern sky. He could see the woman's disappointment that he wasn't leaving with her.

Corvette still felt the vestiges of adrenalin inside him from his poker victory. It wasn't so much the amount of money that he had won, which was small by his experience, but the fact that his win had graced him when he was in a long slump and nearly broke. He needed confidence to play in some high-dollar games before the World Series of Poker coming the following week. Several months earlier, he had qualified for the Final Table at The Rio the following Monday. Each day as the tournament grew closer, Corvette's nervous energy wouldn't give him peace. He could have danced longer this evening, but the band began packing up. His stomach started to growl an insistence that he find steak and eggs and coffee. He ate a long, happy breakfast alone. He played a few slots in a couple of casinos. Finally, feeling like he had an hour of play left in him before he would crash onto his bed, he headed toward The Oasis Hotel and Casino. He liked the greenery and the artificial mist sprayed in the casino, and he thought that environment would calm him before an enjoyable day's nap in his hotel. He was due in the evening at the MGM Grand for a game with a few poker celebrities arriving in town a week early to watch the World Series of Poker.

This is how it came to be that he was amid the congregation of tourist sheep heading to the entrance doors of The Oasis. Because he was bobbing as he walked, he assumed that was why he saw shifting reflections of light and shadow on the glass doors of the casino entrance. He was still thinking about the tribute which he had just paid his father in the form of that tongue-in-cheek prayer. Corvette realized that he always thought about Rogelio whenever he was manic from the wins of his poker tours.

His father had been a Mexican child born in the United States of illegal immigrants. Inexplicably, the last name of Corvette's grandparents was Fuego de Noche. To Corvette, it didn't sound like a natural name in Mexico, but it was the name his biological grandparents had used when they lived in the United States before he was born. When he asked his father about them, Rogelio became vague and said he was uncertain about the exact circumstances of his parents' deportation to Mexico when Rogelio was two years old. For reasons not explained, they left Rogelio behind in the hands of a Texas rancher couple who took responsibility for raising him. They were well into their fifties, Rogelio had told Corvette, and they only said that they offered to raise Rogelio because they cared about him and didn't think that his parents would ever return. The ranchers didn't speak Spanish, so Rogelio grew up knowing only English and some limited Spanish from amigos in Texas.

The couple never adopted Rogelio, which Corvette always thought was odd, and Rogelio never spoke much about them. When he was thirty-one, Rogelio anglicized his name to the translation of Fuego de Noche: Nightfire. Madeline and Corvette's names were changed legally as well.

Such a cool-ass name, Corvette thought. *Dad used to love Corvettes so much that he insisted I would be named Corvette. He certainly must have known that he was giving me the greatest name anyone could have in this American life: Corvette Nightfire! Gracias, St. Rogelio!*

Later, when he thought back on what was about to happen that morning at The Oasis, Corvette realized how perfect it was that he would be thinking about his father just when the commotion began that would change his life. Since his father died, whenever major events interrupted Corvette's life, Rogelio, his proud and loving father, stayed glued to Corvette's side like a protector angel. Corvette believed this fervently.

It began when Corvette noticed that a couple of the glass doors of the casino entrance were jerking because of something happening on the other side. The partial openings and closings of the doors were causing light reflections to play on the glass. The first people to arrive at the doors when the tumult began halted their approach. They froze like confused deer sensing danger, but a few began to shout warnings to people around them. They began backing away, bumping into others who were still advancing toward the casino.

A chubby, middle-aged man wearing yellow shorts, pink polo shorts, and flip-flops was the first to see what was happening inside the doors. He shouted, "Guys have guns in there!" He accelerated his retreat.

Then a college-aged kid yelled, "There's a mother-fucker of a fight inside!"

Now the people coming up the sidewalk began bunching with the ones retreating from the doors. The reaction time of the latter group had been slow. It was as if the craziness of Las Vegas had suspended everyone's common sense so that it took longer to discern anything unusual, like danger. Some of them were still boozy from a night that didn't end when the sun rudely arose and stoked their headaches. The crowd was beginning to form a pool of awakening panic.

By then Corvette also had approached closer to the commotion. He had a strange thought at that moment: *I always think that life is good. I never expect bad things to happen.*

Suddenly, popping sounds of gunfire inside the casino set off an eruption of screaming. Corvette's instinct was to run and crouch in the lush shrubbery lining the walkway to the casino. Others panicked and ran to get as far away as possible. Some hid behind cars. Corvette was tall and didn't want to be a target, but he did want to know what was happening. He squatted low behind the bushes. He could hear sirens in the distance. He wondered if Oasis security had alerted the police. He stared intently at the two middle doors of the entrance and could make out a tangle of frantically fighting people. It looked like a to-the-death brawl even after the gunfire stopped.

His attention got commandeered by a slender young Hispanic woman emerging from the entrance door. She paused, glancing around frantically. Suddenly, the door behind her opened and struck her back. She spun around. Someone on the floor inside pushed a green canvas duffle bag through the door. Corvette saw the girl hesitate, but then she reached down, felt the bag, and picked it up cautiously. It was obviously heavy. She heaved the bag in front of her. She quickly surveyed the loading area and the driveway to Las Vegas Boulevard. To Corvette, it appeared as if the girl were expecting someone. He watched as she darted her eyes from person to person around her. She checked out the cars and taxis. Her eyes started turning in Corvette's direction. They met Corvette's for a split instant and then moved on, looking beyond him. Suddenly she straightened, and her eyes rapidly returned to him. She focused her gaze. Corvette was surprised, because the look on her face clearly was one of recognition.

She lifted the bag and held it in front of her. As she came toward him, the weight of the bag shifting from side to side gave her a bit of zig-zag. Yet the sense of purpose in her approach made Corvette stand to await her. Clearly she thought that she knew him, and he wondered why.

Maybe she's seen me in the poker circuit, he considered.

He had acquired some minor celebrity status in Las Vegas. He thought that perhaps she was one of the groupies who hung around the tournaments and had tried to engage him in conversation. He couldn't figure out any other reason why she was singling him out at this moment. Perhaps he knew her too. He strained to recall.

The girl had both hands gripping the handles as she struggled with the bag. She was wearing white sneakers and blue shorts. Her white cotton blouse had just enough transparency to reveal that her body was light brown and sensuous. When she got close enough, Corvette saw that she was wearing little make-up, but the thickness of her long eyelashes darkened the pool of her deep-brown eyes. Her beauty was natural and didn't need the assistance of paint. He might have loved to stare into her eyes, except that, strangely, the girl's arms suddenly grabbed Corvette's attention. They looked familiar.

Although she was lithe, her toned arms looked as if she exercised with weights. There was something about her sun-bronzed skin and her lovely arms that convinced Corvette that he had met her before. But when the girl arrived in front of him, she startled him from his thoughts by grabbing his left arm and thrusting the suede leather grips of the bag into his hand. Her left hand was holding a flat car-key fob. She seized Corvette's right hand and jammed this into his palm and enclosed his fingers around it.

She stooped to meet his gaze, because now he was looking down at his hands. She urged him something in Spanish. What Corvette heard was "Booska el ow-toe! Koray!" What the girl actually shouted in Spanish was, "Busca el auto! Corre!" She gave him a firm push as if to tell him to get going. Then she ran.

Corvette's astonishment immobilized him. He watched as the girl bounded down the casino driveway to the street like an antelope. Without realizing that he was doing it, he slipped the car-key fob into his cream-colored linen pants pocket and lifted the bag. People were running helter-skelter, but the girl leaped through them with the grace of a ballet dancer.

Maybe she's a show girl? he wondered. He saw her hesitate when she arrived at the street curb and looked both ways. Then a few seconds later, a midnight-blue Lexus sedan with darkened windows suddenly jumped lanes and screeched in front of her. The driver apparently leaned across the seats and opened the passenger door. The girl peered inside a moment and then jumped into the front seat. By this time, the police sirens had become much louder, sounding perhaps a couple of blocks away. The Lexus took off heading south on The Strip.

The sirens and the girl's disappearance jolted Corvette. He had to make an instant decision. The girl's shout of "Koray!" and her subsequent sprint pulled a Spanish word into his mind that he did know: *Corre!* It meant, "Run!"

He became aware of the heaviness of the bag. He set it down and felt the contents through the canvas.

Like paper bricks, he thought.

The impression on his fingers gave him a hunch that made his heart race. If he were correct, he didn't want to open the bag in front of people. He didn't want anyone to see the contents. He knew two things for sure: He wanted to keep this bag, and he needed to get the hell out of there.

He lost his opportunity to run because suddenly four city police cars wheeled sharply into the driveway and sped toward the casino entrance. He didn't want to attract attention. People began shouting warnings to the police about the gunfire that had occurred. The police cars maneuvered around parked and suddenly abandoned vehicles that littered the driveway to the entrance.

They aren't interested in me right now, Corvette noted. He picked up the bag and tried to affect a natural walk toward Las Vegas Boulevard. It was difficult. *This thing has to weigh at least forty pounds,* he thought.

His hotel was next door, but that was a bit of a hike. There was a parking deck in between the two, so he had to cover a length close to three or four city blocks. He planned to punch up his pace to a near run as soon as he put himself a little distance from the police and the commotion behind him. He carried the bag in front, near his waist, so that no one from behind might see it. Its weight put a little burn in his shoulders and forearms after a few moments of carrying.

When he heard the opening of the police car doors, he risked a glance back. He saw the policemen emerging in a rush with guns drawn.

But something else drew his attention. In the same doorway from which the girl had exited stood a tall Hispanic man dressed in black shoes, pants, and shirt. Even in the distance Corvette could make out the young man's lean athletic build and the intensity of his stare. He cut an impressive appearance. He appeared to be in his mid-to-late twenties. The young man was so focused on Corvette that he didn't notice the policeman rushing him. The cop pushed him back inside the hotel as he charged in. Suddenly there were a few shots again, then more screaming.

Fuck! Corvette thought. *This is getting worse quickly. I gotta get the hell out of here!*

He glanced around. No one else seemed to be paying any attention to him. It was time to hustle. He accelerated his pace, tugging the green bag and hurrying up the walkway to the casino and hotel where he had a room. He half expected to be shot in the back.

I'm nuts! I'm frigging nuts! he thought to himself as he labored to get to the entrance of Pleasure Island. *Maybe I'll get myself killed for this! I just need to get to my room so I can have a goddamn minute to focus. I'm so damned sleep deprived that I can't think. I feel sick.*

The pain in his right shoulder muscle had become excruciating from the weight of the bag, so he shifted it to his other arm. His sleepiness and his preoccupation with what might be happening behind him made him lose moments of time, but at last Corvette noticed that he was striding through his hotel. He tried to relax his rapid breathing from the effort of carrying the heavy bag. He didn't want to attract attention, but his entire body was now feeling strange. The sweat on his chest chilled in the super-blast of the lobby air-conditioning. He thought the top of his chest felt icy. He was relieved to see the elevators ahead.

The elevator opened just as he got to the doors. Mercifully, no one else was there to get on with him. He punched the button for the fifth floor. He thought about the girl's arms again.

Where have I seen her, damn it?

12

He hadn't looked very long at the girl's face because her arms had caught his attention. But his glimpse took in the long, dark brown hair that blew across her face in the little breeze. She was very beautiful; there was no question about that. Corvette would have wanted to know her better under any other circumstances.

What am I thinking? he realized. *I want to know her now! I have a lot of questions for her. The first one is: Why did you give me this bag?*

He got off the elevator and rushed down the hall. He watched the room numbers for his: five-seventy-three. He was dying to open the bag to verify whether or not his hunch was correct, but a new bodily urgency arose: He needed to take a piss. His shoulders were killing him. He grabbed the room card from his wallet. His hand shook as he clumsily tried to insert it into the lock. Finally, the green signal light lit. He pushed into the room, kicked the door shut behind him, and turned directly into the bathroom. He dropped the green duffle bag beside the toilet. He had held his water so long that the piss wouldn't even begin. It hurt while he waited. Finally, the stream erupted, and Corvette's eyes rolled upward from the relief. It seemed to take forever to conclude, but when he finally finished, he grabbed the bag, rushed into the bedroom, flung the bag atop the bed, and tugged at its tight zipper. The bag was so stuffed that it was difficult to open.

Even though he saw what he expected, the reality of it stunned him. He felt flushed and warm, and the room seemed to darken briefly.

No! I won't faint! he commanded himself. He touched the paper bricks in the bag to substantiate that the rubber-banded stacks of one-hundred-dollar bills weren't a hallucination. He backed away from the bed to see if a new view would change what he was seeing. It didn't change a thing.

"Jesus, Mary, and Joseph!" Corvette announced to the room.

He flashed back in his mind to the moment the girl had said: "Booska el owtoe!" She had thrust a car keyset into his hand. He strained to focus his thoughts because he was feeling physically unstable. He replayed the sounds of the girl's words in his mind. He pulled his father's Hispanic accent from his memory to get a sense of familiar Spanish.

Got it! he thought. *"El owto" means el auto. The car. "Booska?" Get? Find? Take?* He would find out for sure, but he deduced the essence of the meaning: She had told him to find the car.

He began to shake from nervous excitement. He thought, *Why in the world would this girl give me a bag with a fortune in it, plus keys to a car, and then run away and jump into a Lexus?*

He replayed in his mind the moments just after she had emerged from The Oasis door.

She definitely came out looking for someone. Then someone pushed the bag to her. Did she know what was in it? When she saw me, why did she bring the damned thing to me? And why did I accept the bag?

He was trying to stay calm and alert. He wanted clarity of memory about what had happened, but this was difficult because he hadn't slept for over a day. He drew in long deep breaths.

Settle down, Corvette, he told himself. *Try to think about what to do. It would be great to keep this money. It's a crazy idea, but I need it. Who knows I have it other than the girl? Who might have seen me take this bag?*

Corvette closed his eyes to review in his memory the bystanders who were there when the shooting began. There were tourists, hotel guests, and parking staff. There was so much confusion in the ensuing minutes that he believed it was possible that no one had noticed the girl come out and bring the bag to him. As far as he had observed, he was the only one who hadn't started running away when the sounds of the shots first penetrated the morning calm. Instead, he had crouched to keep safe. He really hadn't done anything to attract attention. Later, when the police cars arrived, the officers were intent only upon rushing inside the building. Not one of them had looked his way. That left only the young man who had stared at him from the casino entrance.

Did he do that only because I had turned and was staring at him? Did he notice the bag that I tried to hide in front of me? Who else could know? Think, Corvette, think!

He felt suddenly concerned that someone might see into his room from outside. He rushed to the window and drew the inner and outer fabric curtains to darken the room. He left a small crack in the center to permit a little light. He began yanking the paper bricks wedged inside the bag and tossing them atop the bed so he would be able to count the money.

Who else besides the guy staring at me? Possibly the girl told the driver of the car what she had done, Corvette mused. *I might be lucky that people inside The Oasis didn't notice. The ones in that fight might have been too involved for any of them to have noticed what was happening outside the casino doors.*

That left one other possibility.

What about security cameras? Were there cameras placed around the casino entrance? Could these have shown me and the girl interacting?

That one was a real concern. With the police and the hotel security investigating, how long would it take before they would view the camera recordings of what had happened in the casino?

Suddenly Corvette remembered the keyset. He fished it from his pocket, and when he looked at the key fob, he drew a sharp breath.

No fucking way! he thought as he stared at the crossed race flags in a circle on the fob. He knew the car brand all his life. The fob displayed the race flags of the automobile that was his namesake: *Corvette!* Not only that, but this fob operated the keyless entry to the newest generation of Corvette: the Stingray.

He felt the lightness of his head as the room seemed to rotate him into dizziness. Heat and nausea overcame him like a tsunami breaking through the window. Just before he passed out and fell on the bed, he shouted in his mind:

St. Rogelio, if you're there, please help me!

Chapter 2: Convergence

The Girl
Las Vegas, Nevada
Saturday Morning

It wasn't until the guy pushed the bag through the door to her that the girl took command of her panic and began to make choices that weren't reactions ricocheting off the walls like the bullets. Survival instinct made her take the bag. Then she continued looking for the Corvette that Raúl had paid to remain parked alongside the passenger-unloading section in front of The Oasis Casino.

Just moments before, her world had exploded into a ball of white light, and she had just wanted to live. She could hardly breathe. That's what the girl felt during the incomprehensible melee at The Oasis lobby entrance doors. It was the white light of her confusion, her unaccustomed panic, which set off noisy static that jammed her brain. She was a professional, but for the first time since becoming an undercover DEA agent, she saw someone get shot in the chest, and she saw blood spattering all over the casino patrons who were simply walking by at the time when the shots began. The problem was that the man shot was Josh, her most trusted link to the world outside the cartel. She didn't even understand what he was doing there when it happened. The problem was that he was clearly dead. She heard her own wheezing inhale as she saw her DEA associate...no, her friend...slump to the floor. His death left her alone in the midst of the cartel thugs.

She had been walking through the casino with Luis, whom Raúl always had accompany her to "watch out for her interests." The mood of everyone had seemed tense. However, she had the Corvette car-key fob in her hand and was genuinely looking forward to driving it. It wasn't so much that she liked the car as it was that Raúl had trusted her enough to give her the keyless remote, even if he did send Luis to ride with her. If she had his trust, then she was doing a good job. The previous evening, back in the room, Raúl had joked with her that in the United States he wanted to usher in with the Corvette a whole new kind of narco ride, and that she was so hot that all the Zetas would want to set up their women in Corvette Stingray Z06s.

"They'll be doing Mexicano mods on the Z06s," Raúl had laughed. The girl got the joke. Raúl was El Zeta. His cartel name was Z-30. But a couple of years earlier he had figuratively cut off the dick of El Gato just before that Sinaloan cartel lieutenant had died in a shootout with the Mexican Army. So now Raúl was Zeta Number One. He was the Zeta who had the big cajones to push, guns blazing, into the distribution plazas of the Cartel of Sinaloa in the United States, the very plazas which El Gato had set up. The Zeta's name was Jesús Raúl Espinoza. People often called him "The Zeta" now, as if he personified all the qualities of the Zeta Cartel. But he told the girl to call him Raúl. That had been the first sign of trust. Or lust. The second sign was the key fob she held in her hand as she approached the entrance doors with Luis. Raúl had chosen the Corvette to impress her because there was a Z model.

As they walked through the main path of the casino, the girl was thinking about the irony of it all, because "Z" was also the name of the paramilitary guardian group that had arisen to challenge the violence of the drug cartels in Mexico. However, that "Z" derived from the Spanish word for fox: "zorro."

Just ahead of her and Luis were three more of the cartel "thugs," as the girl thought of them. They crossed a small indoor bridge leading to the casino doors. On the left was the artificially-misted rainforest under the solarium. Just beyond this mini-jungle, on the left, was the entrance to the lobby where guests registered for their rooms. The middle thug was lugging a green canvas duffle bag. The other two carried overnight bags. They wanted to make it look like they were guys just checking out of the hotel. The girl saw ahead on the bridge that two Mexican men who had been waiting now fell in with the three walking in front of her. They all acted as if they weren't together. *Five cartel thugs now,* she thought. She was guessing that the bag held the cash that she had heard Raúl mention in English to someone who had come to their suite. Probably Raúl had arranged that there would be vehicles for those five men and for him and Horacio, who were following behind her and Luis.

Just before she noticed anything amiss, she looked behind to check on Raúl. He and Horacio were indeed there, but they had fallen back a distance. There were lots of people in between, but, in particular, she noticed young Hispanic men dressed casually. They were interspersed among gringo and Asian families and tourists. The casino was crowded even this early in the day. She smiled at Raúl, but he didn't seem to notice. He was observing everything around him while talking to Horacio. He looked focused and alert. He and Horacio, as well as the cartel men ahead of her, were all wearing casual jackets that concealed their pistols.

In my two days in Vegas, I've been in Raúl's closest circles, she realized. She was proud.

Two mornings earlier, the girl had flown into Las Vegas from Monterrey, Mexico, on a commercial airline. Luis had been there to pick her up. He had greeted her in Spanish. She was nervous. She felt alone that morning, cut off from the DEA colleagues with whom she usually worked. She was a citizen of two countries, Mexico and the United States, but she had been using a cover of being a business woman in Monterrey during this DEA mission. Her "business" was event planning for major corporations in Monterrey. She had family and an apartment in Monterrey, but the DEA was, in fact, her employer.

She had scored the big catch. El Zeta, Raúl, had been pursuing her since meeting her a couple of weeks earlier at a narco-party replete with la música norteña and the car lot full of standard-issue Monterrey narco-vehicles: black full-sized SUVs. The Zetas had announced their arrival by popping AK-47s into the air. That was a special arrogance considering that the party was hosted by the young son of the police chief of Monterrey.

She had arrived late and had caught Raúl's eye. Since the night of that party, she had been as coy as she could with him, trying to put off the inevitable insistence he would have that she sleep with him. She had been with him on two "dates," which were other narco-parties around Monterrey. She had played the straight and innocent, university-educated Mexican business woman who was excited about the potential of her expanding event planning services to international corporations headquartered in Monterrey. The Zeta seemed turned on by her reception of him as if he were a father figure. He had acted fatherly toward her, but she could see by the look in his eyes that this was an act intended to lure her over time into intimacy. It was what she wanted him to do. She held his interest with short tight skirts and revealing blouses.

Then came the invitation to be in Las Vegas with him. It coincided with intelligence reports gathered by the DEA that there were big movements of cash originating in that city for money laundering purposes and that Z-30 sometimes went there to review operations. The DEA wanted to catch El Zeta in the act of transporting cash. The source of the intelligence hadn't always provided reliable information. But the girl, the agency's own undercover operative, would be with the big man himself, and she would be eye-witness to what he would be doing in Las Vegas. She was young and relatively unseasoned, but if successful in this operative, she would have the type of score that built careers in the DEA.

When she first met Luis upon her arrival in Las Vegas, she judged him to be in his mid-thirties. He was short and thick-necked. He stood next to her completely silent in the baggage claim area. His sun glasses prevented the girl from reading his eyes for clues about his personality. She decided not to try to engage him in conversation. She didn't want to make any mistakes on this trip. When her bag began to circulate on the belt, she pointed it out to Luis, and then she saw his powerful biceps flexing as he retrieved the heavy suitcase. He lifted it as if it were filled with cotton balls. *This guy's short, but he's muscle*, she noted.

He led her outside where a late-model Ford Explorer awaited. The driver of that vehicle was one of the thugs walking ahead of her now. This man didn't look Hispanic; however, he told her in Spanish, "Welcome to Las Vegas. Please get in the back." Apparently Raúl had informed everyone that the girl spoke only Spanish, which was what she had led Raúl to believe. She did this as part of her cover story as having grown up in Monterrey, but never having learned English. The DEA had been surprised when she reported that she had done this. She told them that Raúl might relax into speaking English with his comrades around her if he thought she couldn't understand them.

It turned out that had been a good decision. In the suite just minutes before they all left to stroll through the lobby to their vehicles, the girl had overheard Raúl talking about a meeting that they were going to in a small casino off The Strip, in Henderson. Raúl had been speaking to a Latino man who had arrived in their suite. She hadn't seen this man before. Raúl had led him into one of the bedrooms of the penthouse and had spoken to him in English in a low tone. It was the bedroom that she was using. She could see him standing near the closet, inside which was a safe. Raúl was in the closet.

"This will boost the table-win percentage," she had heard Raúl telling the man. She knew that he was showing the man some cash. "I'm going personally this time because apparently there has been a little leakage at this casino. I want to have a small pep talk with administration. I'm afraid we're going to have an employment vacancy in management this afternoon." She saw the man nod understanding.

"Go get me a green canvas duffle bag from the closet floor in the other bedroom," Raúl told the man.

The girl had turned her back as the man came out of the bedroom. Her data phone was lying on the glass table in front of a café-colored sectional sofa in the living room. She had left it

21

out in the open most of the time when she was in the penthouse so that Raúl could inspect it and see that she had made no suspicious calls or sent messages. She knew that someone in the cartel had tinkered with her phone. Someone had disabled the GPS inside it.

While the man was getting the bag, she had picked the phone up in a casual way as if she were going to check messages or use Facebook. But surreptitiously she had pulled up a girlfriend's name out of her contact list and had typed a message: "CM." She had sent it and then quickly had erased the message.

The message had gone to Laura Elizondo in her phone contacts. That name actually had the number for a person in the DEA. It looked like a Mexican phone number, but it rang an agent in the Las Vegas office of the DEA. The notation, "CM," was the code for "cash movement."

Now as they all got closer to the exit doors, she studied closely the faces of the people walking nearby and ahead, standing near the doors. She wondered if as a result of her message, she might see undercover DEA agents who had come to observe and report the exit of the cartel contingency from The Oasis. She was guessing that the DEA would follow them to their destination. Then might come the moment when the agents would try to effect the capture of Z-30 and his associates while they had the cash. However, she saw no one whom she recognized until, finally, she spotted Josh dressed in cargo shorts, tennis shoes, and an oversized Hawaiian print shirt. He was standing near the doors. He was her closest associate in the DEA. He had been somewhat of a mentor for her. Seeing him, she relaxed.

This was the first time that she had seen Josh since her arrival in the Las Vegas airport. Then he had been standing outside in the passenger pick-up zone when she got ushered into the Ford Explorer. He had climbed into a taxi just as the Explorer departed. At the time, she was certain that the taxi driver was also an undercover DEA operative. She didn't have to look back. She knew that Josh and the driver were following them.

They had left the airport and had quickly arrived at the site of a car agency specializing in the rental of exotic sports cars. The Explorer had lurched into a parking spot. There awaiting her was Raúl, El Zeta himself. When she had emerged from the SUV, he had swept her into a hug against his broad, barrel chest and had planted a kiss on her cheek as if he were an affectionate godfather. He hadn't been overtly sexual yet, but the girl knew that he was trying to seduce her with restrained manners while he lured her with presents, favors, and holiday trips.

"Look what I found for us," Raúl laughed with delight as he pulled the girl over to a green Corvette. "This leasing company has the new seventh generation 'Vette. It's the Stingray. Not just any Stingray, this is the Z06. Crazy car has 625 horsepower! Lime-rock Green. This is a not-so-subtle announcement of our arrival in Vegas, mi vida. Do you like it?"

She had cringed inside when this gross pig of a human being had referred to her affectionately as "his life." She also noted that he had selected a two-seater car, so there would be times, apparently, when they would be alone in the car.

While she was effusing fake enthusiasm for the Corvette and for being with Raúl, the driver of the Ford Explorer handed the Zeta a pocket-sized ledger book. He didn't say anything, and Raúl barely acknowledged receiving it as he continued talking to her. When the girl and Raúl got in the Corvette to head to The Oasis, he put the book in the center console.

That was the memory in her mind when suddenly she saw Josh standing near the doors of The Oasis entrance. Seeing him snapped her out of her musings. Beyond him through the glass doors were cars pulling up to disembark passengers. She peered past Josh, expecting to see the Corvette, but it wasn't there.

She remembered that a couple of days earlier when she and Raúl had arrived at the hotel in the Corvette, Raúl had pushed a number of hundred dollar bills into the palm of the valet manager, who obviously knew him. The money had bought the Corvette a parking place alongside the driveway directly in front of the hotel. The girl had looked back to observe the bellman removing some bags from the trunk. She didn't want Raúl to remember that he had put the ledger book in the center console, so she had come up with a distraction:

The valet manager was young and cute, probably about twenty-seven, her age. So even though he wore a wedding ring, she had flirted with him just a little, in a way that could be both innocent and deniable. She did observe a slightly jealous shadow passing across Raúl's face. Her scheme worked: It made him forget about the ledger. She had wanted it to remain in the Corvette in case any opportunity might present itself for a DEA agent to get into the car and examine it and perhaps even photograph its contents.

Raúl had responded to her flirtations with the young man by showing off. With a dramatic tone in his voice, he had presented the key fob to her.

"Hold on to this, princesa" Raúl had said to her, using the Spanish endearment. "I made a deal with the leasing agency to give me two fobs because I want you to have this for your very own, and the other is for the valet service here to keep." He was bragging. "So this car will be right here in front of the hotel in case you want it to explore Vegas. This isn't permitted for just anyone, you know. I guess I have a few connections in this town," he had laughed. The girl knew that Raúl wanted to make a statement to the young man that he was out of his league and that she would be off limits to him or anyone else. Then he had handed the other fob to Alex, saying, "Alex, be careful not to leave this in the car. The car won't lock when it's inside it. The car will beep three times to let you know the fob is still there." He had said this in a condescending way.

But now, in the limited view she had of the parking area just beyond where Josh was standing, she didn't see the Corvette where it should be. She did see some SUVs with men leaning against them as if waiting for passengers to come out of the casino, as well as taxis and a limousine in the multiple lanes of the driveway outside. *The men are probably cartel guys*, she surmised. She wondered if it would be Raúl or Luis who would join her in the Corvette during their trip to the casino in Henderson. Raúl was letting her drive. She had learned not to ask questions but just to let happen what Raúl always decided.

He hasn't defrocked his jewel yet, she thought, *but if the Zeta takes me, I'll be no more than his whore of the moment. That could be what he thinks of me even now. I'm sure I'm just as expendable as any of the other women he has fancied. God, how I hope we plan this so I don't face that awful moment when the slime-ball begins to undress me!*

It was at this moment when the strange things began to happen. She had noticed two men who looked like tourists standing outside, but she hadn't paid them much attention. Suddenly they whirled around and rushed through the doors into the hotel. One of them seized Josh and pushed him toward the party of advancing Zetas. He had Josh's arms pinned behind him with one arm. He was rifling Josh's pants pockets with the other.

That action caught the attention of the guys who had been standing by the SUVs. Startled, they dashed into the hotel. Simultaneously, from the lobby on the left, five or six men came rushing toward the Zetas and pulling pistols from underneath their shirts as they advanced.

The girl spun around to find Raúl, but what she saw first was a group of young men rushing toward her and Luis from behind. Glancing beyond them, she observed that Raúl wasn't on the bridge which she had just crossed. Instead, she glimpsed Horacio hustling Raúl through the maze of slot machines on the casino floor. She could see that Raúl and Horacio were going to disappear among people and the machines. They were moving in the opposite direction from the young men advancing toward her and Luis.

She spun around to see what was happening ahead of her now, but the sound of a gunshot behind her made her turn to look back once more. She didn't have time to see anything, because Luis seized her arm and began maneuvering her quickly forward, toward the left bank of doors at the entrance.

Now she and Luis were caught up with the Zetas ahead. They had pulled their guns, too. The girl quickly calculated that all together there must be at least a dozen men with weapons drawn. She felt like she was seeing everything in slow motion.

The young guys behind her and Luis suddenly took running jumps upward. When the girl looked up, she saw them airborne. They threw themselves down into the mob of pistol-wielding thugs. She thought that they looked like a human twister. They jumped, kicked, and punched their arms furiously in martial arts movements. Someone pitching forward knocked the girl into the whole collection of all of these people as they became a cloud of human chaos. The young men who had jumped managed to bring several of the various gunmen down and had separated them from their pistols. They themselves didn't have guns.

Dios! she realized. *No guns? These guys must be Zs! Mother of God, what are they doing here?*

She knew who the Zetas were. She was with them. She now understood that the jumping young men might be Zs.

But who are these other guys who came running at us with murderous intent?

That was her last coherent moment until she managed to get outside later, because when the guns started popping, she lost it. The first thing she saw when the bullets began was the huge hole in Josh's chest. The man who had been holding him spun him around and shot him point blank and then returned fire on the attackers. She saw Josh's blood spray people close to him. One was a child. The shock of seeing it threw her into what felt like white-static panic. All she could think was to get through the doors, but now they all were bunched up in front of the middle section of the doors, and she was pressed in. The men were fighting furiously. Some managed to pick up pistols from the floor, but in the madness of the human pile-up, their shots were errant and desperate. Soon the shots ceased altogether as they were all disarming one another and the

26

combat became totally hand-to-hand. The girl gasped for breath in the close quarters. A violent push sent her to the floor with a couple of men and pistols, while above her, other men fought brutally with their fists.

Her terror intensified when she realized that she could be trampled to death. She was on her back. She thought that she saw young Zs jumping on men from above again. She knew that if she didn't do something, the weight of the human mountain was going to bear down and crush her. Her fear gave her desperate energy that enabled her to twist her body so that she was on her stomach.

She got her head up and saw a hole through which she could crawl in the jumble of pants legs and shoes! She had to act quickly. She could see Oasis security guards running toward them with weapons drawn. It was going to get worse. She exerted all her strength to slither through the hole and escape before the guards arrived. When she raised up unsteadily, she was at the left-end door. She leaned against it and shoved it open with her body.

The blast of air conditioning from inside colliding with the furnace wind of the desert heat outside jolted the girl from her panic. Quickly her brain reverted to logical thinking:

I can't blow my cover. I have to think and come out on top. I have to get out of here and contact both Raúl and the DEA!

She heard the sirens of the police cars. These reminded her of the Corvette, and she looked around the driveway, but she didn't see it.

God! Why isn't it here?

She began to review the people outside. They had scattered when the shots began, and now they were everywhere, taking cover on the sidewalk, in the car lanes, and in the shrubs. She tried to focus on faces. She didn't see any Zetas or DEA agents whom she knew.

Something hit the back of her heels from the door she had just exited. She whirled around. A badly injured man with blood all over his face and chest had pushed open the door from a

27

crawling position. He had struggled to shove the green canvas bag to her through the door. He muttered incoherently to her in Spanish. She couldn't distinguish what he said in his low, muttering voice. The man's face looked battered. There was blood on his sports jacket, and his movements were weak. Suddenly she recognized that he was Luis! He looked in terrible shape.

The girl reached to accept the bag from him. When her hands squeezed the end of the bag, she felt its contents. It had to be the cash that she had heard Raúl mention to put in a bag. She bunched together the two leather handles and discovered that the bag was damned heavy. As she struggled with it, Luis retreated fully inside the doorway before slumping into a lifeless posture on the floor.

When she picked up the bag, she felt the key fob still in her palm. It hurt her, and that was when she realized that throughout the whole ordeal, she had squeezed the fob in her hand so tightly that it had made a rectangular impression in her palm.

She thought: *If I'm getting away from here, this bag's a complication. It'll slow me down. Do I leave it? No, Luis gave it to me, so he must have believed it's what Raúl would have wanted. Raúl would kill me if I leave it behind, and the DEA would think I've lost my mind.*

The police sirens were getting louder.

She slowed her breathing to try to keep calm and to focus her thoughts. She searched faces around her again. *Surely there would be DEA agents here*, she thought. But she saw no one familiar, and neither did anyone seem to have any interest in her.

Okay, no DEA agents and no one from a cartel out here right now. I have to get moving. Someone from inside is going to want this bag!

She visually measured the distance down the driveway to Las Vegas Boulevard, the "Strip." While doing this, her eyes took in a good-looking Latino man squatting in the sidewalk by the shrubs, but she looked past him to the street. Suddenly, her brain screamed a recognition:

That's Corvette Nightfire!

She looked again.

It is Corvette! What the hell is he doing here?

She remembered something Raúl had told her about him after he had picked her up from her evening dancing. It wasn't so much his words as his tone that had chilled her.

"That boy doesn't know it yet, but he's coming to work for me."

Now she didn't know if seeing Corvette was a good or bad thing, but it seemed to be a destined thing. She realized, *Shit, Corvette is going to be involved whether I'm the one to involve him or not!*

His presence was confusing, but she understood what she had to do now. She engaged his eyes and grabbed the bag's handles with both hands and started to lug it toward him. When she did, he stood up.

The police sirens now sounded like they were just blocks away. She was running out of time, but there was no way that she could run with the bag. Corvette didn't appear to recognize her, but he understood that she was coming to him. She knew that he would figure out later who she was. She also knew that when he did, he would keep the cash. She was counting on that. She would have to get the cash back to Raúl. It would be messy for the police to find her with the money. The DEA would have to explain it, and there would be increased risk that her cover would be blown. The DEA wouldn't want her to have the cash. They were hoping to catch Raúl with it. If that was going to happen in the future, then she needed to keep her cover and to retain Raúl's trust. Something had gone wrong back there, and the DEA would still need her undercover inside Raúl's inner circle. And that wouldn't happen unless she could return the money to him. Under the circumstances, the girl reasoned, there was no other thing to do. She had to give Corvette the bag. She would know how to find him later.

As she got closer to him, she formulated her plan:

I'll tell him to run when I give him the bag so he'll understand the bag is important. I'll warn him that with the bag he has to run for his life. When he sees me running, he'll get the picture.

Then she remembered something about him: This good looking Latino didn't speak Spanish! It was ridiculous. Part of her cover was that she didn't speak English. She had to remain true to that even now. There could be eye witnesses of what she was about to do, including even someone from the cartel. She would have to keep her message simple.

Busca el Corvette! came to her mind. *No, that will confuse him. He'll think I'm talking about his name. Busca el auto! That will do it. Besides, he'll see the type of car on the key fob.*

Wherever the Corvette was, if there was a chance that the ledger book was still in it, she wanted to get her hands on it. Corvette Nightfire would probably have more freedom to look for it than she would have in the next hours and days. She decided that she would run into the Venetian Hotel after handing Corvette the bag. From there she would execute her next moves, which would be to try to contact both Raúl and the DEA. She thought about her phone, and, miraculously, it was still in her shorts pocket. She had picked it up from the table when she left the penthouse. She could feel the bag bumping the phone against her leg as she hurried toward Corvette.

When she got to him, he was staring at her arms. She bent down to catch his eyes.

"Busca el auto! Corre!" she shouted as she gave him the bag and the key fob. He looked at her with total confusion. She saw that he would hesitate a few precious moments. She pushed him to emphasize that he should run, and then she began her sprint down the driveway toward The Strip.

She felt on top of things now. Her panic had subsided. She got to the sidewalk and took a moment to look up and down The Strip, to see if there were any sign of Raúl or anyone from the DEA. Her mind felt clear now that she had made decisions to take action.

And it was clear enough to understand immediately that the Lexus speeding toward her and cutting across traffic lanes was going to stop for her. Her heart jumped into her throat. She couldn't believe what she was seeing. It was a car that she knew. She checked the license plate as it got closer to verify her suspicion. The car bore personalized Texas license plates that said, "ZINC." The girl knew who the driver would be: the same driver who created the irony of the message on the plate. It did not mean "ZINC." It stood for "Z Inc."

The Lexus screeched to a stop beside her with a loud protest of the tires. The girl yanked open the door, and she saw that, yes, the driver was her aunt, Ana Valdez.

Ana Valdez, the originating founder of the Zs with David James.

Ana Valdez, the onetime Interim President of Mexico.

"Tia!" the girl squealed with astonishment. The word meant *aunt*. "What are you doing here?"

"Dios!" shouted Ana. "Valentina, what the devil have you done? Get in the car!"

Valentina jumped in, and they shot off southbound on The Strip as the police cars bore down on The Oasis Hotel and Casino.

Chapter 3: A Transfer of Riches

The Zeta, Z-30
Monterrey, Mexico
Two Months Prior

The Zeta commanded that he be alone in the frigid, sparsely furnished office upstairs in Los Piratas Casino for his meeting with Horacio. Downstairs was casino elegance with dark wood paneling, low hanging chandeliers, and gaming areas set off from one another in European-styled furnishings. Each room was decorated in themes of different European countries and places: Monaco, Spain, Italy, France, Greece, and Portugal. The Zetas had put *mucho dinero* into this property. The casino manager was a good trooper who paid his "piso" on time and with transparency of reports. He was smart. He knew how to keep his life and maintain his family. He reported promptly any sign of entry by someone from a rival cartel or any suspicious activity, and the Zetas took care of the problem before it could worsen. Monitored security cameras were everywhere. In fact, the security guards manning the camera monitors were Zetas in crisp uniforms. Outside, hawks kept watch on the traffic for blocks around the casino. City police were on the payroll and helped the neighborhood be secure for Zeta meetings. Z-30 had established a reliable reporting system in Monterrey for the movements of the Marines and Army in the city. Before he went anywhere, a vanguard of scouts checked the roads for checkpoints. He felt safe in Monterrey. He relaxed in his casinos.

His bodyguards stationed themselves outside the door. It was almost noon on a Saturday. He only had to wait a couple of minutes before Horacio arrived and eased his large frame atop the cushioned stool across from him. It looked ridiculously small beneath him. Both men were built powerfully and seemed to take up more space than anything else in the room. Horacio had more body fat. The Zeta had a large frame and rocklike muscles from a lifetime of lifting weights. He was forty-eight but appeared younger. He could intimidate a room full of people with the power of his thick and imposing body. He liked to dominate a woman as well when he had sex. Underneath him, they couldn't move in his embrace. Some told him they felt secure when he had them. Those were the women he liked.

"Qué tal, jefe," Horacio greeted him. "How was your sleep? Did you have the dream again?"

"Sí, I followed the red rivers of the pigs from Sinaloa across the border once again, but this time I slipped into some kind of tributary that went into the desert. The water got too shallow, so I had to walk in the hot sun until I came to a huge American city."

"Bueno, Raúl, it is because you have all these casinos in your mind and your dream takes you to Las Vegas. But your rivers are still red?"

The Zeta nodded and thought for a few moments about El Gato, the ascending star in the Cartel of Sinaloa. He remembered the windy, philosophical lectures that El Gato had given him a few years previously, during those daring days when together they had planned and had succeeded in the freeing of Pedro Navarro, the President of Mexico, after he and his family had been taken hostage by the military coup. It had been El Gato's idea to undermine the support of the military coup by rescuing the elected President of Mexico and delivering him to the United States. Although the Zeta had admired the cleverness of El Gato's plan, he had despised the man for ordering the murder of his nephew in one of the confrontations between the Cartel of Sinaloa and that of the Zetas. Ultimately, the Zeta had avenged the death, but El Gato didn't suffer the lifelong torture of the soul which the Zeta had planned for him. That was because El Gato had died in a shootout with the Mexican Marines just a couple of hours after the Zeta had betrayed him. The betrayal had been sinisterly brilliant and had changed the course of Mexican history: Z-30 personally executed President Pedro Navarro, the First Lady, and their two young sons just before they were to be ferreted to the United

States by El Gato. The Zeta had destroyed El Gato's dream and had blown a mortal hole through his spirit.

The Zeta remembered how heady El Gato had been from his successes of establishing "plazas" (markets and distribution centers) for Sinaloa throughout the United States during a three-year period. He had done it by working in stealth. Sinaloa had been relatively unopposed by other cartels and local police forces of the United States There was no attention-grabbing violence during those years in the USA like there had been in Mexico when the President of Mexico preceding Pedro Navarro had declared war on the narco-bosses. The resulting blood bath in the streets and mountains of Mexico had demolished public safety. Five years of near-civil war had led to the overthrow of the corrupt federal and state governments by the Mexican Armed Forces.

It was during this time, when El Gato had proposed to the Zeta that they rescue the Mexican President from his imprisonment, that El Gato had waxed on to the Zeta about the importance of toning down the brutality of violence which attracted headlines. The cartels should employ the business models and technology of international corporations in the business lines of the cartels, El Gato argued. He pointed out that the violence in Mexico had led to the military coup and to possible invasion by the United States. The Zeta agreed with El Gato philosophically, and, in fact, he favored flying under the radar as much as possible. Z-30 differed from most Zeta leaders in that he preferred to execute dispassionately and not sensationally. However, the Zetas were presently muscling into the narco-plazas in the United States that had been expanded by Sinaloa, and warfare was unavoidable. So the rivers of product and cash flowing into the North were crimson with blood, more in the United States than in Mexico.

The Zeta sighed. "Sí, the rivers are red," he answered Horacio. "I see no immediate end to the bloodshed. Many of us Zetas come from the Mexican Special Forces. We're warriors trained in tactics of brutality, Horatio. We're known and feared for this. We get our respect through terror and physical and psychological torture. We won't be able to modify our ways until we eradicate the Cartel of Sinaloa in the United States. We'll accomplish this by corrupting police and judicial agencies in the USA, locality by locality, as we have done in Mexico. We need gringo law enforcement as allies against Sinaloa. We'll get their cooperation through money and bullets. It'll be costly. Operations are much more expensive in the USA. There's a much higher standard of living in that country, so it'll take mucho dinero to make the cops fat and the judges happy there. As for weapons, things will be much the same as in Mexico, except that in the USA, more often the bullets will get fired through silencers."

He liked that Horacio understood the uniqueness of his style and personality within the cartel. Horacio was well suited to work closely with him.

He added, "I must admit that my old nemesis, El Gato, was right about many things, despite his Achilles heel favoring perversions. Once we control the plazas in the USA, we'll institute less bloody, corporate violence. We'll develop super-efficient operating and information systems enabling us to have more targeted violence. I favor using more sweeteners like money and lifestyle benefits for recruiting and retaining human resources. We have to do this. The police forces and the federal agencies of the gringos share data banks, and their multiple agencies are much more collaborative with one another than ours in Mexico. The gringos are more technologically advanced. Shit, they even work with those kids of Ana Valdez and David James, the Zs, with their data phones and tablets and kick-ass ways! They're becoming more problematic for us."

"The battle of the Zs," Horacio responded. "Zetas versus the little flying foxes."

"The world is fucked up," the Zeta answered. "So tell me the story, hermano. Tell me in the way I like to hear it." He closed his eyes to listen.

Horacio was used to this. He told the story as it had been related to him by his captive:

Ignacio Lopez, information technology wizard and Vice-President for Special Accounts for El Banco Noreste, was wrapping up his long day in his office at the bank on Friday when he phoned his fiancé, Lili, to tell her that he would pick her up at her home in San Pedro Garza Garcia in Monterrey in about an hour. It was already dark, and he was the last person in the branch. He asked her if she would mind if they might enjoy a relaxing dinner in a restaurant so he could unwind before they would go to the fiesta of her niece's fifteenth birthday party in the country club on the National Highway. She told him that it was a wonderful idea and that she would greet him with delicious kisses at her door.

"Not too many, cielo," Ignacio had cautioned, "or we'll never make it to the restaurant and the party."

Looking back on it, he thought it ironic that the last business call of the day had been a phone call from Enrique Santos, the young man who led the Zs for Ana Valdez and David James. Although The Z Foundation had a head accountant, Enrique was the contact in matters of large financial transactions. Enrique had been in law school but had postponed the continuance of his education for a few years after the Zs had been left a fortune upon the death of Eduardo Ortíz. Ana and David had objected to Enrique's leave of absence from school, but in the hectic months after Eduardo's death, they had discovered that they needed Enrique's special attention to detail and his insider understanding of operations in The Z Foundation, now operating in two countries.

"I was just calling to congratulate you for the excellent report of investment earnings this month," Enrique had told Ignacio. "Great job! You know, Ignacio, the young people joining the Zs are coming to us in record numbers. We need these types of investment earnings. They're fired up and inspired. We don't pay them, but we need to offer them something for the sacrifices they make."

"The foundation is offering all those scholarships and work credits," Ignacio responded with genuine enthusiasm. "The work credits, especially, are effectively incentivizing employers to hire. To help business owners to be able to employ young people when they wouldn't financially be able to do it otherwise is a win for everyone. When the business grows subsequently, the work credits are no longer needed. These credits and the scholarships are the perfect solutions for the future of Mexico, Enrique! So many of these kids come from poverty. They have to work to help their families just survive. This is why I've always been excited about the purpose of The Z Foundation. It's my pleasure to assist you in growing its assets."

"Gracias, amigo, I appreciate your help. Perhaps next week we can have a meeting to discuss a couple of things? I want to standardize the application processes for the scholarships and work credits across all regions, including the United States. The interest in joining Zs there is mushrooming because, unfortunately, there's a big increase in homicides as the cartels have decided to operate more directly in their cities."

(When Horacio told this part of the story, a frown creased the brow of the Zeta. Enrique's words affirmed what he suspected. The Zs gave dreams and opportunity to the poor. Poverty was the fertile breeding ground for cartel recruitment. The cartels fed on the despair of youth. They turned to gang life because there was no other exit for them from miserable lives. No access to education. No jobs. When they felt powerless, the cartels were there to put an automatic rifle into their hands and money in their pocket. But in the past few years, the Zs were there too.)

He opened his eyes and looked at Horacio. "To get this level of detail from Ignacio Lopez, your men put big fear into him. Go ahead and continue the story."

Ignacio and Enrique made an appointment to meet in the following week, and then Ignacio filed some papers in his desk before preparing to leave. He was hungry and looked forward to dinner with his lady. Unfortunately, Ignacio never arrived at the door of his fiancé's house for those delicious kisses. He soon found out that she wouldn't have been home anyway.

What happened was that, as he was logging off his computer, his cell phone rang, identifying the caller as Lili.

"Qué pasa, darling?" Ignacio answered.

For three or four seconds he heard a woman shrieking horribly in the background as if someone on the other end of the call were holding the phone for him to hear. Then a calm male voice said to him, "We have Lili in our van. She's in a little pain at the moment. It can get a lot worse for her unless you pay attention very carefully. Do you understand me?"

Ignacio felt his blood drain. *God, please, that can't be Lili!* He could still hear the screaming. He struggled to focus on the man's voice.

"Sí, sí, I understand! Please don't hurt her! What do you want?" But he kept hearing Lili scream. She sounded hysterical. Ignacio felt his gut wretch.

Then the smooth voice said, "You have your office shades open. Keep them open so we can continue to watch you. There are several of us. At the front door a nice customer in a business suit is arriving. Set your cell phone on the desk and put it on speaker. Go and open the door. Greet the man with a warm handshake. Bring him back to your office, gesture for him to take a seat, and we'll go from there."

"Okay, okay, I'll do it! Stop hurting her! I'll do what you want. Please! I'm going to the door now."

He glanced out the window and saw a white courier van and a black SUV in the parking lot. He hurried to the front of the building.

He was terrified. He had a knot in his stomach and could hardly breathe. Yet at the door stood a handsome, smiling man who shook his hand warmly when Ignacio opened it. The polite greeting was terribly out of sync with Ignacio's terror. The man made some apology about being late and said that they still should contract the business upon which they had agreed. In a lower voice he commanded Ignacio to leave the front door unlocked. Then, resuming his amiable chatter, he followed Ignacio to his office. Ignacio remembered to gesture to the man to have a seat. He tried to tack a smile onto his face, but he felt so scared that he was on the brink of tears.

"We're here," said the man to the speaker on Ignacio's cell phone. Then he told Ignacio, "Turn your computer on, and after you're logged in, turn the screen so I can see it as well. Do this as if you're going to show me something."

Ignacio guessed that the theatrical performance of the man was geared to security cameras that might be filming outside and inside the bank. He logged into his computer. "How is Lili?" he asked. "Please, don't hurt her anymore." His voice cracked, so he repeated it loudly. For the moment he didn't hear any screams, but he thought that he heard her crying in the background.

"She's a little better because you're doing fine so far, "said the voice on the phone. Ignacio knew that the suave voice masked the soul of a sadist.

The pleasant man in the office said, "Okay, let me see the screen. What I want you to do is to bring up the accounts of The Z Foundation. I want to see the amounts in their cash fund, their money markets, and their investments in stocks and bonds. We're going to make transfers to some accounts which I'll give you."

Oh my God! Ignacio thought. *If that's what this is about, then Lili and I are really in grave trouble. This is a cartel.* His fear surged. His hands were shaking visibly. *God, poor Lili! She doesn't deserve this.* The gloomy realization came to mind that neither of them was going to come out of this alive. Even worse was what they might have to bear before being murdered. He would do anything in his power to try to make the outcome be the best possible for them. He couldn't stand the thought of Lili in pain.

"Okay," he answered loudly so the man on the phone could hear him also. "I'm working with you. Please be patient with me. I'm nervous and trying to think. I won't play any games with you. I have to think about which funds have restrictions. Some transactions don't go liquid right away. There are market settlements for some that take three business days. We'll have to figure out how to do these without the transaction notifications going to certain parties when you make transfers." He hoped by offering that information that he was showing his willingness to help them so that they would stop hurting Lili.

"Eyyy! This is good. You're cooperating, amigo. You're being the hombre for your woman," said the voice on the phone.

The pleasant man in the office said, "Yes, we know these things, and you're thinking well. We know also that you have power of attorney to conduct the transactions for the investments and to make the cash transfers for The Z Foundation. We want you to purchase some publicly traded stocks which we'll identify for you. We want you also to transfer the amounts currently in cash to some private accounts that we'll give you." He smiled. "So this may not go too badly. You and Lili will be our guests during the days that the transactions are clearing. Lili will be a little under the weather the next few days, but she'll recover if all goes well."

Ignacio had calmed just enough to think about the implications of the man's words. He remembered that he had sold some investments for the foundation in the past week at a good profit, and that the proceeds from those had cleared that day and were in the cash account. Therefore, there was a lot of liquidity which could be transferred to other bank accounts. When the voice and the man found out how much, they were going to be pleased.

But if the purchases of "publicly traded stocks" are still in the name of The Z Foundation, how is that going to benefit these people? How will they get the investments in the name of their accounts? Do they expect me to be able to do that somehow?

And then it hit him: *Maybe they're more interested in destroying The Z Foundation than they're in getting cash from it! I wonder what kinds of stock investments they're talking about.*

"While we're waiting for the accounts to pull up," said the man sitting across from him, "we understand that you and Lili have plans for the evening. It's a good idea for you to call now and let her niece's family know that she's feeling badly and that the two of you, unfortunately, won't be able to make it to the fiesta tonight."

The man pointed to Ignacio's office phone. "Go ahead," he continued. He pulled his chair closer to Ignacio's desk and studied the computer screen.

"I'm nervous," Ignacio repeated. "I can't remember the number of Lili's sister. I have it in my cell phone." He was stuttering a little bit.

But the voice on the phone had heard him, and the voice demanded the number from Lili. She spit it out in sobs that were heartbreaking for Ignacio to hear.

The pleasant man in Ignacio's office spoke in calming tones. "She'll be okay as long as you do exactly what we need you to do. So while you're talking to Lili's sister, go ahead and pull up the summary screen of the investment accounts for The Z Foundation."

"I have a spreadsheet linked to the online investment brokerages that the Foundation uses," Ignacio managed to explain. "So I'm pulling that up so that you can see the summary. All the cash and the multiple types of investments with different firms roll up into their classifications of investments in the summary. Each investment firm is listed. The cash and investments with each firm are added together. Then the spreadsheet provides sub-totals by classification of investments. The spreadsheet has a feed from the investment houses, so it is real-time with the investments."

"Okay," said the man, smiling. "Ah, I see you have it on the screen now. Go ahead and make your call."

But as Ignacio punched the telephone numbers of his fiancé's sister, he saw the expression on the man's face suddenly go from smile to astonishment. He leaned closer to the screen and read for a few seconds, and then he reached for Ignacio's cell phone, which was still on the desk. He clicked the speaker off. Ignacio was now talking with his future sister-in-law and was trying to sound convincing to her that Lili had suddenly developed terrible stomach cramps and was vomiting. She was besieging him with questions, but Ignacio also turned an ear to the man and the conversation he was having with the voice over his cell phone. He heard snippets from the man's conversation:

"This is richer than we thought. We're talking $6.7 million in cash alone...I don't know, it looks like stock sales cleared today...the other investments are mostly in mutual funds. There are small amounts in stocks and bonds...okay, yes, also more than we thought. We're talking $36.3 million in addition to the cash. He has a notation at the bottom that there are also properties."

The Zeta's eyes flew open wide. "Wait! Stop the story! Horacio, where was the cash sent? Cayman Islands or Barbados?"

"Jefe," Horacio answered, "they did what you originally instructed. You had said to put it in the numbered account in the Cayman Islands bank, unless the cash was more than a million, in which case to put it in the private bank in Barbados. So it went to Barbados. That's beefing up that account significantly."

"When did this happen, exactly?"

"We got a confirmation from Barbados about ten p.m. last night."

Raúl straightened in his chair. He puffed up. That was what he did when he wanted to intimidate someone. He tensed. It made his body seem more massive than it was. Horacio had received his wrath a few times, but, importantly, he had earned the Zeta's trust over the years. Horacio had learned to remain calm during these preliminary postures of his long-time associate. Already the Zeta could see that Horacio would have the right answers to his questions because the man looked confident and at ease.

"You didn't call me because I told you not to interrupt me last night when I was with the girl," stated the Zeta, but it was a question too.

"That's right, jefe," answered Horacio.

The Zeta noted Horacio's tactic of deference. For Horacio to call him "jefe" was sometimes a term of loyalty and sometimes a statement by Horacio that he knew when the Zeta was in the role of boss.

"You made a good decision about the cash. But the mutual funds and other investments are far greater than I anticipated. I hope you made the right decision about those, despite what I had instructed you."

"When I heard how much those were, I decided not to do anything until I could talk to you. It's one thing to send off a million or two into stock purchases of dubious nature, jefe, but it seemed another thing entirely when the investments of The Z Foundation turned out to be much more than you had expected. I thought that if you knew, then you might have other ideas about what to do with that money. So this is why I'm meeting with you now."

The Zeta released an exhale that deflated his body. He thought for a few moments, and then he said, "Where are the Lopez man and the young woman?"

"We took them to the farm. We're keeping them nervous. That smart, pretty-boy bank manager started crying like a baby after we made the cash transfer. He's a Z lover. It's Saturday morning now. We can keep him and the girl there over the weekend. On Monday, we can send him to work to do whatever you decide needs to be done. We can instruct him to act like business as usual. The problem is that there are all sorts of

43

people who will get transaction notices when he makes investment changes, sales, or purchases."

"Who in the foundation sees them?"

"As you would expect, Raúl: their head accountant, the Santos kid, Ana Valdez, and David James. This guy Ignacio says that usually the ones on top of these notices are the head accountant and Enrique Santos. They get e-mail notices in addition to paper copies, which arrive later."

The Zeta took his time thinking. He got up and retrieved a couple of Tecates from an ice cooler that was on the floor against a wall, and he handed one of the beers to Horacio. He sipped a while and then said, "I don't want to move that money to our corporations that are publicly traded in the stock exchanges. It's too attention-grabbing and traceable. The companies will get investigated for money laundering if authorities suspect that the money for the stock purchases came from cash hijacked by a cartel. I had thought that it would be a good thing to waste the foundation's money on bogus investments, but this is too much money. We can use this."

"Yes, that's what I thought you would say," replied Horacio.

"I was going to have the kid commit suicide after he learned about the death of his fiancé in an automobile accident," the Zeta continued. "The sequence was going to be that he would move money from those mutual funds to investments in individual companies' stocks, and then he would be dead before anyone could ask him the purpose for the change in investment strategy. I was going to have him record his reasons for the changes in a memo to file that authorities would find later. You know, of course, that the companies are shells, and that they have been misstating the books to support the current stock prices. They're houses of cards. When The Z Foundation would get around to doing due diligence on their stock purchases made by Lopez in those companies, they would learn that the stock is almost worthless. However, now we have to re-think this strategy because the kind of money that the foundation has in total could really help our expansions in the United States."

He saw the light of understanding flicker in Horacio's eyes. He thought, *Horacio knows I'm talking about financing the war against Sinaloa in the United States. He anticipated correctly that I would change my mind if I knew how much money was involved. Shit, there are so many Zetas I can't trust. Either they want my job, or they're incompetent in financial understanding and useless to help me. But this man here is one fucking loyal hombre who understands numbers and also knows how I think. I hope I can keep this one.*

"So, sell the investments, leave the proceeds in cash, and move the cash to where?" asked Horacio. "Barbados?"

"Exactly," the Zeta agreed. "Once we get it there in the private trusts, no one can trace it. We'll move it from those to multiple banks. From the banks we'll withdraw cash in paper currency as we need it. 'Efectivo' (cash) is still the operating currency in our businesses."

"What will we do with Ignacio Lopez and the girl he's all sobby over?"

Yes, Horacio thinks ahead. He's helping me to think everything through so I don't make any mistakes.

"Well, we'll kill the girl," answered the Zeta. "But this young man is smart, verdad? I hear he's gifted in computer programming skills. I need someone also who can build a data base from all the information coming in paper ledgers from the streets in the USA. Maybe we can also use him in hacker work and intelligence. We'll send him up north. He can be one of Mexico's 'disappeared,' but, like many of those, he'll be working for us.'"

"But if the girl is dead, what is our leverage over him? He loves Zs. He may try to contact them."

"He has family, including a mother and a sister," the Zeta pointed out. "He'll be afraid for their lives. We'll break him in. If he's a good boy, we'll get him plenty of women to help him through his grief. He'll get over this one. He'll learn that pussy is all the same. He can live as long as he plays ball with us. We'll use him until he wears out or his usefulness is over. It's so fucking hard to recruit IT experts, engineers, communications people, bankers, social media managers... Madre! Educated people are too afraid to come work for us. We have to take them."

The Zeta paused to sip his beer. He formulated a plan:

"Okay, let's dress Lopez in his suit for work on Monday, as you said. He'll know that the life of his woman is in his hands. He'll sell the mutual funds and stocks of The Z Foundation. He'll send e-mails to all interested parties that he's re-balancing the portfolio of the foundation and is increasing the stock allocations and decreasing the mutual funds. He'll explain that in the next days they will see transactions taking a conservative stance, i.e., cash, until he can meet with them and show them the prospectuses of the companies that he's recommending. He'll request a meeting with them in the following week to discuss his proposed investment strategies 'to take advantage of rapidly changing market conditions.' For three days he'll go on bogus client calls. These will explain his absence from the office during the days that the sales transactions are clearing. We'll keep him out of the office as much as possible so that his co-workers don't notice any signs of stress. When all the sales actions have cleared, he'll transfer the cash to Barbados. That should be next Thursday. Then he'll disappear."

"How will he disappear?" asked Horacio.

"He'll simply vanish. He'll leave a suicide note after he learns of the death of his fiancé that day, just to confuse things, to buy us time while we move him. No one will ever find his body or know what happened to him. I'll use him in the USA," responded the Zeta.

"And how will we know that he writes those e-mails correctly and doesn't screw up?"

The Zeta emitted a small laugh. "That same pleasant 'client' with whom he met last night can be his companion to observe him. During that meeting, our young banker can make his transactions and write his e-mail correspondence to the people who will receive transaction notices. After that, he'll explain to

46

his office that he's doing a focused series of calls upon clients over the next few days, and we'll keep him out of the office."

"What about his fiancé?" asked Horacio. "Certainly her friends and family will want to know where she is."

"Well, Sr. Ignacio Lopez will tell them that she's sick and that he's taking care of her. She's in bed with a fever. Perhaps she has a virus. Her true love is concerned for her and seeing to it that she rests and takes her medicine. He'll pass along to her their messages for her recovery. We can cover this for three days."

"Good, Raúl," responded Horacio. "You've thought it out well. You know me. I would be ready to just go in and take out the top leadership of the Zs with our bullets."

The Zeta noted the smooth way in which Horacio had fallen back on using his name.

He feels a certain friendship with me, but that's something we can never trust. He's respectful of my position and stays on his side of the line. What a clever man, really. He knows I once killed the President of Mexico, his wife, and two sons with my own gun. He never speaks of this. No one does. I love the Mexican propensity for denial. It helps us get away with murder.

He answered Horacio this way:

"There are still many in Mexico who believe that it was the Cartel of Sinaloa that was responsible for the assassinations of Pedro Navarro and his family. Look how that pig from Sinaloa, Navarro, was glorified after his death. The murder made him a martyr! Then Ana Valdez became the Interim President of Mexico, but she wisely declined to run in the elections. Yet, because of her work in victims' rights movements and the founding of the Zs, she's held up as if she's a living saint by stupid people in our country and even in the United States! The Santos kid too. And the fucking gringo that everyone likes, this David James. A gringo, por Dios! No, Horacio, let's not be the ones to make them martyrs. Instead, we'll suck them of their life blood, their money, which they give to people to war against us. Take their money, make them powerless, and their supporters will grow impatient and turn their backs. Eventually we'll kill them. When we do, we'll do this in a way that the Zetas are not blamed. Let's be patient. Success comes with patience."

He saw that Horacio was looking at him in an approving way. He stood up and stretched.

"This pinche air-conditioning is too cold for this little room. Let's get out and do some work in the streets of Monterrey. I love this city! Horacio, come with me to the big fiesta tonight. The son of our police chief is having his engagement party at the ranch house of his dad near Santiago. Some three thousand people are expected. A couple of Monterrey's finest DJs are going to play tribal guarachero music. Some of our Zeta boys will dance in their pointy boots. Our own group, Las Zapata, are coming late, and they promise to play a new corrido they have recorded in my studio. All of this makes me horny for women and eager to dance."

"Eyyyy, estoy contigo, I'm with you, boss," Horacio laughed, and he touched fists with the Zeta. "You have a date tonight, or you want me to have some women for you?"

The Zeta was already feeling lighter. "No, carnal, I'm tired of the whores. Tonight I want to find me a beautiful virgin, one who likes to dance and who admires older men. I'll check out who's there. You know, I need to cultivate more the image of a business man, especially now that I make so many trips to the United States. It's time for me to take a wife and set up the nice suburban life. I don't want to marry a whore, hombre. I need to find a sweet young girl who likes the good life and won't want to stick her nose too much into what I do. So maybe I'll have some luck at this big party. But if there are no virgins there, you can bring me the whores."

He slapped Horacio on the back, and they laughed. They went out of the casino with their entourage of body guards into the sweltering, concrete beauty of Monterrey.

Chapter 4: Blood Money

Ana and Valentina
Las Vegas, Nevada
Saturday Morning

If two people could create hysteria in a car, then hysterical would describe the scene for the first thirty or forty seconds in the Lexus after Valentina jumped in and Ana accelerated into the early morning traffic of The Strip. Valentina was still recovering from the shock of the shootings and her near stomping death in the casino. Ana's nerves were jagged from just having received texts from Enrique reporting that Valentina was in the casino lobby with men from the cartel and that shots were being fired. Ana had been nearby, ready to pick up Enrique, because they were following the Zetas accompanying Z-30, whom David had tracked to Las Vegas. Z-30 had come on David's radar during his investigations after the theft of the money from The Z Foundation. Valentina's presence in the casino with Z-30 and his men was a shock to Ana.

Both Valentina and Ana experienced mind-numbing astonishment that the other was there. In the initial moments in the car, when both were already emotionally wrought, the incomprehensibility of the other's presence confused them. On top of that, neither knew why there was shooting in the casino or who was shooting whom. In the mayhem and its aftermath, aunt and niece discovered one another. A giant "Huh?" hung in the air between them.

So it was a very distraught Ana Valdez who had shouted to Valentina, "Dios! Valentina, what the devil have you done? Get in the car!"

"I'm working, tía Ana!" Valentina responded when she jumped into the Lexus. Valentina's head snapped backwards when Ana stomped the gas to get into the lane of traffic. Valentina quickly adjusted her seat belt, an action from habit, not intent. She was still trying to focus on what needed to be done to salvage what looked like a disaster back there. She was already beginning to question her decision to give Corvette the bag of cash. She had to think clearly and act quickly. The decisions that she would make in the next minutes might mean more than whether or not she blew her cover. They might determine whether she would live or die. Now she realized that her jumping into the car of her aunt added another level of complexity to the high-stakes game that she was playing.

What is she doing here? Can she help me? Valentina wondered. She began to gush her story to Ana at the same time that Ana began spilling hers explaining why she was there. When they realized that they were speaking at the same time, Ana yielded.

"I'm doing my undercover work for the DEA, tía. I'm with Raúl Espinoza, the Z-30. He was moving us to a meeting in a casino out in Henderson when some guys attacked with guns. He was taking a lot of cash to the meeting, apparently. When the fight broke out, some young guys behind us rushed up and started doing some Z-style fighting. I had thought that they were Zs because they flipped into the air and struck with their feet and hands. They weren't dressed in black, so I wasn't sure. It became a big mess! I saw my DEA partner, Josh, take bullets. I'm sure they killed him! I fell under a horde of people and thought I was going to be trampled, but I managed to get outside!"

Valentina looked out the darkened car windows and had a new worry: *We're rushing too far from the casino. I can't get too far away in case either the DEA or Raúl looks for me.*

But Ana's words jolted Valentina from her pensive distraction. Ana was speaking Spanish rapidly and loudly because she was upset. She reported, "I'm in town because I came to Las Vegas with David and Enrique. We've been following the money paths of the Zetas in Mexico and the United States. Yes, those *were* Zs you saw back there! David has been working with your employer, the DEA. You know him. He has resources everywhere. Enrique and the Zs helping him were going to follow the Zeta entourage wherever they went this morning. I was on standby for Enrique to do whatever might be needed for them. David is at the DEA office here in Vegas. Then suddenly I received text messages from Enrique. He was inside The Oasis. One of his texts told me that you were walking through the casino with the Zetas. The next one said that shootings had begun. I didn't know you were in Vegas! I was a few blocks away and sped over here to see if I could help you or Enrique."

"I didn't see Enrique!" Valentina responded.

"Well, he's back in there, dressed in black!" Ana answered. She sounded irritated, as if she thought Valentina should have seen him and would be able to say if he were okay or not. "And you never told me that your work in the DEA was doing this type of undercover operation! Have you lost your mind, Valentina? Do you know what the Zetas do to people?"

"God, tía Ana, we have to keep calm. Please, we can talk about this later. Right now, help me think!"

"Okay. Where were you running to when I drove up?" Ana asked. Valentina took her aunt's new tone of voice as agreeing that it was important to calm down. Ana also slowed the Lexus. Valentina saw that her aunt was ready to make a course correction if necessary, as if they were presently on a course to anywhere. In truth, their get-away had simply been just that: flight to get away.

"I was going to run into the Venetian and call both the DEA and Raúl from there," Valentina answered. She thought she saw her aunt shoot her a quizzical look when she used the Zeta's first name. "So please don't go far now. I should stay in the vicinity of The Oasis! I'll need a believable story for Raúl about where I went when I ran. For certain he can't know I was with you!"

Ana put on the turn signal and moved into the far left lane. They would be turning onto Tropicana Boulevard. Valentina saw that her aunt was addressing her concern that they should return to the area of The Oasis.

51

You can't possibly be thinking about going back to the Zeta," Ana said with a decidedly reprimanding tone. "That man will slice off your head! He can make you disappear off the face of the earth and no one will ever know what became of you. I can't believe you let your work put you in this position! I'm sorry, I have to say this. I know we haven't seen each other much recently, except last month when I sold you my car. You could have told me then that you're doing this!"

"I decided to do this work, tía, but, please, there's no time for arguing about this now. I do want to save my life. You have to help me think! There's something important you need to know: I managed to get from under all the men fighting and made it to the casino doors. When I stepped outside, the bodyguard assigned to me, Luis, pushed a canvas bag to me. It was loaded with cash, I'm sure. He looked badly injured, and after he slid the bag toward me, he slumped backwards. He looked lifeless. I had seen Oasis security guards coming, and I heard police sirens getting louder, so I had to run. I could hardly carry the cash. The bag was heavy. I saw this guy I had met, Corvette Nightfire, and I gave him the bag of cash and also the keys to a Corvette that the Zeta had leased. The Corvette was supposed to be in front of the casino, but it wasn't there."

Ana spun her head toward her. "Eyyy, you did what? Why was Corvette Nightfire there?"

Valentina saw the shocked confusion which her revelation had produced in her aunt. Surprised, she asked Ana, "You know who he is?"

"Yes, he's the poker player! Why in the hell did you give him the cartel's money? He's working for the cartel? Why was he there?"

"No, tía Ana, and I know this sounds weird, but I have no clue why Corvette was there. He doesn't work for the cartel. I danced with him one evening a few nights ago when the Zeta went to a meeting with some men somewhere." She chose to call Raúl "the Zeta" now because she had seen her aunt's sensitivity about her familiarity with the man. "I didn't want to stay in the hotel suite like a prisoner. You know how I love to dance. The Zeta agreed to let me go because he's trying to make me think he's a nice man, a business man, so that he can seduce me later." Valentina said this to emphasize to her aunt that she wasn't having sex with Raúl and that she fully understood his intentions. Ana glanced at her.

Valentina continued, "The Zeta told Luis to take me to the Magnifico because a Mexican band was playing there. He probably thought that Luis would dance with me. I knew that Luis was somewhere watching me the whole time until the Zeta came to pick me up. Corvette asked me to dance almost as soon as I got there. I was standing alone because Luis had gone to the bar. We danced a couple of hours. I didn't see Luis, but I knew he was there somewhere observing everything. When the Zeta came in, he saw me dancing with Corvette. The Zeta took a big interest in Corvette after that. He told me that he soon would recruit him for his business. He said that in a very intimidating way."

"What do you think he meant?" Ana asked. "What kind of business does he tell you he has?"

"He told me he manages many different lines of businesses and that one of them is casinos. Knowing that Corvette is a poker player, I assumed that the Zeta would want to use Corvette in the cartel in some way having to do with cash. All the meetings that have happened among the Zetas on this trip have occurred in casinos. The Zeta talked about the cash that Corvette won and lost. It was a very sick thing, the way he talked about this. He tried to make it sound like he admired Corvette for the type of work he does, but his eyes were mocking. I could tell. I think he was jealous that I danced with Corvette, even though he had told me to go dance. But, because he had made it sound like he admired Corvette, when I saw Corvette at The Oasis, I thought I could give him the cash and later make the claim that the Zeta had told me that he would recruit him. Therefore, what I did would seem like a logical thing for me to do. I could say that I was trying to get the cash out of the casino and away from the police who were coming."

Ana put on the left turn signal and zoomed toward Koval Lane, a road running parallel to The Strip and behind its casinos. "So Corvette knew you when you gave him the cash," she said. "What did you tell him to do with it? Aren't you endangering his life by giving him this money?"

"Yes, tía, but I'm sure Corvette is in danger anyway because the Zeta has noticed the kind of work he does and because he danced with me. I'm not certain that Corvette recognized me right away. I spoke to him in Spanish, and he doesn't speak Spanish. On that night we danced, I had on evening makeup. My hair was up in a bun, and I dressed very elegantly. God, look at me now! I look a mess. I think he didn't know me at the moment I gave him the bag. Everyone was in panic because of the shootings. By now he probably has figured out it was me. I told him in Spanish to run and to look for the car. I gave him the car key too."

She saw that Ana was shaking her head incredulously. She needed to explain more, and quickly, because they were running out of time.

"I know where he's staying, tía. He's lodging at Pleasure Island this week while he's in side games with professional poker players who have arrived in Las Vegas ahead of the World Series of Poker, which is next week. Okay, I see you're confused. Here's what happened: Corvette asked me to dance that night. I kept my cover by telling him I didn't speak English. I knew Luis would be watching me. I danced with Corvette because he's so cute and I really liked him. He was very charming. He kept talking to me in English through the night, even though he believed I couldn't understand a word. It was like an amusement for him to do this. It let me know what his personality was like. I just smiled, and he kept talking."

Ana let out a low, soft chuckle. "Men!" she exclaimed. "Well, I think that the Zeta isn't the only one who would be jealous to know you were dancing with Corvette."

54

That comment interrupted Valentina's memories of her evening dancing. She asked, "What do you mean?"

"I'm talking about Enrique," Ana answered.

"Enrique!" Valentina exclaimed. "He has barely met me, and I recall that I didn't make any impression on him at all!"

"Enrique would never let you or any woman know his feelings," Ana said. "His life has been different. He has been closed up because of the big hole in his heart that's there from when his best friend, Israel, was murdered. But I know he sees you in his heart because of one comment he made. He said to me that you were very beautiful. I've never heard him say anything about any woman before."

"Wow," Valentina responded. "I would have no clue. Enrique is muy guapo. Those eyes! He could steal any heart."

Valentina looked out the window. She saw that the casinos on The Strip seemed to be passing beside them quickly. Ana was driving very fast.

She gets it, Valentina realized. *She's worried too. She knows we can't waste any time and that we have some important phone calls to make.*

Valentina continued, "Anyway, that night I learned a lot about Corvette. He told me that he was staying at Pleasure Island. He said that he had lost a lot of money in recent months, but that he had enough left to finance games this week before playing in the World Series. He said that he had grown up in San Antonio, but that when he was fifteen, his father got a job managing a resort in Barbados. So his family moved there. He said that his mother was a tall British woman who had married his short Mexican father because he had won her over with his dancing and his charm when they met on a cruise! I guess this is why Corvette looks like a handsome, tall Mexican. His mother loves Barbados. It was a British colony and the climate suits her. She's still alive, apparently, but his father mysteriously died in a motorcycle accident in Barbados when Corvette was eighteen years old. He said that they never knew the reason for his father's accident. He had gone for a ride in the middle of the night, and they found him beside the road with his overturned bike. Corvette just kept talking to me, tía, so I felt I knew him very well by the end of the evening. The thing is, I think he developed a big crush on me that night. Maybe he's like his father, a man who can fall in love with a woman at first sight! This is why when I saw him, I felt like I could give him the cash and that he would keep it safe until he heard from me. And I know that probably the first thing he did was to go to his room in Pleasure Island."

Now she saw understanding pass over her aunt's face. Valentina had calculated that Ana would understand because her aunt knew about love and passion. Tía Ana and the gringo, David James, had fallen in love six years earlier, and they still gazed at each other as if they couldn't wait to visit the bedroom. If Corvette was like David and had developed a thing for a Mexican woman, he would want to do anything to please her.

"Okay," Ana said. "Then one of the first things we need to do is to call this Corvette Nightfire's room and tell him to stay put and keep the cash out of view. Put it in the room safe if it'll fit. He shouldn't move unless he hears from you, because, obviously, his life is in great danger. If he calls the police or FBI, he'll have to tell them that you gave him the cash. It'll leak out and everyone will know. Worse, the cartel's cash will be taken away by the police. The cartel won't forgive either of you for losing their money. The cartel will kill him and you if that happens. You don't take money from a cartel without terrible retribution."

Valentina saw in her aunt's face how genuinely worried she was about her. Then suddenly she looked puzzled. Ana glanced at her and said, "Valentina, I don't understand why Corvette was at The Oasis entrance just when the Zetas were about to leave the building. Are you sure that he isn't already connected with the cartel? Why would he be there?"

"I really don't know, tía, but everything about this man tells me that he's an innocent and that he's here in Las Vegas because of the poker tournament. He seems like a completely guileless person to me." Valentina sighed. She continued, "But you're right, tía Ana. His life *is* in danger! Maybe I shouldn't have done what I did. Maybe I should have just left the cash at the door and run. But I knew the DEA wants to catch the Zeta making a money transfer. I had seen Raúl getting away, and he didn't have the cash. Suddenly I had it. I thought that I could return it to him later. And since he had told me that he wanted to talk to Corvette, I would be able to deliver Corvette to Raúl as well."

But inside, Valentina wondered, *Did I make a hasty decision and now I'm justifying it?*

Ana asked, "Is it possible that no one saw you give Corvette the cash?"

"I don't know! There's that possibility. Everyone was occupied with the fighting when I escaped. Luis would know, but I'm sure he died after he pushed the bag to me."

"Okay," Ana said. "I guess we can't know for certain if you were seen. Right now, we're losing too much time. We should call Corvette and tell him to stay and wait for us. Since he thinks that you don't speak English, I'll call him and tell him that you're with me. Then I'll put you on the phone. Maybe you can use some broken English, enough to let him know that it's you. Tell him something from your evening together so he can be sure. Say some things in Spanish and continue your cover of not knowing English."

"But I also need to call the DEA and the Zeta!"

"Yes," Ana replied. "So we have to hurry. We'll call Corvette first. Also, I need to contact Enrique to find out if he and the Zs are okay. Dios, please! Who attacked the Zetas? It had to be the Cartel of Sinaloa. The cartel killings keep escalating in the USA. If Enrique and the Zs are okay, they can help protect Corvette while we determine our plan of action. David can help with this. He'll know what to do. He's been working not only with the DEA, but also with the FBI and Homeland Security. They helped him track Z-30 to Las Vegas. I don't know if you heard, but The Z

Foundation had its money stolen. Almost all of it. We're working furiously to find it. So it seems that all of us are chasing cash."

"Dios, tía Ana! No, I didn't know about this! Oh my God! Do you know who did it?"

Ana gave her knowing look. "We feel certain that the Zetas did it."

Valentina released a heavy breath. "Then this cash we're talking about belongs to the Foundation."

"No, not directly," Ana responded. Ana crossed Sands Avenue and pulled into a parking lot. She said, "I'm going to pull in here briefly so we can call Corvette and Enrique. After those calls, we'll know more about what's going on."

"Okay," Valentina agreed. She was starting to feel a fresh wave of nervousness. There was a nagging question in the back of her mind, and as her aunt began to enter the parking lot, she asked, "Tía Ana, you said David has been working with the DEA. I wonder why he didn't know about my undercover work with the Zeta."

"That's a very good question, mi querida," Ana answered. "Perhaps he knew and didn't tell me. Perhaps it wasn't shared with him because of compartmentalization in that agency. That's something we'll find out from him."

Ana pulled into a parking spot. But suddenly they could hear sirens again even over the noise of the car air-conditioning fan. Lots of sirens.

"Oh my God!" Ana exclaimed. Valentina noted her aunt's habit to use that expression in English whenever she was surprised by something. She did the same thing. It was as if she and her aunt shared verbal DNA. "Those would be the ambulances," Ana pointed out. "There must be multiple injuries. Valentina, we should just go directly over to Pleasure Island before they begin cordoning off the streets. Traffic around here is going to be horrible. We'll get stuck."

"Yes!" Valentina agreed. "Let's go! Tía, just drive. I'll try to call Corvette. If he answers the phone, I'll say, 'Es Valentina,' and I'll use a few English words and then put you on the phone. You should try to call Enrique now while I'm doing this."

"Okay," Ana answered. She was already exiting the parking lot and turning right on Sands. The two women heard the sirens becoming louder. Valentina pulled out her phone and dialed information to get the number for Pleasure Island. Ana began to fumble inside her purse with her right hand as she drove. Just as she found her phone with her hand, it began to ring. At the same time, Valentina was requesting the number to Pleasure Island. She turned to see her aunt looking at the screen of her phone.

"It's Enrique!" Ana mouthed silently to Valentina. Then Valentina heard her aunt answer the phone by coming directly to the point: "Enrique, are you okay?"

But Valentina was interrupted by the voice of the Pleasure Island receptionist on her phone asking how she could assist her call. She asked to be connected to Corvette Nightfire's room. While the phone rang, she listened to Ana's side of her conversation with Enrique. "Thanks God!" she heard Ana say in English. That was how her aunt always used that expression. It didn't matter how many times Valentina had told her that this was not grammatically correct in English. Then Ana asked Enrique, "They're all okay? All the Zs?"

In Valentina's ear the ringing of the phone in Corvette's hotel room continued with no answer. She decided to disconnect and to call back. Perhaps an annoyance factor of a phone ringing, stopping, and starting again would prompt Corvette to answer, if he were in his room. Valentina just *knew* he was there. She re-dialed the number and asked for Corvette's room. The ringing began again.

She heard Ana asking Enrique who were the people who began shooting at the Zetas. Then she asked him how many people were shot. In her phone, Valentina continued hearing the ringing with no answer. Her aunt looked over at her, and Valentina made a gesture to show that Corvette wasn't picking up the phone in his room. Ana nodded her understanding.

Valentina disconnected, and then she heard Ana say, "Enrique, listen to me. As soon as the police finish with your statement, get your guys and come over to Pleasure Island. Right now Valentina and I are on the way to the lobby there to try to find someone."

There was a pause for some question by Enrique, and then Ana answered, "Yes, Enrique, she's with me. We have quite a complex situation, and I'll explain it to you as soon as I see you."

It was at this very moment, as Valentina began to deal with a new despairing feeling because she had neither the cash nor Corvette to bring to the Zeta, that she saw a look of shock appear on her aunt's face as she listened to Enrique.

"How do you know about the bag?" Ana asked him.

Valentina sat upright when she heard this.

"Yes, you're correct," Ana said. "We're looking for the person she gave it to. He has a room in Pleasure Island. Did anyone else see?"

Valentina struggled to hear Enrique's answer to her aunt, but Ana was holding the phone too closely for Valentina to hear. She thought that Ana suddenly looked pale. Then she heard Ana say, "Okay. I need to reach David. If by chance you talk to him before I do, make sure he knows that Valentina is with me and that we're heading to Pleasure Island. I think he's still in the DEA offices on Main Street right now. I'm sure the DEA also wants to know where Valentina is. Enrique, free up as soon as you can. We can probably use some help from the Zs, so bring some with you and meet us at Pleasure Island. Call me when you're on the way, and I'll tell you where we are."

As Ana clicked off her phone, Valentina felt like her aunt was going to give her bad news.

She did it with a sigh. Ana looked at her and said, "We really have to find Corvette. There were three deaths in the casino."

Valentina inhaled sharply and began counting: "Luis, Josh, and....?"

"Enrique believes the third one is Raúl Espinoza," her aunt answered. "Z-30."

Valentina hadn't even recovered from shock when Ana's phone rang with a call that would change their plans.

Chapter 5: A Heart Defeated

Corvette Nightfire
Las Vegas, Nevada
Saturday Morning

To the rhythm of the Latin music, the girl's arms swayed in spellbinding dance. Corvette saw nothing else in the dim light of the ballroom except these seductive, bronze-colored charm snakes writhing sensually, interpreting stories just for him. She sparked him. He felt a charged pulsing in his chest from some orchestra she had discovered inside him. She scored her stories to music, and at times the girl conducted the orchestra to a crescendo, and the percussion section boomed vibrations through his skin and bones. It made him dance with sexy, loose abandon that released him from gravity. Every now and then, when her arms receded a bit into the darkness, Corvette glimpsed the smile of the woman and the deepness of her brown eyes. Those eyes were knowing. He could tell that she saw the joy in his heart.

He hoped that the evening would never end. He imagined that she would forever be his partner of arms, and he smiled. Those wonderfully toned and elegant limbs of this magic woman were directing his every move on the dance floor. He wished he could sing to her in Spanish, but he couldn't. Instead, he spoke words, the words of his life, English words that he knew she wouldn't understand; but he wanted to sing his whole life to her in these lyrics. So he told her everything about his life: his dad, his mom, his hopes, his dreams, his life in Texas and Barbados, his wins and losses of poker. He told her how beautiful were her arms, and that sounded so absurd; yet there they were, dancing with Latin ease; and her smile became even more dazzling after he said it. He felt that this girl was exciting him to a slow and powerful orgasm in his heart, and that his whole body was going to ejaculate promises to her of world riches and a lifetime of devotion.

Her name came back to him: Valentina. Such a perfect name for this exotic woman sashaying and telling stories through her dance! A woman whose body swirled through time while her slender arms and coquettish smile held Corvette transfixed in a moment...such a woman should be named Valentina!

Corvette was used to stunning girls pursuing him. This had happened as long as he could remember. Women lost their sensibilities around him. They liked him. Yet this evening, this enchanting night, he had met the first girl for whom he wanted to sing the words of his life from a heart so happy that he thought it was going to burst.

But then the music became weird. It became not music at all, but a ringing sound, very insistent. The arms quit dancing when that happened. They posed, as if expecting something. The ringing stopped. Corvette peered beyond the arms into the darkness to try to discern the face of Valentina again, but he didn't see her. The ringing started once more. It was such an annoying ring. If that wasn't bad enough, the sound of sirens joined it. Suddenly when he looked, he saw that the arms were extending a green bag to him.

He jolted awake, cold. Drool was trailing from the side of his mouth to the bedspread. The room was dark except for the crack of light coming from the window. From his prone position he could see the stacks of hundred dollar bills that populated the cover of his bed.

Jesus! Of course! The girl who handed me the bag was Valentina! I remember her arms from our night of dancing. How could I have forgotten that?

Corvette squinted in the darkness, as if doing that would sharpen his memory. He tried to recapture the memory of the girl's face when she had handed him the bag. Yes, the eyes were just about right. The girl in front of the casino didn't have any make-up on, and she looked like she was dressed for jogging or something, but....

She was Valentina!

He also saw that the cash on his bed was as real as it could be. He jumped up and stared at it. Then he noticed the phone on his night table.

That was the ringing. Man, how long was I asleep? The voice message light wasn't on.

It was just after nine in the morning. Corvette wasn't sure what time it had been when he came into the room, but unless he had slept an entire day, he didn't think he could have been asleep more than twenty or thirty minutes.

He turned to the source of the crack of light in the room. He walked over and parted the curtains a little more. He had a view of Las Vegas Boulevard. There were police cars and fire trucks everywhere. The road had been cordoned off to traffic. He saw three news helicopters circling overhead. The sidewalks were filled with the curious: a mixed crowd of tourists, guests, hotel and casino staff, and convention attendees who had come out to see the commotion from various hotels.

This is not good! How many injuries? he wondered. *God, did anyone die?* The thoughts startled him into being fully awake.

There was ample sunlight in the room from the widened curtains. He saw the TV remote on the nightstand and fetched it. He pointed it at the television, and in just a couple of clicks of the channels he had a live broadcast with an aerial view of the front of The Oasis and the mayhem of people and vehicles outside the hotel. A banner at the bottom of the screen proclaimed "Three reported deaths in gangland shootout inside Oasis Hotel and Casino." A commentator in a small window in the top right corner of the screen was summarizing what was known so far:

"We only have been able to talk to a few eye witnesses who have very conflicting reports about what happened here approximately at 8:30 am inside the entrance to The Oasis Hotel and Casino. We're trying to get confirmation of numbers of injuries or deaths after what apparently was some kind of shootout and fight at the entrance doors and off the lobby of The Oasis. We have not been allowed into the casino. The city and state police are inside, along with the City of Las Vegas Fire and Rescue teams. We have been promised that there will be a statement as soon as possible from the Sheriff. That would be Sheriff Paul Robertson, who heads the police department for Las Vegas and Clark County. But we also have seen state police and FBI vehicles here, indicating, of course, the presence of those law enforcement units. A very concerning and tragic occurrence here in The Oasis. Witnesses have said that there are three persons who were killed in the melee and that the lobby was filled with tourists and guests, including children, who witnessed what happened. Apparently there also were many injuries, but we have not been able to confirm any of the numbers yet."

Corvette half listened for the next few minutes as different commentators droned on, having no new information to report. One word kept flashing in his mind:

Gangland! What did that mean? Mafia? Why did they say "gangland?"

He looked at the cash on the bed.

I have to be nuts! How much is that? Valentina gave me gangland money?

It didn't make sense to him. He tried to reconcile that thought with the feelings that his sweet and innocent Mexican dance partner evoked from him, and those two things didn't jive. He suddenly felt like he needed to hurry and do something, but he didn't know what. The easy thing came to him: he should count the money.

He put several stacks side by side on the desk near the window and saw that all the stacks were uniform. He counted out one hundred bills in one of the stacks. Each stack therefore was ten thousand dollars. He counted the stacks. There were two hundred thirteen stacks. He had two million, one hundred thirty thousand dollars.

He pulled the desk chair out and let himself fall into it.

Oh shit.

He thought about the girl who gave him the money: Valentina.

Why would she do this to me? Or for me?

He reconstructed in his mind what had happened:

She came out of that mess in the casino. She stood there a moment, but then the door opened and hit her and she turned around. Someone pushed her the bag, but....I don't think from the way she was acting that she was expecting that. Then what did she do? She reached down and felt the bag. Then she picked it up. It was heavy. She set it down. But she probably knew what was in the bag. And if someone pushed it to her, then that person knew her and trusted her. So she knew the guy. So she was one of them. Then she looks around for someone. She doesn't see them, but she sees me. She recognizes me and brings me the bag, tells me to run, find the car, and then she runs away. So she was trying to get away, probably even when she first came out without the bag.

Okay. Fine. She's scared and trying to get away. She knows what's in the bag and gives it to me. What does she think I'll do with it? Hmmm, she thinks I recognize her. Let's say that she gives this to me because she trusts me, not because she's trying to screw me. I just don't get a bad vibe from her like that. Maybe she gave it to me because she's going to come join me. How will she know where I am?

He got up and poured himself some water. He thought of something he could be doing while he thought things out: He gathered the stacks of cash on the bed. His dream about Valentina's arms came back to him. It made him think about the night they danced. He wondered what happened that night, besides the fact that he felt like he had fallen head over heels for a woman who couldn't even understand what he was saying to her.

Damn! Yes, I told her everything about me that night, including where I was staying. Maybe she doesn't understand English, but she would understand 'Pleasure Island.' She knows I'm in this hotel. When she gave me the bag, she knew where she could find me. That has to be it!

66

Suddenly Corvette had an overwhelming feeling that at any moment gunmen would come bursting through the door of his room. His heart began to race. He stared at the door. Then he looked at the phone.

I was dreaming. Did my phone really ring? Twice? Was that her?

He tried to remember more about the night they danced. He had seen a man come in, and Valentina had nodded acknowledgement to him from across the dance floor. He was older, old enough to be her father, Corvette recalled. He was a tough looking dude, a Mexican man from his dress and appearance, and solidly built. He had looked at Corvette coldly, but Corvette had become distracted by the sweet voice of Valentina as she excused herself from him in Spanish. Then she had taken the man's arm as if he were a father, and the two of them walked out. Corvette remembered seeing another man, short and muscular, leaving behind them. He had a Mexican appearance as well. Corvette strained his memory for details of the looks of the two men.

They didn't look like pleasant men. They looked...mean. Mean-looking, gangland, Mexican men. Gangland? In Mexico, that could only mean drug cartels. Who else would be carrying around a couple of million dollars in cash, even in Las Vegas? What was Valentina doing with those guys?

His throat still felt dry so he retrieved his water. Then he tried to answer his questions:

This morning, she apparently was running away from them. She came out expecting to see someone who was going to help her get away. Instead, she saw me and gave me the bag, told me to run, and then she fled. When she got to the street, someone did race up and rescue her, and off she went. So I don't know who she's with now or what the business is about the Corvette, but she probably has tried, or will try, to contact me. Maybe she's going to know what to do about the money. She heard the sirens like I did. She could have given the bag to the police, but she didn't. So she wanted to avoid the police. She

67

preferred to give the bag to me. I need to know why before I do anything, and that means I need to talk to her. So maybe I don't know everything, but I know a lot more than I did ten minutes ago. Now I need to grow some balls and deal with this.

It was precisely that kind of thinking that helped Corvette realize that Valentina was dealing with some heavy shit. If she could do that, then so could he. He reviewed his options: He could succumb to panic and make knee-jerk decisions that he would regret later, or he could be a poker player and make some bold moves even if he was scared.

Bluffing is what I do, he remembered. *I just need to find out who the other players are at the table.*

If it were possible to keep the cash, he wanted to. He needed it. His mother needed it.

It was time to take action and be a person in control of things. One thing he needed to do was to get out of that room with the cash. The first inklings of a plan began to come to him.

If that was Valentina on the phone calling me, she would have asked for the hotel operator to ring my room. The hotel wouldn't give out my room number. So the next most logical thing would be that she would come here. I wonder how we'll communicate if she doesn't speak English? I guess we would muddle through it. Maybe she would communicate with me with the help of the person who was in the Lexus.

Corvette looked at his watch. He realized that possibly enough time would have passed for Valentina to come to the hotel if that had been her calling earlier. She would probably come to the lobby. Possibly there she would ask that the room be rung again. He should discreetly go to the lobby and see if he saw her or anyone suspicious. He would do that in just a few minutes.

First, he had someone to call to start his plan of action. He searched his pants pockets and found his phone. He pressed a speed dial number. While the phone was ringing, Corvette saw his image in the mirror on the closet door. He was wearing cream colored linen pants, a white cotton shirt, and a casual, linen jacket almost the same color as his pants. He had on his watch with a silver band and a matching man's bracelet. His dark brown, almost shoulder-length hair looked oily from sweat and the battering of a long, past twenty-four hours.

I've got to change clothes and look very different, he thought.

A voice answered the phone. It was Raymundo, his private taxi driver and sometime-gopher whom he hired whenever he was in Las Vegas. Raymundo had an appreciation for Corvette's semi-celebrity poker status, his crazy hours, and his needs for personal errands during odd times, usually when Corvette was in play. Raymundo was a new young father and planned to marry his girlfriend soon. Corvette had enjoyed many long talks with Raymundo in his taxi-van during jaunts around Las Vegas and to and from the airport, and the two had become fast friends. Raymundo usually teased Corvette about being a Mexican-American who couldn't speak Spanish and would give him lessons in the form of short phrases which he could use to "communicate" with the señioritas, but Corvette was a reluctant student. Raymundo had friends in all walks of life, and he knew how to keep secrets and be discreet. Corvette trusted him completely.

"Raymundo, are you off today?" Corvette asked him.

"I'm available all day for you, amigo," Raymundo answered.

That reminded Corvette that Raymundo spoke Spanish. *Maybe he can help me communicate with Valentina,* he noted. "Gracias, amigo. Listen, I have special work for you today. I'm under a lot of pressure and this work must be done quickly and with absolutely no one but you knowing about these things. I have some serious money for you for this work, and I know you will do it with absolute professionalism. Let me ask you something. Do you have a credit card with a little room on it? I may need you to charge things, and, of course, I'll reimburse you all expenses when I see you."

Raymundo was young, and Corvette wasn't sure if he would have credit, but he gave it a shot because Raymundo was his own businessman and displayed some hustle in his work ethic. He also was a technology addict, always fiddling with his data phone and searching the internet for businesses, restaurants, hotels, and places of interest for his clients, and checking his e-mail and social media pages.

"Sí, sí, within reason. I'm not a wealthy man like you, but I can accommodate a few things perhaps. What do you have in mind?" Raymundo answered.

It was an ironic statement, Corvette thought. Raymundo assumed that he was a wealthy man, which he wasn't at all. He recently had been broke. Now, however, he possibly was wealthy again. The question, as usual in his life, was would he be able to keep this status? Any status of life for Corvette changed suddenly and often.

And now there's a new question, Corvette thought. *Can I keep my life?*

"Good," Corvette answered. "Where are you now? Are you near The Strip?"

"No, I'm at home, not far from there. I can be anywhere you need quickly. Where are you?"

"I'm still at Pleasure Island, Raymundo, but I need to get out of here, and I have to go into hiding. That's hard for me, as you can imagine, so I'll need your help. I'm about to meet someone here in the next few minutes, I think. I'm going downstairs to look for her. While I do this, you can be doing a few things for me right now: Search and find when there are flights today out of Vegas and out of Reno to Barbados, or to Miami if there are no available flights today to Barbados. Write down or print the schedules. Check availability on those flights. I need to go as soon as possible. If the only available flights to Barbados are later in the day, say, late afternoon, then I need you to find me a hotel room I can use to wait in. Somewhere off The Strip. Don't put the room in my name. I would want you to rent it in your name. That's why I asked about your credit card. We can talk about this more after we know flight schedules. Will this be possible?"

"That's no problem, Corvette."

"Okay, as for the flights, I'll only have one carry-on luggage. I won't check bags."

"Okay."

"Next, there's a form for declaring money when you travel. Search it. I think it is called something like FinCen 105, a report for international transport of currency. I used it once a long time ago, but I can't remember how I got it. See if you can find it online and print it."

"FinCen 105. Got it. I've heard clients talk about this," Raymundo answered.

Corvette continued, looking at himself in the mirror. "If I have time, I want to get a haircut somewhere off The Strip where no one will recognize me. I need to change my look and style. Pick a place for the haircut. Also, I need you to get me a few clothes. I want to dress like you. My shirts are size sixteen neck, and thirty-six sleeve if you get me long sleeve. Extra-large shirt otherwise. In pants, size thirty-three or thirty-four waist, and length thirty-six. If you want to do me right, go ahead and get shoes or boots. I'm size eleven."

Raymundo burst out laughing. "You're good with numbers, not surprising for a poker player. You got the face for Mexicano, mi amigo. You want to be one hundred percent Mexican like me today?"

"Sí," Corvette answered.

"You need my underwear?"

"Very funny, Raymundo," Corvette replied. The comment relaxed him a little. He was amused.

He remembered the first time that his friend had told him his name. "Seriously?" Corvette had asked him. "In English, your name is Raymond?"

"Sí, and everyone loves me. Well, a corrupted translation from Spanish would be 'world lightning bolt'" Raymundo answered him. Corvette had seen from the speed by which Raymundo got things done, it was an apt name.

He returned to his instructions to Raymundo: "If I catch a flight quickly, we won't worry about the clothes. You'll get these if I have to wait somewhere. Obviously, these will be very quick purchases."

"Anything else?"

Corvette said, "I'm scheduled to be in a poker game this evening. I'll need you to call and make an excuse for me, but I'll tell you later exactly how to handle that. Just remind me about it. There's an etiquette about not showing up, and I'll want to compensate the guys and the casino as a courtesy for putting up with my withdrawal."

"Okay, bueno, I'll remind you."

"Go ahead and get started on these things. I'll call back in a little while after I do some things here," Corvette replied. He always felt good about Raymundo's attention to details. He felt tremendous relief just knowing he had someone helping him with his plan. He added, "Gracias, amigo. I always count on you and trust you. I'll make today's work worth your while, I promise you."

"You always take care of me, compadre," Raymundo answered. "I'm not worried about this. Hasta luego."

When he hung up with Raymundo, he had a slight feeling of satisfaction that came from doing something. Yet, there was a nagging in his heart, a small ache, which he knew had to do with Valentina. She had given him something that morning. It was more than just the cash. His feelings about this surprised him. He felt a bond with this girl because in the middle of some calamity still not understood, she had chosen to take a big step that involved him. He wanted to believe in her. He wanted to believe that she was good. He was dying to see her so that there could be some explanation for what happened at The Oasis. If he could help her in some way, he wanted to. He was praying that she wasn't one of the bad guys. To Corvette, everything in his life was like poker. He went all in when he thought the hand was with him. He always wanted the big pot, or nothing.

But when life or death is at stake, it's important to be prepared for anything, thought Corvette, *even the possibility that Valentina is a snake.* He had a few things he needed to do to write an insurance policy for himself: He had to get some items that he would need from the convenience store in the hotel. He had to race time. He decided that he should go downstairs to see if he saw any trace of Valentina, and if not, he would make his quick purchases in the convenience store and then return to his room to grab a fast shower and change clothes. He would make another change later with the clothes that Raymundo would bring.

He got a brown sports cap from his closet and pushed his hair up in it. He took off his jacket and checked himself in the mirror. He wanted to spot Valentina without being recognized by her or anyone else if he could, just so he could assess the situation. He thought of his sunglasses and put them on. The hat and the glasses definitely gave him a different look, but to be safe, Corvette decided to change shirts as well. He chose a dark brown, short-sleeve cotton shirt that coordinated well with his crème colored pants.

This is as generic as I'm going to look with the clothes I have, Corvette sighed. He knew that his height didn't exactly let him blend in the crowd, but for Vegas, he thought that he had a conservative look.

He did a quick run-through of the lobby, the entrance, and nearby sections of the casino, but he saw no trace of Valentina. He hid briefly in several strategic spots to survey the people around him, but he didn't see her or anyone who set off alarms inside his head. So he strode to the convenience store, made his purchases, returned to his room, stripped off his clothes, showered, shampooed, and dressed again. All this took twenty-five minutes.

He had just finished packing the green canvas bag and putting the last stack of cash inside it when the telephone in the room rang. The sound made him jump. He lost balance and fell against the mirrored closet door.

"Shit!" Corvette yelled out. He felt his heart racing. "Geez, get your act together", he admonished himself as he raced for the phone. He felt embarrassed by the startle, and he was angry with himself. He didn't want to be afraid, but he was.

When he answered the phone, he expected to hear a woman's voice, but instead it was a man's. This made Corvette stand erect.

"Is this Corvette Nightfire?" asked the voice. It had a Hispanic accent.

He hesitated for a moment, but he knew he was cornered. "Yes," he answered tentatively.

"We need you to come to the lobby. Bring the green bag with the cash."

Corvette was expecting some kind of discussion, but the voice was so to the point that it jarred his thought patterns. A surge of fear seized his chest. When he didn't answer, the voice said, "Do you need assistance with this?" But the man asked in a way that sounded sinister rather than helpful.

"No," Corvette answered, but his throat was dry, causing his voice to crack. He knew he sounded weak. He became pissed with himself again, so he repeated forcefully: "No." Then he effected a sarcastic tone. "I don't need assistance."

"We'll see you in five minutes," replied the voice.

"How will I know you?" Corvette asked.

But the man disconnected, and the silence of the phone line left Corvette feeling defeated.

Valentina has slipped out of reach, he thought despondently. The discouraging sadness that he felt was more powerful than the painful knot of anxiety in his chest due to his fear. His sadness about Valentina was rooting inside him.

He sighed. It was time to make a decision.

Play this like poker, Corvette, he suggested to himself to calm his nerves. *Think of the odds and the probabilities, make a choice, and when you get downstairs, bluff if you need to.*

He visually surveyed his room. He saw his sunglasses on the bed and his sports cap on the bedside table. He decided to go downstairs with his hair down. There was no need to disguise himself right now. He looked at the green bag, considered it for a few seconds, and then picked it up. He left his room and headed to the lobby.

No one rode down on the elevator he caught, and there were no stops on other floors. He was arriving in less than five minutes. He stepped off the elevator, and four persons got on, and then the alcove to the bank of elevators was empty. He heard the casino beyond and proceeded to walk toward it.

He didn't have to go far before meeting his party. Five young guys suddenly encircled him. One said, "Come with us."

The group walked him a short distance along the wall to a section of the casino clear of people. They brought him to a tall Hispanic man dressed completely in black. He had straight, onyx-black hair almost as long as Corvette's. His brooding black eyes bore into him. Corvette thought he had movie star looks. He had seen him before. He was the young man who had stared at him from The Oasis doorway when Corvette was making a retreat with the green duffle bag. For some reason this familiarity caused Corvette to relax slightly. The other young men backed away as if to provide a little meeting space for Corvette and the man with the appraising stare.

Corvette decided to make the first move without hesitation, as a way of communicating that he didn't feel intimidated by the group. But he did.

"I saw you before," he said. "You were staring at me when I was leaving The Oasis. Valentina had given me the bag and had told me to run. She took off, and I did what she said. I saw you when the police were arriving. Why isn't she here? Have you hurt her?"

From the man's reaction, Corvette saw that his strategy had worked and that he had caught the guy off guard. A look of disgust came on his face. He let out a small, disdainful snort, and answered impatiently, "No, we didn't hurt her. Hand me el maldito bag."

Score one for me, Corvette thought. He clenched his fist tightly around the handles of the bag. *He knew her by name. My bet is that Valentina and this guy are on the same side.*

He decided to press. He ignored the man's demand and asked, "Where is she? I expected her to come. She's the one who gave me the bag."

The guy's glare became darker, more impatient. "She's in a safe place. I came instead. There's not a lot of time. You have to give me the money right now."

Corvette made a show of looking at the five young men who stood around him. All of them looked Hispanic. He saw their bodies tense with the possibility that they might have to intervene to take the bag.

"Are you cartel?" Corvette asked.

The guy's patience was spent. He didn't answer. He put out his arm and started to step forward. Corvette dropped the bag to the floor and postured as if he were going to push it to him.

"Valentina gave me the bag. I would rather give it to her. You could be her enemy." He had stooped his long frame over the bag but kept holding the man's gaze. He thought that if this guy and Valentina were on the same side, his statement would make the guy keep talking to him. He wanted to get as much information as possible.

The man beckoned with his fingers for Corvette to shove him the bag. When he did, the man answered his question while he partially unzipped the bag and looked inside. He said, "We're not cartel. We're not her enemy."

Corvette could see the tops of cash stacks through the small opening. The man quickly re-zipped the bag.

"Did you count it?" the guy asked.

That surprised Corvette. "No," he answered quickly. "I looked and left it just as I received it."

The man lifted the bag as if weighing it. He set it down again.

"Is there any way I can see Valentina? I want to tell her some things," Corvette said.

The man emitted another snort and the look of disdain appeared again. "Do you speak Spanish?" he asked mockingly. He and the group looked ready to leave.

So he knows something about me, Corvette observed.

"I didn't grow up in a Spanish-speaking household," Corvette replied quickly.

"Hombre, look at yourself in the mirror. You're Mexican. You should speak Spanish. Anyone looking at you would expect you to speak Spanish. I didn't grow up in an English-speaking household in Mexico City, but I'm talking to you."

Geez, he seems actually angry about this! This is crazy. A light-bulb went off in Corvette's head. *This guy is all personal about me. Maybe he likes Valentina! I have to keep him talking.*

"I do want to learn Spanish," Corvette said. "My father was Mexican. I regret not learning. You seem to know who I am. What's your name?"

The guy stared again. "Enrique," he finally answered.

"Enrique, if you're not cartel and you're Mexican, then I presume you're not Las Vegas police or FBI or anything. So who are you guys?"

"We're Zs," he answered. His tone was such that he didn't expect Corvette to know who Zs were.

But Corvette did know, and he could feel the look of astonishment that reddened his face. He saw that Enrique noticed it too. Corvette looked again at the five other young men. They were lean, muscular, and obviously physically fit. A flood of information and memories washed over him. It had been a while, but he had been interested in the many articles about the Zs that were on internet news and features sites. In particular, their physical training impressed him.

"Z for zorros," Corvette returned quickly. "I've read a lot about you. You fight the cartels in Mexico, and you live by some rules of life. Clean living. You also do training which is like parkour or free running. It is like the American Ninja Warrior competition. They have a park here in Las Vegas and places around the world. When Mexico had the military coup a couple of years ago, the Zs were helping people during the transition time to elections. I remember all this. There was an American who was down in Mexico, and he helped form the Zs, right?"

Corvette saw that he had scored. All six of the guys were now looking at him with explicit interest.

"Sí, he's a United States citizen," Enrique answered. "His name is David James."

A new voice suddenly announced its presence from behind Enrique and the Zs. None of them had noticed the man behind them, and Corvette hadn't seen him either. He walked up to the group. Corvette saw that he was another physically fit looking man, but older, perhaps in his late fifties or early sixties. He had close-cropped white hair and a tanned face. He was definitely a gringo, Corvette decided.

The man said, "I hear my name being mentioned." The group of men was obviously surprised. Enrique let out a small exclamation and then gave the man a sideways hug. The others smiled and acknowledged him respectfully.

The man grinned a little and said, "Enrique, I take it that this gentleman turned over the cash to you?"

"Sí, David," he answered, but he had a sheepish look, as if he wondered how much of the conversation with Corvette that David had heard and was unsure if he had handled things well. He added, "Thanks for talking to the police and the DEA so I could get away from The Oasis and come over here."

David responded, "No problem, Enrique. I arrived here as soon as I could. Lots of traffic, and the streets are blocked off outside."

David then held out his hand to Corvette and said, "I'm David. Do you mind if I call you Corvette?"

The man's friendly approach and confident air made Corvette feel safe for the first time since the meeting began with the group of Zs. Relaxed a little more, he shook his hand warmly and said, "Thank you, sir. Yes, please call me Corvette."

"Good," said David. He looked around. "Listen, we all need to get out of here. There were some deaths over in The Oasis.

78

The leader of the Zetas may have been killed. A DEA agent died. So did a Zeta cartel member. Some others from the Zetas and some from the Cartel of Sinaloa were injured and have either been taken to the hospital or have been taken into custody. We don't know how many escaped before the police arrived. It looks like the Sinaloa cartel was trying to ambush the leader of the Zetas at a time when he was transferring cash. We don't know if they knew about the cash transfer at the time or if they were just trying to kill the leader known as Z-30 and by coincidence picked a time that money was being moved. In any event, the cartel members are all over Vegas, and it is better if we're not seen together now."

David looked hard at Corvette. He added, "You could be in big danger, son. You took the cartel's money."

Corvette responded, "I didn't know what I had. This girl Valentina I met a few days ago gave me it and the key to a Corvette. Do you think someone saw?"

"Enrique did," David answered, "and there's no telling who else. There are security cameras everywhere at The Oasis, and we think that in Vegas many of the security guys are taking money from the cartels now for favors. "

"I gave the money to you. What's going to happen to it? Does it go to the Zs?"

"No, Corvette," David replied. "The money is going to the DEA. It belongs to the United States Government now. I do consulting work with the DEA and have been with them this morning. They have their hands full right now with their agent's death. The DEA also knows about the Corvette. They're looking for it."

"Do you need the key fob? I have it in my room."

"If you don't have it with you, we won't worry about it right now because the car was a leased car and we can get another key from the leasing agency." He smiled and added, "Let us know if you see the car anywhere."

Corvette could sense that they were all about to leave, so he was trying to get as many questions answered as he could from this man who was much more friendly and communicative than Enrique. He pressed forward with the question he wanted answered the most: "Is there any way I can talk to Valentina? Or is she a member of a cartel? Please, I want to know this."

David's face became completely impassive. Corvette didn't know that the man had a lifetime career of guarding secrets. He did recognize such a face from poker; however, and he had to learn the "tells" from his opponents in order to guess what kind of hand they held. David definitely was wearing a poker face. He took the time to measure the words of his answer.

"You can't ask about Valentina, Corvette," he said at length. "You can't talk to anyone about her. No one should be aware that you even know her. You could get her killed. You're in this kind of danger yourself. I have some serious advice for you: First, don't mention Valentina again. Second, hire yourself some bodyguards for a while. You're slightly a public figure, and you and your family members have increased risk of being targets of organized crime because of your connection with Valentina and your knowledge of the money. You're going to need to be extremely careful."

Corvette felt instantly devastated. He hadn't realized how much he wanted to see Valentina again. Now David's words were alarming him greatly. Both Enrique and David were staring at him. In particular, Enrique was observing the reaction Corvette was displaying to David's advice. David's expression turned contemplative, as if some question had come to mind about him.

In fact, David's question did surprise him: "Tell me, Corvette, about your curious last name. I have heard that you had a Mexican father. How did you arrive at your name?"

"Well, I'm told that my paternal grandparents, who were from Mexico, originally had the last name, 'Fuego de Noche,' and that my father anglicized it legally. He said my grandparents were deported from the United States to Mexico when he was two years old. A Texas couple raised him. I don't know any other relatives in Mexico. I was never told about any."

"Where in Mexico did your father say his parents were from?"

"He said they were from Chihuahau originally."

"Interesting," David commented. "I'm not aware of any such name in Spanish in Mexico. And your first name?"

"Oh, my dad loved Corvettes all his life. I also have had a couple."

"Well, that's one thing we have in common," David explained with enthusiasm. "I'm quite a nut about Corvettes myself. In fact, I have one of the new Stingrays, a red one."

But David apparently remembered his concern about time and cut the conversation short after glancing as his watch. He reached for his wallet, pulled out a card, and handed it to Corvette.

"If you need to reach me ever, here's my contact information. We need to go now, Corvette. Please take my advice about the bodyguards. A couple of our Zs can stay with you until you make these arrangements, if you like."

But Corvette wasn't in a mood to accept help from the people associated with Enrique. He didn't think that Enrique liked him very much, and it had something to do with Valentina. He didn't want to lose any more face with these guys. He had already surrendered the bag to Enrique.

"No thanks, David, but I certainly will consider your advice."

"Okay, then. Take care of yourself." He shook Corvette's hand. Corvette wanted to see if Enrique would turn his back or also shake his hand, but David patted Enrique's shoulders and began leading the young guys away. Corvette was suddenly alone again but without the green bag.

And he was with very bad feelings:

He didn't want the money to go to the United States government. He needed it more. So did his mum.

He hated the idea that he might need bodyguards. However, he played poker with a lot of cash in very public places. His name was Corvette Nightfire. He was due in nine

81

days at the Main Event Final Table of the World Series of Poker at The Rio. How could he hide?

He wanted to dance with Valentina again. He wanted to dance with her a thousand evenings like the one they had shared.

So, standing alone in the casino, he felt very sad; but he decided that he had made the right choice in his room before he came downstairs. Now, because of what he had just done, he had to get away, and fast.

He grabbed an elevator and jogged down the empty hallway to his room. He pulled the one overnight bag out of his closet, the one he would take on the plane. He got his sports cap and sunglasses. He picked up the one paperback book that he had bought from the convenience store and hadn't put into the green bag, and he tucked it under his arm. He had put all the others under the bricks of cash he had layered inside the top of the green bag. He had selected books that were about the thickness of a rubber-banded stack of one-hundred-dollar bills. The purpose of the books was to make the bag heavy.

Inside the overnight bag that he was taking with him, he had one point eight million dollars in cash. Inside his pants pocket was a Stingray key fob which would now be a souvenir for good luck. The book under his arm was entitled, *Living Your Life with No Regrets*.

He punched the speed dial to Raymundo's number on his phone as he left his room with his items. With luck, Raymundo would have found him a flight to Barbados that left soon. David's questions about his past had aroused a dim memory, and now he had questions for his mother.

Including some questions about the private banking that she used in the past when she had money, he thought.

Then, when Raymundo answered the phone, Raymundo didn't answer saying, "Bueno" or "Hola" or "Hello." Instead, he said, "Amigo, if you want to leave quickly, I have quite a surprise for you."

The luck that had arrived for Corvette two days earlier was continuing its run.

Chapter 6: The Return to Monterrey

Valentina
Monterrey, Mexico
Sunday Afternoon

Valentina couldn't recall any time in her life when she was as angry as she was in the present moment.

Or as scared.

Or as anxious.

Or as incredulous.

Never again would she allow any man to make decisions for her, not even supervisors in the Drug Enforcement Agency, her employer. Not male friends, not husbands of favorite aunts, not hot, con-man poker players who dance like a dream, and certainly not drug cartel bosses who would suck you with them into the vortex of inhuman cruelty and depravity.

In the past twenty-four hours, every man of note in her life had either screwed up and had made ridiculous mistakes or had disappeared. The only person who had displayed any common sense at all was her always intelligent and overly protective aunt, Ana.

I would have looked thoroughly through the bag when Corvette handed it to me, Valentina fumed. *I wouldn't have let six hours go by before discovering that the bag had more paperback books than stacks of cash. Good God! Six hours!*

She was on the Aeromexico Airlines flight to Monterrey from Las Vegas. Her anger had been simmering for a day, but once she got into the solitude of her seat and closed eyes, it tipped to a churning boil inside her stomach. In the air she stared out the window at tranquil-looking, cotton ball clouds that suggested the world was a peaceful place loved by God. She resented the deception of the clouds. The view was so out of synch with her mood that the very idea of a lovely planet only made the bile in her throat taste more bitter. She might have put her foot down and insisted that she was going to remain in

Las Vegas until they clarified whether Raúl was dead or not, except that Ana had convinced her why it made sense for her to return to Monterrey. Valentina hoped that her aunt would be right. Her silent cell phone was making her insane. Raúl had neither called her nor answered her calls. His cell phone was turned off. Was he dead or had he just disappeared? Was she a target marked to die by the Zetas, or was her cover still intact? Had any of them seen her give Corvette the cash?

She and Ana should have stuck with the original plan that the two of them would go to Pleasure Island to search for Corvette, she thought, even if they would have had to pull over the Lexus and hoof the rest of the way there. Instead, they had sat in the car, stuck in the gnarl of traffic, and had listened with despair to the police and emergency service sirens, and then helicopters. While they sat there, David called Ana. He was at the DEA office with Special Agent-In-Charge Zolinsky on Main Street, and they were leaving for The Oasis and then Pleasure Island. The two of them didn't think it was a good idea for Ana to be seen with Valentina.

"The area could be crawling with cartel men from Mexico," David had said to Ana on the phone, and agent Zolinsky had been in agreement. "Valentina needs to act like a scared rabbit and hide. Her cover should continue to be that she's an innocent young woman from Monterrey and is being courted by this dubious Mexican businessman. When the fight broke out, she was nearly trampled. She wanted to get away. When someone pushed a heavy bag to her, she got rid of it as soon as she could and then got the hell out of there. That should be her story. She should hide and wait for Z-30 or someone from the Zetas to call her."

From the passenger seat, Valentina had protested that probably Corvette was expecting her to contact him. "I should go to Pleasure Island and find him. I'm the one who gave him the money. He'll want to see me."

Then David had conversed in a side conversation with Zolinsky, and what came next was an order: "Yeah, listen, sorry,

85

Valentina, but agent Zolinsky wants you to go to The Venetian and wait to see who contacts you."

Ana had put her phone on speaker. "I talked to Enrique just minutes ago, David, and he said that he thought that Z-30 had been killed. If that's the case, obviously he's not going to contact Valentina. In the meanwhile, Corvette could leave if he doesn't hear from her," she pointed out.

"There's confusion about Z-30's death," David replied. "The body had identification on it with a name used by the Zeta in the past, and its appearance is similar to the known appearance of Z-30, but there are some questions. The victim was shot in the face to the degree that he's unrecognizable. A 'Z' was witness to the attack. Agent Zolinsky received this information when he was talking to the police via radio."

Valentina had remembered that Horacio and Raúl had dressed similarly. Both had worn jeans and white shirt. Raúl had on a pale yellow sports jacket, and Horacio's had been a light beige. "I can probably identify the body," Valentina intruded.

"You may be needed for that, Valentina," David answered.

Then he continued, speaking directly to Ana, "I tell you what, cariño, you're right that Corvette could run. We're thinking it would be a good idea for me and Agent Zolinsky to clear Enrique with the police over there at The Oasis so he can go and find Corvette. We'll talk to the police by radio while we're on the way there. Already, two DEA agents have arrived on the scene to help sort things out about the agent who was shot and killed. We'll send Enrique and some of the Zs over to Pleasure Island now. They can scare Corvette from his room if he's there, make him think they're from a cartel, and get the cash. Technically, he hasn't committed any crime. Someone handed him a bag, and he accepted it."

"He can be in serious trouble, David," Ana broke in. "And what am I supposed to do? Sit around in my car?"

"Ana, not many people in the United States would recognize you, but there are Mexicans here in Las Vegas who, sí, would know you and who would guess that I'm here as well. We talked about this yesterday. Come downtown to the DEA office and work with a couple of the agents who are trying to verify and identify Cartel of Sinaloa members who might be in Las Vegas. We suspect that they initiated the attack this morning. This event is going to get very hot, baby. The press is sniffing big news that the wave of cartel-related violence in the United States is quickly gathering strength. Believe me, the news organizations will connect the dots from city to city. Some have great investigative reporters who will follow the trail of money. The stories coming out will be political hot-potatoes for Donnie and will get over-the-top sensational. The gun freaks, the gun control advocates, the people screaming that the country is too soft on crime, and the ones who want to ship all Mexicans back to Mexico will clamor for their moments of fame in the media. With exposure intensifying, I'll have a harder time working under cover with the DEA and the FBI to find the money laundering centers in this country and Mexico. Too many noses under the sheets with me." David's reference to "Donnie" was to Donald Austin Blair, the President of the United States and the best friend of David since their days as roommates at The College of William and Mary.

And that was it! thought Valentina contemptuously as she stared from the passenger jet at the cumulus cotton balls forming a sky-size mattress that blocked the view of the scrappy northern Mexican desert below. *That was how I got cut out of having any say on how to deal with Corvette!*

"Quieres algo de beber?" asked a flight attendant. Her question jolted Valentina briefly from her thoughts. It reminded her of when she had been dancing vigorously with Corvette that evening, and how he had asked her in English if she wanted something to drink while making a gesture of drinking with his cupped hand.

"Sí, agua," Valentina answered the fiftyish Mexican attendant who had dyed her hair blonde even though it didn't go well with her dark skin. She had given Corvette the same answer, and she saw that he did know a few words of Spanish.

He had adopted a surprised and bemused look, as if he had been expecting her to request a glass of chardonnay instead of water.

This memory of him released a pang of hurt. Suddenly she suspected that the pointed ire she was feeling toward men had its roots in a wound. Her eyes glistened, and she was surprised and annoyed that she might be angry because she felt hurt. She turned to look out the window at the clouds again so the flight attendant wouldn't see her eyes when she extended her arm to accept the bottle of water. She gulped a few swallows and then set the plastic bottle on her tray. She closed her eyes to examine her emotions more clearly. She scrubbed through the angry feelings, and there it was: the wound. It looked like a vision of Corvette leaving the city instead of trying to find her. She had given him a green bag of trust, but he had discarded this and had returned the bag filled with his declaration of independence. He was gone. She felt hurt and stupid for misreading him, and now she saw that much of the irritation she had was with herself. Something deeper was bothering her about Corvette, but on the jet she couldn't discern it.

She got it in the Monterrey airport, however, when she saw a poster on the wall in the long walkway leading to the baggage claim ramp. She encountered it after her brief discussion with the customs agent. When her flight was landing, she had seen Monterrey shimmering in the Mexican mid-afternoon sun and the flag of Mexico flapping in the breeze at the airport. Disembarking, she was able to go through the much shorter and faster customs line for returning Mexican citizens. She was a citizen of both the USA and Mexico. She felt half and half. It was a feeling she liked. She thought that the best of both cultures was inside her. Dual citizenship brought so many advantages when traveling back and forth between the two countries.

So her examination by the customs agent was pleasant and perfunctory.

"Bienvenidos, welcome home," said the agent, who appeared in a mood to practice his English. He glanced at Valentina's passport. "So how did you do in Las Vegas?"

"Not so good," Valentina answered truthfully. "I'm coming home a little sooner than expected."

The agent laughed. "I'm sorry, señora. Well, you can have much better luck next time. Las Vegas is like that."

"Maybe so. How are things in Mexico?"

"Bien, bien," replied the agent. "Better now that you're home." It was a bit of a flirtation, Valentina realized. He was an older, married guy simply enjoying a quick chat with a lady he thought was pretty. It did make her smile. He handed back her passport, and she was on her way.

That's when she saw the poster that caught her attention at some subconscious level, and she stopped to examine it. It was advertising a travel service specializing in excursions in Mexico and the United States. In the picture, the flags of both countries flew closely beside each other. It was a sharp, crisp photograph of the Stars and Stripes of the USA and the red, green, and white flag of Mexico with its coat of arms. Valentina stared at the coat of arms. An eagle with wings elevated perched with one claw on a blooming prickly pear. In the other claw, it held a snake that it had caught. She thought about the coincidence that in both countries the eagle featured prominently in their national identities. Then she noticed that the airport speakers were playing a romantic ballad that she and Corvette had danced to a few nights earlier.

He had been very gorgeous and charming, and he danced like a seducer, but that isn't what enticed her to weave a spell to capture him. He told her that his father was Mexican and his mother was British. So Corvette was like her. He was a half and half. The difference was that he had grown up mostly like a gringo, and she had grown up mostly like a Mexican.

So that night, she decided to show him what he had missed. She would bring him Mexico. While he prattled on in English about his life in the belief that she couldn't understand him, she did her charm dance. She didn't do a dance performance for him; no, it was an *interpretation* of her spirit. She began by showing him the eagle of the flag and the serpent it clutched. She was low and slow, like the snake, but then she raised high to reveal the eagle, her arms extended into the sky. Her body swooshed low suddenly in a dip that mimicked the eagle snatching the surprised serpent, and then she ascended, turned, and rolled. Her dress hugged her round parts in ways that made him draw his breath. She smiled. She had him.

She wanted him to live the colors of Mexico: to smell them, to inhale them, to ingest them. She did indigenous dances. Indigenous people south of the border dressed in colors that astonished peacocks. She converted her dress of flowers into a projector for a light show. Using the musical movements of her body to toss her dress into the breezes, Valentina made its flowers come alive in glints of reflected illuminations that changed hues with every turn of her dress. Her pirouette of colors in the air set different moods for each interpretation of story and history. Corvette may not have understood Valentina's stories exactly, but he knew that she was doing something extraordinary by the turning of her arms and the expressions of her face. Sometimes, as he told her about his world, he stopped, breathless in reaction to her moves.

Not every story she told in dance was romance. Once, Valentina paused with her head tilted back. Her right arm held a pistol that only she could see, and she fired it into the air. Corvette's imagination caught the image. She shot this and other weapons to recount the history of Mexico, its wars for Independence, its wars with the United States, and its war against the narcos. She hinted also about her personal training, the firing on the pistol ranges, her athleticism, and the single-mindedness of her resolve to rid the world of some of its evil.

She paraded for him, a parade of the Day of the Dead, a slow rumba forward, like the Katrina in a funeral procession. She drew in her cheeks to look like a skull. She went high on her toes in order to simulate stilts. Now she was almost as tall as he.

She marched the slow, step-by-step cadence of the costumed people going to the cemeteries to honor their family members and other ancestors. She picked up a candle in a glass cylinder from one of the tables and marched ritually around Corvette, to lead him to the fiestas in the cemeteries. The other people on the dance floor were unaware that she had set them also in her play, but they watched her, fascinated. If she had commanded, they would have followed her to the cemeteries with their gifts and flowers for the people who had passed on. Corvette saw this in the way people were looking at her.

Then Valentina danced a jaguar: sleek and catlike. It made Corvette primitive in his hunger for her. The night had worn on, and there was a certain amber madness in his eyes. She knew that he understood what she was, one of the rare black jaguars with iridescent yellow eyes. If he had climbed aboard her as jaguar, she would have raced him across northern Mexico along wilderness paths on moonless nights. He would have clung to her for his life.

And at this moment of Corvette's highest enthrallment, Valentina bestowed him a special gift: the smiles of all beautiful women in Mexico. Each time she emerged from the shadows cast by the palms on the dance floor, she dazzled him with a different smile and look in her eyes. He was transfixed and wanted her. But that night, she would be an elusive dream for him. When the ugliness of the cartel showed up in the form of Raúl, she threw a sheet of Spanish words over Corvette and disappeared quickly, hoping that the magic of her charms wouldn't be spoiled by someone so "feo" as the Zeta.

Yet, in spite of the enchanted evening which they had shared, Corvette had chosen to take the money and run.

Did I misjudge him so completely? she sighed. *He had filled that bag with books and had given it to Enrique? If he thought I was coming for the bag, is this what he intended for me? Why didn't Corvette say to Enrique that he wanted to know where I was? When I asked Enrique about this, he kept silent. I guess Enrique didn't want to see me hurt.*

She took a last look at the poster. For some reason, seeing the two flags together gave her a reassured feeling. She only had a short walk from there to the escalator that ascended to the room where baggage was retrieved. There was one door out of that room to the main airport lobby beyond. Valentina knew that at that door would be a customs agent with a security X-ray machine which surveyed the luggage exiting the airport to Mexico. Valentina lived in Monterrey. She knew what the customs people there were like.

They're more expectant of people to bring plants or personal items that need to be declared than anything truly dangerous, she thought with an ironic feeling. *But usually it's the people passing through who are truly dangerous. These guys really don't know who they're greeting. For sure, they don't expect undercover DEA agents.*

On the escalator, a worry surfaced that she hadn't thought about until that moment: If Raúl were alive, and he probably was, what if he were somehow awaiting her in the airport lobby? She was, in fact, in Monterrey with the hope by her and the DEA that he would contact her, but if he were in the airport, she needed to prepare. She would have to act incredibly glad to see him and happy that he was alive. He would have to believe her act. Her life might depend on it.

Her instructions were to get her luggage and to go to the food court in the lobby and wait to be contacted by someone new for her in the DEA, another undercover agent she would work with. She had been surprised that there was another one in Monterrey. She had been unaware of him. His name was Juan Ramirez.

Her large leather bag arrived on the belt within a couple of minutes of her arrival. She saw that the customs agent, a young man in his late twenties, was standing by the X-ray machine and was joking with a family who were apparently acquaintances of his. He showed little interest in the bags coming through other than quick reviews of the screen.

Dios, customs can be so much more relaxed here than in the United States, Valentina sighed. *I guess there isn't much concern that terrorists are coming in to destroy Mexico. This country has different kinds of problems.*

The agent and family were laughing loudly as she rolled her bag past them through the exit to the lobby. He glanced at her and nodded his head. The lobby was extremely crowded. Valentina took a second to get her bearings and to survey faces. It was a habit of training. She didn't see Raúl or anyone whom she knew. She maneuvered her bag toward the designated restaurant in the food court at the far end of the lobby. She was, in fact, starving. She got in line at a fast-food Mexican vendor and bought burritos con carne with mole and limes. There were only a couple of tables available, and both were next to a gringo-looking man with glasses and a shaved head. He wore a light-brown business suit, white shirt, and thin green tie. The other tables were filled with Mexican families. No one there looked like they would be Juan Ramirez. She saw a teenage kid in the other food line taking a picture of the lobby with his phone. Valentina took one of the empty tables and then watched the terminal lobby to see who might approach and possibly be Juan Ramirez. The gringo guy was checking his phone, and that reminded Valentina to turn hers on. She pulled it out of her purse and set it on the table. She continued woofing down her burritos.

"Hola, Valentina," said the gringo at the next table. He didn't look at her as he said it. He continued scrolling his phone. "Soy Juan Ramirez."

Valentina almost spit out a mouthful of food with surprise and laughter. When she could manage it, she said, "You're Juan Ramirez?"

"Sí," he replied.

Now Valentina allowed a chuckle. "I'm sorry," she told him, although he still wasn't looking at her. "But you look more like your name should be John White."

"I grew up in Monterrey," Juan answered. "My parents worked for the government." He had switched to English. Valentina noticed that he did have a slight Mexican accent.

"Of the United States?" Valentina inquired, although she knew what he would answer. Her question was a bit of a joke.

"Yes. My father was from Maryland, near D.C., and my mother was Mexican and became a citizen. Both ended up as government employees."

"Working in Mexico," Valentina added.

Juan looked at her now with a slightly amused look on his face. "They told me you were very beautiful. I see that's true."

She laughed just a little. "Gracias."

"You actually have a business in Monterrey, I understand, in addition to your employment." He began looking at his phone again. "Maybe you shouldn't look directly at me."

"Okay. Yes, I own an event planning business. I do work in it some, but I also have a manager and a staff who do wonderful work when I can't be present. My mother's sister and I have been very close since my parents died when I was a young girl, and my aunt actually did event planning for many years. I was fortunate to learn from her and pick up some of her corporate clients."

"That would be Ana Valdez of whom you're speaking?" asked Juan.

"Yes!" Valentina replied, pleased. "I see you've been well briefed. But she and I have covered up our relationship somewhat since the days that she began speaking out against the cartels and their violence publicly. It is enough that she has to fear for her own children, and I started my career with the government. The same government as you."

She glanced and saw that he stifled a smile. Juan was making an effort to talk in a low voice without looking at Valentina too much. He lifted his phone and waved it slightly and said, "I have just e-mailed you my phone numbers and contact information. Given the people with whom you associate now, it's important that we work closely and get to know each

94

other. Put me as a contact in your phone as your cousin Juan. Ramirez isn't my real last name. That's a little joke that everyone wanted to have with you, but everything I told you is true. Someday I'll tell you my real last name and you will laugh. But for now, it's good for you to know me as Ramirez and list me in your phone that way."

"Okay," Valentina replied. She looked at faces in the lobby again. No one seemed interested in her or Juan at all. The teenage boy had apparently decided not to get food and had meandered to a bench nearby. Like everyone else, he seemed busy with his phone. Juan continued to examine his phone as he spoke.

"Since you're in the events business, there's a band you should check out. I put their name in the e-mail: *Los Zapata*. You can use your business as a cover to introduce yourself and get to know them. They're good musicians playing corridos norteños (northern ballads) at events and in clubs and private parties. They're building a name in Monterrey. I noticed them because I play drums in a little band that gets together occasionally for fun. What I noticed is that they play a lot of parties given by guys we know to be in the Cartel of the Zetas. Eventually, this will attract the attention of other cartels."

"Dangerous," Valentina said.

"Sí, sometimes the musicians are just these poor guys who are desperate for money and to make a name, and they're not too careful what gigs they accept. But knowing *Los Zapata* could help us understand better the map of the parties and clubs in Monterrey, which ones are owned or are taxed by which cartels, and who's enforcing the 'pisos.' We think that some clubs and casinos are receiving laundered money from the United States. It's an ever-changing landscape."

"I'll check them out." Valentina pulled up Juan's e-mail, entered his contact information, and deleted the e-mail. She would remember the name of the group.

"Let me know as soon as you receive any contact from the Zetas regarding Z-30, or anything unusual where you might need backup. Sometimes I might be lurking in your background scenery when you need help. For now, it's probably a good idea for you to work in your business and to live a normal young woman's life in Monterrey."

"And what do you do in Monterrey?" Valentina asked. She knew that agents from the DEA or any of the intelligence agencies of the government and armed forces of the United States officially had no business in Mexico. Whenever something happened to expose the presence of U.S. operatives, the Mexican government issued public statements of protest or declarations that there would be a thorough investigation. There was a weird form of denial in Mexico. The Mexican people were very sensitive that their government would allow U.S. personnel to work in their country, given the aggressive and meddlesome police and military actions that had happened throughout history. Also, from the viewpoint of the Mexicans, the United States was a country that felt it was the policeman of the world and would have no qualms about bombing any country into oblivion if it defined a country as threatening to its interests. More than that, the general suspicion was that the U.S. wanted the natural resources of other nations, particularly oil. Mexico had a lot of it. The U.S. had already taken half of Mexico in the 1840s and had made military incursions since that time. So Mexico jealously guarded its oil reserves and remained wary of United States' intentions.

But the fact of the matter was that the Mexican government always had an on-again, off-again cooperation with the United States in terms of secret missions and intelligence, particularly with respect to the activities of the drug cartels and their leaders. The game was that the Mexican government would keep the U.S. at arm's length and would be in control of all covert operations. When the Mexican people did not want the United States involved in anything at all, then the Federal Government of Mexico would deny the presence of the country altogether. No one actually believed this.

Yet the truth was that the United States participated in many joint activities with the Mexican government and with its intelligence agencies and armed forces. The USA also had operations unknown to the Mexican government. There were people like David James who were private citizens working with Mexicans in consultation with U.S. governmental agencies. David even married Ana Valdez, a Mexican woman who led the peace and victims' rights movements and who had for several months been Interim President of Mexico after a military coup had overthrown the corrupt government of Pedro Navarro.

That woman, my tía Ana, understands the complexities of the Mexican national character very well, Valentina thought. *She's one of the few leaders whom people trust in this country.*

"I'm a computer and telecommunications network installer for Sabiduría Electrónica," Juan responded to her question.

"That might be a more dangerous occupation than working for the government," Valentina said.

Juan chuckled but didn't look at her. "Pues, sí," he agreed. "Several corporate computer programmers and telecommunications experts have been kidnapped or have disappeared in recent years."

"Tell me something," Juan continued. "I was given a briefing about what happened in Las Vegas while you were there. What isn't so clear to me is how Corvette Nightfire got out of the country with so much cash after he had handed over a bag supposedly containing all of it to the DEA. Do you know how this happened?"

"Do you know who Corvette Nightfire is?" Valentina shot back. Juan's question quickly resurrected her irritation and indignation over the whole stupid carelessness of the DEA in that matter.

"Yes, I like to play poker, and I follow the guys who play in the World Series of Poker throughout the world."

Valentina harrumphed. "Okay, I'll tell you. Corvette tricked everyone, and no one expected this from him. After the shootings and fight in The Oasis, in which we lost our agent Josh

Bailin, the Special Agent-in-Charge of the Las Vegas office of the DEA, Zolinsky, authorized David James and the Zs to receive the money that Corvette had accepted from me when I put the bag in his hands right after the shootings. Zolinsky has known and has worked with David James many years. David was once an employee of the CIA, but lately in Mexico he has done a lot of freelance consulting work with the Mexican Armed Forces and the DEA in tracking cartel leaders and money laundering trails. At Pleasure Island, Corvette turned over the bag to Enrique Santos, who heads the Zs, just as David arrived. Enrique opened the bag to check to see that the cash was in it. Corvette had put a couple of layers of stacks of hundred dollar bills. The bag seemed full because he had placed paperback books underneath the cash. There was even a Gideon bible in the bottom of the bag. The cash in the bag totaled about three hundred thousand dollars."

"When was it counted?" interrupted Juan.

"Hours later," answered Valentina with obvious frustration. "Enrique and David turned the bag over to Zolinsky, who ordered a couple of agents to take the bag to the office for lock up and accounting. There was so much emotion and confusion in The Oasis. All of us were very upset over Josh being shot and killed. His wife somehow turned up there because she saw news on television and hadn't been able to reach her husband. So it was a mess. I remember that someone said that they knew Corvette Nightfire was going to be in a poker game at the MGM that night. So the cash just kind of became overlooked in the chaos of the day. It's pretty routine to confiscate cash. You know that the Las Vegas office of the DEA is small, and the regional headquarters for the office is actually in Los Angeles. So there weren't many agents unoccupied that day. Most were in The Oasis and handling the aftermath of the gun battle there. It was madness."

"What happened when it was finally discovered that the bag wasn't full of cash?" Juan asked. He still looked at his phone and glanced around the lobby instead of directly at Valentina.

She answered him by pretending to talk on her cell phone as she looked in another direction from him. The teenage boy had gone to the food line of a different vendor. She caught him looking at her and then quickly looking away.

"More confusion!" sighed Valentina. "Corvette had said that he didn't count the money. So the first question that came up was: did he receive the bag with the books in it? That question led back to me. Did I know there were books in it? Of course not, I answered. So there were phone calls back and forth between Zolinsky, who was with David and the FBI, and the agent in the office who discovered the books in the bag. What condition were the books in? What kind of books? All this ate up time. There were several copies of the same books, and they all appeared brand new. Where could they have been bought? The bible was a clue. Finally, an agent turned up the sales clerk in a store in Pleasure Island who had sold Corvette the books that morning. So then the hunt for Corvette Nightfire began."

"And he got to Barbados somehow?" Juan asked, to verify what he had already been told.

"He caught a flight out amazingly fast," Valentina replied. "It took time to find out on which airline and from which airport he flew, and he was long gone. He filed a declaration that he was carrying one point eight million dollars in cash. He carried it on the aircraft. He said it was gambling winnings. He caught a flight to Mexico City, where he also declared the cash. From there he got a flight to Trinidad, and from there to Barbados."

Valentina saw Juan shaking his head. "Sooo..." he said, "the guy was smart enough to declare the money so he wouldn't get in any trouble for not declaring it."

"Exactly," Valentina answered, and she felt the anger again. She knew she shouldn't, but she was taking Corvette's actions very personally. "And he has committed no crime. I gave him a bag with money, and he left with it. He didn't steal it or anything."

"No, but he has a world of worries now, doesn't he? He has money taken from the wrong kind of people. He's a celebrity on the poker circuit. How is he going to do that now? He'll have to look over his shoulder every minute of every day."

Valentina sighed. *Why do I even care about this?* But she attributed her concern to the fact that she was the one who had involved Corvette in the first place. *Maybe I just feel guilty.*

After a few minutes of silence, Juan said, "I see you've finished your burritos. You should leave, and I'll sit here a bit and continue to check my e-mail on my phone. Where are you going?"

"I'm taking a taxi home," Valentina responded. "I'll catch some sleep, and then tomorrow I'll go to my office."

"You have family here?"

"Just my tía Ana, when she and David are not in their home in San Antonio. Most of my cousins are in Mazatlán and Guadalajara. I grew up with my father's mother here in Monterrey. But my grandmother passed away. I have many friends here who are like family.

"And none of them know what you do."

"No."

"So you're really alone in a sense right now. This is why it is important that you communicate well with me," Juan pointed out.

"No problem," Valentina said. "We work this way." She couldn't help wondering, however, if Juan had received instructions to keep her on a short leash. She wondered if the DEA regarded her giving Corvette the bag of cash as a colossal mistake. *Wouldn't that make sense?* she thought with frustration. *They might need a scapegoat for their own comedy of errors which permitted Corvette to get out of the country with the money.*

Without saying goodbye, Valentina gathered her purse and rolling suitcase and headed to the counter where she bought a ticket for a taxi to take her home. At the airport there were bonded and approved taxi companies that were licensed to take passengers to and from the airport. In Mexico it was important to take a bonded cab. There were many unofficial or illegal taxis in the city, and some of them were operated by organized crime. These sometimes were vehicles for kidnappings of unsuspecting or careless people. Valentina selected the taxi company on the computer screen shown to her by the concession agent, a pretty young girl whose smile wasn't diminished by her crooked teeth. Valentina paid, received her fare ticket, and went outside the terminal to the curb where she got in the line of the taxi company which she had selected. There were only three parties ahead of her, so her wait wasn't long. The sidewalk attendant put her bag in the trunk of the taxi. The driver had opened it from inside. Valentina got in the back seat with her purse and phone.

"Buenas tardes, señora Bonita," greeted the driver, who looked like a kid not more than nineteen years old. He was calling her pretty. He had the ticket given to him by the attendant with Valentina's address, and he verified it with her. "We're going to La Calle Montaña Verde in San Pedro, verdad?"

"Si, gracias," answered Valentina.

But she never made it home.

Chapter 7: Rapid Fire

Apparently Horacio had the same instinct as the Zeta. He was slowing his pace and looking around more intently as they got closer to the entrance doors of The Oasis. The Zeta had subconsciously slowed. He saw Valentina and Luis ahead and the two Zetas whom he expected to be waiting on the bridge in the little indoor rain forest. The walkway they were on was crowded. The strange thing that he observed was the Hispanic-looking kids who had come in separately from different places in the casino. They acted like they didn't know one another, but there was a homogeneity to them that struck the Zeta. Their random casualness betrayed a barely perceptible synchronicity. They were between him and Valentina and Luis. He turned his face to use peripheral vision to see if he would notice others behind him, but he couldn't be sure. It was then that Horacio placed his hands on his shoulders and began pushing him off the walkway and deeper into the casino. He heard Horacio mutter, "Madre de puta!" Then he heard shots. They were coming from near the entrance. Horacio pushed him to go faster in the opposite direction. They were moving down an aisle perpendicular to rows of slot machines. The Zeta and Horacio both glanced behind them, and that's when he saw that dog from Sinaloa charging toward them with his pistol drawn.

The Zeta had fought them, tortured them, and soaked his hands in their filthy blood for so many years that he could smell one when he saw him. For over a hundred years certain Sinaloan families, originating in that state's mountains, tightly controlled the marijuana cash economy that thrived because of the United States' insatiable appetite for their product. They often decided by murder or intimidation the winners and losers of political races not only in the mountains, but also in the important cities, such as the capital city of Culiacán and the beach resort city of Mazatlán. The Sinaloans had helped Pedro Navarro, a native son, attain the Presidency of Mexico just months before the military coup had toppled his government. Fate had put that man in the hands of the Zeta. He had put a bullet in his forehead in front of his wife and young sons, and then he had executed them.

The cartel men from Sinaloa loved to pose in photographs with their family, friends, weapons, and cars. The Zeta had yet to meet one who didn't have a portfolio of such pictures of himself. Always they included photos of groups of guys smirking over the carcasses of animals or people they had killed and mutilated. To the Zeta, they looked like brawn, tattoos, and ignorance. He would tell people that he could recognize a man from the mountains of Sinaloa because of the facial structures that came from too much inbreeding.

This man who had run up on him and Horacio appeared older than most. Life expectancy of the members of the cartels of Sinaloa and the Zetas, in particular, were quite short because of their fierce wars in Mexico and the incipient fighting in the United States. The Zeta judged this guy to be about thirty-two. He looked experienced and professional. His weapon was a semi-automatic Glock twenty, like one the Zeta owned, with forty caliber bullets designed to murder or stop a victim instantly. He was looking directly at the Zeta. The Zeta understood that this man recognized him and that he was the intended target. The dog had the advantage in that he already had his weapon drawn and was bringing it up for aim when he got to Horacio and the Zeta.

But Horacio had seen him coming before the Zeta did. Horacio moved his big body with lightning speed between him and the assailant and hurled himself at him. He took the bullets for the Zeta. There were three so rapid-fire that they sounded like one. They smashed into the center of Horacio's face and blew it beyond recognition. Horacio's large frame jerked backward from the impacts. The Zeta was now reacting and had drawn his own weapon. With luck, he might be able to get some

103

shots at their attacker before the man could turn his weapon on him.

Except, a crazy thing happened. One of the Hispanic kids whom the Zeta had noticed earlier suddenly came from behind the gunman and from a spin kicked a powerful blow to the kidney area of the man's back, and this sent the Glock thumping across the carpeting of the casino. It came to rest near the Zeta. The man grimaced in obvious pain and pitched forward. He might have fallen, but he kept his legs moving with the forward momentum, so he ran clumsily until he crashed against the side of a slot machine. This allowed him to stabilize and support his back against it momentarily. He got a quick-second look at the Zeta and the kid who had assaulted him, and then he took off running, bent over to the side from his pain.

Now the kid stood frozen, his body tensed, in front of the Zeta. Raúl realized who he was. He knew the young man could flip or strike within a microsecond. He holstered his pistol inside his jacket, stepped back from the Glock on the ground, and briefly raised his hands to show he wouldn't use weapons.

"He got him," he told the kid in Spanish. "That's who they were after. He got Z-30."

The kid stared intently. He looked a little uncertain and surprised that he was being addressed. He glanced nervously toward the lobby where there had been shots. Screams could still be heard.

"I'm going home," he told the kid. "My work is done. I know who you are. You're one of the zorros. You're a Z. You're Mexican. Where are you from?"

The kid was backing away. He looked unsure if he should answer. Then he said, "I'm from Las Vegas."

"No. Your parents, then. Which city in Mexico?"

"Puebla," the boy answered.

It was almost as if the Zeta knew that would be the kid's answer. "I'm from Puebla," he told the kid. "We're people then. You're Mexican. Your parents are from the city of heroes. Maybe this is why you're a hero today. Always remember your people and where you come from." He nodded his head toward the lobby where the commotion continued. The kid took a last look into the Zeta's eyes and then darted in that direction.

The Zeta stared down at Horacio and hated to see him like that. A thick pool of blood was expanding from Horacio's face into the carpet. He shook his head and muttered, "Madre de puta," to honor Horacio's last words and his act of heroism in defending his boss. He looked around, but any customers who had been playing slot machines nearby had run off in panic. He looked up in the ceiling and didn't notice any security cameras in little glass bubbles.

Horacio had been carrying the Zeta's passport in his jacket pocket, along with his own. These were phony, of course. The Zeta bent down and pulled out the two passports. He verified that Horacio had been using one that had an old name which he, the Zeta, once used. He put that one in Horacio's back jean pocket. He fished Horacio's pants and found his phone and his wallet and took those. He turned his and Horacio's phones off. He bent down and pulled Horacio's jacket from his body. The front of it had blood spatters, so he folded it over to hide them. Horacio's pistol was still holstered on his chest. He removed the weapon. He walked over to the Glock twenty that the dog from Sinaloa had dropped, and he lifted it from the floor. He draped Horacio's folded jacket over his arm and hand so that the weapons he carried couldn't be seen. Then he calmly strolled along the walkways in the midst of a mob of people to the self-park garage at the north end and exited the casino.

Zs and Sinaloa, he thought angrily. *Here at the same fucking time. Who has my cash?*

He recalled that stupidly he had left the ledger book in the Corvette. He would have to get that.

He slipped his left hand under Horacio's jacket and transferred the weapons and the jacket to his other arm. He remembered Horacio saving his life. He remembered the kid who saved his life.

It's one thing to find a fight in a plaza we're taking over from Sinaloa, but if Zs show up for the fight while I'm here, that can only mean that David James is in town, and so is the fucking DEA, his whores.

He would have to take care of that problem, and soon.

Chapter 8: Island Secrets

Madeline Nightfire
Bridgetown, Barbados
Monday Morning

Corvette's mother awoke at her usual seven in the morning to the sound of an obviously straining air conditioner and her small single-story home in Holetown being a degree or two warmer than she liked it to be, and she liked to be warm. She stretched her tall and lean fifty-one-year-old body upon standing, extending her arms to the ceiling and raising up on tip-toes for as long as she could stand it. The mirror above her dresser reminded her that she had slept in skimpy black cotton lingerie, so she gathered her ocean-blue summer robe from the bedpost and slipped it on. Her feet guided her automatically to the coffee pot. She got it brewing while she visited the bathroom for her morning relief. It was in there as she sat on the john that she recovered enough from her sleepy haze to remember that her son had shown up the previous morning at her doorstep, fresh from his taxi ride from Grantley Adams International Airport.

Only he didn't look so fresh. Corvette had been traveling since the previous afternoon, he told her, and before that he hadn't slept for a day. Therefore, she hadn't been able to have much conversation with him about his surprise visit before he apologized and said that he simply had to crash for a few hours. Now Madeline realized that Corvette had been sleeping in the other bedroom of the house for almost twenty hours.

His visits were the joy in her life, but he never had paid a surprise visit home before. He had appeared with only one overnight bag, and he had whisked that off to the bedroom with him. He kept some clothes in the bedroom ("island clothes," he called them) for the weeks when he would be off the poker tour and would come home to de-stress, eat healthier, and surf.

She was in the kitchen pouring her first cup of coffee when she heard him come out of the bedroom and zip into the bathroom, the only one in the house.

"Good morning, mum!" Corvette shouted. "Going to shower. I'll be with you in a minute."

"I'll heat you some muffins," Madeline yelled back.

She didn't have a good feeling about his being home unplanned and unannounced. She knew that his luck had gone south. About ten days earlier, Corvette had confided in her by phone that his sizeable gambling funds account was almost gone. He had enough to play some games in Las Vegas ahead of the World Series of Poker, he had told her, but he needed to win there.

Wait a minute! she thought. *Doesn't that start in just a few days? What's he doing here? This must be bad!*

She heated muffins with Barbados cherries picked from a small tree in her yard. She had made these the evening before so Corvette could have them for breakfast. There was a salty morning breeze moving inland from the ocean, so she decided to give the air conditioner a needed rest. She cut it off and went through the house and opened the windows and doors while Corvette showered. In Corvette's bedroom she observed that he hadn't even pulled back the sheets when he slept. The depression of his long body was still in the rumpled bedspread of the twin-sized bed. Seeing the small suitcase unopened at the foot of the bed, she decided to unzip it and determine if he had clothes that needed washing or to be put away. She swung it on top of the bed. She noticed that it was heavy and packed tightly.

Maybe he's not planning to stay long and intends to go back to Las Vegas, she told herself.

When she pulled back the zipper, cash bulged out. Madeline jumped in retreat. She was perplexed. She suspected that the rubber banded bills entirely filled the bag. She returned to the bed and unzipped the bag a little more. Feeling inside it, she confirmed her suspicion. She became instantly nervous for her son.

Tell me he didn't travel with this much cash in a carry-on! she exclaimed in her mind.

Quickly, she re-zipped the bag and placed it at the foot of the bed precisely where she had found it. She grabbed onto the hope that perhaps Corvette had had a sudden change in luck for the good, a thought that brought her some comfort, but she definitely would have some words for him about traveling with that kind of cash on his person. She knew that it wasn't out of the ordinary to have a large amount of cash on hand inside a casino in a place like Las Vegas, but to leave a hotel with that kind of money was insane.

She heard him bumping about in the bathroom and knew that he would be coming out soon. She hurried back to the kitchen.

I don't want to spoil his surprise for me about his winnings, she thought. *I'll wait until he shows me the cash, and then I'll let this kid of mine have it!*

But Corvette didn't bring up any talk of winning it big in Las Vegas, a subject that Madeline assumed he would want to spread joy about right away. Instead, he gulped his coffee and stuffed down muffins as if he hadn't eaten in days. He seemed fidgety. His smile looked forced. He chattered in a distracted way about how delicious the muffins were, how great it was to be back on the island, and how he felt like getting some new clothes and a haircut. The last comment surprised Madeline and got her mind off discussing the money momentarily.

"You're actually telling me that you want to get a haircut after I've been trying to get you to do this for years?" Madeline asked in mock astonishment. She couldn't suppress a chuckle of delight.

"Yeah, mum, I'm twenty-seven now. Maybe I could lose the surfer look and go with something more conservative. You know, try to be a little more handsome."

Madeline shook her head and replied, "Corvette, your hair is black to the point of almost midnight blue. You've never looked like a surfer. You just looked like you didn't want to grow up. Yet you've been spending your young adult life hanging out with the older professional heavyweights of poker all over the world."

"Some of them look pretty radical, mum," Corvette answered. "They're not exactly businessmen keeping banker hours, you know. Do you even watch the poker tournaments on the tele?"

Now they were talking about poker, and Madeline saw an entrance to the subject of the cash.

"Not that often," she admitted. "Are you wanting a more successful look for any particular reason? Has there been a change in your circumstances that you want to tell me about?"

The question made Corvette fidgety again. He answered, "Yes, something I need your advice about, mum. Something new for me." He got up and poured himself another cup of coffee and then returned to the kitchen table. What he brought up for discussion wasn't what Madeline expected.

"Remember how you and Dad used to tell stories about how you met? And how you fell in love on a cruise ship after one night of dancing? I used to love those stories. I thought they were so funny, and from the look in your eyes, I knew you weren't exaggerating. But Dad... you know how he liked to embellish things! One thing I always knew is that you guys really loved each other. You've always been very straightforward. Dad would reveal some things about his life in minute detail, but then he could be so closed and mysterious about others." Corvette let out a sigh of remembrance, shook his head, and repeated, "Dad!" in admiration of his character.

"You mean St. Rogelio?" laughed Madeline. She said it to relax Corvette some.

"Haha," her son answered, "yes, I still pray to him."

"He loved you to death. You were his boy." Madeline got up, gave Corvette a sideways hug in his chair, scuffed his hair, poured herself more coffee, and returned to her seat across from him. Now she had a different intuition about what he was going to tell her. She decided to help him by telling him a story.

"The night your father and I met was a night of bewitchment for me," Madeline said. Her eyes looked faraway to a distant time, and she could feel Corvette following her journey to that night. "Yes, it sounds like a funny story. Can you imagine it? I was a proper British girl getting away from my horribly stuffy family for the first time, on a cruise with girl friends in the Caribbean. In one of the night clubs on the ship, on the very first night of the cruise, out comes your short, drop-dead-handsome Latino father dancing with some girl he just went up to immediately and asked. He did these sexy moves with her that left me breathless. Me and the girls were giggling, and they noticed I was blushing because he seemed so naughty, but I couldn't take my eyes off him. Then, oh my God, your father spotted me looking at him, and he gave me this big smile and looked back at me with every turn. On the very next set, he came over and asked me to dance, and I about died. I knew we looked so funny out there together, me being so tall and blonde and all, and him being so short and tight, but before long we had everyone's attention. My girlfriends stopped laughing and watched us in amazement. He did something to me that freed me. He was sexy, and I felt this inside myself for the first time. We danced so hot that we left scorch marks on the dance floor!"

She saw that her unusual exuberance about that night emboldened Corvette, which is what she wanted to do. Usually she described that evening in a demure way, but she had learned that at times you have to let people see the passion inside you so that it confirms the passion they feel in themselves.

"Well, this is what I want to tell you, mum. I think I've fallen for a girl I met on a dance floor, and she's Latina too. But this seems crazy to me, because I've never had this kind of attraction before. She's from Mexico."

Madeline laughed and reached for her son's hand. "Well, son, don't be so surprised. I don't think it's crazy. You're a blend of me and your father, but with your own unique qualities. Your father was Mexican. You have a little bit of my English reserve in you. This is why I gave you all those years of dance lessons, because I think dancing frees emotions that get stuck inside. I'm not always good at talking about my feelings. Dancing is a powerful way to express them if you can't say the words. You always loved the Latin dances, which are especially sexy. So tell me about this girl. She must be rare because you're seldom impressed enough to continue relationships. Am I right? Did you meet her in Las Vegas?"

"Yeah, Las Vegas," Corvette answered, but she noted the heaviness behind his enthusiasm for the girl. The heaviness turned out to be a sadness. "I think I already blew it with her, and, I don't know, she might already be taken. She's not married. Well, she'sn't wearing a wedding ring."

That puzzled Madeline. "You didn't ask her?"

"I couldn't," Corvette replied. "She doesn't speak English."

Madeline jerked slightly in surprise, looking at him. "Well, unless you've learned Spanish and didn't tell me about it, how did you communicate with her?"

"That's what's crazy, mum. But it's exactly like what you just said about dancing. We danced the whole evening to a Mexican band in this very elegant lounge at the top of The Magnifico. When she danced, I swear, she told me stories! She did things with her arms. God, she's so beautiful, and she has these lovely arms. We were dancing lambadas and salsas and tangoes, but sometimes she broke away with these moves that seemed native in some way. She created images with them! It made me feel so alive, and so then I couldn't stop talking to her."

"In English," Madeline verified.

"Sí," Corvette answered, to be amusing, "but I felt like somehow she could understand me because of the way she looked at me with her eyes, and because of her smiles. So I told her everything about my life, including how you and dad met. It was the most magical night of my life, and I wanted to ask her name and how to reach her, but the evening came to an abrupt end. All of a sudden this older man showed up who seemed to be her father by the way she acted with him. She quickly gave me a goodbye and then left."

"You don't know her name?" Madeline asked, but it was really an exclamation.

"She told me her first name: Valentina."

"Oh my God, love. Isn't that just a perfect name? So what happened? You did see her again, didn't you?"

Now Corvette visibly gulped. He told her that he needed yet another cup of coffee. When he sat back down, he said, "Mum, you're not going to believe what I'm about to tell you. You're not going to like it. I know you're going to be so upset with me, but I really need your help in a practical way and hope you'll keep calm. The story will sound crazy, but just remember all the mystery novels that you write and how strange things can happen in this world. I got desperate for money, and you need it also, and then this happened. Plus, I have some questions about Dad that I wonder if you know the answers to."

Madeline's heart began to pound instantly. He was going to come around now to talking about the cash, and she realized he wouldn't be telling her a story about winning it in poker. She tried to steady her breathing and to sound composed when she said, "Okay, son, you have me a little scared by this introduction, but I'll do my best to stay calm."

"Well, yes, I did see Valentina once again," he began.

As Corvette laid out the story about the next time he saw Valentina when she gave him the cash and he didn't recognize her, Madeline realized that it wasn't going to be easy for her to stay cool. She tried to put herself into the scene, when there was so much shocking confusion with shootings and police response, in order to understand how Corvette had made a quick decision to walk off with a bag of cash during what obviously was a disruption of law and order. It wasn't so much that he might have made a bad choice in a moment of emotional stress that worried her. It was that she always had worried that Corvette carried inside him the same thing as his father: a certain dark side with secrets. Was he descending a steeper path? His poker life style kept her worrying, and now this revelation was heightening her anxiety. As she listened to Corvette, for the first time she questioned something she had done for years:

I've protected him from certain truths about his father. Maybe Corvette had a right to know these things. Maybe if he'd known, it would have helped him understand that there's DNA in his background that makes him attracted to reckless things. Maybe I've made a horrible mistake! I loved Rogelio so much! I love Corvette like crazy. Maybe I've done them both injustice!

She heard him coming to the part of the story where he made the decision to turn over only part of the cash to Enrique so he could escape from Las Vegas with the rest.

If I can understand this decision, maybe I can get a reading on the condition of my son's soul, she thought.

So she interrupted him and demanded, "Son, explain to me exactly your reasoning for not giving the money to Enrique. Be truthful with me. This is so important."

Corvette's voice had been breaking from nervousness, and he seemed grateful for the opportunity to pause a moment. He swallowed more coffee and then said, "Okay, Mum, I guess a few things were going through my mind. I have to admit that some of it was that I've been panicking about not having money. When I made the Final Table in the WSOP, they paid me several hundred thousand dollars. That, plus other winnings that I had from previous months, got my bank account up to about two million dollars. I got all cocky about my ability, and then I lost it. I hit a losing streak and I'm not sure it has ended. Playing poker has been my life, you know. It's the only experience I have in making money in the real world. I started here with Dad in Barbados with the little private games he always had going. I studied business in college, but you know my heart was always in the game, and even in those years I was traveling and playing. But the thing is, to play in the big leagues, you have to have a bankroll to finance staying in the tournaments. I'm down to such a small amount. I was feeling like I would never play again in the big tournaments, and maybe I had lost my game. The night I went dancing with Valentina, I had won seventeen thousand dollars, and that was the first time in quite a while. I was happy to have some before the World Series that's starting next Monday, but I need a lot more. I was going to be in a couple of games before the weekend with some good players. Suddenly, I had my hands on a lot of cash. I at least wanted to have back the money I had lost. Plus, I know that you need money, and we can talk about that. But if I'm honest with you, there's a stupid reason I wanted to keep the money, and it is the most compelling reason by far."

"Good. I asked you to be honest. So hit me with it. Your taking the cash was stupid. So the reason why can't be worse than the fact that you actually did it."

Corvette replied, "I asked you please not to get mad."

"I'm not mad in what I just told you, son. So go ahead and let me know what was behind your decision to do this."

"Well, it was Valentina who gave me the money, and I didn't know these guys who showed up demanding it. This guy Enrique seemed like he was hiding something about Valentina from me, and I didn't like that. If Valentina came and somehow she could explain to me about the money, I would have gladly given her back all of it. Enrique said they were Zs, but at first he let me think they were a drug cartel or some bad guys. Finally, this man David James showed up, and I knew who he was from different news items I had seen. But he told me that the money would belong to the United States government via the DEA, and I knew it wasn't their money. As far as I was concerned, Valentina had the claim to it, and he told me that I shouldn't even ask about her again, that by just doing that I could put her life in danger and mine. I figured that her life and mine were already in danger. I really want to talk to her, Mum. I want to see her again. I want to hear from her if there's some way I can help her if she's in danger. I want to put this money in a safe place. It's here in the house. I'm sorry to get you involved, but I thought you're the only person I can trust and that you can help me figure out what to do. If anyone comes after me here, well, this is a very small island and everyone knows us. We'll know if there's a stranger in the neighborhood."

His words were like a stab in the heart for reasons he wouldn't understand unless she explained it to him. Once before there might have been a stranger in the neighborhood and she didn't know it. She supposed that it was becoming time to share her suspicions about his father's death. But for now she answered:

"Never underestimate the stealth of evil, luv."

They got silent for a while as Madeline thought and Corvette puzzled over her remark.

"Son, you really think you're in love with this girl?"

"Mum, I would do anything to see her again."

"What is Valentina's last name?"

Corvette winced. "I don't know."

Madeline shook her head. "Somehow I thought you were going to tell me that."

He said, "I need to figure out a way to contact her without tipping off anyone that I'm going to do it."

"Well, this girl knows who you are. You took her money away, and she isn't too happy with you, I imagine. It might be easier for her to get in touch with you. Did you ever build that website I told you that you need for your fans, or a Facebook page?"

"Mum, I was going to do all that, but I've been so busy and just haven't taken time for that. Maybe it's a good thing I haven't, now that there are probably a lot of people interested in knowing where I am."

Madeline considered what Corvette said. She began thinking out loud, "Anyone who does research on you will know that you live occasionally in Barbados. We don't have a land line here at the house, so calling information won't help, but probably somewhere you have put your cell phone number that's discoverable on the internet. We can do some searches and try to find out. There's another way, though, that people can find you. I have a website and fan pages, and it is well known that I live in Barbados. There have been articles published on the internet that mention you're my son. I don't have any phone

116

numbers on my pages, but I do have contact forms and a public e-mail address. Valentina can find us. So can anyone else."

She saw that Corvette was looking gloomy.

"I'm sorry, Mum, maybe coming here with the money wasn't such a good idea."

"The bad idea was taking the money," Madeline scolded. "We could turn it over to the police here."

"Mum!" Corvette got up and leaned against the kitchen sink and stared out the window. Madeline saw the breezes blowing his hair and his face that looked so much like Rogelio's. His body was lean and muscular. He looked like a big man-child. She knew there were things she should tell him. She was trying to figure out a place to begin when Corvette began speaking.

"This is a nice home, Mum. The yard looks great. The flowers inside and out have your touch, I can see that. But when Dad was alive you lived so much grander. We had the tropical mansion and the pier with the boat and the swimming pool and the other rental houses on the island. We had all those parties. Everyone in Bridgetown knew about us, and they all loved Dad. That lifestyle required a lot of money, Mum. A lot of it. You know, I didn't think too much about that after Dad died, and I was younger and in high school and then in college. I just thought, 'Well, bad luck. We don't have my father's nice salary to pay for everything.' All of a sudden, the money wasn't there, and you sold everything and drastically cut back on expenses of living. We moved here to this small house. I was busy and then away, and I didn't think too much about what you were going through. About what you're still going through. In the last year, though, I've been feeling older and have more experience in life. I'm noticing more things. I saw what it's like to have money and then lose it. One night, about a month ago, I couldn't sleep. I was thinking that some things didn't add up, and this kept me awake all night. For example, after you sold all the properties and the boat and the cars, where did all that money go? You said that you paid off debt. Okay, maybe so. But for over ten years your books have been selling well. I know you must have a decent income from that. Certainly, enough to afford more than this. I was in a small store recently in my hotel. It had a little book section, and even in their limited selection, there were three of your mystery novels. And then I thought something else: I meet a lot of resort managers in my travels on the poker circuits. I stay in some very nice places. These managers work very hard, like Dad did, and they make good money. But they don't make the kind of money that permits a life style anywhere close to what we lived. You know what I mean? So, I'm wondering about that, Mum. How did we have that, and where did all the money go after Dad died?"

He turned around and leaned back against the sink counter. He stared at her with dark green eyes that were sympathetic and slightly misty. Madeline didn't answer him because she could see that he wasn't finished speaking yet.

"I remember that you know a lot about banks, Mum. Even back when I was in high school here, you used to tell me about the international banks in Barbados, particularly the Swiss ones that have private, numbered accounts. I've read what you've written about these in a couple of your novels. So I'm guessing that you still have accounts like this, or you know about them. I have one point eight million dollars in cash. It's in the bedroom. Can you help me get this somewhere safe, and fast? I know you, Mum. You have too much mischief in you to want to give this money to the police. You can act all British and proper sometimes, but the truth of the matter is that you married a short little Mexican man who danced away with your heart, and you love mystery, secrets, and romance. Maybe I'm a lot like my Dad, but I'm also a lot like you. So help me out here."

Madeline let out a big sigh. She wanted to give her son another hug. He was making things so much easier for her. She began her answer by telling him about Rogelio.

"You call him St. Rogelio. He was no saint, Corvette. He had some character flaws that got him in over his head. He did have a good heart, and I loved him madly."

"How did he get all the money?"

"I'm not entirely positive, but I think I'm ninety-nine percent positive. I believe he was laundering money for organized crime through the hotels he worked in. I think he didn't really want to do it and that he wanted to stop it, but I think he was threatened that things would happen to his family if he didn't cooperate."

"Say what?" Corvette exclaimed. His jaw fell open. He sat back down in his chair.

Madeline nodded, anticipating this reaction. She explained, "I did see his pay checks, and there was no way they would cover all the things we had. This started back in Texas. It began soon after he became interested in learning about his parents and what happened to them. The ranchers who raised your father told Rogelio that his parents were Mexicans who got deported from the United States and that they had made a quick decision with them to raise him. So Rogelio started obsessing about it. This was when you were still very young, maybe about four years old. It didn't take long for him to find out that his name, Fuego de Noche, was not a Spanish name used in Mexico. Rogelio got very interested in this because of you. He wanted his son to know something about his roots. On my side of the family, my parents and sister pretty much wrote me off after I met your father and married him. They're dull, boring, and mean people set in their ways in the little English village, and I broke all the rules by running off. They don't want anything to do with me, and I really don't get a thing out of going back to that place. I tried for a few years, but their indifference and meanness to me was just something I didn't feel I had to put up with. So Rogelio saw this, and he agreed it wasn't healthy for us to visit my family, but he did say, 'Well, our son will grow up without experiencing grandparents.' So he became interested in knowing more about his family tree. Unfortunately, by this time the Texas ranchers who raised him had passed away. They were an older couple who didn't have much energy by the time that their little agreed-upon-son was a teenager. You can just imagine, love, as crazy and explorative as your father was, without anyone strictly supervising him, how many opportunities he had to try things well beyond his years. Thank God, somehow he had a strong work ethic."

"So what happened?" Corvette asked impatiently.

"Your dad started making trips to Mexico to find his parents. He was doing pretty well managing a hotel in San Antonio back then. We lived modestly. He had two or three days off here and there, and he would go to Mexico. A couple of longer trips took him to Sinaloa because he thought the couple had told him his parents came from that state. He searched archives in libraries and churches and all sorts of public records, but no one had heard such a name. He came to believe that it had been a name just made up, but it was on his birth certificate in the United States. Then one day someone suggested to him that perhaps it was an indigenous name. That led him to some tribes in the state of Chihuahua. Among the Tarahumaras, he once found some people who said they knew of a family that used a name in their language that meant something equivalent to "fire of night." However, they didn't know where these people were. This seemed to satisfy your father in some sense. He gave up on the idea of finding his natural parents, but he decided to anglicize his name. So he had your name legally changed at that time. We all did this. I guess this gave him a legitimacy that he sought. But after those last visits to Mexico, your father began working very long hours, even more than usual, and I hardly saw him. After that, I noticed our income in the bank started to increase."

"You think he was on the payroll of organized crime?"

"I do now, Corvette. He met a lot of people in Mexico, and he definitely had opportunity because he was spending a lot of time in the two states of Sinaloa and Chihuahua. Then, only once, he said something odd to me. He said that it was strange that his natural parents would give him up so easily when they got deported back to Mexico, and why were they deported? He said that maybe it was because they were under suspicion of running drugs. That Texas ranch where they lived was very close to the border, he said. But he never mentioned it again, and when I brought it up, he blew me off."

She saw her son visibly shaking, as if the breezes from the window were making him cold. He was looking at the window, but Madeline knew the air wasn't the source of his goose bumps. This story had to come at the pace which Corvette could handle, so she paused when she sensed he needed to digest, and she waited for his next questions.

"Mum, how did we end up in Barbados?"

"Pretty much like we have explained in the past, son. Your dad and I had visited here on cruises a few times. I absolutely adored this island because it was a British colony at one point, so I had that connection. Also it is tropical here. Your father had a great reputation as a resort manager. The man who owned The Colonial Inn and Resort here had an extended stay once in your father's resort in San Antonio, and he was very impressed by Rogelio. He needed a manager here in Barbados, and he offered the job to your dad. Your father seemed very enthusiastic about leaving Texas and coming here, and he knew I would love it."

Corvette's next question surprised her.

"I don't remember the owner of The Colonial Inn," he said. "Was he Mexican?"

"Noooo..." Madeline answered, drawing out the word as if to ask, "Why that question?" She added, "He was from Colombia." And she thought, *My son would be a worthy investigator in one of my mystery novels.*

Corvette dropped his head. She suspected that he was trying to withhold tears. She fought to keep her own emotions under control.

Quietly, he asked, "Where does your money go, Mum?"

She told him quickly. "I make payments to a trust in a private bank here in Barbados. When your father died, a lawyer visited me and showed me that Rogelio had a lot of debts that needed to be repaid. He had a good idea of the income I was making from my novels. He knew the market value of all our assets. He suggested a plan of liquidation, a living budget for me, and payments to a trust account for the future. He gave me a little time to find alternative ways to pay everything off, but he said I would find that his assessments were on the money. And he was right. So I have been complying with his plan."

Now Corvette's head snapped up. "Jesus, Mum, what the hell kind of debts were these? How much? Were they enforceable? Did you get your own lawyer? Couldn't you have declared bankruptcy or something?"

She answered him very quietly, to calm him. "Love, these debts were personal loans to your father. They had exorbitant rates of interest. They were several million dollars. It was a situation that bankruptcy wouldn't solve."

"What were the loans for? All the things we had?"

"The properties and vehicles were all financed through conventional loans, Corvette, and the sale of those things pretty much repaid those debts. Your father and I received those loans based on the strength of our income and worth of our assets. But I didn't know about these other liabilities."

"What were the liabilities for, Mum?"

She hated to tell him. But now she realized that she had to, and probably it was coming too late to have made a difference in the situation he was currently in. Had he known, she thought sadly, maybe he would have done things differently in life.

"Different personal things, honey. But mostly for gambling debts."

"Oh my God!" Corvette exclaimed.

Now she saw the water in his eyes and she could feel the tears in hers. She knew what he was going to ask her next.

"Mum," Corvette whispered, "do you think...is it possible...I mean, Dad's accident was just that, right? An accident?"

"I'm not sure, honey. I'm not sure. I guess, to be honest, I came to think that it wasn't."

"Did that lawyer or anyone threaten you in any way?"

Madeline brushed away a tear scrolling down her cheek. "Everything about the lawyer was understated. He's the only one who ever contacted me. He explained to me about private banks and that my payments would go to a trust that disburses to the owners of your father's notes. He told me that if I complied, the interest portion of the payments would remain reasonable. He had a way of talking that seemed courteous and efficient, but I was able to imagine an undertone of threat that scared me."

"How much is owed now?"

"There's a balance of a little over a million dollars."

"God, Mum, why in the world didn't you tell me?"

She was so scared. She couldn't tell him. She couldn't answer him. She continued to brush away tears."

"Because of me," Corvette said, breaking the silence. "You were afraid someone would hurt me."

Madeline buried her face in her hands. "I couldn't stand that," she replied. "I still haven't recovered from your father's death, and I'm not sure it was an accident."

"We've got the money right here, Mum," her son said softly.

The statement snapped her back to taking control. "We don't know who that money belongs to, Corvette. From what you've told me, it probably belongs to a lot of innocent people somewhere in its lineage who are victims of God-knows-what horrible things."

"Okay, look, Mum, you're not in your situation alone anymore, and I got you involved in mine. So we're going to work together to get us out of our messes and do the right thing. I think we should start with Valentina. That's what I want to do. Maybe from there we'll know where to go. How do we find her?"

Madeline wiped her eyes. She said, "I think we have to start with David James. You don't know anyone else who knows her, except for the guy you don't like named Enrique. So, we'll start on the internet digging up information on David James and find a way to contact him. I'm sure he'll be glad to hear from you for some not-so-good reasons. We need to gain his trust and get him to tell us how to contact Valentina. But I'm not as confident as you that she's a person on the right side of things, Corvette. If you want to start there, let's get busy."

"David James actually gave me contact information, Mum," Corvette said, remembering the card that David had handed him.

"But I already know he's adamant that he won't help me find Valentina. He wants me to forget her."

A silence hung between them for a minute as both thought. Then Corvette asked, "What do we do about this cash?"

Madeline shook her head. "It's not a good idea for me to show up at the bank with nearly a couple of million dollars in cash, especially under the circumstances."

"I declared it as gambling winnings when I took it out of the United States, and I reported having it when I traveled through Mexico."

"And I'm sure there's a trail of people who know where you went with it," Madeline answered, thinking it out. "So the money needs to go into an account in your name. Most banks don't accept large deposits of cash in new accounts unless they know a person and where the money comes from. They worry that it is from organized crime and that is illegal for them to accept deposits."

"I'm still using my Barbados accounts, and as recently as nine months ago I had two million dollars in it. It didn't last long, though."

"I didn't realize you had that much at any point in time, Corvette. That's astonishing. Well, I have some friends in our bank. It's a Swiss bank. I've talked to them through the years about their numbered accounts when I did research for my novels. I do have a good relationship with Johann Wolfgang, who manages some of those accounts. We'll visit him together and tell him about your gambling winnings and ask him how we can get your cash safe and secure and private. It's possible he'll help us."

"Can we do that now?" Corvette asked anxiously.

"Yes," Madeline agreed. "I don't think we have lots of time before bad things start to happen. I'll get dressed, and we'll go over there."

"Then I want to hurry back home and start finding out what we can about Valentina. I want to find her, Mum!

"Then the next thing I think we should do is to enroll you in Spanish classes."

Her remark made them both laugh. Hers was a laugh of relief. It felt good not to have secrets from her son anymore.

The boy is growing up, she thought. *We'll get him a haircut and make him look like a man. Then we'll work on this case together. Who knows? This might make excellent material for my next novel.*

She got up and told him that she was going to shower quickly and then jump into her clothes. As she zipped to her bedroom, she had a sudden, unexpected remembrance about David James. Maybe she was going to be able to help her son find Valentina after all!

Chapter 9: The Lead to a Dead End

Enrique Santos
Las Vegas, Nevada
Sunday Morning

Despite what the guy had done, Enrique felt something good for him, and this was driving him nuts. He hated him, but maybe he liked something about him too. Corvette seemed like a pretty-boy gringo: spoiled, selfish, and immature. He played poker for a living, Dios en cielo, and the shallow media of the United States was falling in love with photographing him dancing or capturing shots of the sexy young girls watching him in the card games. Games, in a world full of spilt blood and desperation! How in the hell did it happen that this guy got to spend an evening dancing with the one woman in whom he finally felt an interest? Enrique had imagined having a romantic evening with Valentina. And how did it slip by Ana and David that Ana's niece would be doing undercover work exposing her arguably to the most dangerous man in the world: Z-30?

But Corvette showed some spunk in dealing with me, Enrique observed. *He was a little clever and we were a little stupid. He got away with the money. So why would there be anything in me that would want to like him?*

In the past couple of weeks Enrique was beginning to feel like God was mocking him. It was as if the Creator were trying to suffocate him in a world of Corvettes. He was sitting in the passenger seat of David's new Stingray as David weaved through the mid-afternoon traffic of Las Vegas from their hotel to the office of the DEA. David had a passion for these cars that seemed to go past respectability. He had scared the parkour out of Enrique one night in Texas by taking him out at one in the morning to a deserted highway and catapulting them to something close to a couple of hundred miles per hour. In the ambient glow of the dash, David's face had radiated some type of mad furor. Enrique had imagined that they might have whooshed unknown numbers of small animals crossing the highway into the cosmos. They had been traveling too fast to tell. A couple of sign posts had seemed to curve as they flicked by, as if to confirm Einstein's theories of relativity. The experience was surreal. He had never seen David exhibit this kind of behavior before. The man was always so composed, calculating, and pleasant. That's what scared him the most that night.

But then Enrique had a memory that once before he had seen this same expression on David's face. It was when he first was getting to know him, and David had thundered knocks on his door in Mexico after the police had released the men whom they had arrested for murdering Enrique's best friend and soul-mate, Israel. He was a young friend of David's, too. David had just found out, and his veins bulged in his temple like he was about to have a stroke.

"We have to stop this shit in Mexico!" David had yelled when he opened the door. He had caught Enrique in a moment when he himself was reacting in furor from the news: He was in the midst of throwing furniture against the wall of his condo. Yet the anger in the gringo had surprised him. It was primitive, like his, at the limits of frustration that could no longer be restrained.

He had slammed the door against the wall when he permitted David to enter. He had yelled in response, "Tell me how we're going to do it, David, because I swear I'll kill them all! Come in and tell me! Tell me a lot of things, like who you are and how you always know who to call in Mexico! Tell me what we're going to do, because I'm in. I'm tired of being afraid."

From that moment they were bonded. With Ana and Eduardo Ortíz, the man who in death became the financial benefactor of the Zs, they entered into a commitment of blood to resist the expansion of the narcos throughout the continent of North America. Enrique never would forget Israel, his friend-of-roots in Mexico City, who had mentored him and had protected him during their adolescent years of skateboarding and urban free-running. Israel had mapped the paths for him and Enrique to obtain their college education in Monterrey. In Monterrey, Israel was murdered, leaving Enrique alone. To Enrique, Israel was a brother-in-soul who would live within his heart the rest of his life. His surprise was that Israel's torture and murder had moved David to a dramatic re-direction of his life too. He came to understand that to David, Israel symbolized all the innocent victims mutilated and killed by the drug lords during his years working with the DEA and the CIA. Israel was the tipping point for him. He had claimed a place inside David's heart also. From the grave, Israel's quiet cries for justice seemed to transform the lives of everyone who remembered him.

The memories and the thoughts about Corvette were making Enrique fidgety and disquieted. He absent-mindedly opened the center console of David's Stingray and snapped it shut. It made him think about the other Corvette, the one everyone in town was trying to find.

What had Valentina said to Corvette when she handed him the key fob? Busca el auto? Look for the car? Yes, because she was clever and didn't want to confuse him. She knew he would recognize soon enough the crossed race flags of the Stingray on the fob. And I'm a little jealous and a little pissed that the car would have to be a Corvette, having the same name as the gringo kid. What kind of name is that for a person?

The previous evening, David, Ana, and Enrique had managed to break away to have a quick fast-food dinner with Valentina. She was upset that she had been pushed out of the field of action and that everyone else was making decisions that she felt she should have been involved in. She was steaming because no one had checked the bag to discover that most of the cash was missing and that Corvette had managed to get out of the country with it. Enrique had tried to get in her good graces by lending a sympathetic ear, even though he was the one who had had the job of contacting Corvette about returning the cash.

When the quick meal was over, Enrique didn't have the feeling that he had made such a good impression on this girl. She had made him confess something:

"Did he want to turn over the bag to you?" she had asked him.

"Not really," Enrique admitted. "We were trying to scare him by letting him assume we were cartel."

"Of course he didn't want to give you the bag! I'm the one who gave it to him. I'm sure he would have wanted to return it to me, or at least he would have wanted to ask me questions," she replied pointedly.

"How would he do that? He doesn't speak Spanish, and he thought you don't speak English."

That had been the wrong thing to say to her. She cut him a glare that frosted him quiet.

David had then intervened: "Valentina, I think we're all sorry. You've been doing an ultra-good job, a dangerous job, in great service to both Mexico and the United States. Enrique, Ana, and I have been tracking the Zetas' money laundering and just happened to be in Las Vegas when you were here with Z-30 and the Cartel of Sinaloa decided to pick this time to try to assassinate him. They may have succeeded. We don't know for sure, yet. But your associate got killed and the whole thing has been a fiasco. I'm very sorry about Josh. I'm sure that must be weighing on your mind tonight along with other things."

Those remarks had seemed to pacify Valentina a little bit, but Enrique could see that she was a Latina woman and that it would take her a little while not to act angry. Ana had been somewhat quiet during the meal. Enrique thought it was because she was worried about her niece, but there were several things on her mind.

"I'm starting the drive home to San Antonio tomorrow for a couple of days to check on the kids," she told Valentina. "I'll need to go to Monterrey after that because I'm co-leading a march there with Carlos Limas, the poet. It's a prelude march to drum up enthusiasm for another caravan of peace promoting community action, one that would march into the United States. I'm not sure if you can be in touch with me there, but just know that in a week I'll be in Monterrey for about a week if you need me."

Valentina had nodded and had thanked her, and then Ana had added, "I miss the kids. We relocated them into schools in San Antonio, and now I fear I'm away from them too much. I've been gone from home a couple of weeks, making appearances at non-violence rallies on the way here to Vegas. David has been away from home even longer. He was in Phoenix before coming here. I think the kids miss him more than me!"

Enrique had recently seen Ana's children from her first marriage. Her husband had died soon after elections which had ended Ana's short time as Interim President of Mexico. Rafael Jr. was now fifteen years old and finally a little taller than his short mom. Paula, however, was somehow tall and, at seventeen years old, she already showed the poise, grace, and stunning beauty of her mother. Enrique had caught the way that Paula snuck glances at him. She acted so much older than she was, and if she were, in fact, a few years older, she would be a serious contender with Valentina for his attentions. He had never commented to Ana about this because he was afraid it would seem perverse in some way.

Although Ana is married to a man twenty-two years older than she is, Enrique observed. This still amazed him.

They had finished the meal when David pulled out his phone and brought up some photographs. He handed the phone to Valentina and told her to scroll through the four or five he wanted her to see.

"These are not the most pleasant pictures to look at, Valentina, especially after just eating. They're pictures of the body taken in the casino this morning. Are you able to say if these are photographs of Jesús Raúl Espinosa, Z-30?" he asked her.

"Dios, son horribles," Valentina had whispered as she studied them. "I really think this is Horacio, but I can't be one

130

hundred percent certain. His jacket isn't there, and I would have recognized that. This body looks more like Horacio's, but it's difficult to tell. They're big, bulldog men, both Horacio and Raúl. I didn't pay attention to the boots they were wearing. These guys always wear boots. I want to tell you that this is Horacio, but I can't be sure."

David had sighed. "That's fine. That's what I thought you would be able to say. No one here is certain. The Z who disarmed the man who killed this guy said that the other, unharmed man stated that the victim was the Zeta. The body is carrying identification that the Zeta once used. Then a few minutes ago we learned from the Sheriff's Office that they're receiving threatening calls from people in Puebla, the Zeta's home town in Mexico, who say they want the body returned to Puebla immediately. Apparently, people in the home city of the Zeta believe that the man shot was Z-30."

"And the other man hasn't been found," Enrique had added, trying to re-engage in the conversation with Valentina.

She had nodded and had sat pensively a few moments. Then she had asked, "What about the Corvette? Has it turned up anywhere? There was a ledger book of some sort that Raúl had put in the center console."

"Negative, so far," David had answered.

"I can't figure out why the car wasn't there," Valentina replied. "It's just strange."

The car still wasn't found the next morning, and Enrique kept thinking about it. If he could find it, that would impress Valentina. He wanted to do that for her. He wondered if the ledger inside contained important information about money laundering that would help David with his work. He didn't want too much time to get lost without tracking it just because everyone was so busy in the aftermath of the shootings and fighting the previous day. The national media was all into the shootings in The Oasis because drug gangs in a number of United States cities had been waging bloody attacks and reprisals against one another, and now congressmen and senators were vying for sound-bytes on the subject.

But Enrique got David's attention that morning when he pointed out something:

"Suppose the Zeta is alive. Suppose he doesn't know who got the car either. So then he would be wondering two things: Who got his money, and who got his ledger book, if, in fact, it is a ledger book that's important. Wouldn't he be looking for that too? Maybe our search for the car will run us directly into him. That would be good if he's not going to make any attempt to get back in touch with Valentina and we can't get to him that way."

David patted his back. "Good point, amigo. I do want to know what's in that book. Look, the police are trying to find the Corvette, but who knows what kind of job they're doing? I'll tell you what I noticed, Enrique: That parking staff manager at The Oasis sure looks Mexican to me. Maybe the Mexican leader of the Zs can get him to be forthcoming, eh? These guys know everything. He has got to know what happened to that car. I know he was interviewed yesterday by the Sheriff's Department, and he claims cluelessness, but why don't you give it a shot?"

"Okay. Do we know anything about him?"

"Yeah. Valentina says he knew the Zeta, like he had dealt with him before. The Zeta stuck some hundreds in his palm to let the car stay out front. There were two sets of key fobs. She said that the Zeta made a show of giving her a set and the other set to the manager."

"It's hard to believe that the car could be missing without the parking staff knowing about it," Enrique said.

"The feedback we got from the police is that no one claims to know where either the key fob or the car is, neither the manager nor the staff they interviewed."

David drove Enrique to the entrance of The Oasis in his Corvette. Enrique might have appreciated the irony in that, but he was busy observing the activity of the parking attendants near the doors. He got out so David could disappear with the car a few minutes and he could work alone.

Enrique had chosen to wear what he considered his working Z outfit: He had on black sports shoes, socks and pants. He had put on a black silk T shirt that had the Z logo: a silver "Z" inside a triangle where a left shirt pocket would have been. It was actually a logo that Ana had designed, and The Z Foundation supplied these shirts to the young people who liked to wear them when they did community service. The flexible clothes Enrique always wore permitted free running and parkour jumps without hindering or binding him.

He sought out the manager and was told it was Alex. Alex walked over from behind a stand at the entrance to greet him.

"Good morning, sir, how can I help you?"

Enrique put a folded hundred dollar bill in his hand from his personal money and spoke to the guy in Spanish and English.

"Qué tal, Alex? Soy Enrique. Can we be friends a few minutes? I'm not police. Soy de Ciudad de México, but I live in Monterrey now. Don't know if you're into the parkour that there is here in Vegas, but if you are, you might know what the Zs do. I lead the operations of the Zs in the United States and México."

Alex broke into a big grin and replied in Spanish, "Sí, compadre, conozco muy bien quién eres. Soy de Monterrey." He told him that he knew very well who he was and that he also was from Monterrey. "I see your emblem on your shirt," he added. "We're seeing these outfits in Las Vegas now."

"Okay, did you live in the United States when there was the military coup in México?"

"Sí, I'm a citizen of the United States. I carry ten years living here."

"Good, Alex, but you know that our home country struggles in the shadows of the USA. We're good people, resourceful, from a land of resources; and the future will be brighter for all Mexicanos. However, we have to take care of some very bad problems. Problems that are coming here to your new country now. So I'm not going to mention specifics out here. You can relax, because I know you're under the microscope in many ways. I do have some questions, and hopefully you won't say to me, 'I've told the police all I know.' This has to do with the missing car."

Enrique saw that Alex was adopting an impassive face. He gazed past Enrique, as if he were watching his staff attend the guests arriving and departing. He spoke in a low tone without looking at him.

"Look, it's just that the hotel lawyers now have come out and said we're to talk to no one about anything unless they're present or we have it cleared."

Enrique noticed Alex's wedding band. "You have children, Alex?"

"Si, I have three little ones. The youngest is three and the oldest is five."

"Then I'm sure you worry about the safety of your family, and also your job is important to you. I understand. Let me ask you a different kind of question then. Do you have any new employees who maybe didn't come in today?"

A slight smile appeared on Alex's face as he continued to stare in the distance. "Good question, amigo. The answer is sí. Why did you ask me that?"

"Pues, the new people make mistakes, verdad? Maybe they do stupid things, like move a car and bring it back and then leave the key fob inside, so anyone could walk up and start it. Or maybe they aren't so careless. Maybe it's just that someone has paid them for the favor of leaving the key in the car. The bad thing is, you would have no control over that. It's best to keep those things quiet."

"Sí, and that's a very interesting trail of logic," replied Alex. The smile was a little bigger.

"So, my gift to you in your hand for a name, Alex. Perhaps someone not here today."

"We had a new employee who was here just three days. He didn't come in today."

"Nombre?"

"John Turbowitz."

Gracias a Dios, thought Enrique. *There can't be many Turbowitzes in Las Vegas.*

"Y este tipo vive en Vegas?" Enrique asked. *And this guy lives in Vegas?*

"Sí, with his parents, he told us. He's just a college kid here."

He spent a few more minutes chatting with Alex so that the young man might relax about his provision of information. Enrique told him that he needn't worry and that he wouldn't come back with follow-up questions. Enrique pulled a card from his wallet. He bumped fists with Alex and then opened his palm. "Bien, muchas gracias, Alex. Here is my card. We have a Z training facility here in Vegas. If you ever need me or would like to look into the Zs, give me a call. You look like you could be a fit guy."

Alex chuckled. "That sheet would kill me." He mispronounced the word for Enrique's amusement. Then he said, "Do a jump or something," and he chuckled.

But Enrique thought he would get the last laugh. "You see the gringo driving the Vette up the driveway toward us?"

"Sí"

"Okay." Enrique kept talking to Alex as David slowly pulled up the drive. Just as David was arriving, Enrique stepped backward in front of the Corvette. David's reaction time to stomp the brakes wasn't quite as fast as Enrique's backward flip out of the way. David thumped his fist on the steering wheel.

"He's pissed," Enrique mouthed silently to Alex as he walked around to the passenger side door and then got in the Corvette. He saw Alex turn his back so that the gringo wouldn't see him laughing.

"Damn it, Enrique!" David said to him as he began to pull away from the entrance. "I'm going to take that as a sign that you had some success."

"Yes, sorry, David. I showed off a bit. You're right. I played a hunch that someone on the parking staff might have taken the new Stingray for a spin. So the easy thing to do is to set the keyless remote on the seat or in the console and then push the start button of the car. When you get back, it's easy to forget and leave the fob inside the car. The car beeps, but if you're in a hurry, say, to attend a customer who's suddenly present, maybe you don't hear the beeps because you're on the run. Whatever the situation, now the car is in the driveway with the key inside, and all anyone has to do is to push the start button and go. Now, a classy place like The Oasis is going to have a competent parking manager. So I guessed that maybe someone new and not so experienced might have made a mistake like this."

"So who's our suspect?" David asked.

"We're in luck. He has a unique name, John Turbowitz, and he's a college student who lives here in Vegas with his parents. He only worked three days and was a no-show today. The manager confirmed what I was thinking, to the extent that he felt comfortable doing it. The corporate lawyers have told the employees to shut up to media or outsiders unless they're present."

The visit to Alex had been a couple of hours earlier. David had phoned in the name of the Turbowitz kid to Zolinsky in the DEA so that he could be checked out. Zolinsky had told David that he would run it by the Sheriff's Department to locate the young man.

Enrique and David had stopped at an Appleby's for lunch, and both had spent much of the time on their phones checking messages and e-mails. Ana had phoned to say she was en route back to San Antonio and that there were no problems. Zolinsky had called David just a half hour ago and had reported that Valentina had safely landed in Monterrey and had been contacted on arrival by their agent, Juan Ramirez.

Now Enrique and David were on the way to the DEA office where David would meet with Zolinsky and the Chairman of the Nevada State Gaming Control Board, whom they had invited to

136

discuss possibilities that there were new ways drug cartels might launder money through casinos in Nevada. David had promised Enrique to relieve him of the responsibility of having to sit through the meeting, or of having to pore once again for hours over detailed gaming reports to look for inconsistencies in the trends of table wins.

Instead, David was going to let Enrique use the Corvette while he remained in the office for the afternoon. Enrique was going to be able to meet with a new crop of Zs in Las Vegas who were presently training at the Z facility in the desert just four miles south of the Las Vegas city limits. Enrique had found that this was the work that made him happiest.

But even as David pulled over on Main Street in front of the DEA offices, he received a cell phone call from Zolinsky.

"Where are you?" Zolinsky asked. Enrique could hear him through the phone speaker. There was anxiety in his voice.

"Just pulled in," David reported. "About to come inside. What's up?"

"Valentina," Zolinsky answered. "She seems to be missing."

Enrique felt his heart fail.

"And something else: that kid, Turbowitz. The State Police just found his body shot to pieces outside his car on a street near an exit from I-215, a little south of the airport. It appears whoever did it tore through the vehicle looking for something."

Chapter 10: Among Women and Lovers

Valentina Garza
Monterrey, Mexico
Sunday Afternoon

The nineteen-year-old taxi driver had gotten on the autopista, the toll road, without Valentina even requesting it. She was glad. It was fast and safe, frequently patrolled by the State Police of Nuevo León, the Federal Police, the Army, and the Marines. At present, the road was lightly traveled for Monterrey because it was mid-afternoon and the infamous rush hour traffic clogged this peripheral highway from six to eight-thirty p.m. Valentina guessed that she should be home from the airport in about forty minutes.

The driver was flirty and chatty. He had a fresh-scrubbed appearance that made him cute. He was asking Valentina a lot of personal questions, as if he were leading up to asking her for a date.

The boldness of some kids, Valentina chuckled to herself. She tried to pay some attention to what he was asking her just so the boy could feel good about his effort. She liked his innocence. Her world was now so far removed from innocence that when in crowds, she sought people with bright eyes and smiles as a way of remembering what her life had once been.

But she was distracted and thinking about a lot of things at once. She might have to return for a while to the more mundane career of supervising her events planning business. She remembered when she had thought that handling annual corporate employee conventions with multiple, huge display screens and the logistics of snack breaks, meals, banquets, and concerts or dances delivered over-the-top stress. Normally, that work didn't put her in life-or-death situations like her work in the DEA did, unless one took seriously the threats of irate corporate executives when something went wrong. After at least a twelve-hour sleep, she would be in her Monterrey office again receiving updates from Lila and Marta, who ran things in consultation with her through Facetime, Skype, e-mails, and phone calls.

She also kept thinking about the ledger book that had been left in the Corvette. *Did it have anything to do with the recording of drug sales and cash*, she wondered, or *perhaps it listed names, phones, and addresses of persons in the business.* She never actually saw its contents, but she had an intuition that it was important in the drama that had unfolded in Las Vegas, beginning with the shootings in The Oasis.

Suddenly the taxi driver announced in a changed tone of voice, "Señorita, I think this is very strange. There are some SUVs behind us that seem to be following us. When I slow, none of them pass; and when I speed up, they keep up with me."

She heard the anxiety and suspicion in the youth's voice, and a chill passed through her. In Monterrey and in other cities of Mexico, the taxi drivers were often targeted for death because they transported rival gang members. There were occasions when trucks and SUVs arrived at taxi-stands, and delinquents armed with semi-automatic rifles got out and murdered all the drivers sitting in their cars as they awaited fares. So there was nothing unusual for this young man to be observing vehicles carefully through his rear mirror as he chatted hopefully with the beautiful young woman in the back seat.

Valentina turned and looked out the rear window of the Altima taxi. She observed three SUVs just behind them, all with Nuevo León license plates. They were in the same lane that the taxi was traveling. A few other cars and a minivan were in the passing lane. She could only see men in the SUVs. None had a happy family inside.

She quickly put her phone into her bag. She pulled out a wad of currency in pesos. She leaned forward to see the name of the boy driving her. It was José.

She said in a calm but emphatic voice, "Listen to me carefully, José. The men behind us may have business with me.

139

If these SUVs start to pass us and surround us like they want to stop us, I want you to pull over to the side of the road and stop. Please don't try to be a hero. I'll get out of the car and go to them. They will want me alive, I'm sure of this. When you stop, I want you to lie down across the front seats of your car, and don't look. You don't want to be a witness. You don't want to give them any reason to hurt you. I'll get them away from you. Don't get up until you're sure everyone is gone. When you pull the car over and stop, press the button that opens the trunk, where my bag is. The reason is that if they want my bag, they can get it without involving you. Okay? Me entiendes?"

"I understand," he answered, clearly scared now. He kept his eyes on his mirror.

Valentina handed him the money that she had pulled from her bag. "Here. This is to compensate you for this stress. Put this under your seat, or hide it in some way."

The young man accepted it. Valentina returned to looking out the rear car window. The SUVs weren't making any changes in their file behind them. After another couple of minutes went by, an idea occurred to her.

"José, go ahead and put on your turn signal, and then pull over to the side of the road. If they're following us and want me, they will pull over as well."

He answered, "Don't you think it's a good idea just to keep going? Maybe we'll see some police."

Valentina let out a small sigh. "We're not going to see any police," she said.

"Okay," José agreed. He flipped up the turn signal lever and slowed the taxi along the shoulder.

Valentina looked back, and, yes, the SUVs slowed as well. In the first vehicle behind them, the man next to the driver was pointing at their cab while the driver was talking on a cell phone. That SUV and the second one pulled ahead of the taxi. The third followed them along the shoulder.

"Bueno, José," Valentina instructed, still holding her composure to sound confident and in charge. "Now come to a stop, press the button that opens the trunk, and lay down across the seats."

"Good luck, Señorita," José tried to answer bravely. "Gracias for trying to help me." He braked the car to a stop and popped open the trunk before lowering himself.

Valentina quickly emerged from the back seat and stepped in front of the taxi's driver window to block José from the approach of any of the men getting out of the SUVs. She had her purse strapped over her left shoulder.

"I'm Valentina Garza!" she shouted. "Don't hurt the driver of this taxi! He's not looking at you! I'll come with you peacefully, if that's what you want. My bag is in this open trunk."

Two men who had emerged from the vehicle behind them began to approach the trunk. She turned and saw two more men approaching from one of the SUVs ahead of them. She extended her arms in front of her and shouted to them, "Stop there! I'll get in whatever vehicle you say."

To her surprise, the men stopped and hesitated, as if she were speaking to them with authority. When she saw their hesitation, she made a show of putting her arms in the air and walking toward the guys approaching the rear of the taxi. One strode up to her and took her purse.

"Which SUV?" she asked.

"Get in up there," he responded, indicating the men from the first vehicle.

Valentina changed course and walked quickly toward those men. As she passed the driver's window, she said, "Stay down, José, everything's fine." The two men ahead awaited her. She glanced back and saw the men behind her removing her bag from the trunk. Then they shut the trunk, peered briefly into the taxi through the rear window, and began to stroll back to their vehicle. She resumed her march to the front SUV, and one of the men ahead escorted her and opened its rear passenger side door. Valentina climbed into the seat and took her place next to a skinny, acne-pitted man who stared appraisingly at her. She heard the doors of the SUV shutting behind them and then the sounds of three engines starting. The driver of the SUV she was in pulled back onto the autopista. Once they were up to speed, she risked a glance backwards and saw to her relief that all the SUVs were in the highway and that the taxi was becoming a speck in the distance. José had been spared harm.

She thought it best not to speak. It was quiet in the SUV for a few minutes, and then the driver said, "Bueno, let's all just sit back and relax. We have a bit of a ride ahead of us. Unfortunately, it is in the other direction, and I'll have to get off the autopista and turn around."

The man in the front passenger seat was texting someone. Valentina let her back recline against her seat. She imagined that in the SUV behind them, one of the men was rummaging through her suitcase. They wouldn't find anything interesting, unless they were into women's panties.

They're being hands-off with me, she observed. *They're taking me to Raúl. They don't want to mistreat me and have to answer to him. They also didn't expect me to have any gun. They still think I'm just the girl from Monterrey.*

Then she realized that she had forgotten to send a message to Juan Ramirez before she was taken.

Ana Valdez
En Route to San Antonio, Texas
Monday Morning

From Las Vegas, Ana had driven to Deming, New Mexico, halfway to her United States' home with David in San Antonio. It had been a boring ride alone, nine hours, and she had arrived to stay in a Hampton Inn just before sunset. The town of fifteen thousand people glowed red in the low evening sun as the shadows from the Florida Mountains yawned and stretched across the desert toward the community of single-story homes. Ana was driving I-10, and she was aware that in Deming, she was only thirty-three miles from the border with Mexico. Now

142

on the second day of the trip, she soon would be passing through El Paso, which shared the border with Ciudad Juarez. Just a few years earlier that Mexican city of one-and-a-half million people had been called the most dangerous city in the world because of the battles of the drug cartels and the street-gang homicides that marred the daily lives of people. The violence was everywhere in the city, from the poor barrios to the central district of offices and night clubs to the residential areas of working class homes. Unidentified bodies piled up in the city morgues. For over at least the preceding decade, young girls in "Juarez" had disappeared by the hundreds, either murdered or kidnapped into a life of enslavement as prostitutes or drug runners. Meanwhile, El Paso, Texas, in full view of Juarez, was one of the safest cities in the world with a very low homicide rate. *Is it fair that a wall and a bridge could make such a difference in lives, love, and pain?* Ana wondered. The inequities of human existence challenged her faith in a loving God at times. Eventually she concluded that God worked miracles through people who committed to help others. Some risked their lives daily to do so.

That's how God shows love, she was thinking as she drove. *We can see it in action through ordinary heroes. Our leaders are not heroes. Our leaders are weak and corrupt. Now in our dangerous world, we need heroes who lead.*

Those were her reflections when she was startled from her thoughts by the first of two phone calls that would catapult her into social activism and crime fighting to a degree that she hadn't experienced since the days of the military coup in Mexico. She was approaching the city limits of El Paso. When the ringtone sounded, she grabbed the phone distractedly from the seat beside her. The call was from David. She could tell in his greeting that something was off, so she came to the point: "Cariño, what's wrong?"

David inhaled a deep breath, and then he said, "Honey, yesterday when we talked, I told you that Valentina had landed safely in Monterrey. She had a conversation at the airport upon arriving with an undercover DEA agent there."

"Yes, and?" Ana demanded.

"She told him that she was going home to catch up on sleep and that today she would go to the office to work. Apparently, she hired a taxi to take her home, but on the periphery autopista, the taxi was intercepted by some SUVs. The taxi driver reported that Valentina surrendered herself to the men in the SUVs and saved the life of the driver by commanding him to lie in the cab while she dealt with the situation. She left peacefully with the men. The taxi driver says there were three SUVs that pulled over, and they all left together after taking Valentina. He didn't look at the men, as she had commanded him, but he heard the whole business. He said that she simply asked the men not to bother him, and she asked which vehicle they wanted her to get into."

"Mother Mary!" Ana exclaimed, instantly agitated and worried. "David, has anyone heard from her?"

"No, darling, not yet. The driver does know that she had her phone with her. We also know from the DEA agent in Monterrey that she has his contact information in the phone and that he's listed as her cousin. There's a full-scale search going on right now in Monterrey by the state and federal police and the Army, Ana."

"David, why didn't you tell me yesterday?"

She was trying to hold her temper. She knew David could feel the fire in her tone.

"I'm sorry, sweetie, but what could you have done? I wanted to get all the information first before calling so I wouldn't alarm you unnecessarily while you were driving. It took until the evening to discover exactly what happened and to put together the search efforts. I didn't want to give you a sleepless night before another hard day of driving," was David's answer.

"David, you know perfectly well that our marriage, our partnership, no funciona así. It doesn't work like that. Neither of us makes decisions about what the other person can handle.

You don't really know what I might have decided to do had I known earlier, or maybe I would have ideas about how to find her or where she is."

He had blown it and he knew it. "God, Ana, you're right. I'm really sorry, honey."

An uncomfortable silence prompted David to continue.

"What do you want to do, Ana? My thought is this: I think that Z-30 got back to Mexico, or he's getting back, and he arranged to have Valentina picked up and be taken to him. The fact that it has been a day and we have not had any kind of word from Valentina might mean that they're holding her in wait for him and that she doesn't now have her phone or a way to contact Juan or us. I'm sure she'll find a way to send out a message when she can. She's resourceful, and if anyone could figure out a way to buy some time with the Zeta, it would be Valentina. Women of this caliber run in your family."

"Well, that kind of talk isn't going to get you back into my good graces, David," Ana said. She was furious. "But I do agree with your assessment. Right now I'm at the border in El Paso and could easily run down to Monterrey."

"Yes," David answered carefully, "but one of us should get back to the kids at least for a couple of days. Do you want me to go back to San Antonio and then come to Monterrey? Or do you think you should go home?"

Anna sighed. "Damn," she said. "I may know a lot of people in Monterrey, but you're just as connected now with the kind of resources that can help find Valentina. The DEA has people in Monterrey."

"A few," David answered, "and also I'm aware of some military intelligence in the city at the moment."

"And you know General Alvarez and others you can contact in Mexico. It's probably best if you're in Monterrey and I come down in a few days as planned. I just don't know if I'm going to be able to stand being out of the action in looking for Valentina."

"I tell you what, Ana. I'll park the car in Vegas, and Enrique and I'll hop a flight to Monterrey and get involved. I'll call to inform you of every development. You can help us from home until you get to Monterrey, and then you will be in Mexico to prepare for the peace march on Saturday. We'll all be together in less than a week."

David's comment about the car jostled a memory of something she had thought about on her long drive and had intended to ask him.

"Speaking of parking the car reminds me about the missing Corvette. I meant to ask you this yesterday and forgot. Was it determined that the car was leased?"

"Yes."

"Which leasing agency?"

"The police are trying to track that down, Ana, and I have been so frigging busy that I haven't followed up with them. A kid who worked for the parking staff at The Oasis was found shot dead in his car near the airport. He may have borrowed the Corvette for a small pleasure ride and left the key fob inside the car when he returned it to The Oasis. Remember that Valentina said a small ledger book of some sort was inside the Corvette? Well, someone who murdered the kid ripped through his car as if looking for something."

Ana shook her head as she drove. "That's terrible, David. That poor boy." That news heightened her fear for Valentina's life. "Listen, there can't be that many car rental agencies that lease Corvettes, even in Las Vegas, right?"

"Yes, you're right."

"Well, remember that your Corvette is tracked by a roadside assistance satellite? Wouldn't the leasing agency or the manufacturer be able to have that track the exact location of the car?"

She heard David draw a breath. "Dios, Ana, yes! Oh my God, I feel so stupid!"

"Too much work and sleep deprivation, mi amor," Ana answered. She knew he was sorry now that he had avoided talking to her about details since the previous afternoon.

"I'm going to track that down right now! Maybe the Sheriff's Department already knows this." He waited just a second and then asked her, "So, are you going to San Antonio or Monterrey?"

Good, she thought. *My decision. He learns fast. Again and again. I really love this man.*

"I'll go to San Antonio and be with the kids. The nanny is there, but she's not the same as me or you being with them. They need us. You're right, David, I can help you from home until I can be with you and Enrique in Monterrey."

"I promise you, Ana, we're going to find Valentina."

"We have to hurry, David. Valentina and I didn't see each other so much in the last three or four years, but she did do a lot of work with me in my prior life of event planning. She learned the business from me. She has a different last name, but if she's with the Zeta, it may not take him too long to discover that she's my niece!"

Madeline Nightfire
Bridgetown, Barbados
Monday Afternoon

Corvette had been fidgety and had paced around the house while Madeline pored over internet images on her computer. She saw that her son was losing patience with her, but she had surprised him a couple of hours earlier when she told him, "I remember something interesting about David James. He's married to a woman named Ana Valdez who was the President of Mexico briefly, and I recall that she leads a lot of peace marches."

"Okay," Corvette had said. "I don't know how you know these things, but how is that information going to help me find Valentina?"

"I know these things because I research news, current events, and crimes for story ideas for my mysteries," Madeline explained. "As for what this information has to do with Valentina, you already told me that David James commanded you to forget Valentina because you might get her killed. So it's true that he's not likely to tell you anything about her even if you call him up and tell him that you will bring back the money...which isn't a bad idea, I might add. But if I talk to Ana Valdez, woman to woman, she just might say that she'll convince David James to help you. Sometimes a mother talking to another mother is a communication with power that can't be equaled by any other means. She needs to know that you're serious about finding this girl and that you want to talk directly to her before making any decisions about the money."

But he had still looked doubtful. "This is taking too long, Mum, and I don't know the reasons why they wouldn't tell me where she is. Maybe your talk won't help."

"Let me search to see if I can find any contact information anywhere for Ana Valdez."

Madeline had found an overwhelming wealth of material on Ana, including hundreds of blog articles Ana had posted and endless photographs of her at campaign rallies throughout Mexico. There were also pictures of her and her former family when she was "society" in Monterrey and was married to Rafael, who died later. There were photos of Ana at parties and events that she had helped organize. Then, in the society section of the Monterrey newspaper, Madeline found the one photograph that made her squeal and call out to Corvette to come beside her.

"Hurry!" she had commanded when he was coming too slowly.

Now he was standing over her and looking at the picture she had on her computer screen. It was a picture of Ana and two other women and a young lady. It had been taken several years prior. The women were listed as organizers of a juvenile diabetes fund-raising gala. The smiling ladies were in formal gowns and were holding bouquets of roses that had been presented to them. The caption under the picture proclaimed the successful charity a "family effort," and it identified the women as Ana Valdez; her sister, Rosa Valdez; her cousin, Oralia Salva; and her niece, Valentina Garza.

"Read the names and look at the picture closely," Madeline told Corvette as he started to study it. "It's in black and white." She pulled back and let him lean in to look at the laptop screen.

It didn't take long. "Holy shit, Mum, that's her! That's Valentina!"

"Positive?" She remembered that Corvette hadn't recognized the young woman when she handed him the bag of cash.

Corvette continued staring at the screen. Then she saw him clearly become excited.

"Yes, I'm positive! She's younger, but she's dressed up and wearing her hair up similarly to the way it was the night I danced with her. God, Mum, look! She even has a flower in her hair in the same way!"

"She's a stunning girl, baby," Madeline said.

"You should see her now," Corvette replied, but he wasn't removing his eyes from her picture.

Madeline chuckled and retrieved the computer. "Let me search for contact information for Ana Valdez that's something better than e-mail."

It only took her about ten more minutes to find it. Madeline saw that in her work with the Zs, Ana wanted to be accessible. On one of the webpages for the Zs, she found contact information that included a cell phone number.

"Incredible," she whispered under her breath. Then she looked at Corvette. "Are you ready? It's time to try a call."

Ana Valdez
Just outside Fort Stockton, Texas
Monday Afternoon

It had been over three hours since David's call, and Ana's anxiety regarding the status of her niece was threatening to turn into panic. She worked on keeping herself calm, but she wasn't a person who easily tolerated being unable to control things or having periods of inactivity. Her worrying about Valentina completely overshadowed the joy she expected to feel on the way to seeing her children again. The only consolation that she could hold onto while she wasn't receiving any news was what David had said: Valentina was a resourceful young woman who thought well on her feet in times of crisis. Ana had a thin hope that Valentina was okay, wherever she was, but she also believed that time wasn't on Valentina's side. She needed to be found.

Ana had resisted calling David again just because she was anxious. *God, why doesn't he call back with some news, even if it is when he and Enrique can catch a flight to Monterrey,* she thought. *I'll feel much better just knowing they're there to push the search along.*

So when the phone rang the second time that day, she grabbed it and answered it without looking at the caller identification. She was so lost in her thoughts that she just assumed the call was coming from David.

"Hola, cariño," she answered.

There were noises on the other end of the line for a few moments, but finally a female voice blurted, "Excuse me, is this Ana Valdez?"

"Speaking," Ana replied loudly. She felt disturbed by her misjudgment of who was calling her.

"Señora Valdez, I'm Madeline Nightfire. I'm the mother of Corvette Nightfire. Would you have a couple of minutes to speak to me?"

The mention of the Nightfire name, so unexpected, jolted Ana into acute alertness.

"Yes, certainly, Ms. Nightfire," Ana answered. "You sound a little far away. Are you on speaker?"

"Yes, I was about to tell you that. I'm calling from my home in Barbados, and my son Corvette is here with me. Please call me Madeline, and thank you for taking the call."

"Hello, Señora Valdez," Corvette chimed in.

Ana was shocked to find herself on the phone with the man who had fooled David and Enrique and had taken the money. *Stay calm, Ana. This has to be a good thing,* she told herself.

Then she answered, trying to sound casual and open, "And please call me Ana. I must admit I'm surprised by the call and don't know how you reached me. How can I help you?"

"Obviously you know Corvette's name, and your husband probably told you what Corvette did, Ana. Corvette knew who your husband was when he met him in Las Vegas. When my son showed up on my door here in Barbados, he told me that he had met David James. I remembered that David is married to you, and I explained this to Corvette. Then I did a bit of research on the internet to try to find a way to contact you. There's so much information about you there, of course. One of The Z Foundation websites listed your cell phone number. We took the liberty of using it. Please forgive this intrusion, but what we would like to discuss with you is very important."

"Okay, I understand. Certainly, I would like to talk with you both," Ana answered. "Please go ahead. I'm listening." She noted with interest that the woman had a distinctly British accent.

She could hear Madeline Nightfire take a long breath on the other end of the line, like a breath of relief.

"I'll come straight to the point. Corvette arrived here with almost two million dollars in cash. He had wanted to deal with the situation back in the states, and he had wanted to make a decision about what to do with the money by speaking directly to the person who had given it to him, the young woman named Valentina. From the stress and the emotion of what happened in the casino in Las Vegas, Corvette didn't trust anyone to discuss the money with except Valentina. He didn't know who the money belonged to. From his point of view, he only knew

151

that the money belonged to Valentina and that she was the one who gave it to him. He was hoping to see her again, but that possibility disappeared when the young man named Enrique and your husband came for the money. Corvette was warned that he shouldn't contact Valentina. He still wants very badly to talk to her. He's having second thoughts about taking the money, but it is an issue he wants to resolve with Valentina."

I wonder why this woman is doing all the talking and not Corvette? Ana wondered. *Maybe his mother has told him that he has to give the money back. Maybe she's the force at play here.*

"Madeline, do you understand where the money came from?" Ana asked.

"I assume, and so does Corvette now, that the cash came from a drug cartel."

"Yes, and this particular cartel is extremely vindictive and murderous. I have to alarm you, in fact. I'm speaking of the cartel known as the Zetas. Their fingers reach worldwide."

Madeline said, "I know, Ana. That's very scary. Look, let me tell you something so that we don't have to dance around an issue. When I was researching how to find you, I discovered an old photograph of you at a charity event in Monterrey, and Valentina was in the photograph with you and was identified as your niece. So I assume that Valentina isn't in a drug cartel."

Dios, mother of God! Ana thought as a dread seized her entire body. *If this woman can find this information so easily and casually, how can the Zeta overlook it?* She took a moment to collect herself, and it was long enough that Madeline said, "Hello?"

"I'm here, sorry," replied Ana, trying to keep her voice even. "You're right. Valentina isn't in a drug cartel. But seriously, I can't discuss her status regarding this or the money."

Then Corvette stepped in.

"Señora Valdez," he said, choosing still a respectful entry to the conversation despite Ana's request for informal address, "on my part, there's so much more to this than me wanting to speak

152

to Valentina about the cash. Obviously, that's important to me. There's a personal reason that's driving me insane. I know you don't know anything about me in terms of what kind of person I am. My leaving with the money probably doesn't speak well to you. But I want you to know this: I spent an evening dancing with Valentina when we were in Las Vegas, and I haven't been able to get her out of my mind since that time. I don't speak Spanish. Yet the whole night we danced, I talked to her in English. We had a magical evening, and I wanted to find her again. I only knew her first name. The next night, I went back to the place where we danced, hoping to find her. I stayed up all night. I was so sleep-deprived and tired that I didn't recognize her at first when she gave me the cash. But I did figure it out. And that's the thing: she saw me and gave me the bag of cash. She trusted me and gave it to me, and I just knew she would get in touch with me about it. Later when the phone rang in my hotel room, I was sure it was going to be her. It wasn't. It was this Enrique guy, and I thought he could be some thug or cartel guy at first. I didn't know. Then your husband David showed up. I had read about him and have lots of respect for what he does with the Zs. I asked him to let me speak to Valentina, but he refused, warning me that it was dangerous and that I could get her hurt. But I'm not going to get her hurt, and I'm not going to rest until I find her. Now I know her last name, thanks to my mum. I'm just begging you, if there's any way possible, put me in touch with her or let me know where she is. I just want to talk with her, and then I'm sure we can resolve the money issue. But this isn't just about the money. It is a thing of the heart."

Ana was stunned. She was surprised not so much by what he said, but by the sincerity of his words. She was moved.

"Corvette, what would you do to try to find her? Almost anything you could do would be reckless, and you wouldn't even be aware that you were causing harm until it was too late."

"Then help me, Ana." He used her first name this time. "If you don't help me, the only thing I can do is to go blindly to Monterrey. That's where she is, isn't it?"

153

Ana ignored the question for the moment. She addressed her next remarks to Madeline: "Is he serious? He would go to Monterrey, Madeline?"

"Ana, my son does whatever he wants to do, and as you can see by what he did in Las Vegas, he makes his own decisions. He plays in world poker tournaments..."

"I know," Ana added quickly.

"...and he's quite comfortable traveling the world even with large amounts of cash. I would say that Corvette knows something about taking risks."

"Please, Ana," Corvette came back into the conversation. "I'm going to Monterrey on the next flight I can get there. I know it sounds crazy, but Valentina is the woman I want to talk to, and that's it. I don't even know how I'm going to communicate with her, because we don't speak each other's languages, but somehow I'll find her and we'll talk."

All the discussion about Valentina and Corvette's interest in her was making Ana sentimental. She felt herself wanting to cry. However, Corvette's determination to go to Monterrey was ringing alarm bells everywhere in her head. She decided to make some decisions on the phone without first discussing it with David.

Corvette is too impulsive. I can't risk him going to Monterrey and running his English mouth all over the city. He'll get killed before the first day is over, and, yes, he'll get Valentina killed too.

"Wait, Corvette and Madeline," Ana began. "Listen to me carefully. There isn't good news. Are you both listening?" She asked this for emphasis.

"Yes," they replied simultaneously.

"I'm currently driving to San Antonio to our home. I have been on the road from Las Vegas the past couple of days. David and Enrique are still in Vegas. I just learned by phone from David earlier today that when Valentina arrived in Monterrey, on the way to her condo by taxi, the taxi was stopped by armed men who took her hostage and drove off with her."

"Oh my God!" from Madeline.

"Shit!" from Corvette.

"So I don't know exactly where Valentina is. She's my niece. I'm deeply worried that the men who have her, who probably are the Zetas, will discover the connection that she has to me very soon, and the consequences of that would be horrible. So Corvette, you can't go unprepared into Monterrey asking about her, especially when you don't speak Spanish. I've seen pictures of you. You might look Mexican, but a man who doesn't speak Spanish and who's well known on the poker circuit is going to have a short shelf life in Monterrey if he crosses purposes with any of the drug cartels."

"God, Ana, what can I do? Please don't tell me to just sit and wait. I'm not built that way. I can't do that, and now I'm too anxious for Valentina."

"Yes, yes, I get that, Corvette," Ana replied. "I'm like that. I'm also a pretty good judge of character. I believe you're very sincere and feel something for Valentina, but you're impulsive and naïve when it comes to what is going on in Mexico. So if you must do something, you're going to have to do it under the direction of my husband, David, and even Enrique; and I'm going to have to talk to them."

"Enrique?" Corvette asked in surprise.

"Yes, Enrique is the chief operations officer of the Zs internationally, Corvette. He's a wonderfully committed young man."

"I don't think he liked me much."

"Well, Enrique was trying to do the job of getting back the cash you had, and I'm afraid that among David, Enrique, and myself, we got a little overprotective of Valentina. We should have recognized her ability to make good decisions. She wanted to be the one to try to talk to you, and she did call your room. I was present when she tried."

"Wow! Really?" Corvette asked, obviously cheered by this news.

155

"Yes, and there's something else you should know, and this is nothing you can repeat. You can't ask me a lot of questions now when I tell you this. So let me tell you, and then I'll explain to you what you need to do. If you really care about Valentina and her life, you will do exactly what I say."

"Okay, I'm ready."

"First, Valentina speaks excellent English. She's a citizen of both the United States and Mexico."

"Oh...my...God!"

"That's a fact which, if known by certain people, can cost her life. Second, don't make a move until you receive a call from David. I'll try to reach him as soon as we disconnect. Corvette, if you're going to Monterrey, you need David. He and Enrique are looking into flights there now and are going today. They're going there to search for Valentina. They will have a lot of resources available to them, including the police, the military, and the Zs. I want David to pick you up at the airport and direct how you help them. You may have to take direction from Enrique too. I'm coming to Monterrey in several days. We work as a team. We're Zs. In Monterrey, the Z chapter will be out in force helping us look for Valentina. Can you join us and work under these circumstances?

"Yes, I absolutely can," Corvette answered. "That sounds like a wonderful plan. I'll wait for David's call. Please get him to call me soon. I can hardly stand this situation of not doing anything."

"Well, you've been doing things. You found me already. Madeline, you're his mother. You and Corvette might not know what he's getting into. Associating with me, David, and the Zs is extremely dangerous business."

"Yes, Ana, we both understand. I'm no stranger to this type of danger. Corvette's father had some run-ins with the drug cartels of Mexico, and that danger followed us here to Barbados. I think you and I both have a lot more to talk about."

Dios! Ana thought. *Is there no one on earth who escapes the dirty business of the cartels?*

Ana empathized with Corvette's impatience. She was feeling the same in a desperate way. She guided the call to a conclusion, and as soon as the three had given farewell courtesies, Ana speed-dialed David's number. She reached him to discover that he and Enrique were already in the Las Vegas airport.

"I was just getting ready to call you to let you know we found a flight," David told her.

Ana brought him up to date on the conversation with Corvette and his mother and Corvette's intention to go to Monterrey. David sounded confused by the development.

"I'm glad that you got him to agree to work with us," he said, "but I really wish he wasn't coming. One more thing to worry about. I don't understand why he personally has to come. Why wouldn't he just wait until we find Valentina, and he could talk with her then?"

This made Ana smile. "Mi amor," she asked him, "me amas? Do you love me?" She knew that she had a way of asking him this that melted him. The question was a lover's code between them.

"God, Ana," David said in the thick of the airport hustle and bustle, "te amo con locura. Seriously? Corvette Nightfire thinks he's in love with Valentina?"

"It is what I think, cariño."

The next night, a curious David James and a sulking Enrique Santos waited outside the customs area in the international terminal of the Monterrey airport to greet Corvette Nightfire when he disembarked his flight from Barbados via Trinidad and Mexico City. Corvette arrived with one bag, and it wasn't filled with cash.

Chapter 11: Misery

Ignacio Lopez
One month prior to The Oasis shootings
Somewhere in Texas

Lili tenderly massaged his scalp until the skull-cracking headache subsided enough for him to dare to open his eyes. Thank God there was only the dim grey light of early dawn. He could adjust as the daylight brightened. It took a moment for him to focus, but then he had the vision of Lili. She held his head in her lap as she sat in the bed with him, and she hummed softly, soothingly, as soon as she saw him open his eyes. He could hear the sounds of the men bumping around in the kitchen on the other side of the house. He tried to remember what day it was. He realized in a moment that it was another work day. The work had become so tedious lately. He wished that he hadn't remembered so soon. He longed to just be there, having no thoughts, listening to Lili's breaths and hums. Still, even the times that she was with him, he felt the sadness. The sadness at least calmed him. It was the furor that brought on the headaches. They were horrible. He wanted to be dead. No, more than that, he wanted to give the headaches to his tormentors, so they would die.

"It was really bad this time, wasn't it darling?" Lili asked softly. She skidded her fingertips slowly through his thick, black hair. It made a tickling sensation that almost made him want to sleep again. "When we get to San Antonio, I'm going to take you to a neurologist I know there. He can get you better, I promise."

He must have fallen asleep again, because when he opened his eyes the next time, the sun was up and the light in the room was bright, even though Lili must have drawn the curtains. She was already gone for the day.

He didn't remember if he had eaten the previous night because of the headache, but apparently he hadn't, because his stomach was growling like a lion cub. It gave him the motivation to get out of bed. This came just in time, because the ugly Texan redneck entered his room and would have shaken him to get up. The guy didn't give a shit about what repercussions that might have for his headaches. As far as Ignacio could tell, the Texan's only preoccupation in life was when he would "get pussy" next, as he put it.

It had been the arrival of the Texan at the house that gave Ignacio his first clue that he might be in Texas. That had been a surprise. He should have known that he was in Texas. One would think a person would remember a trip from Monterrey there. However, they gave him drugs one night when he had a particularly violent headache, and he felt he had slept a very long time. He awoke in a different house, this one, out in the scruff-grassland boonies. It was similar to the first, a long, one-story ranch that had a hidden cellar. This one had five bedrooms instead of three. When he had first looked out the window, the arid landscape looked like Tamaulipas, the state in northern Mexico where the border divided the city of Nuevo Laredo from Laredo, Texas. The vehicles he had seen parked in front of the house were all from Nuevo León, so he believed that he was in Mexico still. In subsequent days appeared vehicles from Texas and other states in the USA. All the people whom he saw in the house were Mexicans, except for the ugly Texan, but even he spoke Spanish.

He told the Texan to relax, that he was up, that he would get coffee and some toast, and then he would go into the office in the cellar and get to work. He looked forward to the coffee to help keep the headache at bay.

Then he wondered, *How does Lili know that we're going to San Antonio? How does she know a neurologist there?* He had meant to ask her, but he had fallen asleep again.

The coffee maker was a Keurig appliance that made individual cups of coffee. The smell of the beverage as it steamed into his cup reminded him of those days in Monterrey when he was making the funds transfers from The Z Foundation.

He was nervous in his gut every one of those days despite the fact that the cartel seemed to be treating him so lavishly while they all awaited for the confirmations of the fund transfers. One or two men dressed in expensive business suits had been with him at all times. They had spent a lot of time in coffee shops in the mornings and in nice restaurants for lunches and dinners. Ignacio had drunk more coffee on those days than he ever had in his life. All he had wanted to do was to keep Lili alive and out of pain. At night they had taken him to a beautiful home in the mountains off the National Highway somewhere. He wasn't sure exactly where because on those trips they blindfolded him, but he heard them operate a gate at the entrance to the property. Before leading him to his room for the night, they showed him Lili asleep in her bed. She looked like she was sleeping peacefully in a room in a lush resort. They had explained to him that because he was cooperating so nicely, they had been treating her to "relaxing agents" that let her endure those stressful days calmly.

On one of the days, he believed it was the Tuesday, the man who had visited him originally in his office told Ignacio that they were going to have lunch with a couple of VIPs in the organization. He drove Ignacio to a country club halfway between Monterrey and Santiago. They went directly into the busy dining room where they were seated in a corner that had been cleared just for them and the two men who were already there.

Even seated they looked physically powerful. They were dressed in crème colored business suits with blue cotton shirts, and both had necks that appeared as if they would explode through their collars. One had a bit of a gut. His name turned out to be Horacio. The other man, about the same size but with an imposing physique that looked like it was carved from granite, was occasionally addressed as "Jefe." But Jefe had told Ignacio simply to call him "Zeta."

They sat at a table next to a wall of glass overlooking the golf course. In the distance the Sierra Madre Mountains loped high and green, running to the south. The Zeta and Horacio continued a conversation that they were having when Ignacio and the "pleasant man" (as Ignacio thought of him) arrived. They smiled and nodded at them as they sat, but otherwise they didn't acknowledge their presence for about ten minutes. Ignacio and the pleasant man sat in silence.

The one called Zeta ordered salmon stuffed with crab for Ignacio, and after lunch had been served, Zeta became very friendly and conversant with him.

"You've done very well for us," Zeta said to Ignacio at one point. "I'm always impressed by a man who honors his woman. Your work has been so exemplary that it has been a pleasure for us to maintain Lili in high fashion. I'm sure you're looking forward to the wedding. Tell me, exactly when will this be?"

"Next June," Ignacio answered nervously. He saw that Horacio was watching him with a very benign expression on his face. It felt suddenly like he was on a job interview with corporate executives wooing the last couple of candidates. The whole environment of the country club and the luncheon began to separate him from his reality of being kidnapped, he realized, and then he even began to forget that he had discerned this. The Zeta somehow was making him feel comfortable and creepy at the same time. His stomach felt jittery. He had the thought that maybe he wouldn't be able to tolerate the salmon.

"Wonderful," the Zeta answered. He waved his arm to indicate the golf course outside and the gated community of gorgeous suburban homes that spotted the mountain above them. "A smart and ambitious young professional such as yourself probably wants to provide a lifestyle such as you see here for a beautiful and sophisticated bride like Lili. I had the pleasure of conversing with her. She's quite a catch, Ignacio, and she would do wonders both for your family and your career."

Ignacio tried to look as if he thought of Lili in that way, like an asset for his upward mobility. He nodded agreement to the Zeta, but he was too nervous to attempt a convincing reply. He was also shocked that "El Jefe" had talked with Lili.

Is there really hope that Lili and I might live through this? he wondered. He didn't want to let himself believe this, but perhaps the jefe had come into the money-stealing drama with a change in ideas about how things would play out because Ignacio had cooperated so completely.

"I have a lot of work, Ignacio," the Zeta continued, his tone now becoming confidential. "The financial reporting of my businesses are horribly fragmented. I have a lot of people on the payroll with, shall we say, street level skills, and they still rely on paper record keeping. The workers are not really trained in accounting or records administration for the most part. The best ones are using old-fashioned ledgers and notebooks, but many others bring revenue and expense records on scraps of paper, napkins, or paper bags. I can't count on the accuracy of data under these circumstances. In many of our lines of businesses, we're not selling product but are taking commissions from sales of services or products in our territories. Our clients like to underreport their revenue. Not all of them, of course, but still, this is a problem for us. There's no consistent, historical reporting of revenue and no computerized data base. On top of that, my employee turnover rate is high, and that even makes this whole situation worse."

Are you fucking kidding me? Ignacio thought. *Does he want me to be an accountant for him?* If he hadn't been so stressed, he would have thought the man's dark irony was hilarious.

"No, I don't want you to be an accountant," the Zeta said.

Did he read my mind? Did I ask the question? Damn, am I so nervous that I'm missing things?

"Perhaps you can help me find accountants, yes," the Zeta continued, "but I think you have much bigger talents than bookkeeping. What I'm looking for is a person to construct encrypted data bases and financial reporting systems for international and lines-of-business segments. I need a reporting system that rolls up reports from the segments and service lines to top management but permits drill downs to the local units of detail. I need real-time customer and employee profiles that I can trust. The thing is, Ignacio, my business lines are growing fast in Latin America, and exponentially fast in the United States. The business environment is highly volatile and subject to sudden, unexpected interruption. So the unusual feature in the reporting system I need is the ability for the information and reports to disappear immediately upon any intrusion by a governmental, military, or police agency, or by a competitor. I want backups of the data bases and financial reporting on a cloud that can't be found, and which no one knows exists."

Ignacio was stunned by the degree of trust that the Zeta had put in this confidence to him. He found himself reviewing whether he was qualified to design work systems such as this. He was good at deciphering code, but could he construct code that would be impenetrable?

He thought, *Zeta's sharing with me doesn't derive from trust. He knows he can kill me and Lili if I'm not completely trustworthy or if I don't get the job done. Ignacio, try to keep perspective, for God's sake. This man doesn't trust me!*

"I'm good with code, passwords, and deciphering. I did some hacking as a teenager. Nothing major, just for the fun of doing it. To show off for friends. Of course, my degree is in business administration, and I'm an accountant," was Ignacio's response.

"Yes, I have looked into your background, naturally. Very impressive record, Ignacio. But do you know what impresses me the most?"

He took a gulp of coffee. He still hadn't taken a bite of salmon. "What?"

"You have that quality of personality that makes clients trust you. Therefore, important people such as David James and Enrique Santos of The Z Foundation trust you with their money and want you to make investment decisions for them. A person with this quality earns trust because he has delivered. He has a proven track record. People believe him when he speaks."

"Yes, I know that people trust me. I try to listen to them and then advise them appropriately. I'm not that old, but I have learned certain things from a young age. I try to guide people to what is best for them and then provide those things to them."

Both Horacio and the Zeta smiled.

"The ordinary person wants security, Ignacio. Financial security. Personal security. Safety. The extraordinary person wants power, the power to determine how those things are delivered. They're the persons who become leaders. What kind of person are you?"

"Pues, I'm a leader. I always thirst for more. I like to know the meaning of life," Ignacio answered. He was aware that he was trying to make a good impression. He believed that it might help Lili somehow.

The Zeta stared at him thoughtfully as he chewed a mouthful of beef. He swallowed and said, "I'll tell you the meaning of life. Life has no meaning. Nothing. Nada. The only meaning life has is the meaning that you give to it. You're the one who defines the meaning of life, amigo. It isn't something outside of yourself to be discovered. Anyone who believes otherwise is a fool."

Something inside Ignacio's heart leapt in recognition.

"Would you care for more coffee, señor?" the waiter asked.

The memory of that question brought Ignacio back to the present time. He pulled his cup from the Keurig dispenser and took in a couple of steamy drafts. He cut some slices of Italian bread that was on the counter, buttered them, and popped them in the toaster oven. When they were ready, he grabbed a paper towel and took his breakfast downstairs to the office.

A door in the kitchen looked like a pantry door, but it opened to stairs that descended to the cellar. The cellar had the same footprint as the floor plan of the living area above. The office where Ignacio had to do his work was the only finished room downstairs. There was a bathroom in the office.

The rest of the area had a concrete floor and was wide open. At the far end was a commode stall. Along the wall toward the center of the room, there was a stand of three deep stainless steel sinks with faucets in each one. One had a length of hose attached to spray the floor. There were three drains in the floor: one near the office, one near the commode stall, and one in the center of the room. Near the sinks were a heavy duty washer and dryer.

Along the walls there were rolled up sleeping bags, stained single-bed mattresses, and piles of dirty sheets and blankets. On some mornings when Ignacio came downstairs, he found ten or twenty cartel guys sleeping or stirring in various states of drunkenness. Mostly these were young guys, but sometimes there were women, and usually they looked like they hadn't bathed or changed clothes in a week. Always there were pistols and automatic rifles on the floor near the strewn mattresses or atop fold-up tables. These normally bore ammunition cartridges, knives, holsters, and sometimes boxes of small envelopes that contained cash. The people came and went. When they left, trash and fast food bags littered the floor.

On some days two young girls came and cleaned up. Ignacio thought that they were about fourteen years old. They would move the sleeping bags and mattresses to the wall, like they were arranged this morning. Occasionally they threw the sheets in the washer and dryer. More than once Ignacio saw the girls servicing cartel guys when he came down the steps. The girls looked at him with a bored, distant gaze as some brute grunted atop them.

Today the office door wasn't locked, which meant that Sergio was in there already working on one of the computers. Sergio was a wiry man in his early thirties with a face pitted from ancient acne. Sergio came every couple of days or so and brought Ignacio his work assignments. He usually stayed for the morning. He reviewed Ignacio's work. He hardly spoke except to tell Ignacio that he had done his work correctly. By noon he was gone.

The other consistent visitor was the ugly Texan who came and went throughout the day. He retrieved cell phones, radios, weapons and ammunition from the locked supply closet, or he

165

brought new items in. Sometimes he sat with a laptop at a beat-up, small square oak table and typed. Ignacio assumed he was writing e-mails, but he never saw the screen to know what the Texan was doing. He suspected that he worked there sometimes just to be certain that Ignacio wasn't doing anything that he shouldn't be. Ignacio was aware of spyware on his computer that would allow others on another computer to view the software he was using and the entries he made.

Ignacio's work space was a computer desk set up with a desktop computer connected to a modem that delivered the internet service. Connected to that was a wireless router. Ignacio noted that it was a boosted model that could provide wireless access throughout the whole house. All around his desk were dozens of cardboard file drawers stuffed with ledger books or scraps of paper. These were the information sources as the Zeta had described them. Ignacio organized them, analyzed them, and entered them into the data bases and financial spreadsheets that he had been constructing. It was tedious work that led to the headaches every evening. The Texan or one of the other guys living in the house would bring him lunch every day, but at dinner time he could eat upstairs in the dining room if he weren't in too much pain.

After dinner he went to his room because the headaches started up, and only Lili's private ministrations seemed to soothe him. She came in after her day at work and massaged his head. She would do this until he fell asleep, but sometimes when he awoke in the night, she would be gone. He felt that she wasn't in the house. Sometimes he thought that she was back in the early mornings until she had to go to work again, but he didn't want to think where she went when he couldn't see her. From what he saw of the outside, the house was in a remote part of the country. Somehow she was always there when he was in pain.

Ignacio had earned the privilege of doing the office work. During the days of the beatings back in Mexico, he had learned to have the correct attitude. He would never forget what happened during that time:

Things had changed drastically after he had transferred the funds from The Z Foundation to the trust accounts of the private bank in Barbados. Ignacio and Lili had been brought to a single-story house somewhere in the outskirts of Monterrey. The Zeta, Horacio, the pleasant man, and the other couple of nicely dressed men disappeared. Instead, Ignacio's company in the house were kids still in their teens and a couple of older guys who never wore anything fancier than stained shorts, tennis shoes, and faded T-shirts. They were ignorant thugs, Ignacio thought. They seemed to confuse their pistols with their cocks. They beat him beginning from the first day with absolutely no provocation and no predictability. They kept him mostly tied on top of a mattress in the cellar. They threw food at him at irregular intervals and often let too many hours pass before taking him to the bathroom. When he shit or peed in his pants, the guys would become furious and start beating him on the head with their pistol butts. That was usually his punishment, although one kid had a fondness for extinguishing his cigarettes on Ignacio's arm.

He stopped begging them to let him see Lili or pleading that they not hurt her. They kept her upstairs. Sometimes he heard women screaming with sounds of sex, but none of them sounded like Lili. When he asked about her, they answered by taunting him, telling him how sweet she was and how much she wanted it from them.

"She don't want you no more, pretty boy," one said to him constantly. "She's getting the good stuff now. Why do you think she never asks to come down here?"

And they would all laugh. He never believed what they said about Lili.

He wasn't sure how many days or weeks passed, but at one point the headaches began. Then one night, inexplicably, the Zeta showed up.

"I can't believe they have been treating you like this," the Zeta said. "Are you ready to come work for me now?"

Blood was streaming from Ignacio's nose to his mouth. He nodded.

"I need to move you to a new place to do this."

"Please, take Lili with me. I need to see her!"

"Yes, of course," answered the Zeta. "I see you're ready to do something productive now." He handed Ignacio a handkerchief for his nose. "You need medication," he told him.

That night, they gave him an injection for his headaches. He wasn't sure how long he slept. He was only in the cellar another day or two when they gave him the medicine that apparently made him sleep for days, and they moved him to the new house. He was ecstatic to know that he had a bedroom and that Lili was permitted to visit.

He shook off the memories of the horrible stay in Mexico in that first house and returned to the present. On this day, they brought him lunch as scheduled in the office, but in the mid-afternoon he began hearing muffled voices above. The men seemed agitated about something. He heard car doors opening and closing and people coming and going in the house. He knew that some of the muffled speaking was cell phone conversation because Ignacio only heard one person talking.

Then, just about dinner time, he heard a number of vehicles pulling up close to the house. He thought he heard the Texan, very excited, shouting instructions to someone. He got up to go upstairs, which he was allowed to do at dinner time. Normally the Texan would come down and announce that he could eat, but Ignacio's inner clock notified him just as reliably. But this time when he got to the door of the office, he found that he was locked in. That hadn't happened before.

Suddenly he heard the cellar door opening above and then the sounds of feet descending the steps. Lots of them. "Rápido!" someone shouted. "Hurry!" When the voices were just outside the office door, Ignacio pounded on it to remind any of them that he was still in there.

He heard a key in the lock, and then the Texan threw open the door and screamed at him, "Keep quiet, Fuckhead!" Ignacio noted that the Texan was so agitated that he yelled this in English. Then Ignacio saw the people who were coming down the stairs.

They were women and girls, some young teenagers and some as old as their late thirties. They had their wrists tied with cord behind their backs, and they came down the steps slowly because they were blindfolded. Some were crying. They looked either terrified or emotionally numb. In the cellar and above the women at the top of the stairs were young guys whom Ignacio had never seen. They looked absolutely filthy and sweaty, with oily hair flecked with dust and plant fragments as if they had been in the desert sun for days. The guys in the cellar were busy rolling out the sleeping bags and mattresses for the women. They grabbed them and pushed them on top of these. Ignacio stood in the office doorway. He was too shocked and confused by what he was witnessing to speak.

One of the new young men, who apparently was their leader, came down the steps and continued an argument that had evidently started outside. The young man appeared indignant, and the Texan was furious.

"We had to shoot the men who were with the women and leave them at the border," the young man told the Texan. "I didn't want to bring the ladies here, but El Gordito said his place was full and he couldn't move his people until tomorrow. He specifically told me to bring the women here."

"Chinga tu madre, you know El Zeta said what? Never, never, never bring the people here to this place. There are reasons for this!"

"Ok, ok, relájate, hombre! Calm down! I can get them out of here in the morning and move them north to the Gordito. It is one night. No one has to know. What the fuck can I do if the fat one tells me to bring them here?"

"Sleep under a cactus, asshole," the Texan said in English. Ignacio noted that the Texan kept falling back into English.

The young man apparently understood, but he responded in Spanish, "We walked the fucking desert two days before we got to the truck. Everything screwed up back there. But look, we found this merchandise and stole it from coyotes who had no business in our territory. So these whores are not costing the Zeta anything. You don't have to say anything to the Zeta. Tomorrow we can let him know from the other place. He'll be an impressed and grateful man."

The Texan looked really nervous. "The Zeta knows everything. He's everywhere. If he finds out about this, I'll fucking kill you." This also came out in English.

The young man glared defiantly. "We'll be out of your hair before daylight. Look, your men probably need some sweet pussy by now. How long have they been out here in these boonies? Have you looked at some of these ladies? They're mostly from Honduras. Let's just relax and party tonight. We picked up refreshments on the way in."

Ignacio saw a couple of the Texan's men already stroking the hair of two young girls. All the women were downstairs now. They cowered atop the sleeping bags and mattresses. Ignacio knew what was about to happen, and he didn't want to see it.

The recommendation of the young man that they enjoy the women fell on favorable ears. All the men of the house were clamoring to have the women, and they looked threateningly at the Texan. Ignacio took advantage of the dramatic moment to go up into the kitchen. No one was paying attention to him. He had begun to worry about Lili. He thought it was too early for Lili to be at the house, but he searched the rooms anyway. No one was upstairs to stop him. He found no sign of her.

His stomach felt queasy, and his head was beginning to hurt as it usually did when the sun got low. He found milk in the refrigerator and poured himself a glass. Three of the young men who had been downstairs emerged from the cellar and hurried out the back door. They returned moments later with cases of beer and tequila and headed back down the steps.

When the women began crying and screaming, Ignacio went to his bedroom. His head was beginning to pound. He couldn't wait for Lili to get home. He tried to ignore the sounds of the men hooting below and the terrified protests of the women. He had become very anxious for Lili. The new men in the house would definitely like her. He tuned in to the sounds outdoors, listening for the approach of a vehicle that might be bringing Lili home. His headache intensified. When eventually he did hear a vehicle arriving, he thought he had fallen asleep because suddenly it had grown dark in his room.

He managed to get himself up so that he could go to the living room to warn Lili when she came in. A surge of pain at the top of his head stopped him cold when he arose. He had to pause a few moments until it subsided. Then he hastened to the living room. It was a strange experience because he had never been unsupervised in the house before.

He got to the living room just as the front door swung open wildly. To his surprise, he didn't see Lili. Horacio came through the door, followed by the Zeta. They didn't look happy. They looked just as surprised to see him.

But Ignacio found some words: "They're all downstairs."

The two didn't say anything, but they turned and went out of the house. Ignacio walked over to the front door which they had left open, and he saw them retrieve AK-47s from a white Ford Explorer. They brushed past him on the way back in, went to the kitchen, and headed down the stairs to the cellar. He went down behind them and positioned himself to watch from the door of the office near the bottom of the steps.

He saw the controlled fury behind the commands which El Zeta gave. Horacio stood beside him with his weapon pointed in the room. A number of men had their pants down, and all were scrambling to get themselves together. They now looked as terrified as the women.

171

"Get them out of here and off the property," the Zeta said to the young leader of the men who had brought the women. "Get them loaded into the truck."

The man started balking orders to his men. When they began to put the blindfolds on the women, the Zeta impatiently told them to do that in the truck. Ignacio saw the expression on the Texan's face when the Zeta said that. The Texan hadn't taken that as a good sign.

"You men, get in the back of the truck with the women and put their blindfolds on there," the leader repeated to his guys.

Horacio stood at attention, awaiting a signal from his boss.

When the men and the women had ascended the stairs, the Zeta stopped their leader as he began to follow them. "Wait here a minute. I want a word with you," the Zeta said. Then he nodded to Horacio, who went up the steps.

El Zeta said to the Texan, "Take our guys upstairs, and then come back down here for our little talk."

But the Texan didn't have to advance far. The men of the household got the message and hurried up the steps. The Texan came back and stood beside the leader of the group who had brought the women.

The Texan said, "I swear, Jefe, I told this fuckhead not to come here with those women." He said it in English.

The other man said, "It was only going to be for one night, Jefe. El Gordito didn't have room. He commanded me to come here. We had the opportunity to steal these women for you."

"Shhh...," said El Zeta. "Listen."

There was silence for about sixty seconds, except for the sounds of the people outside getting into the cargo area of the freight truck which had brought them. Then came a long chain of sound: that of an AK-47 firing without ceasing. Someone upstairs in the house shouted, "Oh, shit!" There was silence again, then the sound of the truck's cargo door being pulled down, and then the sound of the truck starting and driving away.

Ignacio saw that the young man who had brought the women now looked sick with terror. He knew what was coming. The Zeta raised his semi-automatic and fired three single-shots into the young man's heart. The Texan jumped back, startled, but then he stood erect, waiting. El Zeta put four bullets into his chest.

The Zeta turned around to look at Ignacio. Ignacio didn't hesitate. He strode over to the Zeta and said, "I'm ready to do much more than this busy work I've been doing. I have been analyzing in particular the casino reports, and I have ideas how you can push through ten times the cash you're doing now. You have a problem because cash is coming in much faster than you're getting it out. That's too dangerous in the United States. They will find you. They will take your money. They'll freeze all your assets and those of everyone in your organization. They'll search even for your private bank accounts in other countries and pressure the bank owners to give up information on you. I know how to avoid all this."

Ignacio said all this as if nothing unusual had just happened, as if he hadn't just witnessed the Zeta murder two men.

The Zeta stared into his eyes a few moments. "Good," he said. "I was coming tonight to get a progress report from you on your work. On the way here, I heard about this shit, these whores from Honduras being brought here. I can't have anyone working for me unable to follow simple instructions. I'm sorry you had to see this, Ignacio, but you seem to be handling it in a very mature fashion."

"I understand business, Jefe," Ignacio responded, and he nodded at the two bodies on the floor. "I can help you. There are virtual locations where money can go and never be found. I have researched this and know how to do it. I do need some help with my headaches so I can do a good job for you. If you move me, I want Lili to come again. She helps me a lot with those. She says she knows a good neurologist in San Antonio."

"No problem," the Zeta answered. "From what you just said to me, I think you already know where I need you the most."

173

"Las Vegas," answered Ignacio.

"Yes, exactly. I'll need a couple of days to make the arrangements." He turned and looked down at the bodies of the two men he had shot. "It'll be a while before Horacio gets back. He'll be taking the truck to dump its cargo in a place where it can't be found. Let's go upstairs. I'll get the guys to clean down here."

They headed up the steps. In the kitchen the Zeta asked him, "How is your headache tonight?"

"It's really bad, to be honest with you."

"All right, let's get you some medication to hold you until the morning, bien?"

Ignacio awoke the next morning feeling the fingers massaging his scalp. "Mmmm, good morning, Lili," he said, eyes still closed. "That feels so good."

"Good morning, honey," a voice spoke softly. It was a voice sweet and melodious, but it wasn't Lili's.

Ignacio opened his eyes wide. At first the woman looked like Lili, but then his vision focused, and he saw that this woman lying across his body and stroking his hair was young, with large green eyes set far apart and fine black hair that hung to her waist. She smiled warmly. She wore a white cotton blouse that from his view revealed breasts round and nurturing. She brushed his cheeks with the back of her hand as lovingly as a mother caressing her newborn baby. He might have been startled by the stranger's presence, but she handled him with calm and poise. He studied her a few seconds. She was undeniably gorgeous. He whispered to her, "Where is Lili?"

"Let me tell you about that," the girl responded quietly. She lightly brushed a strand of hair from his forehead as she explained, "Zeta was very happy with your decision to work with him in Las Vegas. He called Lili where she was working, and she's thrilled because he told her that she would be there with you. He needed her to complete her project where she is, and then he's bringing her to you in Vegas...if you want that. In the

174

meantime, Zeta is very concerned about your headaches, and he asked me to come take care of you for a couple of days until you relocate. I know about migraines and what people need, honey. So it'll be my pleasure to be with you until you leave here. I'm going to take good care of you."

"I see," Ignacio answered. Her fingers massaging his scalp felt wonderful. He thought that possibly she did it even better than Lili. "Well, good, thank you so much. I want to feel better."

"I promise that you will,' she answered, and she kissed him tenderly on his cheek. She added, "My name is Andrea." She breathed this into his ear.

Chapter 12: A World Gone Nuts

Corvette Nightfire
Monterrey, Mexico
Late Tuesday Night

Damn, David drives like a bat out of hell, Corvette observed from the back seat of David's 1969 restored Camaro as they tore from the airport to David and Ana's house in Cumbres in the northwestern frontier of the metropolitan Monterrey limits. *I should call him "Batman."*

In the cramped rear seats designed for people who were child-sized, Corvette leaned his long frame forward to participate in the conversation with David and Enrique. That is, he tried to hear them above the wind and engine noise. David had put the convertible top down in the late October chill of the mountains precisely for the reason of Corvette's height. This at least provided visibility to Corvette as they zipped past the lights, signs and cars of Monterrey on the way to David's home. Everywhere he saw billboards and placards. He couldn't read them, but it amused him to be surprised that all the road signs and advertisements were in Spanish.

I'm such an English-oriented, Mexican gringo! he laughed inside. *I guess a border does make a difference.*

The "conversation" was mostly David shouting in English above the road and wind noise so that he and Enrique could hear him. Enrique replied in Spanish and then repeated it in English, as if he had to keep remembering that Corvette didn't speak a language that he should know. Corvette was sure that Enrique was doing this on purpose to mock him, but he let it slide. He was in a good mood to be in Monterrey because his being there alleviated his desperation to do something to find Valentina.

"We don't know a whole lot more yet, Corvette," David yelled. "Enrique and I are just here one day ourselves. No one has heard from Valentina, and there's no sign or clue about Z-

30, who, we presume, has something to do with her being out of contact."

"Well," Corvette shouted back, "you guys haven't explained to me exactly why he would want her. I have some guesses, but I think you should tell me. I really want to help find her, and I want you to trust me."

How is that for coming to the point? Corvette thought.

"Yeah, you're right," David answered. "Enrique and I have been discussing that. You're here with us now, and we're going to level with you. We'll trust you. We want to show you some things in the morning, a kind of orientation for you. It'll help you to understand things. To understand us."

"Us? You mean the Zs?"

"Yes," David replied. "We're going to bring full Z resources to the effort of finding Valentina. It would be good for you to see what the Zs are all about, what we have, and what the Zs can do. There's a lot happening in the next few days. We can't move fast enough."

"Yeah, I'd appreciate that. I don't fully understand what I'm involved in, and, on top of everything else, I have an important decision I need to make in the next couple of days."

It was a decision worrying Corvette, but there was too much wind and engine noise for him to bring it up now. He wanted to discuss it with them soon, however.

The opportunity came at David and Ana's home in Cumbres after David gave a tour of their medium-sized, modest home. Corvette had expected something grander, considering the status of its owners, but he saw that they had furnished it elegantly. The artwork in every room celebrated Mexican culture, except in David's office, where a United States flag stood in the corner, and pictures of restored classic Corvettes adorned the walls. They had once been owned by David. The house had three levels, each with ceramic tile floors accessed by glistening marble stairsteps. Corvette was amazed that cement houses could have detailed and stunning architectural styling. Dark mahogany beams ran parallel across the ceilings of the living area on the second floor. Tall windows rose from the ground through all three levels in the front of the home. Because the house was on the highest lot on the mountainside of the suburban development, it provided vistas of Monterrey and its lights that reminded Corvette of Los Angeles as seen from its surrounding hills. The views from the home stole his breath.

David brought them upstairs to the third floor master bedroom. That room and an adjacent sala that overlooked the second floor both had sliding doors that opened to a furnished rooftop terrace. David led them across the bedroom to step outside. He flipped a switch by the door, and soft music began to play through outside speakers. "Ana and I like to come out here to dance late at night," he said smiling. Enrique walked to the edge of the terrace and stared across the city. Corvette noted the outdoor lounge furniture and tables and then joined Enrique to admire the view. The full moon was high. He felt the freshness of the autumn breezes.

"What an astonishing city!" Corvette exclaimed sincerely. "I had no idea Monterrey was so big."

Enrique glanced at him and nodded; then he pointed and said, "I live close by, just off that main road there. Do you see that cluster of six-story buildings? That's the condominium complex where I live."

David came up beside them. He added, "I lived there once also. That's how I met Enrique. He and his roommate, Israel, and I used to work out together in the gym there. Sometimes we grabbed some tacos and beers afterwards. Israel had long been Enrique's best friend. They grew up together in Mexico City and came to Monterrey to attend university. Israel fell in love with a young woman who didn't tell him that she was married to a drug cartel leader here in Monterrey. She was trying to leave the guy, so she hid from him in Israel's and Enrique's condo. Israel didn't have a clue that she was married. She and Israel only knew each other a couple of weeks when the cartel kidnapped him and murdered him. She disappeared and has

178

never been found. After that, Enrique and I became closer friends. Ana and I were in the early stages of the development of the Zs when this happened to Israel. The Z project helped Enrique and me work through anger."

The quick story shocked Corvette. He realized that David had stepped in to explain something that probably was too emotional for Enrique to talk about. Corvette looked at Enrique. He was tall like he was. He had a rugged, brooding handsomeness and a tough-looking demeanor, but his eyes betrayed that his soul was sensitive. Those black eyes hadn't cut Corvette any slack, but as Corvette observed him now, he realized that Enrique used the darkness of his eyes as a way to hide pain that he wanted to remain private.

"I'm really sorry to hear this," Corvette said quietly. What else could he say? He hoped that his words conveyed to Enrique the sincerity that he felt.

"Well, Corvette," David said, "we're planning to get up early to go to the regional Z training facility in the morning. I think you should join us. I have an extra bedroom on this floor of the house. You're welcome to stay with me, or you can stay at Enrique's place. Your choice."

"I'll go to Enrique's place tonight," Corvette answered. "I would like to see it."

Enrique glanced at him, obviously surprised by his decision.

"Bueno," David answered. "You guys up for a beer? I have them in the fridge right here. We can chat a few minutes and then call it an evening."

They nodded agreement, and David retrieved ice-cold Modelos from the stainless steel refrigerator next to a large outdoor grill. The three took seats at a bar in front of the appliances. They made small talk a few minutes, although Enrique mostly was quiet. Then David brought up the subject that was the perfect segue for Corvette to reveal the decision he needed to make. He had been worrying about it ever since he had taken the cash in Las Vegas.

179

David asked, "So, Corvette, have you given any more thought to my suggestion that you hire bodyguards? You're with us right now, but I know that you're getting well-known on the poker circuit. Do you plan to continue playing? If you do, I think you need to have good security attendants."

"Yeah, that's something I have to address soon, David," Corvette answered, "and it brings up something I need to tell you. I really could use some advice from you guys about this. Have you followed my career this year? Do you know my current poker status?"

Enrique was staring at him keenly.

"To be honest," David answered, "before last week, I had never heard of you." He let out a small chuckle. "But I've been briefed on you, and I know that you're a budding celebrity in the poker world. You're scheduled to play at the Final Table next week at The Rio."

Corvette sighed. "My luck has been strange. In the early part of this year, yes, I did exceptionally well; but in the last three months I pretty much lost most of what I had won. When you play against expert players who've been on the circuit for years and who've won a lot of tournaments, you need to have a good bankroll to finance the size of betting that occurs. I'm down to pretty much nothing, except I do have a chance for a huge pay day next week.

"Earlier this year, I won an entry into the World Series of Poker's Main Event. The Main Event this year had over eight thousand entrants. Over the period of one week, these entrants narrowed down to what's called the "Final Nine" players who would, in November, play for the WSOP bracelet and the big jackpots. With a combination of skill and luck, I managed to stay alive day after day until I won a place at the Final Table. So, yes, I'm in the Main Event next Monday night. On that night, the Final Nine play down to two or three. Then on Tuesday those two or three play for the trophy, the bracelet, and the cash. All of this is live on ESPN."

Corvette caught Enrique's frown as he and David glanced at one another. He guessed that Enrique was trying to figure out the implications of this divulgence.

Corvette continued. "In case you don't know, the chips that a player wins during the tournament are not actually dollar amounts owned by the players. The chips are more like points. But all the cash generated by the ten-thousand-dollar buy-ins from the approximately eight thousand people entering the tournament goes into a pot which funds the prize money paid to the tournament winners at the end: those who come in first, second, third etc. Going into the Final Table, I have twelve million chips. That sounds like a lot, but it isn't. Only one of the nine players who will be at the Final Table has less than I do. The player in the lead has thirty-two million chips. So, you see, I'm beginning with less, and, theoretically, I have a higher probability of elimination. Of course, skill can defy the probabilities, especially the skill of bluffing."

They were quiet, digesting this. Corvette took a couple of sips of his beer to give them time, and then he continued, "As I said, the play down to the Final Nine happened this past July. I was feeling very heady and full of myself after I qualified. I went back on the road playing in other tournaments. At that point, I had well over a million dollars of my own from the early part of the year, but I got reckless with my betting. I was overconfident from my wins in Vegas. Frankly, my luck dove into a long losing streak. I couldn't get good hands. I started betting larger amounts believing that my luck was overdue for a change to the better, but it didn't change. By the end of last month, September, my million dollars was pretty much all gone. I played a small game the night I met Valentina and won seventeen thousand dollars. I was ecstatic. I took it as a sign that my losing streak finally had ended."

He paused to assess their expressions. Enrique's frown had become an accusing look. His expression said, "That's why you took the money!" David's face appeared to be processing the

181

information revealed by Corvette with a hundred other thoughts.

After a few moments, David was the one who broke the silence. "Corvette, first, congratulations for your achievement in Las Vegas! That's pretty amazing, and it does open up many things to consider. To be honest with you, everything has happened so quickly that I didn't even have a moment to bring Enrique up to speed on you. I'm really glad you brought this up to discuss with us. It shows trust. Tell me something. If you lose in the tournament, for example, if you're the first one of the final nine players eliminated, do you win any money?"

"Well," Corvette answered, "the total pot this year is about thirty-seven million dollars. The share for the one who wins will be about eight million dollars. Everyone at the Final Table has been guaranteed at least seven hundred thousand."

"Then, basically, all you have to do is sit down at the table and play a little while. Worst case scenario is that you receive seven hundred thousand just for showing up," Enrique said.

Corvette caught the judgmental tone which Enrique had tried to mask. "There's one small problem," he replied, "When we made the Final Table, they gave each of us seven hundred thousand dollars, an "advance" which will be deducted from our winnings. In other words, the ninth place finisher gets nothing. The other eight will get to keep their winnings minus the "advance." But I'm determined to win, no matter what competition I'm in. Winning the World Series bracelet is very prestigious, and I could certainly use the cash!"

David jumped back in, apparently catching Enrique's tone, and delivered what was actually a reminder message to Enrique: "Sometimes we have unexpected destinies, Corvette. For example, Enrique and I also came into a large amount of money, and neither of us would have foreseen it. Enrique, Ana, and I worked closely in the early stages of the Zs with a wonderful Mexican patriot named Eduardo Ortíz. He died serving his country during the military coup. He had no children remaining at his death. Both his children had died, as well as his wife. He

182

had a huge fortune because he was a family shareholder of Mexico's largest private international cement company. The three of us, and the Zs, were like family to him at the end of his life. He left the bulk of his estate to The Z Foundation, and he left some money to me and Enrique. I won't speak for Enrique, but in my case, it was much more money than I ever thought I would see in my life."

Corvette glanced at Enrique and saw him looking down. He wasn't sure if this was from embarrassment or shame.

"Tomorrow, Enrique and I'll bring you up to date on what the Foundation does and its current financial problems. This information relates to the Zs, so in an indirect way, it relates to finding Valentina. Let me think about what you have told us tonight. That tournament in Las Vegas is less than a week away. I'm sure you must be wondering what to do about it."

"Yes," Corvette answered. "It's probably pretty dangerous for me to return to Las Vegas. I'm sure I have enemies there, and I don't even know who they all are. Besides Mexican drug cartels, I don't know what United States agencies or the police would do if I'm back there. I want to play in the tournament, but I'm conflicted about finding Valentina versus running the risk of going there."

"Okay, we'll talk more about this. For now, I think we're all tired. I want to sleep on what you've told us and think about what might happen to you if you go back to Las Vegas. So let's call it a night," David suggested. "We roll out early in the morning."

Corvette turned to Enrique, who was staring at his empty beer bottle. He asked quietly, "Enrique, still okay if I crash at your place?"

"Sí," he replied, nodding his head. "Vámonos. Let's go."

"I know what that means," Corvette said, attempting humor, but David was the one who chuckled.

Enrique's dark blue Jeep was in David's driveway. Corvette threw his bag in the back and climbed in beside Enrique. They rolled slowly down the steep street to the main avenue, Paseo de Leones. The silence between them felt uncomfortable to Corvette. He didn't want to become angry. He wanted to talk to Enrique. He had planned on the plane what he might say to him. Since they were captive together in the Jeep, Corvette thought this would be a good time to bring up the subject of Valentina.

"I need to ask you something, Enrique."

His companion said, "Okay." He continued to stare straight ahead.

"I've been wondering if you've been going out with Valentina. I thought that maybe you liked her, and this is one of the reasons you don't seem so crazy about me. Were you already seeing her and then found out I danced with her one evening? Is this something that has bothered you?"

He was relieved to find out that Enrique didn't try to dodge the question.

"I've had some problems with you for a couple of reasons," Enrique answered. He sounded slightly angry. "The first one is that you took the money. I don't think that's right. You did it in a very underhanded way. Maybe I wasn't exactly straightforward with you, but you still shouldn't have taken the money. And I'll admit to you that I have been a little jealous that you had an evening with Valentina, yes. It's because I was getting up the nerve to ask her out. I haven't had much of a social life with women. I've gone to school, studied hard, worked, and I've devoted my life to the Zs. She gave you that bag of cash. She must have liked you to some extent. Yes, that has bothered me."

The stoplight they had been at changed to green, and Enrique shifted gears and made a left turn. He continued, "Ana told David that she thinks you're in love with Valentina. And here you are in Monterrey to help find her. So there must be some truth to that."

"I haven't been able to get her out of my mind, Enrique. When I met her, she told me that she didn't speak English. That whole night we danced, I felt happy; and I told her all about my life even though I didn't think she could understand me. Now I

184

know that she speaks English, which is weird; but the thing you pointed out, that she brought me the bag of cash, made me feel very bonded with her. Finding her and asking her about this are things very important to me to do. If I can help her in some way, I want to. It has become my obsession to find her. Listen, I haven't had many serious relationships with women either. A lot of them try to follow me around while I'm playing poker in different cities, but I don't really know them, and I'm always leaving for the next city. I never felt a stirring in my heart for a woman like I did on the night I met Valentina. I can't explain it. Do you know, my parents met on a cruise ship, and they fell in love while dancing! My father was Mexican and my mum is British. They seemed like a very unlikely pair. Who knows about life, Enrique? It can be so strange."

"Sí," Enrique answered with a sigh. "For me it has been dark and serious. I don't think I know how to have fun. That friend David told you about: Israel. He was like a brother to me, and he knew how to have fun. I haven't been the same since they murdered him."

"Well," Corvette replied. "I can see that you're brave and strong. I'm feeling pretty scared, to be honest with you."

That made Enrique turn and look at him. A half smile came to his face. They arrived at the automatic gate to his condominium complex. Enrique inserted his card and parked in a space close to the guard shack. He cut off the engine, and then he looked again at Corvette.

"Don't worry," he said. "I'll look after you."

Wednesday Morning

At five in the morning, Enrique awakened Corvette from the doorway of his dark room. Smells of coffee and omelets loaded with red peppers motivated Corvette to rise and grope for something to put on. He still felt sound asleep.

"You'll need running shoes, some jogging pants, a T shirt, and a light jacket. I can loan you a jacket if you need it. The day starts off cold here, but it'll warm up quickly, especially if you're active. I have breakfast ready for us; then we need to hurry. Probably David is already on his way there," Enrique told Corvette.

They headed out Highway 54 past the Monterrey international airport. Before reaching Cerralvo Municipality they turned west into the hills and found a narrow private road that sloped upward several kilometers until they came to a ranch. They waited behind a bus and a van at a security gate where a guard checked identification of the passengers coming in, but he greeted Enrique with some joking banter and motioned them through. Corvette noticed that the ranch was named "Los Gemelos," which Enrique said meant "The Twins." There was a tag written underneath the name of the ranch on the sign at the gate. Enrique interpreted it for Corvette to mean "The home of the Zs."

"This was the first Z training camp," Enrique explained. "The ranch was the home of Eduardo Ortíz and his wife. Their children were twins, brother and sister, whom David met when they all were in their early teens. The Ortíz family had moved to Virginia at that time while Eduardo was expanding the operations of their cement factories in the United States. David became engaged to the daughter, but she was killed in a horrible car accident that the two of them were in. Her brother became a notorious leader of the Cartel of Sinaloa after he returned to Mexico. He was called El Gato. During the military coup a few years ago here, El Gato kidnapped Ana while he led a small army to free the former President of Mexico, Pedro Navarro, from the imprisonment he was in at Los Pinos in Mexico City. He was helped in this by the Zeta, Z-30, who betrayed him at the end. El Gato died in a shootout north of here at the border. He was shot by his own father and a soldier. David, Ana, and I were there. Eduardo also died from a gunshot wound there. He left most of his fortune and this ranch and some other properties to The Z Foundation."

The driveway forked near the entrance to the ranch and became a narrow road winding through hills to a compound a couple of kilometers away. As they bumped along that road, Enrique continued to explain:

"You'll see soon a huge clearing of land where the training facilities are. Before the military coup, Eduardo let the Army and Marines of the Mexican Armed Forces use his land and equipment here for Special Forces' training and for the planning of secret missions, especially against the drug cartels. Sometimes the DEA and military intelligence units from the United States had agents and soldiers here to work with the Mexican forces. David had a lot to do with that happening. He had spent his career in the CIA helping Latin American governments do battle with the cartels in Colombia and Mexico, and in other countries as well. Later he had his own consulting firm serving intelligence agencies of the USA and corporate clients who wanted to provide safety for their employees and families in Mexico. He and Eduardo were dreaming up a kind of paramilitary-public-safety organization to help protect citizens from the blood baths in the streets caused by the cartels when David met Ana. She had been leading peace and non-violence movements and demonstrations for justice throughout Mexico. She had put together some ethical and moral rules of life for an organization that she was dreaming up. When she and David came together, their ideas merged, and the Zs were born. You will be meeting many of them in a few minutes."

My God, I'm really in a different world now, Corvette realized. He felt a little knot of anxiety in his stomach. Not even a week earlier he had been in his element: playing poker, bandying jokes with Raymundo, and dancing in Las Vegas. How had he suddenly become involved with paramilitary groups fighting drug cartels in Mexico?

The knot tightened when Enrique added another piece of information that astounded him even more:

"One of the things you should know about David, if you don't already, is that his best friend is Donald Austin Blair."

What? "The President of the United States?" Corvette asked.

Enrique laughed, pleased that he had shocked him. Apparently he was enjoying the reaction that his briefing of Corvette was producing. "Sí," he answered. "I still marvel at that too. They were roommates at college in Virginia at a school called William and Mary. They became best friends and have been that way throughout their lives. The President seems to trust David's opinion about things here in Mexico more than he does the intelligence agencies, and when David needs something, the President usually gets him the help he needs. That may be something that will happen this morning. David has a call scheduled with the President to update him about the cartel activities in the United States, especially as it relates to money laundering, which David has been tracking. David is going to take the opportunity to ask for help in finding Valentina."

They rounded a curve in the road and turned into an entrance to the Z Training Facilities. Corvette thought that he was looking at a Hollywood set. He saw an unpaved parking area, and just beyond that, to the left, a mock-urban-street scene with cement buildings two to four stories high. These lined both sides of a street that had cars, a bus, and a couple of pick-up trucks. The buildings were unfurnished shells that had steps between them and staircases and landings inside them. Corvette could see a couple of dozen or so young people milling in small groups in the street with team leaders giving them instructions or some sort of pep talks. It was only just past six in the morning.

Beyond the street scene were three one-story buildings. As they parked, Enrique began to explain to Corvette what he was seeing.

"The reason for the urban setting there is because much of the fighting with cartels and so many of the public safety problems occur in the cities. Many of the young Zs are kids who come from the poor barrios, and they're at home running and jumping around the concrete and the cars. This part of the training is a lot like the sport of parkour or what is called urban free running. The Z philosophy is about defensive violence. The Zs don't carry guns or knives. If they get in trouble with enemies who do have these weapons, they need to be able to dodge an attack and get away fast. The Zs put themselves in life-or-death situations to help innocent victims. Here in this training facility they learn to 'fly' in a sense. When you see them jumping and running, you will understand what this means. When I first met David, he told me that he that he has been 'flying' since he was a little boy and that he still does, and I laughed. I thought he was an old man. Then I saw him doing it and stopped laughing."

They pulled into a parking space beside the van that had preceded them through the gate to the property. A group of four young guys and a couple of girls were retrieving bags from the back of the van.

"Those kids will be staying overnight, possibly a few nights, depending on which program they're in. The first building you see up there is a military-style barracks that sleeps eighty persons. The building in the middle has a kitchen and dining area and a simple auditorium for large group meetings and talks. The third building is a technology center, and it houses several offices. I see David's Camaro, so he's already here and probably in that building. He was going to be talking to the President at six a.m. Let's get up there."

As they strode rapidly toward the technology building, Enrique pointed out the steel communications tower beside it and explained that it was for cell phone coverage and radio communications. On the flat roof of the building sat a large satellite dish. "These buildings have been constructed since Eduardo died. During the military coup, he let the Armed Forces use his house as a headquarters for operations in the Northeast of Mexico. Where you see the fields over there is where helicopters would land and where a lot of military vehicles remained until deployed for missions in the area. I'm talking large craft. Black Hawk helicopters of the United States' Army, for example, and Black Hawks purchased by Mexico from the United States' manufacturer landed here. Since that time, The Z Foundation has cleared more land for the athletic fields. You can see a lot of physical training equipment up there on the left: the rope structures, the weird bars for arm development and climbing, the tires and pits for jumping, and a lot of other challenges. Then farther are the three fútbol fields. The kids who stay here a few days love to play, of course, even after the hard days of activity. During the day you can see them looking longingly at the fields."

Enrique pointed to an opening in the trees beyond the field with the athletic equipment. He explained, "There are running and hiking paths with exercise stations in the forest. We put some scary footbridges and cables across steep ravines in there for wilderness-type training. Sometimes it's good to be in the woods, especially on the hot days. It's so much cooler in the shade."

Corvette was dumbfounded by what he saw. He found his morning voice and said, "This blows me away, Enrique. It's not what I imagined when you said that we were going to the Z training facilities. Who pays for all this? Are there other centers like this in Mexico?"

"Sí," Enrique replied, "although none of the others are as large as this one is. We have them in Mexico City, Guadalajara, Juarez, and in many of the larger cities throughout Mexico. The money has come from the earnings of the investments of The Z Foundation and from annual donations. This one here has had a lot of funding from the Armed Forces budget covertly in the past because of Eduardo's involvement with them, and some funds have even come secretly through agencies in the United States which do undercover work in Mexico."

Geez, thought Corvette.

They entered the attractive, metal modular building that housed the technology center. Enrique led Corvette to the first room on the left of a small lobby. It was an office which David was now using to speak to the President of the United States. David motioned for them to sit down in two chairs in front of the desk where he was seated as he talked on the phone. David looked crisp and relaxed. He addressed his long-term best friend as "Mr. President" and, occasionally, as "Donnie." Corvette sat listening, trying to wrap his mind around the fact that the person on the other end of the phone was often referred to as the leader of the free world. He envisioned David handing him the phone and saying, "Corvette, would you like to speak to Donnie?" This made him laugh out loud, and Enrique glanced at him curiously.

But the conversation soon became more serious than it was when they first had entered the office. David became quiet. He picked up a pen to jot a few notes on paper as he listened. His expression grew solemn. Finally he said, "Well, that information really clouds who might have Valentina, doesn't it?" Corvette felt his heart race when he heard this. He strained to hear what the President was saying to David, but he couldn't distinguish the words.

David told the President, "Enrique arrived with the young man who received the bag of cash from Valentina. They're sitting in front of me now. I'll bring them up to date; then I'll call Zolinsky in the Las Vegas DEA office to exchange the latest information with him. Thanks for your help in speaking to the directors of the FBI and the CIA regarding finding Valentina. You're right, Mr. President, we don't know with any certainty if she's in Mexico at this time." He glanced at Corvette.

That's strange, Corvette observed, *why didn't he mention me by name to the President?*

Just before signing off, David made a cryptic remark that Corvette thought might be referring to him. He said, "I'll definitely talk to him about that when the time is right. He'll probably be feeling a little overwhelmed by the end of today."

Then, after the response of the President, David said, "Yes, Ana is coming here to Monterrey Friday afternoon. She's bringing Paula with her. Paula wants to see the rally Saturday morning when her mom speaks to the audience in the Macroplaza. These rallies against illegal weapons sales and drug consumption are being planned in the United States also, as a continuation of this kick-off in Monterrey. A caravan of activists will leave here after the rally and head to the United States. The caravan is going to make stops in cities across the country on its way to Washington, Mr. President. Celebrities and other speakers are being booked in the cities to try to get media attention. Ana plans to be at a couple of the early rallies in Texas. With the violence from the cartels escalating in the states, I'm getting increasingly worried about Ana's safety when she participates in these things."

Suddenly Corvette had a memory of an event he had seen on television a few years earlier. He had learned from his mother that Ana was the woman who had been appointed by the military coup for a brief term as Interim President of Mexico until free elections would be held. Now he recalled the televised scene on the International Bridge between Laredo, Texas, and Nuevo Laredo, Mexico, when Ana led Mexican civilians to meet the President of the United States and the First Lady half-way. It was a ceremony to celebrate the re-opening of the border after the days of tension following the coup. During the coup, the United States was considering a military invasion of Mexico to restore order in a country that seemed on the verge of civil war. Corvette now sat stunned by the insight that the people he had been with in the last few days were international leaders who had been playing major roles in the shaping of history. This realization made him think of St. Rogelio.

Rogelio, I asked you to help me. Is this how you're doing it?

When David disconnected the call, he sat silently a few moments and then shook his head. Looking at Corvette and Enrique, he said, "There's new information that has added to the mystery of where Valentina might be. I don't think this is good news. That DEA agent who was killed, Josh Bailin. His wife came forward yesterday when she found unexplained bank

192

deposits to their account. She told Josh's boss, Zolinsky, because she was afraid it might have bearing on what had happened in The Oasis. The follow-up investigation by the DEA with the bank and a review of Josh's office files and cell phone records turned up that the deposits were made in cash and have been ongoing for the past year. The evidence in other records points to the fact that Josh was a paid informer for the Cartel of Sinaloa. His main contact was a person who has been identified as a leader in that cartel's operations in the Las Vegas area."

"Dios!" Enrique exclaimed, hitting his fist on the desk in front of him. "He could have been the one who informed Sinaloa that the Zeta would be at The Oasis!"

David nodded glumly.

"Sinaloa could also know that Valentina was with him!" Enrique added. Then he put his hand to his mouth and looked embarrassed.

Recognizing that Enrique thought he had let the cat out of the bag, David shook his head and said, "Don't worry about it, Enrique. We were going to tell Corvette today. He has probably figured it out anyway." The two turned to see Corvette's reaction.

Corvette felt anxiety tighten his stomach again. He did think that he had figured it out. He was hesitant to say what he thought out loud in case it would sound ridiculous to them, but he risked it: "I'm guessing that Valentina was doing undercover work. She works for the DEA?"

David nodded. "She has an events planning business here in Monterrey, but she's an employee also of the DEA."

"Sooo..." Corvette drew out the word as he contemplated. "We're worried now that either of two cartels could have her?"

"Yes," David answered. "It might be better if Z-30 survived and she's with him, especially if she still has him fooled. If the Cartel of Sinaloa has her, I don't think it bodes too well for her. The President is directing the CIA and the FBI to pull out all the stops to assist the DEA find Valentina, including using intelligence resources here in Mexico."

"What about the Corvette Stingray?" Enrique asked. Corvette noted Enrique's quivering voice. "Any news on that? Is it possible that Josh Bailin was the one who took it? Valentina disclosed that it had the mysterious ledger book inside it. Maybe he got it."

"Not a bad deduction, Enrique," David said solemnly. "The car hasn't been found. You would think that with all the agents and police looking for an unusual car like that, it would be easy to find. No one has seen it."

"What color is it?" Corvette asked. It was an offhand question, but as David was answering, "It's a color called Lime-rock Green," Corvette thought about people in Las Vegas looking for a shiny green Corvette Stingray, and suddenly a face appeared in his mind:

Raymundo's.

"I know someone who can find the car," Corvette said. "He's a man so connected in Vegas that he can get anything I need, anytime. He's my personal assistant when I'm playing in tournaments there. I can ask him to look for it without explaining why. He's completely confidential and discreet. He's the man who got me out of town when I left last Saturday."

"Damn," Enrique said. "Call him." He looked to David for affirmation, and David nodded.

"Okay," Corvette said. "Do you guys mind if I step outside? I can reach him on my cell. He answers every time I call."

"Thank you. Be our guest," David answered, gesturing toward the door.

The sun was starting its ascent above the eastern horizon. It was still chilly, and Corvette was glad to be wearing Enrique's jacket. He moved to the wall of the building out of direct sunlight and shielded the phone with his hand so he could see. He dialed Raymundo.

"Glad to hear from you, compadre," was Raymundo's greeting upon answering. "Although it is early as shit. I was going to call you today if you didn't get in touch. This city is going crazy buzzing about the Main Event at The Rio next week.

194

Everyone is talking about the players, but most of the pretty young ladies are asking about you. I've seen a couple of on-line articles about you, and the writers have mentioned that no one knows where you are. So are you coming, hermano, or are things still too hot for you here?"

"It's getting even hotter, Raymundo," Corvette replied. "Listen, man, keep this between us. I'm making up my mind whether I can come to Vegas or not. I'm in Monterrey, Mexico, right now looking for a Mexican girl who has disappeared. I met her in Vegas last week. Her name is Valentina Garza. Don't talk to her about anyone. It could get you killed. I'll explain all this later. I'll try to get a picture of her and send it to you. She's my age. She's special to me. I'm worried whether she's alive. I'm an enemy of some pretty bad guys now, Raymundo: The Zetas. So if you want to disassociate with me, no hard feelings, bro. I'm telling you that I'm in some heavy shit. If you look for this girl and find out where she is or might be, you need to let me know day or night. Both the United States and Mexican governments are looking for her. It is possible that either the Zetas or another Mexican cartel has her, so be extremely careful. Not trying to scare you, Raymundo, but I'm serious. You might not want to have anything to do with me for a while."

"Mmmm," Raymundo responded in a long, throaty growl. "Sounds like you need protection. I can get that for you, no problem, if you come to play here."

"What kind of protection?"

"Some talented body-guards, carnal, who have lots of weapon experience. They got crazy names like Jupiter and Pluto, like they love astronomy or something. We can work out a good safety plan if you come, I promise you that. Jupiter is a huge white guy, the biggest I've ever seen, the biggest in the solar system, man. Pluto is a short fire pump of a man, a black guy. I hired him right away after I asked him, 'Why do they call you Pluto?' He told me, 'I'm dark and deadly.' I asked him, 'When can you start?'"

Corvette snorted a chuckle. "You're not afraid? This is serious, Raymundo."

"Not afraid, hermano, but my rates just went way up."

"Ok," Corvette laughed, "I think I can afford it now. Gracias, amigo, I'll think about coming and let you know very soon. Give me up to two days. If the girl is here in Mexico and I'm really of some help finding her, it'll influence my decision about the trip."

"Todo bueno," Raymundo answered. "I understand."

"Well, I have another reason for calling. I'm looking for a lost Corvette Stingray, a brand new one. The whole world is looking for it, the same people looking for Valentina."

"What color is it?" Raymundo asked.

Corvette snickered to himself again. *Same question I asked.*

"It's a green called Lime-rock Green."

"I have it."

Corvette paused. "You have it? You have what?"

"The car."

"What do you mean you have it?"

"I found it in the desert. Well, to be accurate, me and CT found it."

Corvette knew instantly who CT was. Raymundo had just a handful of choice clients like him, but the others were international celebrities with long running shows in Vegas. Corvette was his least-known client. CT was a legendary comedian whose stand-up routines had sold out the theaters in two of Vegas' best known casinos over the course of the past fifteen years.

"Jesus, Raymundo, you found a new green Stingray in the desert? When was this?"

"Yesterday."

"Are you frigging kidding me? Where is it now?"

"In my garage."

"Come on, asshole, quit messing with me. Tell me about this."

Raymundo started laughing. "Okay. It was a freak thing. CT was coming back in town from some place, and I picked him up

196

at the airport. He has a ranch out in the desert off Magic Way, past Henderson. He has this service road, this private dirt thing full of holes and ruts that runs around the back of the home. I was helping get his bag out the back of my taxi. We were standing around talking when a bright gleam of sunlight burnt into my eye from something behind a mound of dirt and cactus a hundred yards or so from the house. CT saw me blinking my eyes because they had water in them, so he started being all comical with me and giving me a hard time about being emotional for his homecoming. So I explained that some piece of metal caught sunlight that shone in my eyes. He walked around in his yard until he saw the reflection too. He said, 'Dude, that's coming from a mirror. Let's go check it out.' I didn't even want to go because I was in a hurry, but I trudged up the little sand hill with him. We saw car tracks in the sand. When we got past the little mound, there was the Corvette. I have a feeling it's the one you're looking for. Not too many of those around."

"God, Raymundo, I can't frigging believe this! What kind of shape was it in?"

"Well, the side windows were shot out. There was nothing in the car. It had been cleaned out good. Nothing in the trunk, the glove compartment, or the center console. We checked under the hood, and it had been messed with in there. Not sure yet what was done. But that wasn't the strange thing."

"What do you mean? What was strange?"

"Mexicans must have gone through this car."

"What does that mean, Raymundo?"

"The wheels were missing. That's why CT said he didn't want to fool with it and I could have it."

"That's nuts, Raymundo! Why does that mean Mexicans went through the car? Jesus, you're Mexican. That sounds so racist. Why didn't you notify the police?"

"Are you kidding, amigo? A cleaned out, abandoned Stingray? Do you know how much I can get for this car with a little identification removal?"

Corvette sighed. *The whole world has gone crazy,* he thought.

"Just messing with you, amigo," Raymundo laughed. "The truth is, this car looked to us like no one wanted it anymore, you know what I mean?"

"Okay, just ignoring all that, how did you get the car to your garage if it's in the desert with no wheels?"

"For the same reason! I'm Mexican! I have wheels! Dios, what kind of Mexican are you? You're named after a car by your papacito. You know that Mexico is a car culture. You're a disgrace to your nationality."

Corvette couldn't help himself. He broke out laughing. "I'm not a Mexican citizen," he pointed out.

"Besides," Raymundo continued, "CT helped me. I didn't have keys to start the car, but I have a cousin with a tow truck. So after we put the wheels on, he towed it to my house."

"In the broad daylight, with the whole world looking for it?"

"Noooo," Raymundo answered. "By then it was completely dark."

"Oh my God, I just don't believe this," Corvette said. He tried desperately to focus on what should be the next step. After contemplating a few moments, he said, "Raymundo, listen to me, please. That car is crucial evidence wanted by the DEA, the FBI, and the Nevada State Police. It may contain evidence that would help us find this missing girl I've told you about, such as fingerprints or any other kind of evidence which we can't even imagine. Everyone wanted the car because it supposedly had a ledger book inside it that was small and could fit in the center console. The cartel wanted to find it for the same reason. So you saw nothing like this?"

"No, amigo, I'm telling you, there's nothing in that car."

"Okay. Please don't touch the car again. I'm here with people in Monterrey who talk to the DEA all the time. May I explain this situation to them? I trust them. I don't want you to get into any trouble or be in any danger. I can handle that. You know that kid who was found shot up last week? The one who used to work on the parking staff of The Oasis? Well, that kid had taken the Corvette for a little joy ride, and someone killed him trying to find that car. So this is serious. Who knows you have the car?"

"The crazy man, CT, but he already agreed not to say anything to anyone because he doesn't want me in trouble either. Also, my cousin, but he's family, so he's a stone. No one can get anything out of him. That's all."

"All right," Corvette said. "I'm going to get off the phone with you and go talk to these guys here about what we should do. Hold tight until you hear from me again."

"Bien, amigo, no worries. I'll await your call."

"Be careful," Corvette advised.

They disconnected.

Holy mother of God, thought Corvette. *Wait until I go inside and tell David and Enrique that I know where the car is. They're going to shit in their pants.*

In spite of his nervousness, he started laughing.

Chapter 13: Voice of the Dead

Enrique Santos
Monterrey, Mexico
Just After Midnight Thursday Morning

Score another one for Corvette, Enrique thought that night before he drifted to sleep after the exhausting day at the Z Training Facility. *We have the United States government, the police agencies of Las Vegas and Nevada, the Zs, and at least two Mexican drug cartels looking for a pinche Stingray for days; people are dying in the search; and Corvette tells us in Monterrey that he knows where it is. This is after he fools us all and gets out of the country with stolen drug cartel money. No wonder the guy is in the World Series of Poker!*

He hated the idea that, after observing Corvette all day to figure him out, at night he would still be thinking about him as he lay in bed. What had impressed him was that Corvette had been quiet, reflective, nervous, respectful, and...*sincere!* At one point, Corvette had wiped away a tear while they listened to some young Zs explain what had brought them to volunteer their time, to risk their lives, and to choose the Zs over other alternatives for serving their country or communities. Some of them knew English and spoke it so that Corvette could understand. Enrique quietly translated the Spanish of the others.

The story that had seemed to move Corvette the most came from a compact, nineteen-year-old kid as they sat in a small group after lunch.

"I'm Daniel Flores," he had said. His eyes had gazed mournfully in the distance, as if he could see his own heartbreak in the form of a beast coiled and ready to pounce on him for another devouring. Daniel's eyes were ones of a youth who had aged too soon from a loss that a sensitive heart should never have to endure. Yet he had spoken forcefully, as if to defy the demon threatening him.

"My older brother, Alberto Flores, repaired cars and installed tires. He did this since thirteen years of age to help our mom pay the bills for our family. He was five years older than me. Every day he put his arm around my neck. He told me, 'Come with me, Daniel. You're going to help me work. One day we'll be partners and have our own business.' He worked hard from early in the morning until late at night. He didn't have a place. He fixed cars at the homes of people, and he jacked up the cars to put on the tires. When he came home at night, I would finally let myself fall asleep, but not until he climbed into the bed that we had to share. Our mom gave us four sisters, and we were crowded in our little home. I worried about him all the time because our neighborhood in Monterrey is very dangerous.

"One day Alberto came to the house in the middle of the day, extremely excited. He had rented this old empty building a block away and had set up his own repair shop. He wanted to surprise his family, our mom and me in particular. His friends and some cousins and uncles in Monterrey donated old equipment to help him start up the place. He was twenty-two. He was so proud. He never took a day off from work. He wanted me there some, but he made me stay in school and help our mom with chores and fixing up the house. So I would work with him after school, but by six o'clock he made me go home. He told me, 'Daniel, after you graduate school, you'll be my partner and you'll help me expand so we have repair shops all over Monterrey. I'll need someone smart for a partner. I didn't stay in school, and I don't even read so well.'

"But in less than a year, these cartel guys started threatening Alberto to pay piso. They called it insurance to protect his business from other cartels. It was insurance to protect Alberto even from them, truly. He didn't make enough profit to give them what they demanded. He got very scared at some point because they told him that they would hurt his family if he didn't do better. One night he told me about these things. We knew it was the Zetas because they had come to Monterrey, and that's what they want: piso. He wanted me to know, in case they came. He told me that all the businessmen in the neighborhood had decided to refuse to pay piso. He stopped paying.

"One night in bed as I was waiting for him to come home, I heard people shouting in the street. I ran outside and saw a big fire down the block. I knew it was Alberto's place, and I ran there. It was a huge blaze, and some people said that some guys just drove up and, without saying a word, they poured big cans of gasoline in the door and all around the walls of the building. Two guys ran inside and got Alberto. They did this very fast and put him in a truck, and all of them got in their cars and trucks and drove off. They lit the gasoline before leaving. They did this, of course, as a warning to the other businessmen what would happen if they didn't meet the demands of the cartel.

"So now it is a year later, and my family knows nothing about where Alberto is, whether he's dead or living. Of course, the police investigations turn up nothing, and after a while the police stop talking to you. They're paid by the cartel, or they're afraid. This is the worst terror and pain. This is worse than if they just had killed him. Now always we're stuck with this splinter of hope that somehow Alberto is alive and we just need to find him and rescue him. Every day goes by, and the hope gets a little dimmer. Then one day you hear a story of someone who is miraculously found, and you have the hope again. It is horrible. My mom, she's a skeleton of sorrow and bitterness because of what happened to my brother. She goes to vigils; she puts out flyers with Alberto's picture; and she asks everyone, 'Have you seen my boy?'

Daniel had stopped speaking. He continued to stare off, living memories, when, to Enrique's surprise, Corvette broke his silence and asked Daniel quietly, "And what are you doing, amigo?" But he had picked up a few words of Spanish, and Corvette asked Daniel this saying, "Y qué haces, amigo?"

It surprised Daniel too, and this snapped him out of his daydreaming. He turned and looked directly at Corvette, and he answered, "I put on the black clothes of the Zs. You can't trust anyone else. I follow the Z Rules of Life. I train and discipline myself so I can work with my brother and sister Zs who patrol our neighborhood. I repair cars. None of us who do business or work pay any piso to anyone. The cartels don't bother us since the Zs come to watch over our people."

Enrique saw the slight nodding Corvette gave to Daniel. It wasn't just a nod of approval or understanding, Enrique thought, because he clearly saw grief drawn across Corvette's face. There was some commonality which Corvette felt with Daniel, a loss still undisclosed.

Later, Corvette had asked Enrique if he would show him some of the Zs doing their physical training. They went to the urban street set where some of the young men and women were in pairs running up the steps to the roofs of the shell buildings and then leaping from one building to the other.

"They always work in pairs in the real world," Enrique had explained. "Here they put their stamina and jumping skills to the test. In the cities the Zs might find themselves in situations where they have to advance quickly on someone who's going to fire an AK-47 on people, or they might have to get away quickly from someone who pursues them with firearms. The training for the Zs is to disarm someone with a weapon in a way that incapacitates him. The incapacitation is important because the aggressors must have no second chance to use their weapons. The cartels often shoot and kill indiscriminately. To them, life has no value."

"Are the Zs taught to kill?" Corvette had asked.

"If necessary, yes. The philosophy behind the training is similar to that of Krav Maga. Because of the superiority of the enemy due to their weapons, the Z must use a defense that employs maximum disabling. Killing should be avoided if possible, but if killing is necessary to save lives, this has to be in the skillset of the Zs."

"Why don't the Zs use weapons?"

"The whole purpose of the Zs is to stop bloodshed, Corvette. The Zs were born out of the 'No Mas Sangre' movement in Mexico. No more blood. There were powerful protests against the government and the cartels throughout all Mexico before the military coup. Everyone wanted an end to the violence that completely destroyed public safety in the cities. Blood literally ran in pools through the streets, and the children of Mexico were seeing it daily as they went to school. Too many sons and daughters were lost. The protestors grew in strength and united. They were an alliance of peace movements, victims' rights advocates, human rights organizations, and groups demanding an end to corruption in government and police forces. Ana became a celebrity of causes in those days, although she never intended to be that. But through her writing and tireless public speaking at mass demonstrations across Mexico, she became a strong populist leader. She was always against bloodshed. Her development of the Z Rules of Life fit perfectly with the type of quasi-military training that David and Eduardo Ortíz were planning for civilian units that would assist the Armed Forces in maintaining public safety in the cities. Everything in the history of the Zs - their formation and their rules for living - revolves around the laying down of arms. The objective of their vigilance is peace and security for their communities."

Corvette had grown silent a while as he visually surveyed the simulated city street and then gazed at some Zs who were working out on the equipment in the field.

Suddenly he had said, "I recently found out from my mum that my father may have been involved with the Mexican cartels. He might have been forced to launder money for them through the operations of the resorts that he managed. His last job was in Barbados. One night, when I was eighteen, he strangely went out for a motorcycle ride at three in the morning and was killed when his bike went off the road. I always thought it was a freak accident, but my mum just told me that she has been making payments for my father's gambling debts to a trust. Some attorney contacted her just after the accident, and she thought he represented people who might have murdered my dad by forcing him off the road. When Daniel was talking earlier, I thought how bad it was to be one of the disappeared persons that people talk about in Mexico. It is also awful when you're not even sure if your loved one was murdered or not. I grew up believing there was an answer in justice for everything, but now I'm starting to see that there's not."

Corvette's revelation had caught Enrique completely off guard and had astonished him. But before he could gather words for a response, Corvette quickly said, "Could you take me for a little run?"

They had warmed up with some stretches, and then Enrique had lead him on a jog of several laps in the street, weaving around the vehicles parked there. Corvette pointed to a building on the end and said, "Let me try running up." Enrique had sprinted up the four-story staircase inside the empty edifice to the roof. Corvette had managed to keep up, but he was huffing.

"Stay here. Don't try this until I come back for you," Enrique told him. He then took a running leap across the divide of buildings to the next rooftop. Corvette walked over to the edge of his roof and looked down.

"I don't think I'm ready for this," he shouted with a nervous laugh.

But he had tried other types of land-based running and jumping later on the fields, and this had made a favorable impression on Enrique. Corvette wasn't in shape, but he had a strong build and could make a good athlete if he wanted.

Now, as he was finally about to drift to sleep, he had a final thought regarding Corvette: *Maybe the guy isn't quite the spoiled rich kid that I imagined. He seems curious about things outside his world.*

Corvette had decided to spend his second night in Monterrey at David's house. Enrique had wondered if Corvette would be opening up more to David. He sleepily looked across his dark bedroom to a digital clock on a set of drawers. It said twelve thirty-seven a.m. Then he allowed himself to shut off his mind and fall deliciously into the deep after a long mentally, physically, and emotionally demanding day.

Somewhere in the void music began to play a familiar tune. Enrique just wanted to ignore it, but it kept playing. A dim auditory recognition came to him. It was his cell phone, and his hand reached automatically to the night stand beside his bed and fished in the darkness. He saw the light glow of the caller id. It said, "Unknown." His hand pressed a button and brought the phone to his ear.

"Enrique!"

"Hmmm," Enrique groaned.

"Enrique!" the voice said again. It was the insistent voice of a shout made at below-normal volume.

"Bueno," Enrique managed to say.

"Enrique, soy yo, Ignacio!"

"Who?"

"Soy yo, Ignacio Lopez," said the voice, a loud whisper. "The man who managed the funds for The Z Foundation."

Enrique shot upright in his bed. He suddenly recognized Ignacio's voice, and the shock threw him into coughs. He cleared his throat.

"Ignacio, por Dios!" Enrique whispered in an unintended mimicry of Ignacio's tone. Vives! You're alive!"

"Sí, I'm alive, Enrique, for now. We have to speak quickly. I may have to get off at any moment. I'm calling with a stolen phone. I want to know if my mom and sister are okay first."

Enrique looked at the clock. It read one forty-six a.m. He answered, "Yes, Ignacio, they're fine. I know that they are because we have Zs at their house day and night. When you disappeared, the police produced a suicide note and told them that you had gone somewhere to kill yourself. Your mother and sister never believed that, Ignacio. They knew you would never do such a thing. Your mom got in touch with me. She knew about Lili, and then when you disappeared, she asked me if Zs could guard them for a while. She doesn't trust the police. So I have had Zs there with them all the time."

"Gracias, muchas gracias, Enrique," Ignacio said with heartfelt emotion. "I just figured out about Lili. I didn't have the memory of them telling me that she died in an automobile accident until just a couple of weeks ago. They've given me too many drugs and have beat my head with pistols. I thought that Lili was alive and was with me. I would see her and talk to her. I have horrible headaches that started with the beatings."

"Quick, Ignacio," Enrique interrupted. "Before you tell me anything else, tell me where you are in case something happens that we get cut off."

"For now I'll only tell you that I'm somewhere in Las Vegas," Ignacio responded. "I'm a dead man, Enrique. I'm working for Z-30. I'm building information systems for his money laundering operations through the casinos. This is why they took me: to do this."

"Please, tell me where you are! We can rescue you, Ignacio, we can take care of this! With David's contacts we can do anything in the United States to get you out of there."

"No. Listen to me! You can't save me! If you try, if they know I've contacted you, they'll kill my mother and sister. That's my greatest fear."

"Are you taking a risk calling me now, Ignacio? Can they trace the call? What can I do to help you?" Enrique asked. He felt desperate. He tried to think what questions he should ask to get as much information from Ignacio before something went wrong with the call.

"I got a stolen phone that they overlooked," Ignacio responded "They bring in stolen items all the time. I tried for the last couple of weeks to remember your number, but, I don't know, I think my head just cleared up enough for me to recall your number. I was dialing it incorrectly before, and it was driving me crazy not to remember it until the last couple of days. There are only two guys sleeping in this house tonight, which is unusual, because the other men have been out on a big mission. So I'm taking a chance on the call while I have opportunity."

He said "house," Enrique observed. *That's a clue about where he is.*

"Is Z-30 alive?" Enrique broke in as Ignacio drew a breath. "Does he have Valentina Garza?"

"Yes, he's alive," Ignacio answered, seemingly surprised by the question. "I hear the men talking to him on the phone. I don't know who Valentina Garza is."

Enrique's heart dropped. *What?*

Ignacio started speaking again, obviously in a hurry and with a sense of urgency. "Listen, Enrique, the Zeta had Lili killed. I'm going to destroy him for this. I know how to do it, but I'll need your help. I also can get the money back for The Z Foundation. I need you to give me the banking information for it. I'll expose the money laundering through the casinos, so I need for you to tell David James how it's done and what to look into. I've copied the data base for the transactions of the laundering. I entered much of the data for it personally the past weeks, information that comes from the streets in the form of ledger books and scraps of paper. The data base can't be found because I put it on a site in the Deep Web."

What the hell is the Deep Web? Enrique thought.

Ignacio paused a couple of moments to let his words sink in. Enrique didn't get the opportunity to ask his question aloud because Ignacio began speaking in a rush.

"Ok, pay attention, Enrique, because I'm going to have to get off the phone soon. The cash from illegal operations is given to guys on the cartel payroll to gamble in the casinos that the cartel has under control. These guys are the losers. They lose the cash to the casino. They're hard to track because they're not used in a single casino more than a couple of times. They go to casinos in other areas where they do the same thing. This happens at the gaming tables because there the cartel has men in collusion. In the casino the money is laundered. The money from the cartel losers goes out of the casino to the cartel winners. These are guys who are experts at the games: poker, backgammon, whatever. They win the cash back for the cartel.

It's rigged to make sure they win, of course, but the cartel wants experts with a track record of winning in case anyone looks into an individual winner. The winning and losing percentages of the cartel-controlled casinos are monitored to be in line with ranges examined by the gambling authorities in Nevada and in any other state where the Zetas are doing this, so nothing appears unusual. The casinos report the winnings and withhold taxes. This reporting is how the cash is laundered. The payment of taxes is just regarded as a business cost of laundering. The winners are investors in various cartel trusts and private banks. These invest in expansion of cartel operations: businesses such as commercial building companies, car dealerships, jewelry stores, more casinos, arms manufacturers...any type of business that supports other profitable activities of the cartel, like drug sales and human trafficking. I've copied much of this information in data base files stored on a cloud server in the Deep Web, and I've done this without the cartel's knowledge of the copies. So far. I can provide passwords for opening them. I've successfully hidden my work of copying from the cartel by trying to defeat keystroke monitors and spyware, but eventually they'll detect what I'm doing. That's when I'm dead."

Ignacio paused again.

Holy shit, Enrique thought. *Think quickly. What do I need to ask him before he cuts the call?*

"Ignacio, I follow you. What is the Deep Web? What do you need me to do?"

"Bueno, research the Deep Web. It is where criminal activity can safely hide. No time to explain now. I need you to get David and the United States authorities to arrange asylum for my mom and sister and get them out of Monterrey to somewhere safe and secret in the United States. I don't know or care what the politics are. That just has to be done right away, and you may need to convince my mother and sister to go. This has to be done now, Enrique. My days are numbered. I don't know how long I can be undiscovered in what I'm doing. There are cartel computer experts who do security checks on guys like me. I've fooled the Zeta into thinking I'm loyal to him, that I've been beaten into some sort of conversion to the excitement of cartel life. He isn't a man easy to fool, and I'm not naïve enough to believe I can do this long. I've seen him kill people in cold blood. It wouldn't surprise me if he killed Lili personally. When I was delusional about her, believing that she was alive and with me, he played along as if I were really seeing her. Now he tells me that she has projects elsewhere, and he believes I don't care because they bring beautiful women to me."

"Dios, Ignacio, I'm so worried about you!" Enrique exclaimed. "Amigo, please, maybe there's a way we can get you out and get you protection too."

"No, no, no, don't take any chances on my mother's and sister's lives! I won't permit this! Do what I have asked, or all of this is off."

"Okay, Ignacio, relax! I promise that I'll cooperate completely with your wishes. But we want the Zeta. Will you be able to tell us where he is? Is there a key to predicting him?"

"I don't know where he is now. He shows up to see me randomly. The key to understanding him is this: He always does exactly what he says he'll do. I have seen others misjudge him and think that they can influence his decisions or change his mind, and that has been their fatal mistake. He just listens a lot and assesses people. He lets them believe what they want to believe."

Ignacio drew a breath. "I have to go."

"Quick, one last thing. Did you hear about missing money after a gunfight in The Oasis this past Saturday morning and a missing ledger book?"

He answered with rapid sentences. "Yes, the Zetas are all out looking for the money and the book. That book is similar to others I receive. It could be one that details the collections behind the missing money, the calculations of the piso in a particular territory, and the people behind it. It might support the amount of the cash that's missing. Some ledgers are payroll ledgers that identify politicians, judges, and law officers who are accepting bribes. Once the information is entered into the computer, the book would be destroyed. Now more and more of the collections are entered into computer tablets at the source of collection, so the paper back-ups are not necessary. This was my work: to engineer this change. I've designed shortcuts for the tablets that greatly reduce the number of keystrokes and typing. The tablets are restricted and permanently assigned to a limited number of trained users. They're responsible for the destruction of the tablet if anything goes wrong. The information system I designed recognizes the tablet. The information entered goes to a data base on a cloud server owned by the cartel and can't be accessed again except by certain individuals who are informed about ever-changing passwords. The information is only there for a couple of days for administrative review. They unlock the passwords by inputting a number series generated randomly at time intervals by the computer. If they don't enter the correct number within just a few minutes of its generation, they can't obtain a password. There are also security questions that need to be answered by that individual. I maintain that cloud server. That's how I secretly have made copies of the data base. The original data files pass through a browser that can access the Deep Web and are stored in an undiscoverable site there."

Ignacio stopped his rapid-fire explanation suddenly. "I've been talking too long. I really have to go."

"Okay. Two things, quickly: Did you hear who received the missing money? How do I get back to you with banking information and what can be done to protect your mom and sister?"

"I know nothing about anyone receiving the money. As for my mom and sister, I'll call you back. I don't know when. It could be a day. It could be a week. So, please, just get this done fast. I know you, and you're the person I trust the most in the world. I know David and trust him also, and I know that he has connections to make things happen in the United States. So talk to him, get things moving, and answer all your phone calls in case it is me."

Ignacio disconnected.

Enrique continued to lie in his bed in the darkness. He wanted to let himself settle and to be certain that he hadn't dreamed the phone call.

It was too rich in sensible detail to be a dream, he thought.

He heard the passing of an occasional truck outside on La Avenida Pedro Infante. This would be the only time of light traffic on that street. He heard distant dogs barking, a sound always heard in Mexico. He knew that he was coherent.

That was when the troubling thought came back to him: *What does it mean if Ignacio doesn't know anything about Valentina but knows so much about the missing money and ledger? Is she important to Z-30 or not?*

He felt tears in his eyes. He realized that Valentina was like family to him. She was Ana's niece and very much like her, and his love for Ana had become like love for a close older sister. He had been afraid for Valentina, but now he was even more so.

In the dark room he imagined a time bomb ticking away the seconds. He jumped up and found pen and paper to write down the information that Ignacio had provided him, in case he would forget something later. He didn't trust his memory after being awakened from a dream state.

Then he pushed the speed dial on his phone to ring David.

Chapter 14: Descent

Valentina Garza
Leaving Monterrey, Mexico
Late Sunday Afternoon to Post Midnight Monday Morning

To her surprise, the three SUVs that had intercepted her and had taken her from the taxi drove to the free highway that led to Nuevo Laredo. They were leaving Monterrey. Valentina had assumed that Raúl was in Monterrey, and now she was learning that she was wrong. The driver chose the free highway over the toll autopista probably to avoid Federal Police or Army patrols. Those frequented the toll road often to provide more of a feeling of security to the drivers passing from Monterrey to the dangerous border city of Nuevo Laredo controlled by the Zetas. That city was a short throw over the International Bridge to Laredo, Texas. Just before they turned onto the free highway, they pulled over for a couple of minutes while the vehicle behind them passed and went down the road. In a while the radio carried by the man in the front passenger seat crackled an all-clear.

Three blinded SUVs caravanning along the highway to the border looks suspicious, Valentina thought. *Even though this road is usually covered by the drug cartels, these guys are not taking any chances.*

They wound through the steep green and brown mountains north of Monterrey, but before they arrived at Nuevo Laredo, they turned left onto a narrow two-lane highway that passed through the scruffy semi-desert flatlands to the northwest. After about a half hour they arrived at a small cinderblock house on land that had wire fences, apparently to keep in cattle and horses. The first vehicle was already there and was empty. They waited in their SUV. When the third one arrived behind them, men driving the first vehicle came out of the house carrying a brown leather duffle bag, and they boarded their SUV. Then all three vehicles started off again.

213

There was little conversation among the men with her. That was the norm for the entire trip, which turned out to be much longer than she had expected. When she had first climbed into her seat, she had asked, "Are you taking me to see Raúl?" The two up front had looked at each other, and neither answered for a couple of moments. Finally, the driver had responded, "You'll see soon enough." This led Valentina to consider the possibility that the men were taking her to meet someone else. She decided to remain quiet.

The man in the front passenger seat intermittently kept checking his phone and typing messages. Occasionally, he received brief radio transmissions from the lead vehicle about "all clears." Valentina heard him being called Lorenzo.

The ride was becoming long and monotonous, except for two interesting exchanges of conversation that the men made in English. *Poor English*, Valentina thought when she heard it.

She believed that the first exchange had been a test to verify that she didn't understand the language, because the man seated beside her had stared at her to watch her reaction while the others spoke. The topic was Corvette. Lorenzo had looked up from reading a message on his phone. He made a couple of comments about the Monterrey fútbol team, Los Tigres, and he discussed the potential of several Mexican players. Then he said to the driver, "You know, there's a Mexican in the World Series of Poker this year, some guy named Corvette Nightfire. If he wins, the asshole will leave the table with eight million dollars."

"Shit!" responded the driver. "Verdad? Mexicano? That sounds like a gringo name."

"He's half Mexican," Lorenzo clarified. "Just a gringo kid. He has twenty-seven years. The son of puta plays games for this kind of money while we scrap and lose the life."

"I'll play the gringo," the driver said. "I'll call myself Ferrari. I should play El Corvette after he wins and has lots of money. The odds will be in my favor." He patted something beside him which Valentina took to be his gun.

They laughed. Valentina turned to gaze out her window as if not understanding them and not caring. But she had caught the stare of the man beside her. When Corvette's name had been pronounced, it sounded like "Corfet" with the accent on the first syllable. Lorenzo had said his last name in the sing-song Mexican way that drew out the word "fire" as if it were a lyric in a corrido. They made a couple of other remarks about Corvette and then resumed silence.

Inwardly, she was stunned. *Corvette can win that kind of money?* The fact that they had brought him up in conversation made her think that, indeed, they were taking her to see Raúl.

The Zeta's interest in Corvette isn't a benign one, she contemplated with apprehension.

The second exchange of conversation in English came a few minutes later. Valentina thought that she must have passed the test of not understanding the language because after Lorenzo received a message on his phone, he spoke to the driver in English again.

"Our man won't be at the check point to let us pass to the U.S. side tonight. The gringos gave him a last-minute shift change. That's too bad. We have passports. Even the señorita does. It would have looked fine on the cameras. If we attempt it now, we could get a car check for the bags."

"Fuck!" said the driver. "Then we'll be taking the long way. We're going under the ground."

"Sí."

"I hate that. I presume we're going to the special one? I don't trust those things. I get weird in small places. What do you call that in English?"

"Clausofobeec," Lorenzo answered.

"Sí, eso."

"You can relax," Lorenzo assured him. "I hear it is well built. They started it on the gringo side."

"It goes to the middle of nowhere, right?

Lorenzo chuckled. "Believe me, it goes to a safe place, the finest money can buy."

The driver didn't comment on that, but Valentina puzzled over what he meant.

"What about her?" asked the driver. "Should we blindfold her? She might notice."

"We don't have to worry about her. Those are the instructions."

That was all that was said, but it gave Valentina all the information that she needed to understand where they were taking her. She was totally surprised. She was going back to the United States! She wished so much that she had her phone for any opportunity to get out a message regarding her situation and where she was headed, but, of course, Lorenzo had taken it.

At least I'll get to see one of the famous drug tunnels, she thought. She had always wanted to see one firsthand. The thought of passing through one with cartel men, however, now unsettled her a little. It felt dangerous. She wondered where it was.

Surely not even the narcos would attempt building a tunnel under The Rio Grande River!

They continued country roads to the northwest until, finally, Valentina recognized an intersection with Rte. 1 to Anáhuac, the small Mexican city of streets in concentric circles around its central zone. But just before coming to Anáhuac, the three vehicles turned left on Rio Salado, Highway 23, and headed to the wilderness again. After about twenty kilometers, Valentina estimated, they turned onto a dirt road which led to an open field.

There sat a twin-engine plane.

A half-hour later, it was becoming dark when they took off. Lorenzo and the car's driver had boarded the plane, along with Valentina and the pilot, who had been awaiting them in the field. The guy who had been in the back of the SUV with Valentina had remained behind. So also had the men in the other two vehicles. Valentina guessed that they had come to the field so that the men could provide protection, if necessary, while the plane took off. She had seen her bags and the brown duffle bag be loaded. It reminded her of the bag that she had passed to Corvette.

It contained cash, she remembered. *From now on I'll never be able to see bags like that without thinking about how much money they can hold.*

They had flown over mountains during the remaining rays of sunlight, but low to them, to the point where Valentina was nervous about hitting trees when there was a sudden change in terrain. The pilot, however, seemed to know the route well. Once they had passed these and were flying over desert, the pilot descended and hugged the nowhere land. After it had become dark, Valentina never felt the plane ascend to any large degree. There were occasional foothills, and the pilot kept close to the topography. She had seen by the position of the setting sun that they were flying northwest still. As more time passed, she calculated that their destination would be near the border of either New Mexico or Arizona beyond the reach of The Rio Grande River (which the Mexicans called Rio Bravo). She guessed that they would land near the border in the state of Chihuahua, perhaps near Puerto Palomas and Colombus, New Mexico.

But she was a little off. Nearly three hours later, they landed in the desert in what would have been complete darkness except for the flicker of a light from the ground and the headlight of the plane which came on as it approached a cleared area. The pilot had never radioed anyone. He had studied his coordinates and seemed to know landmarks. In the last half hour, Valentina had only been able to see the red lights on an occasional phone or radio tower and some mounds in the distance which were faintly darker than the blackness of the land. Those were hills or mountains. The pilot must have been astutely aware of other markings in the pitch blackness of the country.

She thought about what Lorenzo had said earlier: "Our man won't be at the checkpoint."

That suggests that the men chose an alternate destination from the one planned. Out here in the wilderness we must be landing near a small place, which rules out Ciudad Juarez and El Paso, Texas, across the border, Valentina reasoned. *With their millions of people, I would have seen lights everywhere, and I saw none of that. So the next crossing from Mexico would be Las Palomas going to Colombus, New Mexico, in the United States. Under ten thousand people in those two cities combined, but, still, I would have noticed lots of ground lights and traffic. They make the trucks from Mexico hauling freight stop on the U.S. side and unload the cargo onto American trucks. Didn't see a busy highway. So, we're not landing near Las Palomas either. We're in the middle of nowhere, but these guys certainly aren't going to risk trying to fly the plane over the border even if there's no fence in these parts.*

She concentrated.

There's a small check point almost forgotten in New Mexico. What is the name of that? Maybe four cars a day crossing the border, no commercial vehicles, and open only until four in the afternoon...

She remembered hearing once Customs and Border Protection officers talking about it.

They said that it was where Highway 81 went to the border and that on the Mexican side, the road wasn't even paved! They said there was little more than a blue and white concrete shack there for Mexican customs.

Then she remembered the name for the Point of Entry on the United States' side:

Antelope Wells, New Mexico. I think we're near that place! If that's the case, then Highway 81 traffic north would be mostly CBP patrols. Interesting! But in the United States, these guys I'm with need a highway if we're going anywhere!

Just after the plane touched down, the pilot turned off the headlights. He brought the plane to a quick stop. They were met by a four-door Jeep which had approached them with only parking lights lit. Those seemed excruciatingly bright in the blackness of the desert. When those lights went out, Valentina needed a couple of moments to adjust to the darkness. The sky was moonless. Despite the uneasiness that she felt, the desert sky, full of seemingly a billion stars, stole Valentina's breath. For some reason, she thought of Corvette.

The men worked quietly and rapidly. The bags went into the back of the Jeep. The driver of the first vehicle in which Valentina had ridden got into the front passenger seat. Lorenzo opened the door of the back seat and motioned for her to climb inside. He took the seat next to her. The Jeep's driver got in. Valentina heard the plane start to taxi away from them, and then her new driver started to bump across the desert terrain with just parking lights on. Valentina heard the plane ascend behind them. No one said a word.

Valentina was on the verge of motion sickness from the uneven and jolting Jeep ride across desert land when, after about ten minutes, they pulled onto a dirt road. In comparison, the ride felt like that of a four-lane highway, so Valentina recovered most of her equilibrium. After about twenty minutes, the driver turned onto another dirt road, but this one was barely more than a dust path across the desert. Valentina was enduring this new jolting when finally the Jeep stopped.

She got out quickly with the others, and the cold air revived her almost immediately. She had a surprise. They had pulled up to a small cinderblock house that looked like it could contain no more than two rooms. It had a door and one shuttered window on the front. Lorenzo pulled the bags from the back of the Jeep, and then the driver guided them by flashlight inside the house. He stopped to open the door with a key.

"Welcome to my castle," he said with a sarcastic laugh.

Inside, he flipped a light switch by the door that powered a couple of lamps. Valentina saw that most of the square footage of the house had an open floor plan with a living area and small kitchen in the rear. There was one wall that had an open door revealing a tiny room barely big enough to contain a bed. In fact, Valentina saw that there was no bed. The light scattering into that dark room revealed a well-worn sleeping bag. Directly ahead was a bulky dining table that looked entirely too massive for the small square footage of the house. It seemed to serve as a separator for the kitchen. It sat atop a rectangular hemp rug. The man who had driven the Jeep walked to one end of the table and then looked at Lorenzo. Lorenzo went to the other end, and the two of them moved the table off the rug. Valentina and the other man had to step out of the way. Lorenzo reached down to move the rug.

Oh my God! Valentina realized suddenly. *This is the tunnel!*

With the rug out of the way, they all stood looking at a square wooden door set inside the concrete slab of the floor. Lorenzo reached for a latch-hold set in the door. He lifted the wooden piece up, and he and the other man moved it backwards to the kitchen area. Then, getting on his knees, Lorenzo felt with his arm inside the rectangular opening in the floor and found a switch to a light which illuminated the descent of a metal rung ladder. The walls on the way down were cinderblock and formed a square made of sides about three feet across.

Why are they letting me see this? Valentina worried.

"Vámonos," Lorenzo commanded, and he began to climb down the steps. He got far enough down where he paused, waiting to receive Valentina's bags and the leather duffle, which apparently was heavy. Each of the other two men handed these to him, and Lorenzo brought them to the floor below. Then they indicated to Valentina that she should go down.

She got on her knees and backed into the opening. Once she found the steps, she estimated that she descended about twelve feet to the floor. At the bottom ran electric cables that powered light bulbs spaced through the tunnel. The floor, walls, and ceiling were packed dirt with regularly spaced wooden beams and occasional wooden panels that ostensibly helped to prevent cave-ins. There was a small clearing room to the side where sat a large generator that powered the lights and ventilation system. There were three small wheelbarrows

220

beside the generator. It was very cold. Valentina looked to the floor. She expected to see rails for rolling flat-beds to carry heavy packs of marijuana, meth, or cocaine, but this tunnel had no rails.

No rails?

Then she spotted the brown duffel bag on the floor on the side, and she made some guesses:

This is intended to be an occasional-use tunnel for moving cash, small groups of people, low-volume drug loads, and maybe rifles, pistols, grenades, and other small weapons. It could even be used to bring hostages across the border...God, like me!

The man who had driven Lorenzo and Valentina from Monterrey now descended the ladder. When he got to the bottom, the man who had greeted them upstairs replaced the wooden door. This left the three of them alone at the bottom of the ladder. The one standing with Valentina and Lorenzo now looked sick. Valentina remember that he was claustrophobic. She decided to try to win his favor.

"So, I'm Valentina and I know this is Lorenzo. What is your name?" she asked boldly in Spanish.

"Marcus," he answered. He looked like he might throw up.

"Can we hurry and go to wherever this leads, Lorenzo and Marcus?" Valentina said. "I'm really scared in small places." She said this to win the sympathy of Marcus.

"Right. I'll lead," Lorenzo answered. He put Valentina's bags in a wheel barrow, but Marcus carried the leather duffle.

Valentina had to stoop slightly. Neither of the two men were taller than Valentina, so none of them were uncomfortable in the height of the tunnel. The light bulbs were spaced apart enough to cast adequate light in the areas where they walked, but their glow in the distance made them squint or shade their eyes to see clearly the dirt floor on which they trod. Ventilation was provided by cheap plastic room fans mounted along the walls. These protruded so that when they passed the fans, they had to move their heads to the side to keep from hitting them. It was a cold night in the desert, and Valentina wished the fans weren't on. She had dressed for a mild day in Monterrey, so she was wearing only long tan cotton pants and a rose-colored short-sleeve blouse. The men apparently hadn't expected a trek through a cold tunnel either.

When they finally saw ahead a well-lit open area in front of a steel rung ladder identical to the one they had descended, Valentina estimated that they had walked a distance of about four fútbol fields. This time Marcus, who was the sturdier built man of the two, went up the ladder and pushed hard on a wooden covering at the top. Valentina saw that everything on this end looked identical to the other, including the cinderblock reinforcing walls around the ladder to the exit. She looked up and again estimated that the floor of the tunnel was about twelve feet under the ground. She had noted on the walk that there was little zig or zag in the path from one end to the other.

A well-engineered tunnel, she thought. She felt the nagging doubt still: *Why are they not concerned about me seeing this?* She didn't like that. *They aren't worried because they know I won't be alive to tell about it?*

Marcus descended again and grabbed the brown duffle bag. Lorenzo motioned for Valentina to begin to climb up. He handed her large handbag to her and allowed her to sling it over her shoulder. Marcus had disappeared into the darkness above, but after some scuffling noises, a dim light flooded the upstairs. Valentina heard Lorenzo struggling with her heavy bag behind her. When she got to the top, she saw the interior of a modest, one-story house comfortably decorated and obviously for masculine tastes. She pulled herself out and stood. The front door was open, allowing a cold breeze to chill the house. Marcus was just outside conversing with a new man in the light-diagonal of the open door. Marcus noticed her and motioned for her to come. She turned first and tugged on the bag that Lorenzo was pushing up from the ladder and dragged it out of his way. Lorenzo climbed out.

"Gracias," he said.

Valentina hugged herself tightly against the cold and walked outside. She was going to ask if she could have a jacket from her bag, but Marcus took her arm immediately and began escorting her to a late model Ford four-door pickup truck parked a few yards away. The motor was running, and when she got into the back seat, it was warm inside. She looked back at the house. It was a ranch-style home as she had guessed inside.

Then her eyes went wide with astonishment. She stared into the darkness to be certain. Parked close to the side of the house was a Customs and Border Patrol Jeep!

They drove to the highway from the house on a dirt road cutting through the scruff desert. Deciding to be bolder in order to glean more information, Valentina leaned forward and tapped the driver's right shoulder.

"I'm Valentina," she announced to him.

The driver turned and looked at Marcus sitting beside him.

"She wants to know your name. She's polite," Marcus explained.

"Timoteo," the driver announced. "Most people call me Tim."

"Gracias," Valentina replied. "Guys, can you tell me where we're going yet? At least can you tell me if we have much longer on the trip? My body is hurting from so much sitting."

It was Lorenzo who answered. "We have about three hours in the Jeep. Then we arrive at an airport for a flight where the pilot actually files a flight plan."

The men laughed.

Then Timoteo said to Marcus, "There won't be a road check up here tonight. There's only one every now and then here, but I made sure that there wouldn't be one tonight. It's so freaking quiet and boring in these parts. Even the Mexicans don't want to come up here."

They laughed again.

Oh my God! Valentina realized. *The house on the U.S. side of the tunnel is owned by a border patrol agent.*

Marcus turned and looked back at Valentina. "Try to sleep if you can," Marcus suggested.

"Yeah, sure," Valentina said.

Marcus and Lorenzo apparently did just that, at least lightly, and so there was no conversation for most of the trip in the Jeep. Valentina felt exhausted, but her survival instinct kept her awake. She soon saw New Mexico highway signs. They were traveling north on Highway 81. From the time estimate that Lorenzo had given her, she became reasonably certain that their destination would be Tucson, Arizona, but they drove instead to a little airport in Benson, about thirty miles to the east of that city. They parked and went into a small hangar adjacent to one for a flight school and walked through it to the door on the other side that opened to the airfield. It was almost midnight, and when she stepped into the brisk night air of the field, not only was she cold, but she heard her stomach growling.

So did someone new standing in the shadows.

"I have some sandwiches for us on the plane," he said. His dark arm swept outward and pointed at a small jet. She couldn't make him out right away, but she recognized his voice. His shadowy form was big, and then he stepped into the light coming from the hangar doorway.

Valentina had planned what she would do if she met him again, but when she threw herself into his arms, it was as much the excitement of relief as it was her intended charade. The possibility that someone else had her had just been eliminated!

"Raúl!" she squealed with practiced delight. "You're alive! God, I have been so worried!"

He took advantage of the moment. He pulled her hard against him with one arm, as if she were a feather, and used his other to seize the nape of her neck and press her head to his. He kissed her full on the lips and held her, and she could neither turn her face nor move her body. She managed to open her hands to touch the sides of his stomach. She thought that this small display of affection, as much as it disgusted her, might be just the thing that would keep her alive. There would be many questions that would come later, she knew, and she would have to be convincing.

When the Zeta finally let her go, Marcus and Lorenzo had already boarded the jet. She didn't see her purse or the bags, so she assumed that they had loaded them.

"I still have lots of things to show you in Las Vegas, mi amor," Raúl told her. "The flight will only take an hour. I'm sure you must be as tired as walking death. You will love where I'm taking you in Vegas. You can soak in a Jacuzzi before bed if you like, and I'll let you sleep as late as you wish in the morning. Then we'll have lots to talk about at breakfast."

Chapter 15: The Price

Juan Ramirez
Monterrey, Mexico
Tuesday

By Tuesday morning Juan was worried. He had left the airport Sunday deciding to let Valentina sleep and rest. The next day he went to work at his cover job with Sabiduría Electrónica and was Monday-morning-busy. It wasn't until just before lunch that he phoned the events planning business where Valentina worked to ask to speak to her.

"She hasn't come in yet," answered a pleasant sounding woman who had identified herself as Marta. "Is there anything I can help you with?"

That was how she had put it, and so Juan had assumed that Valentina had been in touch with Marta and would be coming in later. He relaxed, went to lunch, went back to work, got busy again; and then, just before leaving work for the day, he phoned a second time.

This time the woman answering the phone was named Lila, and she reported that Valentina hadn't come in for the day.

"We were expecting her, but I'm sure she got tied up with errands or some other business. May I have her call you, or can I be of assistance?"

Juan noted the trace of anxiety in her voice despite her attempt to sound professional and casual about Valentina's non-appearance. He decided to push for a little more information.

"Oh, I'm surprised," he said. "I'm her cousin, and she told me yesterday that she would be coming to the office."

"What is your name, señor?"

"I'm Juan Ramirez."

"You must have her number. We have tried to reach her but have been unable to do so."

226

This caught Juan off guard. "Um...sí, I have her number, I suppose, in my contacts. I phoned here because she said she would be working." He thought that sounded like a weak explanation. In truth, he had called the office because he wanted to limit the number of phone calls directly to Valentina's line.

But immediately after disconnecting with Lila, he phoned Valentina's cellphone number. There was no answer.

She's missing. He knew this in his gut. He thought: *If the DEA had any change in plan for her today, I would have been notified.*

He leased a condominium in a high-rise in San Pedro, but instead of going home, he drove to the condominium tower where Valentina lived. The DEA had supplied him with a security card to allow access to the parking deck. He used it to go in, and he drove to the spot assigned to Valentina, where she had left her maroon Ford Explorer before her trip to Las Vegas. It was there. He pulled up close to the rear of her car and cruised slowly by. He could see the chalk mark he had made days earlier on her rear passenger-side tire. The car hadn't moved. He didn't need GPS records to know this.

He knew the building didn't have security cameras. There were a couple of security guards who used a large booth by the automated gate to the parking deck as an office, and one made rounds every couple of hours. They checked guests and delivery trucks in and out. That basically was the security for the complex. Juan knew that the guards had protocols for calling for assistance with public safety from Monterrey's new police force, the Civil Force, and from the Army if there was information or suspicion that members of drug cartels were arriving on the premises.

He found a guest parking space and then used the building steps on the side to ascend to the third floor, where Valentina lived. He knocked a couple of times and waited, but there was no answer.

Okay, he reasoned with himself, *let's say that Valentina came home by taxi from the airport Sunday and did a few things in the house and then slept late this morning. Even if she decided not to go to work, she would have phoned her staff. If she had decided to do errands, her car would have moved. If she were here, she would answer the door. If she were sleeping, my knocks or phone calls would have awakened her.*

Juan had to be a careful man. He was a DEA agent in a foreign country that only off-and-on officially recognized conducting joint missions with the DEA or any of the intelligence agencies of the United States. He had the same Mexican emergency contact person as Valentina in Monterrey: a commander in the Mexican Army who could make back-up support decisions for Juan should he find himself in trouble with the drug cartels. His name was Coronel (Colonel) Francisco Moreno. This colonel relayed communications and requests for information from Juan to his superiors in Mexico City, where the Mexican military intelligence operations was centralized in a department of the Secretariat of National Defense known as S-2. Those senior officers, in turn, communicated and planned operations with Juan's superiors in the DEA.

In Mexico, Juan did not ever carry his DEA identification, pistol, government-issued laptop, or phone with him. Those he kept in a self-storage unit not far from where he lived. On rare and urgent occasions he went there if he needed any of those items. On the way to Valentina's condo, he had been careful to drive around the area where she lived several times to be certain that no one was following him. So now he also took a circuitous route to his storage building. He checked his mirrors continuously before driving into the parking lot where his unit was. He parked in front of it, got out of his car, unlocked the upward-rolling door to his storage room, and went inside. His was in a row of units that were climate controlled, so Juan could cut on lights and work comfortably inside after closing the door.

He set up a small folding table in the center of the room. He powered up a Wi-Fi hotspot device obtained from a mobile phone carrier, and he started his laptop. He filed an encrypted report describing the facts of Valentina's "disappearance" to his DEA supervisor in the Los Angeles office. He then phoned Colonel Moreno and requested a reconnaissance to find Valentina.

"We have not been able to confirm that Z-30 is alive and back in Mexico," the colonel sighed upon hearing the news. "We have been in communication with the DEA in Las Vegas regarding identifying the bodies of the Mexicans killed there and the possibility that Z-30 isn't dead and has escaped. Do I have your permission to talk to that office about the disappearance of Señora Valentina Garza?"

"Yes, of course," Juan answered, but he knew full well that the colonel would do it with or without his permission.

Moreno continued, "There are people in Puebla who are making a lot of noise about bringing the Z-30's body to his hometown. Some persons or groups in that area seem to be inciting his supporters. We suspect that this is being done as a deception to make everyone believe the man is really dead. I have advised the DEA that there needs to be extra security around the facility that has the bodies in the United States. As you must know, in Mexico when cartel leaders are killed, their bodies are often stolen from the morgues or funeral homes, sometimes even during gun battles. If this is attempted in the United States, you can just imagine the impact that would have in a country already upset about cartel violence spreading there from Mexico. If the body alleged to be Z-30 gets stolen before DNA comparisons can be made with relatives of him in Puebla, the ensuing mystery and controversy over whether he's dead or alive will just confuse efforts to find him if he did, in fact, escape."

"Sí, well, I feel that someone has Valentina, Colonel," Juan answered. "I just met her and she made a good impression on me. I liked her and was looking forward to working with her."

"We'll do everything possible to try to find her," Colonel Moreno assured him.

On Tuesday evening as he left his office just after six p.m., they got him.

Sabiduría Electrónica leased a medium-sized modern office building in an office park amid the technology companies lining the highway to General Mariano Escobedo International Airport in Apodaca, a city within the metropolitan area of Monterrey. The industries and corporations there had not had to spend much money on security staffs as in certain other parts of Monterrey because there hadn't been much experience with the violence plaguing other parts of Mexico. Juan's Volvo sat parked in a lot that was for the most part unguarded except for occasional patrols by city police. Juan normally didn't have any apprehensions about walking to his vehicle before and after work, even in the darkness due to the short days of winter.

There were still plenty of vehicles left in the lot when Juan strolled toward his car. His kidnappers had hidden themselves low in the seats of their four-door extended-cab Ford pick-up truck. Juan was absorbed in his thoughts as he paused to find the key fob in his pants to unlock his car door. It was already nighttime. As he stood by his car, three men quickly got out of the truck parked next to his vehicle and accosted him. One pushed him up against the side of the car and put a pistol to his temple and pressed it so hard that Juan gasped a yelp of pain. The man grabbed his key fob from his hand.

"Not one more sound," he whispered threateningly in his ear.

Another man pulled off Juan's suit jacket and handed it to a third accomplice. He then put his hands in Juan's pants pockets and pulled everything out, and then the three men hustled Juan into the truck. Within thirty seconds they had accomplished the kidnapping and were leaving the parking lot. They rolled out to Federal Highway 85. Two men in the back seat subdued Juan by gagging and blindfolding him and binding his wrists as the driver aggressively plowed through the growing rush hour traffic. Juan cooperated, but one of the men struck Juan hard with his pistol and pushed him low in the seat as they began to exit the parking lot.

As it turned out, that was the first blow of his torture.

When his blindfold was removed in the frigid basement room, Juan saw its weird configuration and knew that he would never leave it alive. The tile floor sloped slightly to a central drain. Three connected industrial-sized steel basins lined one wall. The plumbing for those had spigots and hoses for washing, rinsing, and sanitizing large objects. A long rubber hose rolled up on a hanger on another wall connected to a dispenser for wash, rinse, and sanitize as well. He saw a couple of long-handled brushes and squeegees for cleaning the floor. Juan knew this was a room designed to facilitate removing large quantities of blood.

From his wooden chair near the center of the room, he also saw the metal table in a corner that had tools and weapons: hammers, long-knives, pistols, an axe, some rope, and a chain saw. Underneath the table were baseball bats and a can of lighter fluid.

In front of him a man sat at a folding table. He had a benign-looking face, which made Juan even more leery. The other men, about nine in all, stood behind the table. Juan could barely see them because of the glare of spotlights mounted on a high stand next to the table. On the other side of the table, a man operated a video camera supported by a tripod.

Juan had seen hundreds of Youtube videos released by drug cartels with similar scenarios. An interrogator at a table did almost all of the talking. The pleasant looking man was Juan's interrogator. Juan heard him addressed as "Santi" once. Santi asked questions, hundreds of questions, for what seemed like hours to Juan. Santi spoke calmly, but the men who took turns punching Juan or beating him with the baseball bats openly enjoyed their savagery as time went on. They weren't calm.

Santi showed Juan photographs that had been taken of him in the food court at the airport when he was talking to

Valentina. There had been only one time when Juan had allowed himself the luxury of looking at her in an amused fashion as she spoke to him, and that moment had been captured perfectly in a photograph that the man presented to Juan.

He asked Juan the same questions many times as he held up that photograph for him to see: "What was your business with this woman? Why were you at the airport?"

"She was a beautiful girl," Juan explained over and over. "I was flirting with her. I was trying to ask her for dinner. She kept telling me no, and I kept trying. Please! It's that simple. I was at the airport because I had taken a work colleague to catch a flight to Guadalajara and I was hungry!"

The explanation never satisfied the man at the table, and with a simple nod of his head, the men with the knives and the baseball bats and the powerful fists and the hard shoes that kicked resumed their jobs. Someone had removed the wooden chair that Juan had first sat on. He rolled in blood and spit and fingernails and broken teeth. He couldn't understand his own feeble words once his teeth were gone. Eventually he could only utter sounds. He tried to communicate to the man at the table with his thoughts:

She's a beautiful girl, and I liked her. You want me to say who she is or what she does. But I only tell you this about Valentina Garza: She's a gorgeous woman who intrigued me. I liked her. Don't you understand? I had no business with her. I just wanted to ask her to dinner.

"I'll ask you once more," the man at the table said. "Who are you? You look like a gringo. Why are you in Mexico? What was your business with the girl?" The man with the camera continued to record everything.

I told you. I'm Juan Johnson. I'm a technician for Sabiduría Electrónica. You have my wallet, my employee badge, my Mexican license to drive. My parents were Mexican citizens. My dad came to work in Monterrey when I was a little kid.

Santi kept on with the questions, as if he, Juan, were choosing to slur his words and cough blood deliberately, as if he could somehow answer those questions.

I'm going to die, thank God, Juan thought. He still had enough coherence to understand that even if they stopped at that moment, his altered body and his way of life would bear little resemblance to the Juan that had awakened on that sunny morning. And the pain...the pain was a monster that had clawed into his body. It would never leave him. The monster was already talking to him, suggesting that Juan try to live so that it would be able to feed on him in the awful days and years ahead.

My dying is what's going to convince them, he thought. *My death will give Valentina a chance. They heard nothing about the DEA from me.*

He heard the sound of the chain saw starting. Somehow he raised up enough to look through his swollen eyes at the man at the table. Santi had heard the chain saw also and had been distracted enough to look. Then he turned and gazed with curiosity at Juan, as if to evaluate Juan's reaction to the sound of it.

You didn't win, you fuck, Juan told the man. *I still wouldn't trade places with you. I became a Marine to help my country remain free. I joined the DEA to help keep young people free from drugs. I'm about saving lives, and you're about destroying them.*

Juan exerted all his effort through the pain to raise his head even higher from the floor. The man with the chain saw now straddled him. But Juan still held the attention of the man at the table.

I'm the winner, Juan told him with his eyes. *Be a man and come over here and acknowledge me. You know what you should do.*

The man at the table understood! Juan saw him raise his hand and signal the man over Juan to shut off the chain saw. The man cut the engine. Then the man at the table picked up a pistol, got up, and walked over to Juan.

"He has told us what he knows," he told the men in the room. Juan had collapsed to the floor and lay on his back. Somehow he could still see the man through the slits of his eyes. Santi bent over him and brought the pistol close to Juan's forehead.

"You just picked the wrong woman, hombre," he told Juan. "We're the Zetas, and you picked the woman of our leader."

Valentina is doing good work, then, thought Juan. *She has them fooled.*

He was going to be administered the coup de gracia, and he would feel no pain. Just before Santi pulled the trigger, Juan felt amused by a memory from the airport, and he sent a message to Valentina in his mind:

It's Johnson, Valentina - my last name. My real name is Juan Ramirez Johnson. Yes, you should laugh! It's funny!

Chapter 16: Seduction

Z-30
Las Vegas, Nevada
Monday morning, two a.m.

They were going to the luxurious home of the successful Mexican TV and film producer, Yandel Sandoval, Raúl told Valentina. In the car on the twenty-five-minute ride from the hangar in Las Vegas to the home, Raúl was surprised when Valentina fell asleep and slumped cozily against him in the back seat. She had him confused, upside down in his logic, and hard. She could be dangerous for him. Finally! A woman who might be clever enough to deceive him. This thrilled him. She presented him a puzzle with missing pieces. He would have so much delicious fun trying to find them.

Yandel wasn't in Las Vegas, but at the house there was a staff of three servants, one of whom was a cook. Raúl had met Yandel at a cartel-hosted party in Monterrey a year earlier when he was filming a telenovela in that city. The ruse that Yandel pretended to believe was that Raúl was a businessman who owned, among other things, a leasing service for private jets. Raúl had provided aircraft for Yandel because this provided respectability and prestige for Raúl's businesses. In return, Yandel did favors like lending the use of his homes in Las Vegas, Los Angeles, Acapulco, and Mexico City.

Raúl could almost let himself believe that Valentina was sincere in her excitement to see him alive. Her sleeping against him in the car seemed natural, as if she felt he was her protector and was taking care of her. She had told him in the jet to Las Vegas how scared she had been during the shootings the past Saturday and that she had fled in a panic to Monterrey. When the cars had intercepted her taxi, she just knew that he had come for her. She had a shine of admiration and gratitude in her eyes when she told him this.

Or she's an actress worthy of being in one of Yandel's films,
Raúl thought.

There were beefy men outside the mansion in the desert
country when they arrived: Raúl's bodyguards. Valentina roused
herself up, but she looked sleepy-drunk as she smiled at Raúl
and then accepted a female servant's bid to come to a drawn
bath. Valentina looked back. Raúl took it as an invitation to
follow. As he did, Lorenzo, who had driven the car to the house,
handed him a cell phone. It was Valentina's.

The woman showed Valentina to a huge bedroom on the
second floor. The Jacuzzi in the adjoining bathroom steamed
invitingly. Someone had placed oils and burning candles along
the tile steps enclosing the bath. Valentina walked into the
bathroom and grinned.

"Yummy," she whispered to Raúl.

Another servant, a young girl, brought Valentina's suitcase
into the bedroom, and then both the girl and the older one left.

"I'll leave you to enjoy your bath," Raúl said to Valentina.
"I'll sleep in a room downstairs. In the morning we'll have
breakfast together, whenever you feel like getting up."

He pulled the double doors together and stepped into the
bedroom. From inside the bathroom came the sound of a toilet
flushing. A few seconds later he heard sloshing water. He felt
Valentina's phone in his pocket and retrieved it. It had just a
little charge left. He verified that his men had disabled the GPS.
He tapped the icon for her contacts. He saw that Valentina had
hundreds of contacts in her phone. Some had pictures; some
had avatars; and some had no iconic representation other than
the universal silhouette of a man's head.

"Raúl, are you out there?" Valentina called in a soft voice
from the bathroom. Before he thought whether to answer, she
said, "Come in for a minute."

He opened the doors and stood in the doorway.

Valentina was reclining in the water against the rear of the
tub. The heat of the water made her look dreamy and flushed.
Soap bubbles covered the view of most of her body, but the

mounds of her breasts rose enough that Raúl could enjoy the fullness of her femininity. Her skin electrified him. He smelled scents of vanilla in the steam. Valentina was smiling sleepily as she admired the candles and the luxuriousness of the room. He followed the sweep of her gaze. He was dying to get into the Jacuzzi with her, but he knew he had to resolve things with her first. He would stick to his plan.

"I just wanted to thank you," Valentina told him in a voice barely larger than a whisper. "It's so elegant in this place. That trip to come here was awful. I'll sleep like I'm in a coma. Gracias, Raúl!"

"De nada, preciosa," he answered.

But then she laughed. "Couldn't you have just called to let me know you were okay, and maybe invite me back?"

That did amuse him. "I wasn't going to take any chances on your life. I wanted to find you and make sure you would be safe. We'll talk about these things in the morning."

She saw that he was holding her phone in his hand, but she gave him an unconcerned reaction. She stretched her arms behind her and sank lower into the water.

"Buenas noches," she said, and she shut her eyes playfully, as if she were already in a nap.

"Buenas noches," he replied. "Sleep well tonight."

So, is she a good actress, or does she genuinely not care that I have her telephone? he wondered. *Maybe she knows what it's like to be with me and wants me to see that she isn't bothered by changes in her life. Who knows? But I'll find out.*

He backed from the room and shut the doors again. In the bedroom he paused and once more studied Valentina's phone.

It's more interesting who's not in here than who is, he thought. *I see no listing for Ana Valdez, her aunt. No David James.*

He darkened the phone and dropped it into his pocket.

And what about the man who talked to her in the airport? Is he a contact in the phone?

He was fascinated.

They ate later Monday morning at a small breakfast table under awnings that shaded them from the desert sun on a patio outside the large master bedroom that Raúl had slept in during the night. Valentina wore a pastel-blue silk robe over pajamas that Raúl had seen her wear in the suite in The Oasis. It was late enough that the chill of the early morning had already given way to the promise of a warm day. He saw that the freshness of the morning air brought out the natural beauty of Valentina's light-bronze skin. She had applied no makeup, but she looked radiant. His body was dying to fuck her.

When they finished eating, Raúl poured Valentina some coffee from a new pot that the servant had brought to the table. She seemed relaxed, which was good. He wanted to begin his planned conversation in a casual, non-threatening way.

"Mi amor, we should talk about some things so that nothing comes between us."

"Certainly, Raúl," Valentina answered. She stirred some cream into her coffee. He watched her hands for signs of nervousness, but he didn't see any.

"I apologize for being so intrusive with your life. My work demands a high degree of security. I know that you saw me with your phone last night. My men who brought you here separated you from your bags and your phone, and you have been a very good sport about all this. Obviously we snuck you back into the United States. I appreciate your good attitude. By now you must know more about me and the work that I do than what I have told you."

"Of course I do, Raúl," Valentina answered with a direct stare into his eyes. "Well, I didn't know the night we first met, the night of the engagement party for the police chief's son when you asked me to dance and we chatted such a long time. I realized then that you're a successful man. I saw the contingent of men near you who tried to make themselves unseen, and I knew they were bodyguards. You told me that you owned a number of businesses. Raúl, we were at a party given by the police chief, por Dios! Everyone in México knows that there are cartel guests at parties given by police, politicians, and celebrities. And especially in Monterrey! Don't forget, I'm in the business of producing events and big parties. For my clients, safety and public security are my top concerns when it comes to occasions so important to them. I know about these things. I was at the engagement party because it was a very good event for me to make contacts."

"So you have done some research on me?"

"Sí, and I suppose that you haven't lied to me. You do own many businesses, I'm sure. In this world, Raúl, we use search engines of the internet even on our telephones, verdad? So I searched your name, sí. It is said that you're a top leader of the Zetas."

She looked hard at him, waiting to see if he would admit it.

He nodded. "I come from Puebla, the city of heroes. My nephew and I grew up together, closer than brothers. We were the same age and very poor. We loved the parades of Cinco de Mayo celebrating the Mexican victory over the French in Puebla. Especially we loved to see the Special Forces of the Army when they marched in those parades through the city. So my nephew and I joined the Special Forces when we were older. It was a way out for us, a way into the world. We both trained well, and we had skills. We had big dreams. Huge dreams! There was no way to accommodate those dreams in México except by the path we chose, hermosa."

She kept eye contact with him, and he saw in her eyes a disagreement coming.

"The path you have chosen is very scary to me, Raúl. I've spent the past weeks comparing in my mind the charming man whom I met with the horrible man described in stories. I have always dreamed big, and I've been working hard in México to make my dreams come true. Nothing has blocked me so far. I know I'm just beginning. But I've never thought about hurting people on my way to get what I want. That's difficult for me to understand! During the few times I've been with you, you've seemed different from what I expected from a leader of Zetas. Maybe you do a masquerade for me, I don't know yet. I've stumbled into you, and I'm a little afraid. But I thought that I could get to know you and see if you're really the person I met and liked. All this business of guns and kidnapping me and taking my things is pretty high drama, Raúl. I agreed to come on this trip with you because I wanted to see what this life is like..."

"And to see whether or not you could live it?" he interrupted. "But the trip hasn't gone well so far, right?"

She sighed. "People have died. I ran in a panic. I worried myself to death about you. That feeling surprised me. It told me that I really care about what happens to you. Sí, if I'm completely honest with you, Raúl, I think that I've always been attracted to a life of excitement and nice things in a not-so-healthy way. I'm afraid that I'll find myself thinking that I could go down the path with you a bit if I don't know too much about the bad things of your work. I'm worried that I could let myself be charmed by you into something way over my head because you act like a good and loving protector for me. I don't want to think that you kill people. I'm afraid that I'll look the other way and not think about the people who die, not think about their families."

He was surprised. *She's a good fucking actress or she's sincere,* he thought. *This sounds sincere. Either way, she's hot. Oh, I'll protect you, Chiquita.*

"México is at war, my angel, and, regretfully, people do die. I won't lie to you," he told her, "people have to pay the consequences for what they do to hurt our businesses, cariño. There's no justice in our country. You know this. All is corrupt. We have to make our own justice in a world where the laws are stupid and contrary to what people want. If enemies somehow go to jail, they run their operations from the jails. My business world is harsh, with no room for mistakes. My world has its own rules and ethics, and justice is simple, quick, and easy to understand. I can't suffer betrayals. I protect what is mine. I wouldn't want you to know all the things I have to do in a world such as this. A woman like you should live in a beautiful world, with normal cares. You should be loved and respected. When you're with me, you get the best things in life. When you're with me, no bad things can happen to you."

"I had to run, Raúl," she pointed out.

"I found you quickly, in another country, and brought you to be safe with me."

"Am I in danger?"

"We need to talk about that, angelito."

He allowed himself some moments to admire Valentina's face. She had the cheekbones of royalty, he thought. *Men would conquer cities for you, my love. Age will be slow to chip at your beauty. People will see you when you're in your sixties and still describe you as gorgeous.*

She reminded him of the current First Lady of Mexico. In the elections held after the military coup, the country had elected as president, Domingo Artemis, a billionaire businessman married to a popular and stunning opera singer named Crystal Ambia. Whenever leaders of foreign countries paid visits to Mexico, or whenever the President and the First Lady traveled abroad, the media reporters and the heads of state tripped over each other to talk to her. She never appeared in photographs upstaged by anyone else. Even her husband looked like an accessory to her. The Zeta thought that Crystal Ambia brought international respect and style to the Mexican Presidency. That's what the Zeta wanted: a partner with class and beauty, one who would provide a cloak of respectability over his life. Such a woman could distract people from their concerns about his businesses. A woman such as Valentina could make him a family and make their family life look normal.

That is, unless you're working with the enemy, my love, he thought.

"Anytime you're with me, you're in danger, verdad?" he began. "Look, just living in México is dangerous. Tell me, who's dangerous to you? The cartels who want to eliminate me? The police? The Army? Maybe even me. Are you afraid of me?"

"Yes, of course."

"There are things about you that you've not told me," he said.

"Things that you already know, correct? I'm sure that by now you know everything about me, Raúl." She picked up the coffee pot and filled his cup and then refreshed her own. "I have been nervous because of my relative. By now you know that Ana Valdez is my aunt. This raises questions about me in your mind."

Very good. Very good play.

"Sí, amor, she was Interim President of México and is at war with the cartels. She's married to David James, a gringo who once worked for the CIA and who has friends in high places both in the United States and México. I find out that they have been in Las Vegas when the pigs from Sinaloa attacked me and killed Horacio. Now the niece of Ana Valdez keeps time with me."

"You can have almost any woman you want, Raúl. You've had many, I'm sure. You picked me to spend some time with you, and neither of us knew much about the other when you did. What are you going to do, Raúl? Are you going to marry me, or are you going to fuck me and then kill me?"

"You fascinate me, and I want you. Talk to me. Tell me about this."

"My aunt is an incredible woman, a good woman. She cares about our country above all. I grew up without a mom, and Tía Ana was my role model. I spent my early teenage years helping her with events, and everything that I know about this business I learned from her. She got very busy with her causes and politics. She started traveling a great deal. I went to the university and got busy myself. Tía Ana and I fell out of touch. We've been able to greet each other on Facebook and some social media sites. I think I got a little hurt when she got busy. I felt like she was too busy for me. So I don't see her, Raúl. She married David, the gringo, as you put it. They live in the United States much of the time. Tía Ana has a new family, and I have my life with my business in Monterrey. That's pretty much how it is."

"Tía Ana isn't going to be too happy knowing whose company you're keeping."

"That is understatement!"

"Why would you risk giving up or upsetting your family? Women in México don't do this," he said.

"Oh, Raúl! There's a new breed of women in this country! Many of us have very independent minds. Just look at my aunt! And I make my own choices in life. No man helped me begin my business. I like to evaluate things in my own way and then decide what I'm going to do. I'll do this when considering how I'm to be with you, if you don't have me killed."

He chuckled inside. He saw how clever it was of her to deal with him straight on. She knew that he would never trust her, and she also knew that disclosing everything to him would keep her alive.

She pressed ahead. "I know you have to wonder if I'll betray you. How do we get past this?"

He sat back in his chair and gazed across the desert. After a while, he turned to her and answered, "Let's see if we can work together. There are some things you can help me with. Trust-building things. As we go along, we'll know. And you can let me know how I can help you."

"Okay," she answered. "What else do you need to talk to me about?"

"There's missing money. Somehow Corvette Nightfire got it."

"If that was what was in a green bag, then I'm the one who gave it to him."

"Why?"

"Luis pushed the bag through the door to me. It was heavy as hell. I heard the police coming. I just wanted to run. Out of nowhere, Corvette was there. I saw him and figured that if the bag was important, we could find him later. Why would he be there unless you asked him to be? I gave him the bag and told him to run in Spanish. It was pretty obvious what that meant. I knew he would take it and hold it until he heard from me."

243

"Why?"

"Because I could tell he liked me."

Okay, he thought. *Okay. Let's see if she'll let herself be used as bait. Part three of the test. Part two is about to begin.*

The Zeta stood up and walked to her. He caressed her cheek lightly with the back of his hand. She put his hand in hers and looked up at him with a question mark in her eyes.

"Well, I like you more," Raúl said.

He pulled back her chair and she rose. He kissed her softly, and then he took her hand and led her into the bedroom.

Valentina Garza
Late Monday Morning
The Bedroom

She could tell by the way he slowly undressed her and stared at her body that the Zeta wasn't going to be especially rough with her, but he had a sinister stare. His lust sickened her. It would be bad enough to be violated by this man, but she could tell that he had ideas that went beyond her worst fears. She would have to vacate her body.

He removed his own clothing slowly as well, as if this would excite her, and she tried her best to wear an expression of appreciation for his looks. He obviously lifted weights. His chiseled broad body showed unnatural looking vascularity in his arms and legs. His body appeared as if it had been chipped from granite and stained brown. She could envision bullets bouncing off it. The veins even ran across his abdomen like a 3-D road map of Puebla, his home city. She thought he looked grotesque.

He had kept open the curtains while he undressed both of them so that they would see each other. When they were naked, he left her to draw the fabrics across the sliding doors. This cut the light to near-darkness in the room. When he walked, the floor thumped from the heaviness of his body.

He returned and enveloped her in a strong hug. She thought that if he really applied pressure that he would snap bones. He pushed her to the bed with his chest and then flipped her over, putting her stomach down. He set his massive body on top of her and covered her, circling his arms underneath her to put his hands on her breasts. He had her arms locked to her side. He entered her from the rear and it hurt. He moved slowly while talking in her ear, telling her that she needed protection and that from now on she was his and that he would take care of her. His breath was sour, and she was afraid she would gag. She decided to go to Corvette.

She knew that Corvette would be tender and that he adored her. He would whisper in her ear to look at herself with his eyes. When she would do as he asked, she wouldn't be able to believe that such a beautiful woman existed and that it was she. When he held her and put himself inside her, her arms would be free, and she would reach back and let her fingers run through his long hair.

The Zeta raised her and hoisted her to his shoulders. She faced looking behind him and had to hold onto his head for balance. He spun around in circles until she almost felt sick from dizziness, and then he tossed her back on the bed and fell on her. He covered her completely with his body and began to do unspeakable things. But she was far away, dancing with Corvette and showing him Mexico. He talked to her non-stop in English while she cried with joy to be in his arms. When they were done, she sang to Corvette in Spanish a soft song of freedom.

Z-30
Late Monday Morning

He thought that he heard her humming at the end. When he was done with her, he looked at her and could tell even in the near darkness of the room that her eyes glistened with tears. She had a distant far-away look, as if she were thinking of someone else.

He guessed that it might be Corvette Nightfire. When he had come into the ballroom that evening while she and Corvette were dancing, she had ended the dance abruptly and had rushed up to him to take his arm. But already he had glimpsed in her eyes the interest that she had in the young man. Somehow, also, Corvette had been at The Oasis to receive the bag of cash. His men had confirmed to him that Luis pushed the bag to Valentina. The whole thing had been unplanned. Yet, Corvette was there.

Unexpected destinies...fascinating, he thought.

He walked naked to the drapes and drew a crack to let in a small amount of light. Valentina had already crawled under the sheet. She did look at him and managed a weak smile and said, "You have made me so sleepy, Raúl. Would you mind if I spent a little time here in the bed and nap? I still feel exhausted."

"Not at all, mi amor," he answered. "Sleep as long as you like. I'll be in the house today and will be here whenever you awake."

He dressed and headed to a well-air-conditioned solarium filled with plants on the opposite end of the house. He plopped himself on a comfortable white bamboo sofa amidst the mist and sweet smells of the flora. He pulled out his phone and was checking messages when a call came from Santi, the pleasant-looking man with the soothing voice who had visited Ignacio in his office the night they had taken Lili and had forced Ignacio to make the fund transfers. Since Horacio's death, Santi had been the man who had stepped in with efficiency to execute and coordinate the items on the Zeta's ever-changing action list. He had accomplished things for the Zeta even from Monterrey.

As he answered the phone, the Zeta thought:

All guts and ambition, this Santi. Qualities I can predict and therefore trust.

Santi came right to the point. "We found the man at the airport, the gringo who was talking to Valentina. We know

246

where he works: a tech company called Sabiduría Electrónica with offices near the airport. We sighted him from the description of his car by the kid at the airport who followed him out the door to the parking lot. We found his car in the Sabiduría lot. It's just five minutes from the airport. We're working on his identification now."

"I don't like gringos in Monterrey," the Zeta answered. "The ones in Monterrey are usually corporation guys or consultants, but every now and then we have the fuckin' DEA. Find out what you can, then bring him in for the questioning. If he's DEA, I want to know what business he had with Valentina. I want to know what business he had with her anyway. See if he has family here or any complications. I want him checked in but not checked out, if we can do that clean."

"Sí, jefe."

The Zeta felt the pang of familiarity. Santi had used that word in the way that Horacio used to do it.

"Do we know where Corvette Nightfire is?"

"We're working on that," Santi replied. "We're sending a couple of guys to Barbados."

"Find him. I don't want him roughed up. I have a job for him. He's supposed to be in the World Series of Poker next week, and the madre de puta disappeared with my cash. It isn't even as much as he could win, el estúpido. Get him here. I want him face-to-face. I want him at that fucking table."

"I got more good news for you. We have the missing ledger book."

"Eyyy, chinga! You found the Corvette?"

"Wasn't in the Corvette. El Lobo got it. Our man in Vegas. That dead DEA agent had it. El Lobo recognized him as DEA shit in the lobby just before the shooting began. He rushed the guy and grabbed him. Put his hands in his pants like he was going for his cock and grabbed the ledger out of it. Not sure when the Sinaloa pigs were planning to attack, but when El Lobo grabbed the man, that's when the fireworks began. El Lobo shot him

247

point blank in the chest. What the fuck, jefe, there was a party of people there! DEA, Sinaloa, Zs...what's going on?"

"They're all going to pay, Santi. Where's that book?"

"Can be delivered straight to you. El Lobo didn't really know what he had. He laid low with his hombres in his place Saturday and last night reported the book when he saw it was important."

The Zeta gave Santi delivery instructions, and then he said, "Take care of that gringo in Monterrey. Find out where Corvette Nightfire is. Then I want you here with me in Vegas."

"At your service, jefe."

Chapter 17: The Power of Name

Corvette Nightfire
Monterrey, Mexico
7 a.m. Thursday Morning

When he bit into the orange slice, it sprayed all over his face, so his skin tingled in the chill of the late October dawn in Monterrey. Corvette was standing in the driveway of David's home awaiting Enrique and was recovering from the surprise he and David had had at breakfast just minutes before. David was still talking on the phone when Corvette signaled to him that he was going outside to wait for Enrique. He grabbed the orange and took his coffee.

Enrique wheeled into the driveway precisely at seven a.m. as he had specified. Corvette jumped into the passenger seat of the Jeep before Enrique had even come to a complete stop. He was anxious to talk to his new friend. He noticed the circles under Enrique's eyes, but he was jacked up about what had happened at breakfast with David, so excitedly he greeted Enrique and launched right into it:

"God, Enrique, I was up there eating some eggs with David, and his cell phone rings, and I can hear a woman on the line saying, 'Mr. James? Can you hold for the President of the United States?' As if someone would say, 'No!' Enrique, how often do they talk?"

Enrique glanced at him with his tired face, but then a rare smile and a small laugh seemed to restore him. "Well, you're hyper this morning. How much coffee have you had? In fact, David talks to him only occasionally, usually when important things are happening. What was this call about?"

In moments they were on Paseo de Leones, on a route that would take them downtown. Corvette continuously steadied his beverage mug between his legs as Enrique expertly shifted lanes, weaving through the legendary Monterrey morning-rush traffic. He had the windows down and it was cold.

"They were talking about the shooting at The Oasis and what's happened since. The President told David that he might already know, but the DEA all of a sudden had lost three agents. Specifically, the death of Josh Bailin and the disappearance of two agents working in Monterrey: Valentina Garza and a man named Juan Ramirez Johnson."

A deep frown burrowed in Enrique's face. He made another sudden lane change. Corvette grabbed the side grip handle. Some coffee sloshed through the hole in Corvette's mug lid and splattered his pants.

"I don't know that last guy," Enrique said.

"Geez," Corvette exclaimed, reacting to the coffee. "Do you always drive like this? I'm gonna get car sick."

"You have to drive aggressively in Monterrey," Enrique said. "If you don't, it confuses the other drivers and accidents happen."

Corvette snorted amusedly. "Okay. Well, David did seem to know of the agent named Juan, and apparently he was going to be a partner working with Valentina here in Monterrey."

"This doesn't sound good, Corvette."

"I know. The President was really up in arms about murders and shootings in the United States the last couple of weeks. I could hear him talking. He said he has been in constant touch with the FBI, the DEA, and the Treasury and Justice Departments about what's going on. Apparently, a Federal judge was executed in his home last night in Dallas. Also, some innocent people caught bullets in a crossfire late last night in Chicago during a battle where guys were firing automatic weapons at each other in a city residential area. That's all over the news this morning in the United States. The families were huddled under beds with their kids while bullets tore through the walls and windows! A little child got hit. In Chicago the news reports are blaming Mexican cartel rivalries for the shootings."

"What was David's reaction?"

"He told the President that the Executive Branch agencies needed new models of investigation when it comes to the drug

250

cartels and all of the organized crime groups in the world. He said that this was no time for the various executive agencies to stonewall one another on information because the entrenchment of organized crime in our institutions of justice and law enforcement is occurring at a rate faster than it is being dealt with. As for Mexico, David said that the United States had a horrible history with the country and that its people distrusted the gringo government as much as their own. The United States and Mexico must cooperate in data sharing and criminal investigations because the crimes of the drug cartels are not separated by the border. He said that the U.S. attitude of superiority toward Mexican politics and culture dooms effective joint efforts against the cartels. David told him that the cartels don't play by any rules of civility, that they use pure terror in nasty, creative ways, and that you can find the cartels by finding their victims: the people they're extorting and killing."

Corvette sipped his coffee as another memory came to him about the conversation.

"Enrique, it seemed like David was getting angrier as he spoke," he continued. "I hadn't seen that side of him. Then he began to talk about money and started to calm down, as if he realized he was getting too wound up. He told the President that another way to find the cartels was to discover the businesses that seemed too successful, because they're money laundering centers. He said that the cartels use money to corrupt judges, the police and their families, and local politicians. When that doesn't work, they resort to killing them. Apparently, David has developed some sort of computerized data base that maps the flows of cash in and out of money laundering centers?"

Enrique didn't answer for a minute as he focused to fight his way merging into the traffic heading to La Avenida Gonzalitos. The constant chugging of the Jeep's acceleration with the subsequent sudden braking brought the morning eggs up into Corvette's throat.

"Sí, Corvette. More importantly, David has developed computer models that are *predictive* about cartel money flows in the United States and Mexico so that it might be easier to find money laundering points in the early stages and to shut them down. You have to understand about David and why he's so upset: First of all, know that it's easier for the cartels to corrupt people in Mexico than in the USA, but also understand that the cartels know that their business opportunities and margins are much greater if they can operate without having to go through the headaches of crossing that border. The border is very expensive for them. The border makes the prices of goods from Mexico become exponentially higher. People in the United States want their drugs, and they're used to the high prices and will pay them. So the cartels have learned that it is more profitable for them to grow marijuana, make meth, and set up labs, whatever, in the United States. And what has happened in your country is that many people who lost jobs in the bad economy of the past several years are returning to jobs in the recovering economy for much lower pay. The cartels offer money and power to people such as this, people who believe that they will never have these things otherwise, ones who have stopped believing in the American dream. The disenfranchisement of people from the dream creates a perfect environment for the cartels to grow and flourish. Once men and women join the cartels, the only ways out are either death or prison. For these reasons, the Mexican cartels have gained ground in the United States. Therefore, much more than before, the cartels are laundering inconceivable amounts of money through businesses in the USA. David is an expert in finding these laundering centers. He believes that getting their money is the way to shut down the cartels in this country."

"Yes! That was exactly what he and the President were discussing!"

"That's how the cartels tried to shut The Z Foundation down, by getting its money. Specifically, the Zetas did it. They did to us exactly what David is trying to do to them."

"What do you mean?"

"A few months ago, the Zetas kidnapped the investment banker for The Z Foundation and forced him to transfer most of the money of the foundation to a foreign account. It apparently went to an anonymous account in a bank in Barbados. I'm sure this one is a criminal bank with no bricks and mortar. They also took his fiancé that night, and that was how they got him to cooperate. No doubt they tortured her, and he wanted to save her. But they killed her anyway. That's what they do. I worked very closely with this guy. His name is Ignacio. We were business friends."

At the mention of the Barbados bank, Corvette felt his heart drop in his chest.

"The thing is, Ignacio went missing right after the cash disappeared from the foundation. Pretty much everyone presumed he was dead. Then last night, in the middle of the night, I got a call from him! The cartel had kept him alive because they needed him. He's smart; he knows computer code; and he knows financial systems. Ignacio has fooled them into thinking that he's working willfully in the cartel, that he has joined them. He verified to me that Z-30 is alive. He didn't know that you received the missing money, and I didn't tell him. When he talked to me last night, he was extremely stressed and didn't have much time because he was sneaking the call. He was afraid of being caught. He gave me information to pass to David. So I called David and woke him up last night."

Ah! Corvette thought. *I sensed that David wanted to discuss some things privately with the President on the phone. This must be one of them.*

"Enrique, I left and came outside to meet you so David could talk freely with the President. He probably updated him about your call after I left," Corvette explained.

He paused a second to take a sip of what little coffee remained. It had become cold.

253

He said, "You mentioned Barbados. That's where the money went, Enrique...the money from the bag...I put it in my bank in Barbados."

"Hmmm," Enrique said, nodding.

"Is this guy Ignacio okay?"

"No, Corvette. He himself believes that he's a dead man and is only buying time. We're going to try to save him."

"Fucking right!" Corvette answered. But he didn't have a clue how it would be done. He wondered if Enrique did. He decided to ask a question that had been in his mind since the day before:

"Enrique, if all the money from the foundation is gone, how are the Zs operating?"

"Pues," Enrique answered, "there's a little money in a bank in the United States. To be truthful with you, for the last couple of months, David, Ana, and I have been using our own money to meet the financial obligations of The Z Foundation until we can either get the money back or raise money through contributions. Ana is good at that last thing."

"Oh my God! You guys are paying for everything?"

"Sí, mi amigo, we believe in what we do. And we were lucky to be left money from Eduardo Ortíz."

Corvette looked at the brightening orange morning sky and the distinctive silhouette of the mountain that was the symbol for Monterrey: El Cerro de la Silla, which to many people looked like a horse's saddle. Around him he saw so much beauty, but within he felt anxiety and the bleeding of spirit.

"Where is this guy named Ignacio?"

"He said he was in Las Vegas and working directly for Z-30. He verified that the Zeta is alive, but he doesn't know where."

"Damn!" Corvette exclaimed. "Does he suspect where he might be? If we knew that, we might know where Valentina is!"

"I know," Enrique responded sadly. "But he doesn't know...Corvette, I asked him if he had heard of Valentina, and he said no."

254

That hung there a while, a word-blanket of discouragement wrapped around them. Corvette continued to stare out the window at the distant mountains while they slugged their way through the city. He thought about the Saturday incident at The Oasis in which he had played a starring role. He remembered Valentina and how she had instructed him when she gave him the bag of money and then had run as if she had a plan. He thought about how she had flown to Monterrey but had been kidnapped soon after, just a few kilometers from the airport. Could the Zeta have been in Monterrey so soon? How would such a man have reacted after his enemies had attacked him and after he had lost his money to someone named Corvette Nightfire? As he thought about these things and all that Enrique had just shared with him, an intuition formed in his heart.

"Enrique," he said. "I don't think Valentina is in Monterrey. I think she's in Las Vegas!"

"Sí, Corvette. I've come to believe the same thing. We're going downtown now so I can show you the main office of the Zs, and when we get there, we're going to review the Z reports on cartel activities and movements outside of Monterrey in the past couple of days. We'll also call some Zs to see what they observed outside of Monterrey after the time that Valentina was kidnapped."

"Well, I don't know the personality of the Zeta, but if I'm a macho cartel leader and my enemy has attacked me and has caused me to lose my money and my girl, I'm going to go after his balls. I can't think that the Zeta would high-tail it back to Monterrey like a rabbit. He would find the mother fuckers and blood them right into the Las Vegas concrete. And if his girl ran, he would have someone get her and bring her back to him. I don't think the Sinaloa cartel has her. The Zeta does."

Enrique looked at him, and Corvette saw for the first time a type of respect that he hadn't seen before.

"Mierda, Corvette! You're becoming Mexicano!"

He had been pacing while talking on his phone, but when he saw Corvette leaving to go out to meet Enrique, he sat back down at the kitchen table and told the President that Corvette had gone. He had tried to remember to use the formal address of "Mr. President" at times while Corvette had been listening to them, but David knew that the call was a personal one for his friend, the President, to vent some concerns with him.

"Donnie, Corvette has left the house to go off with Enrique Santos. Let's talk about his situation. Yes, he's at the Final Table in the World Series of Poker. He said that he's trying to decide whether to show up to play or not, but, of course, he's worried that the cartel will come after him. They're almost sure to do that. The questions are when they will come, and will it be when he's in Las Vegas. He has a second worry that the DEA, the FBI, or the police will hassle him, detain him, or arrest him, whatever. Can we remove that second worry?"

"What is this kid like? How solid is he?"

"He hasn't had a lot of experience in life other than traveling the world of professional poker. He's naïve in many ways. Enrique and I have assessed him as a young man with a good heart. He has shown a lot of interest in what the Zs are doing. What's incredible about him is that he came to Monterrey to find Valentina and that he was going to do this on his own, so he definitely has guts."

"DEA wants him in Vegas for the World Series of Poker as a lure for Z-30."

"I know. That's pretty dangerous for him, and it could be dangerous for people around him. Innocent people. The Zetas have no qualms about spraying bullets."

"I can handle the Federal agencies, David, so that they let him play. He'll have to be a witness in any criminal proceedings that come out of the investigations of the shootings at The

Oasis. He may not have committed a crime in accepting the money, but in keeping it, he could have some problems with obstruction of justice once he knew what the money was and who had it. He'll have to cooperate later."

"We don't have any evidence that the money specifically was criminal money, nor did we exactly know how much it was," David replied. "People carry large amounts of cash in Vegas." He tried not to have in his voice the tone of the irritation that he felt.

"David, all this can be handled to treat the young man in a legally friendly manner if prosecutions of cartel members come into play. Don't worry about this. I'll handle this part, and you can assure Corvette that none of the agencies or police will bother him when he comes to Las Vegas. In fact, it would be best to keep them away..."

"If we're going to use Corvette as bait," David finished for him.

"I don't like the term, 'bait,' but we have to assume that he's a target. We can load up all sorts of undercover protection around him."

"I have advised him to hire bodyguards. They would be the visible protection that would draw the attention of the cartel and maybe distract them from observing plain clothes agents or police near him."

"You want him to be there, too."

"We all want to find Valentina and to catch Z-30, so, yes, I do," answered David.

There was a little pause, and David recognized the silence as the sound of his friend thinking. He waited.

"David...we all believe that Z-30 got out of The Oasis alive. He would be after the guy who took his money. He would be after the girl he brought to Las Vegas. Valentina is already missing, and so is the agent who contacted her in the airport. Obviously, he could suspect or know that they're DEA agents."

Crap, Donnie, yes.

"And," continued the President, "he had to recognize that the kids jumping and fighting without weapons when the gunshots began Saturday are Zs. So he has to think that you and Ana are behind what happened there, and maybe he even believes that you knew his cartel enemy from Sinaloa would be there."

"Yes, Donnie, and by now if he thinks that Valentina is DEA, he could think that so is Corvette Nightfire."

"Right. This man we're talking about, Z-30, is probably the one who stole the money from The Z Foundation. That was one big warning to you."

"I get that. So I may be personally in the crosshairs now."

"And Ana."

David sighed. For years he had lived with the almost unbearable anxiety of realizing that at any moment his precious Ana could be gone. It was easy for him to feel guilty that he was keeping her in the world of danger like he had known his entire career. When he had brought up this regret to Ana, she had said, "Mi amor, I have lived the same life of danger just by being Mexican. Someone has to stand up to evil. Someone has to lead."

"We're going to get them first, Donnie."

"Do you want protection for Ana?"

"Yes, but she can't know about it. She won't like it."

"I'll take care of that. Your ideas about getting Z-30 before he gets you involve Corvette Nightfire playing in Vegas?"

"Yes. There's one other development that could help. I need to tell you about this."

David filled the President in on the midnight phone call that Enrique had received from Ignacio. One detail in particular intrigued him:

"Ignacio verified to Enrique that Z-30 is alive. He's aware of the missing money, but not that Corvette received it. He knows nothing about the existence of Valentina. The most unexpected revelation was that the information about the finances of the cartel is going to the Deep Web."

"I don't know much about that," the President admitted.

"It's the untraceable area of the web where criminal transactions and black markets exist: Sales of drugs and weapons. Murders for hire. Communications networks for organized crime and terrorist groups. Hopefully, we'll learn more about what Ignacio has been doing when he makes contact again. The immediate and urgent necessity is that we need to assure him that his mother and sister can find safety in the United States. Otherwise nothing happens. His only intention in life is to destroy Z-30 and to lay open the details of his operations to bring down the whole cartel."

"We'll definitely help him do that, David. Whenever he calls back, let him rest assured that the President of the United States will see to it that his family is safe. We have to keep this moving. Do they have to be in the United States?"

"I don't know, Donnie, but we can't waffle on it."

"I'll let you know how we'll handle this. Who are his sister and mother?"

"I don't know. They're in Monterrey. I'll get you that information and send it to you in the usual way. I'll be seeing Enrique and Corvette in a couple of hours at the office downtown."

"Okay, David, let's get to work. Your job is to get Corvette to Las Vegas."

When they disconnected, David felt a strong yearning in his heart. He walked to a window that provided a view of Monterrey carpeting the lower parts of the mountains. The sky was brightening quickly, but many of the lights of the city and the traffic were still aglow. He looked inside himself to understand his feeling, and he realized that he was missing Ana. He felt a desperate need to speak to her. He retrieved his phone from the kitchen table and tapped her speed-dial number.

After the start-and-stop ride downtown, Corvette was glad that Enrique had found a parking spot on the street in the Macroplaza district near the six-story building that housed the international headquarters for The Z Foundation. Enrique kept referring to the building as "Ana's building" because she had owned it for years and had leased several of the floors to small businesses. Half of the first floor was a bank, and the other half housed a fully equipped fitness center for the Zs to use. The latter was greatly appreciated by the Zs who resided in Monterrey. Ana had used an office suite on the top floor for years, beginning from the time when she had an event-planning business. As her involvement in peace movements and victims' rights activities had expanded, Ana had added floor space. When The Z Foundation was created, the offices that included all those activities stretched to consume the entire sixth floor.

The first thing that Corvette noticed when he and Enrique arrived in front of the building was the thick rope. It hung from a scaffolding-type structure on a corner of the roof all the way to the ground. A young man in black was ascending the rope and was about halfway up.

"What the devil is that?" Corvette asked incredulously.

"That rope is how we get to the office," Enrique explained. He had a serious expression.

"The building doesn't have elevators?" Corvette inquired sarcastically.

Enrique spit out a laugh. "Yes, of course it does. I was kidding you. It's a fitness apparatus for the Zs. In fact, that rope is somewhat historical. A few years ago when the military coup in Mexico had taken place, David and Ana were on the roof when a leader of the cartel of Sinaloa burst out of the door up there to assassinate them. Ana escaped by going down that rope rapidly. It's called a 'fast rope.' Using those ropes is part of

260

Z training. That incident was seen internationally because CNN Mexico was here covering demonstrations in the Macroplaza. Their cameras were over there on the roof of that building." He pointed to a six-story edifice across the street. "In fact, the President of the United States saw what happened live on television and sent a rescue mission for David!"

"Good God!" Corvette exclaimed, thinking about the idea of the President seeing his longtime friend being attacked on international television. But then he noticed how rapidly the young man in black was ascending the rope and he became fascinated.

"Enrique, who's that guy?"

Enrique smiled. "I recognize him from his body shape. His name is Diego. It's not his real name because his Indian name is almost unpronounceable to the Spanish tongue. He started calling himself that when he came to Monterrey. He's a little guy who may be one of the world's finest athletes, and no one knows it. He's one of Mexico's many indigenous people. He's a member of the Tarahumara tribe, the reclusive people who live in the Copper Canyon. That's a canyon system in Chihuahau that's larger and deeper than the Grand Canyon you have in the United States. The Spanish explorers called them Tarahumara, but they refer to themselves as Raramuri. It means 'the running people.' You may know them because they're famous for running barefoot long distances in the mountains. Diego is a rare one. He left his home and sought work in Monterrey. He saw Zs here in the city and wanted to do the training. It was hard for him to communicate at first. His Spanish wasn't good. I met him, and we've become friends. I can understand most of what he's trying to say when he speaks to me now. He got a job in a toy assembly plant because funds from The Z Foundation are helping to support jobs that they wouldn't be able to have otherwise in that company. Diego is amazing. He's a rock climber who climbs with his bare feet and hands. He runs faster than anyone I've ever seen. He has been to the training facilities

261

that we were at yesterday and is virtually unchallenged by any of the fitness courses that we have there."

Corvette felt a jolt of recognition when Enrique explained where Diego was from. "Oh, I definitely want to meet him," he told Enrique. "My mother recently told me that my father thinks that his parents might have come from this group of people in Chihuahua!"

"Really?" Enrique said with interest. He pointed to the top of the roof. "Well you're about to get your chance to meet him," he said. "Diego is coming back down. Come on."

He led Corvette to the landing spot where the fast rope was anchored at the corner of the building. Corvette looked up and watched Diego as he seemed almost to free-fall down the rope, but he stopped himself in two places before hitting the ground. He did that by releasing himself with a graceful jump from the rope at the end of the descent, and he approached the two of them as naturally as if he had, in fact, just stepped from an elevator.

"Eyyy, Diego, me alegra muchisimo volver a verte," Enrique greeted him in Spanish, and then repeated this in English so Corvette would understand: "I'm really glad to see you again." Then Enrique did a greeting in a language that Corvette assumed was Diego's native language.

Diego appeared to be in his very early twenties. He didn't stand more than five feet seven inches tall, Corvette estimated. He wore black jeans and a black T-shirt, but now Corvette noted a detail that he had missed before because he was too far away: Diego was barefoot. His small brown feet had lean muscularity, and when Diego moved to take some steps, Corvette thought that his feet made highly refined, flexible movements similar to hands. Right away he could see the shyness about Diego, but the young man had a cheering smile which Corvette thought he used to hide his bashfulness. He shook Enrique's hand, but his inquisitive eyes bore into Corvette's. He stared even as Enrique introduced him. Before he shook Corvette's hand, he said something to Enrique in Spanish. A strange look came over

Enrique's face, and Corvette assumed that it was because he didn't understand the sentence of Diego. The young man looked at Corvette with interest as Enrique finally translated for him:

"Diego says that you have the eyes of his people."

Corvette felt his breath catch with excitement. That simple statement crushed time into a personal singularity. He felt the rush of canyon wind and heard the voice of his father: *Tell him your name.*

But the coincidence of Diego's statement with what Corvette had told Enrique moments before also had stunned Enrique. He exclaimed in a disbelieving way, "Dios, Corvette, you just told me about your father's claim of ancestry from the Tarahumara! This is amazing!"

Corvette extended his hand and moved forward to shake Diego's. He tried a little Spanish that he knew: "Mi nombre es Corvette Nightfire. Like Corvette Fuego de Noche."

He saw Diego look confused by the effusiveness of his greeting. Diego didn't comprehend the personal moment which Corvette was experiencing. Enrique noticed too and began speaking in Spanish to Diego to explain things. Corvette heard Diego using his last name when he responded to Enrique.

He watched as his two companions stood looking at each other in silence for a couple of moments. Finally, Diego spoke again, and then Enrique told Corvette, "He says such a name as yours could live among his people. It would be his honor one day to help you find your family. He says he always wanted a brother as tall as you."

While the three of them laughed, Corvette felt tears collecting in his eyes, tears stirred by unexpected happiness but hidden so that no one might mistake their meaning.

Chapter 18: Gathering Winds

Madeline Nightfire
Georgetown, Barbados
Tuesday Morning to Wednesday Night

She told herself that it was because she wrote mystery novels that she suspected that the two men on scooters behind her were following her. There was nothing unusual about scooters in Barbados, for God's sake. Tourists rented them and rode them all over the island. Usually they kept to the beach roads. The different thing about these two helmeted riders is that when she had driven her old Mini Cooper from the bank to her home on Tuesday afternoon, they had followed her up into Holetown, off the tourist path. When she had turned onto her street, they continued on, so she let go of any worry.

Corvette had begun his flights to Monterrey that morning. She had driven him to the airport and then had stopped for breakfast at the home of her best friend, Kate Pulling, who lived nearby. Kate had moved to Barbados from London after her husband had passed away from a sudden stroke some seven years prior. She and Madeline had met at a local book signing for one of Madeline's novels, and the two English widows had hit it off from the start. Kate was four years older than Madeline. Like Madeline, she was a person who paid attention to details. Almost every Tuesday the two women met at one or the other's homes to play cribbage and to catch up on the latest happenings. Kate, who loved card games, always had a particular need to know how Corvette was faring, and asking about him was usually the first item of discussion. She had only met him a couple of times when he had paid a visit to the island. She joked with Madeline, saying, "I'm smitten with him, you know." Madeline always responded with a stern warning to keep her hands off her son.

Kate had just returned from a month's vacation in England to visit family. At breakfast in Kate's kitchen, Madeline filled her in that in Las Vegas Corvette had danced with a young woman who had seemed to have stolen his heart.

"He missed getting some important personal information about her, like her last name! So he has flown to Mexico to try to find her," Madeline explained. She told Kate nothing about the money Corvette had received and had brought to the island. She did tell her that Corvette had friends in Monterrey who were helping him to find Valentina.

Kate had looked appalled. "That doesn't make a lot of sense, Madeline. I don't want to alarm you, but you do know that Mexico is a very dangerous place right now, don't you?"

Madeline had assured her that Corvette would be safe because he would be staying with Mexican friends who were helping him.

"He needs to get his ass back to Las Vegas and get himself ready for that World Series of Poker is what he needs to do," Kate had responded. "This is no time to be chasing skirts around the world."

"Don't be jealous, Kate," Madeline had laughed. "Besides, I'll be talking to him to make sure he keeps perspective and returns to Vegas."

"Aren't you going out there to support him?"

"I would like to, Kate, of course, but I don't really have the funds for that right now."

"Get out of here!" Kate had responded in mock tone. "What in the world are you doing with all that money you make? If that's your problem, tell Corvette! I'm sure he would be glad to pay your way there. It's so important to the players to have the support of friends and family during the tournaments. You're his mom, his only parent. You should be there!"

They had continued to discuss this because Madeline kept making excuses for not going while Kate looked at her incredulously.

"I know you, Madeline Nightfire, and you're not telling me something. Corvette *is* going to play in the tournament, isn't he?"

Madeline hadn't known how to answer because she didn't like to lie, and she didn't want to admit that she was uncertain whether Corvette would play in the tournament or not. Her hesitation had exasperated Kate.

Kate then had said, "I tell you what, Madeline. Tomorrow night I'm having some of my garden club friends over for cards. Please come, and pack a bag. You can have a sleep-over here. After everyone leaves, you and I'll play cribbage, have some wine, and really take the time with each other to catch up on things. An old-fashioned pajama party, just the two of us. What do you say?"

That had sounded wonderful to Madeline, so she had agreed to it. But after she had left Kate's house, she started to experience what she called her "wall of worry." Kate's concern about Corvette being in Mexico had made her question her judgment in helping him to go.

From there she had stopped by the bank to deposit a book-sales royalty check that had come in the mail late the previous afternoon. Her trusted advisor at the bank, Johann Wolfgang, had seen her come in and had drawn her aside to tell her in hushed tones that the bank's accounts had been the target of a serious computer-hacker attack during the preceding night.

"Luckily, it failed. Our security systems prevailed," Johann had whispered to her, "but to be prudent, you might want to consider changing your passwords on your accounts."

It was on the way home from the bank that Madeline had noticed the two men riding scooters at a distance behind her car. What had first attracted her attention is that the men weren't wearing shorts or light clothing. They were wearing dark jeans, T-shirts, and pointed boots. The boots in particular stuck in her mind as odd. But when the men had passed on after she had turned onto her street and nothing else happened later in the day, she let go of the idea that there was a problem.

I'm hyper-sensitive because Kate brought up that Mexico is a dangerous place, she thought, *and then Johann told me about the hacker attempt. Plus, my nerves are on edge anyway until I hear that Corvette is okay.*

Late Tuesday night, Madeline received a text message from Corvette letting her know that he was safely in Monterrey, that he was already with David and Enrique, and that he would phone her sometime the next day.

"I'm riding in a 1969 Camaro convertible with the top down, freezing my balls off, Mum, and yelling over the wind noise. Not a good time to talk! Hahaha!" he had written.

He called her the next afternoon, full of excitement about the training facility for the Zs.

"I'm getting along great with everyone, even with Enrique, and I'm being careful, so don't worry about me, Mum," Corvette exhorted her.

"I'll try not to, love. I saw Kate Pulling yesterday and told her you were in Mexico, and she got all concerned about you. I think this set me off." She hesitated a second, and then she asked him, "Son, have you given any more thought about the poker tournament in Las Vegas next week?"

"I'm still deciding that, Mum. I just want to spend a little time with these guys here trying to find Valentina. I know I'll have to make a decision about that soon. I'll let you know right away, I promise."

"Thanks, love! Just do me a small favor and check in with me each day, okay? So I won't let my imagination run wild if I don't hear from you."

"I'll do that so you don't worry. No problem."

Everything had been uneventful since the previous afternoon. Then in the car on Wednesday evening, as she turned onto the street where Kate lived, she thought she saw in her rear mirror two headlight beams shut off. She thought they were the lights of scooters.

Shit, Madeline thought. *I don't want to be thinking weird thoughts about this all night.*

She decided to pass Kate's house and take a route that would bring her behind the point where she thought she saw the scooters. She accelerated a little fast for a residential area, made the appropriate turns, and got to the block where she thought they might be. There were no scooters. She didn't see any in her car mirrors.

Okay, I'm just a little jumpy.

She drove to Kate's home. The cars of her guests were parked in a jumble on both sides of the street. She found a spot about a block away where her little car fit. She parked and walked back to the house. Kate and one of her friends greeted her warmly at the door, and as she went inside, she thought she heard the sound of motor scooters passing by in the street. She turned to look, but Kate was already shutting the door.

Ana Valdez
San Antonio, Texas
Thursday Morning, 9:00 a.m.

She had only been awake a couple of hours, but already three persons had brought gifts of love to her.

The first one was Paula. For no special reason that Ana could imagine, her daughter had come to her room before her alarm went off and had put herself in her bed and had cuddled with her. She felt Paula's arms around her, and then a couple of minutes later she heard her reach over to shut off the alarm before it rang.

"Good morning, mommy," Paula said. She never called her "mommy." Already Ana could sense that her daughter was going to be loving and affectionate with her. She responded to Paula with a bright, sleepy-morning smile which Paula could see because she had turned on the small bedside lamp.

With teenagers, displays of affection can never be predicted or counted upon, Ana thought.

"Wow, good morning, honey!" Ana said. "So nice to wake up that way instead of to the radio blaring. Thank you! Why do I have this honor?"

Paula smiled and returned to cuddle Ana. "I don't know exactly," she said. "I know you miss Dad, and he isn't here to be all warm in the bed with you. I'm sure he snuggles with you in the morning, right?" She giggled.

Ana adored it that Paula called David by the name, "Dad." David, by his loving and goofy ways with her children, had won their love.

"Yes, he does," Ana laughed.

This is cautious territory because teenagers are so creeped out by thoughts of their parents making love, Ana reminded herself. That was the real reason she laughed.

"I'm so excited that we're flying to Monterrey tonight, mommy."

Wow!

"I've been thinking about that dress that I wanted to wear to the party tomorrow night. Do you think that Enrique will be there?"

Oh my God!

"Sí, Paula, I'm sure Enrique will be there, but you shouldn't be thinking of him and your dress at the same time! You're too young!"

Paula laughed. "I can't help my thoughts, mommy, and you can't control them either. I just was wondering if you could pick me up from school a little earlier and you would help me find something new before we go to the airport."

Despite the potential for trouble in a conversation such as that, Ana and Paula enjoyed a nice time being amused with each other. While Ana started making breakfast, Paula went to wake up her brother to put him on the road to getting dressed. She returned to the kitchen and said simply, "I love you, Mom. I'm really happy today," and that would have been enough to make the entire day worthwhile.

Except that the second gift arrived just after Ana had let the kids out of the Lexus to go into their school. The cell phone rang, and Ana saw on the caller identification that it was David. He talked to her about his phone call which he had just concluded

269

with Donnie, and he verified her and Paula's flight arrangements to Monterrey. He seemed to be covering all the bases of what they should discuss, except that Ana detected some sad tenderness that he wasn't expressing in his words. It came time to say goodbye, and then David paused, and the silence tugged at Ana's heart.

"Tell me, amor," she said to him.

He couldn't speak right away, as if he were guarding emotions so that his voice wouldn't break. She listened to the silence and had an intuition what he would say.

"It's just that I love you so much, Ana. I have been upside down about you ever since that first time we met, and I still get breathless around you. I would die if anything happened to you, and when I'm away from you like this, I worry so much about you. It's not good for us to be apart. It's not good for me. I really miss you, Ana. Eres mi todo. You're my everything."

Her intuition had been right. "I'm only yours, mi vida," she told him, "and I'm coming to you!"

Not five minutes later, the third loving gift for Ana's heart arrived in the form of a phone call from her close friend, the poet and activist, Carlos Limas. He was going to be leading Saturday's rally in the Macroplaza in Monterrey. When she answered, he greeted her warmly and asked about each member of the family. Then he came to the purpose of his call:

"Oye, Angel, I needed to hear your sweet voice before all the confusion of events begin tomorrow night. I have a very bad case of stage nerves because of the crowds, and the crowds are your fault. I suppose up there in Texas you haven't been aware of all the excitement surrounding Saturday's program in the Macroplaza. The local media and authorities are predicting more than two hundred thousand people, Ana! They're attributing this to you, to your participation in the program. Already people have been pouring into Monterrey, including many from Mexico City. Everyone is so excited that you will be speaking and supporting the peace caravan. You're the heart of our country now, Ana, you know this. You did more to heal our nation in the short time of your Interim Presidency than many had been able to do since the Revolution. I'm not kidding you, Ana. This event Saturday is going to be huge and much more successful than any of us imagined when we first began talking about it."

Carlos laughed. He added, "I'm truly nervous about my speech! I'm a simple poet, Ana. I'm used to a small room of people. I wish I didn't have to follow your address."

Ana was shocked to hear that the crowd might be so big. She said, "Oh my God, Carlos! You're the national icon! You're way too kind to be speaking of me like that. I thank you from the bottom of my heart, but if the program is successful and attracts international attention the way we all want, it'll be because you're the keynote speaker and because of the hard work so many have put into this. Dios, Carlos, this is wonderful news! I'll be nervous too, now. We'll just have to stick close by each other Saturday and give each other mutual support!"

"Sí, let's do that! There's other news, Ana. Domingo Artemis is inquiring if he can make an appearance." He paused to let Ana receive the impact of his surprise.

The President of Mexico might come! Oh my God! is what Ana thought. *I haven't been giving this event enough forethought. How did this get so big?*

Carlos continued, "It is very last minute, and this has sent us and his staff all scrambling in a mad rush to see if the logistics can be worked out. The Macroplaza is small for the size of the anticipated crowd, so people definitely will spill into El Parque Fundidora and into the park that extends to El Barrio Antiguo. He's inspired by the reports of the attendance; he has great respect and affection for you; and, no doubt, he understands the political benefits he would enjoy by his association with the event. He has been stepping up his calls on the United States to control their sales of weapons to criminal elements, you know, and to find better ways to address their issue of drug consumption. So I guess he feels that the event is a perfect stage for him."

271

"Oh, Carlos," Ana replied, worried. "I feel so bad that you've had to deal with all this while I have been in Texas. If I had known, I would have been there to help you!"

"No worries, amiga," Carlos answered. "There's nothing you, nor I, nor anyone could have done differently. This has developed very last minute, like a summer storm seeming to come from nowhere but put together by winds of the four corners."

"You're always the poet, Carlos!" Ana laughed. "Well, now I'm as nervous as you!"

"Jaja, good!" he returned. "So tomorrow night at the fiesta we'll just have to blow out the evening and relax our jittery nerves."

"Oh my God, that reminds me," Ana replied. "I'm bringing my daughter, Paula. She keeps asking me who the musicians are that were lined up for the party, and I don't even know! She can't believe that I don't know. She thinks that this is the most important thing of the party, of course."

Carlos answered, "The original musicians canceled on us a couple of weeks ago. The event planners grabbed an up-and-coming band from Monterrey to take their place. This new group plays both regional norteña music and urban pop. They're popular with the young people in the city. I don't know them, but Paula probably does. They call themselves 'Los Zapata.'"

Madeline Nightfire
Georgetown, Barbados
Thursday Afternoon

Madeline rushed out of her house and jumped into her Mini Cooper parked in front. She locked the car doors. Her hands were shaking so badly that she could hardly put the keys in her ignition. She quickly looked around to see if anyone was coming after her. Like guys who had been hiding in the house. Like two guys on scooters.

Damn, damn, damn! I knew it wasn't my imagination! Shit, what do I do?

She had just returned home from her overnight at Kate's house. Her front door had been slightly ajar. She had pushed it softly, just enough to permit her to see in. Seeing nothing, she took a step inside. The house was a shambles. In her view were the living room, the dining area, and part of the kitchen. The rooms appeared as if they had been ransacked thoroughly but quickly. Even dishes were broken on the floor. The intruders had pulled open all the drawers of desks, tables, and kitchen cabinets. The sofa cushions were scattered as if thrown to the living room floor.

Madeline took a deep breath and held it, listening for about fifteen seconds. She heard no sounds of movement in the house. She only heard the pounding of her racing heart. She backed out silently, pulling the door to its former position, and then she turned and ran back to her car.

Inside the Mini Cooper, she started the ignition and threw the shifter into drive. She drove slowly at first, while she fished her hand in her bag in the seat next to her to find her cell phone. Her hands were shaking, but she managed to tap the speed dial number to call Corvette's phone.

As the phone rang, she began to speed down the street without a clue where she was going. She hadn't gone far when the voice on the other end of the phone answered and said cheerfully, "Hi, Mum, how are you doing? I was just getting ready to call you!"

"We're in trouble, Corvette," she told him.

Chapter 19: The Dance

Valentina Garza
Las Vegas, Nevada
Monday Afternoon

For nearly an hour after she awoke, Valentina remained quiet in bed. She wanted to think and plan. She wanted to absorb the sounds of the household activity. She heard vehicles arriving and departing outside and voices of the guards in the driveway and in various outposts around the house. She didn't look at any clock in the room, but from the light coming through the slit between the drawn drapes, she judged the time to be passing four in the afternoon. She heard indistinct conversations of men on cell phones and the occasional crackling of a radio before and after a transmission. The home had become a hive of activity.

Thug activity, Valentina thought disdainfully. She remembered what Raúl had done to her. She had felt filthy when he was done. When he had left for another part of the house and it was quiet for a few minutes, she had snuck a quick shower to wash his crimes from her. She could have fought him in futile ways. She could have bitten him or scratched him, which is what a normal woman would have done under that kind of siege, but she had acted docile to fool him. Besides, he would have killed her had she done those things. If he wanted, he could have just snapped her neck. She knew that he could do that.

If that would suit his purpose. He's constantly calculating a person's worth.

She was buying herself time. Time to destroy him.

She slipped on lingerie, black jeans, and a white blouse; and she brushed her hair. She applied a little lipstick.

Looking around, she wondered, *Whose house is this?*

She opened the drapes and saw men sitting at the patio table where earlier she and Raúl had breakfasted. On the table

274

lay a pistol, an AK-47, and a cell phone. One of the men saw her staring at the phone, so she gave him a pretty smile to take his mind from that. She retreated, pulling the sliding door closed, and she adjusted the drapes. She surveyed the bedroom and saw that it was a guest room and that there were no photographs in it. She decided to go and find out where Raúl was. She walked quietly down the hall and found a television-and-entertainment sala with custom cabinetry accommodating video game consoles and a seventy-inch TV. The room was filled with family pictures on the walls, tables, credenzas, and stands. Valentina immediately recognized the celebrity family and realized whose house she was in:

Oh my God! Yandel Sandoval!

She felt her heart leap; first, with astonishment that the Mexican film producer would be involved with Raúl somehow; and, second, with joy that she could so easily report her location if she could get her hands on a phone.

She continued through the house, looking in every room for things that might help her escape when the time came and for things that might save her life. She had a photographic memory for details of furnishings and technological apparatuses. She was an event planner who furnished and decorated rooms, and she was a DEA agent trained to have eyes for incriminating evidence, so she was adept at taking in details quickly. She saw that the rooms had no telephones, so the house apparently didn't have land lines. She noted the locations of security cameras above doors and windows and the positions of smart panels with controls for operating the home's environmental and security systems.

She was lucky. She had proceeded through much of the first floor of the house without encountering anyone to distract her from her observations. She did see two men in the entertainment room studying a paper on a sofa table. They looked up and she smiled at them.

"I'm just finding Raúl," she said sweetly. They resumed looking down, unconcerned.

All the men here look Mexican, she thought. She reminded herself to keep speaking Spanish.

She found the kitchen. The woman servant from the previous night was cooking, helped by two younger girls. The three of them looked tense. A small hallway preceding the kitchen served as a mud area off the garage. It had sink basins, storage cabinetry, and stainless washer and dryer.

"Oh! I would die to have the washer and dryer here!" Valentina exclaimed, making a rush into the pass-through to the garage. She did that for the benefit of the servants in the kitchen so she could disappear from their view. She quickly threw open the garage door and perused. She wasn't interested in the Bentley or the Ferrari or the Cadillac SUV. Her eyes sought and found the location of the electrical switch panel on the garage wall. She pulled the door shut again and positioned herself in front of the washing machine and pretended to admire it.

She did it just in time because the servant appeared in the doorway.

"I have a small condo, and my tiny washer and dryer hardly handle half-sized loads," Valentina explained to her.

The woman smiled. "I like those too. Señora, it's good to see you up. May I get you anything?"

"Oh, I would love a bottle of water if you have it," Valentina said. "I just woke up and my throat is dry. I'm looking for Raúl."

"I'll get you the water, Señora. We have plenty. I last saw Señor Raúl in the solarium, just off the living room."

Valentina observed the knife block on the kitchen counter.

"Muchas gracias, querida," Valentina said to the servant when she was handed the water, and the woman beamed a broad smile and made a small bow of the head in response to Valentina's term of endearment.

She saw the arrival of yet another black SUV through the spacious views of the living room glass as she passed to the solarium. Two corpulent men slung with automatic weapons emerged from the rear seats. One opened the front passenger

276

door for a slender young man dressed in dark blue loafers, gold-colored pants, and black T-shirt. He wore four bracelets on his right arm and a thick chain-necklace supporting an ostentatious gold cross that bumped against his chest as he walked. He was carrying some kind of book.

How many lives for that cross? Valentina sighed. She slowed her pace across the room so that she could observe the men and vehicles outdoors. She counted four black SUVs, a commercial-sized, extended-cab pick-up truck, and a dark Mercedes sedan. From what she had observed, she estimated that there were about twenty men on the premises.

I wonder if Yandel knows his home has been converted into a thug house, she thought. She watched the young man with the book approach two guards standing on the marble entrance tiles to the house, and the three of them got into conversation. Valentina entered the solarium and found Raúl asleep in a sitting position on the white bamboo sofa. His mouth was open. His jacket lay beside him. She noted that he was wearing an empty shoulder holster.

She looked for his gun, and that was when she noticed the gold plates on the handle: Raúl's pistol was on the glass-top table in front of the sofa. It wasn't the one he normally carried, but he had shown her this one once in the suite they had in The Oasis. It was another semi-automatic Glock twenty, but the butt of this one had coverings of eighteen karat gold. In the center of the cover, "Zeta" was engraved in ornate script.

When she approached him, the Zeta awoke. He didn't look at her; rather, he made a casual movement to reach for his pistol on the table. He stood and holstered it. Then he turned as if he were just noticing her. A sleepy smile spread across his face.

"Ah, preciosa, you caught me napping. I try to impress you with my young energy. The truth is that my strange work hours require that I sneak an occasional catnap or two." He chuckled. "I hope you're feeling rested now."

Valentina returned the smile, but before she could answer, one of the guards from the front entrance came into the room with the slender man who was wearing the cross.

"Hola, Jefe," said the young man. "I'm sorry to interrupt, but I have this for you, and they told me that it was urgent that I bring it to you." He glanced self-consciously at Valentina as if uncertain that he should have spoken in front of her.

"Sí, gracias," answered Raúl reassuringly to let the man that know that he hadn't committed a faux pas. He extended his arm, and the man handed him the book that he had been carrying.

Dios! Valentina exclaimed in her mind as she recognized the tome from scuff markings on its cover. She had seen it before. It was the ledger book that had been left in the center console of the Corvette Stingray!

Monday Night

Later that night she and the Zeta remained mostly in the entertainment room. The Zeta selected a couple of Spanish-language movies made in Mexico. It soon became obvious that he had put the movies on as a distraction for her while he worked. Valentina reclined against him on the brown over-sized leather sofa. She decided to act sleepy so that, with her head against his shoulder, she could squint through seemingly closed eyes and observe what he was constantly doing with his phone while the movies played.

He made numerous short calls, some of them in English, speaking in code or in vague sentences understood by the receiving party. He stared at the television while he talked, as if he were watching the film, and between calls he consulted the ledger book. She tried to see what was in the book. She caught glimpses of names, addresses, shorthand notes in Spanish, locations, and numbers that probably indicated cash amounts.

Later, when she sensed that he was nearly finished with his calls, she worried what he might want to do with her, so she decided to tease him into doing something that might give her some control over the rest of the evening.

She asked, "Raúl, can we go out dancing?"

"Seriously?"

"Sí, en serio, amor! This is Las Vegas! You work all the time. Take a break and dance with me! I've seen you dance, and I know you like it. I would love to dance for you. I'll put a light in your eyes, baby. You should do this. You should impress your men with how unpredictable you can be! Most of those are young guys out there, Raúl. You have this young, beautiful woman. You don't want them seeing you just watching movies on TV like an old man, do you?"

She saw that she had surprised him. Before he could answer, she pressed:

"Let's spice up our evening, cielo! I've been drowsy all day. It's still early in Vegas! Order us a limo! Please, baby, you can do anything. We can make one stop for shopping. I don't have anything new in my bag. Take me shopping! I'm an amazing woman. I can select quickly. I can get a dress, some lingerie...hmmm? Maybe you'll want to buy me a necklace and earrings? All my good things are at home in Monterrey. Let me thrill you, Raúl! We'll do this, and then you can take me anywhere you're comfortable...a private place or public, I don't care. I just want to dance with you!"

The Zeta chuckled and glanced around as if trying to see if anyone had heard her talking to him in that way. He pulled out a cigarette.

He said, "Dios, Valentina, I'm in the middle of planning the logistics of shipments and arrivals of products. For us to go out like that is an operation. I have to think about security. I have to put things in action."

She got up on her knees on the sofa beside him and brought her body close to him. She gave him a seductive look.

"Oh, Raúl, you have guys to do all those things for you. You can do anything you want. Show them, baby. Give me a good time tonight, and let me dance for you. If you want, bring your phones and your radios and your little books along. You can work while I buy my things. But I promise you, even that won't take long. As I told you, I'm an amazing woman who knows what she wants, and I can buy quickly."

He laughed and blew out a ring of smoke. When he did, she forced herself to give him a long kiss.

They left an hour later in a limo to go shopping and dancing. By the time they arrived at a casino outside of the city, a private room had been prepared for their party, and a band that had finished sets earlier in one of the lounges was on hand setting up to play. Valentina recognized some of the men that she had seen around the house there, already with women.

Hired, no doubt, she thought when she saw them.

Tuesday

When she awoke late Tuesday morning in the spacious master bedroom of the house, she heard Raúl in the bathroom talking to someone on the phone. She recalled that although he hadn't seemed drunk when they had returned to the house, he did fall asleep in his clothes beside her almost as soon as they came into the bedroom. She was upset that she had missed an opportunity to get her hands on his cellphone: Raúl's bodyguard had remembered to take it from him as they came into the house. Valentina had been relieved not to have to face a sexual event with him, at least not that night. Her plan had worked. The plan also had included letting the Zeta see the side of her who wanted nice things so that he might wonder how far she would go to receive them.

Far enough to give up my way of life to be with him, she wanted him to believe.

During the night she had slept beside him in her new lingerie. She had put it on after he was already asleep. That had felt safe, and Raúl later might believe that she had actually wanted to entice him. When she awoke, the sheet was partially pulled away from her, so she knew that he had checked her out

280

before he arose. Now she strained to hear what he was saying on the phone in the bathroom.

He was speaking in English. At first she thought that he was doing this in case she might awaken and hear, but in a few minutes she understood that Raúl was speaking to a group of gringos on a speaker phone somewhere, either together or conferenced in. She couldn't distinguish parts of the conversation because Raúl apparently had his head turned away from her, but after a few minutes Valentina concluded that he was speaking to three men. Apparently, they were policemen in Las Vegas. The subject of conversation was "El Asesino" (the Killer). Valentina knew that he was a high-ranking leader in the Cartel of Sinaloa and that he was rumored to be operating in the United States.

"You're positive that he'll be there at that time?" Raúl inquired, with a hint of threat in his voice. After they affirmed this, Raúl told them, "Stop his vehicle before they get into the city. Set up a checkpoint for drinking drivers beforehand. Separate him from his bodyguards. My men will take him in our truck, which you will have also stopped before they arrive. Let one of your guys get hit if bullets fly. Put him in a vest, I don't care. If a cop is hit, it looks like they have nothing to do with it. Whatever it takes. I want this mother-of-whores for what he did to us in The Oasis. If I get him, I'll take care of you beyond your dreams. There shouldn't be a problem with this. I'll have my sharpshooters take out the bodyguards. Get all of them out of the vehicle so we have clear shots. Let your car videos show the police being surprised and overpowered. You don't need more than three police there, right? You guys handle this. Don't get anyone else involved." There was a pause while the Zeta heard their response. "Okay, I want the bodies of those Sinaloan shits in our truck. But if we have to leave them, we will."

Valentina felt chills permeate her body. *Oh my God! I have to get a message out to Zolinsky, David, Ana...someone!* She pulled the sheet back over her because she felt cold. *I have to get my hands on a phone!*

281

When the Zeta came out of the bathroom after he had finished the call, he didn't return to the bed. Instead, he headed out the room and down the hall. Relieved, Valentina took time to think. She knew that the phones were being jealously protected. She realized that there might be only one way she could get access to a cell phone:

I have to stay close to Raúl's body. I have to keep being intimate with him so I can get my hands on his phone.

She didn't have the opportunity. He left the house and didn't return until late in the afternoon. Even then he remained outside a while. Through the window she watched him talking to men by the cars and occasionally speaking alone to someone on his radio or cell phone. Sometimes he pulled the ledger book from his pocket and consulted it while he talked on the phone.

She had noticed that there always seemed to be men doing something near her in the house. She knew that they were there to watch her, but they apparently had been instructed not to be obvious. Most of the time they were one room away.

To pass time, she got into conversations with the woman servant, and she pretended to watch television and to read magazines while she waited for Raúl to come back inside the house. For the benefit of observers, she tried to appear relaxed and satisfied. After all, the Zeta had taken her out dancing the night before. He would want his woman to look happy.

She had less than an hour with him when he finally came inside the house. She met him in the living room and made a show of giving him an affectionate kiss in front of his men. He looked amused.

"I can take it from here," he joked, dismissing the men. "Have the car ready for me in forty-five minutes."

He led her to the bedroom, but he didn't seem to have an interest in undressing. Valentina guessed that he wanted to be ready to leave and that he was going to show her attention now by talking with her. It felt safe to get close to him. She kissed him and pressed her body to him. She felt his cell phone in his right pants pocket. He left his shoulder holster on, so she let her hands run along his shirt on his back, especially the small of his back. She knew that he was mellowing because she felt him grow hard. She pulled him to sit with her on the edge of the bed.

She wondered, *Is there a pattern to where he keeps his phone? I've seen him carry it in both his pants and his jacket.*

"I loved last night, Raúl," she told him. "Gracias, gracias, gracias muchisimo! I wasn't sure you would really take me out, but you not only showed me an evening, you showed me the moon!"

His eyes told her that he believed she was being sincere. She needed to keep him warm for what she was about to say.

He spoke first. "It was my pleasure, angel. You're a beautiful woman, Valentina. Truly, I think you're the most beautiful woman I have ever been with."

"Mmmm," she answered, and she leaned in to kiss him. He was enjoying it, but she was trying to think about his habits: when he put his phone into his pants, when he stuck it inside his jacket pocket, when he wore his pistol, when he removed it, and when he might instruct his bodyguards to leave them alone.

She broke the long kiss softly and feigned tenderness. She rubbed the palm of her hand on his cheek.

"What do you want in life, Raúl?" she whispered. "Do you want kids? I do."

She brushed her lips against his before he could answer.

"You need legacy, baby. You need a son," she told him. She kissed him again. "No," she whispered, "you need sons. And daughters who are your princesses. You need a home. People should see how you take care of your family. They need to know the kind of man you really are."

He was aroused. This time he came for a strong kiss. She received him, but when she broke the kiss, she continued her thought, whispering in his ear:

"What I know, Raúl: You're true hombre. You come from the city of heroes. You make history. You decide things."

She had him breathless. She wanted him hot, but not so aroused that he would forget the time and forget that he had to leave. She didn't want sex. She only wanted to seduce him into a fantasy of family. It could keep her alive long enough to get his phone.

"You want to give me sons and daughters, Valentina? I have you a long way from home in many ways," he said.

"We're getting along just fine, Raúl," she answered, adopting a contented smile. "I can give you family and the social cover you need. I understand perfectly well what I can do for you: exactly the things you need but haven't had. You've been evaluating me for this job you have in mind. I'm no whore, cielo. I'm perfect cover. I can get people to help you. I also see that you can give me anything I want."

The Zeta pulled away a little. He seemed to be studying her face, but she saw approval in his eyes. He looked at her a while, and then he smiled. "You need to learn English," he said.

He left her on time. He went off with three of his men and didn't return until just before midnight. She was in the kitchen when he returned to the house. She had gone there to look for a drink. Raúl looked dusty and tired when he came in. She was going to go into the living room to greet him, but his cell phone rang, and after he looked at the caller ID, he took the call. He indicated with a nod to his men that they could leave. Two left and one sat down on the sofa. Valentina guessed that he was the nighttime guard. She slid out of view inside the kitchen doorway so that she could listen. He was talking to someone named Santi about a person of interest named Juan. Santi was doing most of the talking.

"Absolutely nothing about the DEA?" the Zeta asked Santi.

There was a long response.

"Sí, I agree," the Zeta answered with a sigh. "It seems he just liked my girl."

Valentina searched her memory in vain to see if she knew who Santi was. Then the other name struck her:

Juan? Juan Ramirez?

Whoever Santi was, the man was talking a lot. Finally, the Zeta said. "The thing with El Asesino is tomorrow. How soon can you be in Las Vegas?"

Valentina had a horrible feeling from hearing the name, "Juan." She had retrieved a coke from the refrigerator, and she decided that now she would try to get back to the bedroom undetected. She felt unnerved, and she didn't want the Zeta to see her looking nervous. She saw the opportunity to slip unnoticed back to the bedroom.

As she went down the hall with the coke, she heard the Zeta say, "Bien, Santi, see you Thursday."

But her mind jumped to the implications of Raúl's question and comment regarding Juan:

Absolutely nothing about the DEA?

It seems he just liked my girl.

She made it to the bedroom and felt her stomach sicken. She ran into the bathroom and locked the door in case Raúl might look for her. She didn't want the transparency of her mood to show to the Zeta.

Dios, she thought, *they wouldn't have asked Juan politely if he worked for the DEA. What did they do to that poor man?*

She knew that he was dead.

She also realized that he had died protecting her identity.

I'm not working fast enough, she thought bitterly.

Chapter 20: Trusting the Devil

Z-30, the Zeta
Las Vegas, Nevada
Wednesday, 10:00 a.m.

He returned to the house from an early morning breakfast meeting in Henderson with a casino director and his senior accounting manager. He was eager to see The Oasis security officer who had come to report to him what the security cameras had captured during the failed assassination attempt on his life the previous Saturday and the latest theories of the police who were working with the security force at The Oasis. The man's name was Jorge Mendez. He had started accepting payments from the Zetas in return for information and future favors. The Zeta had told his men to escort Jorge into the small private office. He wanted Valentina to be on hand as well. He wanted to see her reaction, especially to any reports of people whom she might know. He wanted to observe her face. So he immediately found Valentina when Jorge arrived, and taking her arm in an affectionate way so as not to alert her to what possibly might be an unpleasant surprise for her, he led her to the office with banter and a smile.

Jorge Mendez had worked the night shift and was still wearing his uniform when the Zeta and Valentina entered the room. Jorge had set up a laptop on the front edge of an executive desk and had moved a couple of small chairs to both sides of his. He was standing, apparently awaiting somewhat nervously the Zeta's entrance. Two of the Zeta's bodyguards were also in the room. When Raúl walked in, Jorge strode to meet him with extended arm and said, "Señor, a pleasure to meet you." As he shook the Zeta's hand, he smiled respectfully at Valentina and said, "And you, Señora."

The Zeta appraised him briefly. Jorge appeared to be about forty years old. His crinkled dark eyes radiated intelligence and pleasant manners, but they also registered great reserve and caution. Raúl judged that he was a man who wouldn't go out on a limb unless he was certain of his facts. He looked tired, which might have been from working the previous night on graveyard shift, but more likely it was evidence of fatigue from a stressful and sedentary life. He seemed anxious to get straight to the subject at hand, which pleased the Zeta immensely.

"I thought the easiest way to bring you up to speed on the investigation would be for me to show you some brief recording snapshots taken by our cameras last Saturday," Jorge told the Zeta. "I assembled these into a collage and put it on a flash drive which I'm using in the computer here."

"Excellent," replied the Zeta. He directed that Jorge sit in front of the computer and that Valentina take the far seat next to him. The Zeta stood beside the remaining chair so that he could have clear views of their faces and also the computer screen.

The shots were from cameras in three different places in the ceiling near the entrance doors to the hotel and casino. They could clearly see men rushing into the lobby from outside, one grabbing Josh, the others following, and the men coming from the lobby with guns drawn to confront the Zeta's men. One of the latter men broke away and ran off-camera deeper into the casino. The Zeta recognized him as the man who had appeared from nowhere with a pistol to shoot him but ended up killing Horacio. Very quickly all the men were bunched up in front of the casino doors in a fight, and the young men whom the Zeta had decided were Zs were jumping into the fray.

Two things on the recording especially interested the Zeta. The first was that there was a tall young Hispanic man dressed in black who circled the outside of the fight. He apparently was giving directions to the Zs to exit from there after they had brought the whole group of fighters crumbling to the floor. The young man could be seen pointing, mouthing words, and tapping several of the Zs to get out of there.

When he heard sirens, the Zeta thought, *and probably when he saw The Oasis security coming. I have to admit, those guys*

287

probably saved lives, and probably more Zeta lives than those of Sinaloa. The enemy had surprised my men and already had their weapons drawn.

The other thing of interest to the Zeta was how Valentina had escaped. He saw her scooting out from under the mountain of falling men and running in a panic through the doors. The cameras caught her stopping there briefly, and they then showed Luis pushing the bag of money to her through the door from behind. It was difficult to make out a lot because of the bright light of the sun outdoors contrasting against the darker interior of the casino.

He glanced at Valentina's face as she watched all of this. She looked puzzled when she saw the man in black. She looked horrified when she saw herself emerging from the people who might have trampled her. The Zeta felt frustrated by her reactions.

She could be a mother of an actress, he thought. *She doesn't seem worried what these cameras might show at all.* He tried to throw her by shooting a question at her quickly:

"Cariño, do you know that young man dressed in black?"

She shook her head immediately and then looked the Zeta in the eyes. "No, darling, I can't see him well enough. He's in black and telling those young kids what to do, so he obviously is a Z leader."

The Zeta turned to Jorge, who already looked like he wanted to speak.

"Do we have an identification of him?" he asked Jorge.

"Yes, his name is Enrique Santos, and he's indeed one of the highest Z leaders. The city and state police got statements from him, and then we have seen nothing else of him. Enrique Santos works with David James and Ana Valdez in the top leadership of the Zs in Mexico, and the Z presence has been growing in the United States recently, especially in Latino communities."

"I have heard of Enrique Santos," Valentina stated quickly. "I even met him once years ago at a party. I wouldn't have recognized him in this recording."

She met that head on, the Zeta noted. He asked Jorge, "Was David James present?"

"After the incident, he arrived with an agent from the Drug Enforcement Agency. What we learned is that the DEA had been tracking Sinaloa Cartel activities. One of their agents turned out to be a paid informer for the cartel."

This surprised the Zeta. *The DEA was there because of Sinaloa?*

The Zeta didn't follow up on that thought because he wanted to throw another question out fast while he thought Valentina might still be somewhat off guard. "What about Ana Valdez? Was she present?" He watched Valentina's face carefully while Jorge replied.

"I don't have any knowledge she was around," Jorge answered. "She wasn't around when David James was there."

But the Zeta saw that Valentina wasn't flustered by the question; rather, she returned with a demand to the Zeta:

"Raúl, can I please see you outside for just a moment? I need to tell you something that you need to know."

Now the Zeta felt like he was the one caught off guard. He agreed, and the two went to the quiet of the solarium.

Valentina turned to him. She whispered, "Raúl, everyone in the world must be looking for me! How are you handling this? It is now Wednesday. I'm simply missing since Sunday? And David was here in Las Vegas! That changes everything. Do you realize he's friends with the President of the United States? There could be intelligence agencies of two countries looking for me. I was last seen in Monterrey, maybe, but who would be the prime suspect of taking me? You! And here I am in Las Vegas with you!"

He didn't want to tell her that for the last few days he had been trying to decide whether to keep her alive or not. He just looked into her eyes for a few moments, and that was a mistake because he needed to think clearly. When he looked at her, he wanted her. In those moments he wanted to believe he could keep her. When she wasn't around, he believed he thought more logically. Finally, he replied to her comments:

"I'm handling certain things, Valentina. You speak like maybe you have ideas. I'm listening."

"You have to make them want to stop looking for me, Raúl. You're going to need my help for that to happen."

"Go on."

"If I'm going to join you as a partner, Raúl, then we have to begin the process of making people believe it. I have a right to choose what I want for my life. My tía Ana chose her path. She got busy with her new life and left me behind. I salute her for that. She's a good woman, but I get to make my choices too. She won't believe my choice to be with you for quite a while. But if you truly make me a partner and let me work on some worthwhile projects that help our country, then she and everyone will see that I have set my own course. I'll make believers out of everyone. And I'll try to be an influence on you. I'm smart, and I'll try to help you do things in smart ways so that you stay out of danger. So that you stay alive. There isn't that much time. I don't want to get killed in some gunfight that happens when the damned DEA or FBI or police have figured out where you are! We need to start getting it out there that I'm your woman and that I'm with you by my own volition."

In his lifetime the Zeta had only trusted three or four people. The closest person to him he thought of as "the other." Relatives in Puebla watched this uncle and nephew only a year apart in age grow up together. They often confused them because they looked like fraternal twins with a close resemblance. "The other" was the one person he trusted most in his life, but El Gato had had him killed. He thought of a couple cousins from his youth. He thought of Horacio, who was on his way to being trusted by the Zeta and who, in fact, had sacrificed his life so that the Zeta could live. But never a woman. He had never trusted a woman. To do what Valentina was suggesting would require an emotional investment that he had never considered before. That's essentially what he told her:

"Mi vida, you're naïve in some ways. Not many people can influence my decisions, but, yes, you're very smart. You've figured out what I need at the very time in life I decided to need it. You are, in fact, perfect for the role which apparently both of us have envisioned. This would require very much trust between us. I can't flip a switch and trust you. Maybe you can do this, I don't know. But you're right. We don't have that much time to stay in one place. Let me think about ways in which we can make people suspect that we're together. People like to believe what they suspect. We'll discuss these things. I'm already planning where we need to go to be safe in the short run. I won't trust you for a while. It isn't my nature. Maybe I'll never be able to do this. But you're rapidly gaining my respect for being extraordinarily capable. With me, that's more important than trust."

"Okay, Raúl, fair enough," Valentina answered him. "But I can tell you that my aunt Ana and David are going crazy right now trying to find me. David was here in Las Vegas when you were this past Saturday, for whatever reason. He's good. They might think that I'm in Monterrey right now, but they will discover that I'm not soon. It'll be good for you to trust me quicker than you want to. You're going to need my help."

Her words haunted him the rest of the day. They overshadowed two important occurrences later in the day:

The first was a call from a computer security employee tasked with the job of monitoring and reviewing the work of Ignacio Lopez.

"I can't put my finger on it," said the man to the Zeta, "and the spyware and the reviews are not turning up anything, but something seems wrong. It seems to be taking longer for Ignacio to get things done. My uneasiness has caused me recently to spend more time with him. It's scary what this guy knows. I spent a day with him and made him show me tricks of navigating secret websites. Individual transactions on black market sites in the Deep Web are virtually untraceable, but

Ignacio talked about using probabilities as a way of uncovering certain transactions. When he got into the math, I couldn't follow him at all. He said it was just a theory that he had, but I think he knows more than he's letting on. The guy is super clever. Almost as if he sensed that I had noticed that his work had been taking him longer, he started complaining to me about the processing speeds of his servers. He says that they're too slow for the calculations required by the probability predictions which he's developing. Do you believe that? He's asking for new servers that are very expensive."

"He has no business taking time with that anyway. No wonder his work is slowing down! I'm overdue to visit him and have a chat," the Zeta replied. "I'll come to visit him tomorrow. I have a ledger book of information that I want to give him and explain to him, so your call to me is perfectly timed. But the laptop that he uses...get that away from him just before I arrive tomorrow and have one identical for him that I can present him. Analyze the hard drive on the laptop you take away. Get any flash drives and back-up media from his desk and office. Tell him it is part of security operations. I'll talk to him."

The other important event of the day came late in the evening. He received the phone call confirming that El Asesino had been shot and killed along with his bodyguards at a police road check outside of Las Vegas. The three policemen conducting the sobriety checks also had died as a result of gunshots wounds to their heads during the shootout that occurred. They had been wearing vests.

My shooters did well, the Zeta thought.

Chapter 21: Nuevos Destinos

Corvette Nightfire
Monterrey, Mexico
Thursday Afternoon

He never anticipated what would happen to him, but he felt the stirring of it when he flew over the border that first time, landed in Monterrey, and saw the streets of Mexico from the back seat of David's old Camaro. It was as if the Mexican half of him, asleep all his life, woke up, and from that moment he began to see and understand the world through Mexican eyes. He saw Mexico.

No, not Mexico...México, he told himself.

He thought about that first car ride and the symbolism of it: he was in Mexico, riding in an American car with a gringo owner and a young Mexican who was wary of him. He knew that David came from Virginia, once a British colony. Corvette's mother was British. When he thought about that ride, he imagined that the car was a capsule for the transfer of his destiny. Before, he had been a self-absorbed but sensitive kid who lived in a limited world defined by the poker circuits. The rules were clear and relationships lasted the length of a stay in a city. He had been comfortable in that world, a world he could predict through his instinctive knowledge of the probabilities of getting a poker hand. His anxiety level rose and diminished in inverse proportion to the size of his bank account. That mattered to him only because he needed money to play the game. That was all he knew.

Now things had changed. He actually had a friend. A Mexican friend. And even though Corvette and Enrique had met acting like two snorting rams facing each other with lowered heads, Corvette knew something deep in his heart. He had liked Enrique from the beginning. He liked everything about him: the way he looked, his style, his sullen reserve, the coiled power of his lean physique, his confidence, but mostly his courage and heart. Enrique was a man. He was deep in the ways that Corvette wasn't. Corvette suspected that Enrique's maturity had come from a lifetime of seeing the world through Mexican eyes. He realized that he, too, had Mexican eyes, but he was using them for the first time. He needed Enrique. He trusted him. Enrique had told him that he would look out for him. Then he had spent the time of the last intense days putting Corvette in situations that would forever change the way Corvette felt about life.

None of this, of course, excused the way that Enrique drove. They were back in the Jeep on the way to visit the mother and sister of an investment advisor named Ignacio Lopez, whom, Enrique had explained, had been kidnapped by the Zetas after forcing him to steal the money of The Z Foundation. Enrique told Corvette that the women lived "in the hills," so Corvette knew that he was in for another bout of car sickness.

Not to mention the very real possibility that this Jeep will roll over, Corvette reminded himself. The minute that they began tearing through the downtown streets to head for the hills, Corvette decided that he would distract himself by calling his mother. She called him first, at that moment.

"We're in trouble, Corvette," she told him after he had greeted her. She then reported that the men on scooters had followed her, that Johann Wolfgang had confided in her about attempted security breaches on the bank accounts, and that moments earlier she had discovered that her house had been ransacked.

As he listened to her, he felt his heart assembling puzzle pieces forming a clear picture of what he must do. He remembered the touching story of Daniel Flores and those of the Zs he had met. He recalled the admission by Enrique that he, David, and Ana were giving their money to support the Z operations. He now understood the work that Ana was doing to elevate awareness in the world of the crimes against nature by the cartels. The emotion that he had felt when Diego had said that Corvette's last name could live among his people was rising within him. He admired the courage of Ignacio to risk his life for his family. But the thing that surprised him the most was the connection he felt to Valentina. He knew that he was on a new path in life. He was sure that the path was leading him to her.

As Enrique bumped and jolted to the outskirts of Monterrey, his mother finished her story. Then everything came together for him, pure and simple:

Ignacio is in Las Vegas. I think Valentina is in Vegas. If these guys have been in Barbados looking for me, then they know I have their cash. It's me they want. They can't hurt anyone else because of me! I have to lure them to me. It's gotta be in Vegas. It's all going to happen there.

"Mum, listen to me. Here is what I want you to do. I want you to get out of Barbados immediately. I want you to fly to Las Vegas. I've decided to play in the World Series of Poker. I want you to be there to support me. These people I'm with have offered protection for me, and they will protect you too. In addition, I have a man in Las Vegas who arranges everything for me. I can literally trust him with my life, Mum. His name is Raymundo. He has hired bodyguards for me. I'll call him and have him meet you in the airport in Las Vegas and have him take care of you until I arrive there. I want you to get there ahead of me so it can be kept quiet about your presence in Vegas. Once I get there, cameras are likely to show. I'll arrive Sunday, okay? There's something important here in Monterrey on Saturday that I need to do. But I want you out of Barbados now. Will you do this for me?"

"Yes, son, I really wanted to see you play, and now I'm scared to be here," Madeline answered. "It's just that I didn't have money to come..."

"For God's sake, Mum, don't worry about money. Listen, take down this information I'll give you about my credit card so you can book your flight. Don't go back home. Buy some clothes and a bag. Put these on my card. Book the flight, shop, and go to the airport until your flight departs. Let me know your flight information as soon as you get it. In the airport, stay around people, security, and the police, and observe to see if anyone is watching you. Do the same wherever you have to change flights to Vegas. Then as soon as you disembark in Las Vegas, Raymundo will be there. I'll tell him to say to you that the weather is hot in Trinidad, so you can be sure it's him. Let me tell you what he looks like."

When Corvette finished his conversation with his mother, he turned and saw Enrique look over at him and begin to shake his head.

"Increible! Incredible!" Enrique shouted over the noises of the Jeep and the city. "You keep surprising me, Corvette. So I tell you, mi amigo, if you're going to Las Vegas, I'm going to be there when you are. I have to look out for you!"

Corvette felt a smile spread over his face, but he also thought that he was going to vomit.

"I'm glad," he told Enrique, "but right now you have to pull over. I'm going to get sick."

One hour later, Corvette and Enrique were sitting in the kitchen of the cinderblock house where Ignacio's mother and sister lived. Their neighborhood was a poor community of joined houses even though it was a quarter of the way up a mountain with splendid views of the city. Corvette noted the disparity of living conditions in the city. In some sections, the higher elevated neighborhoods were in gated communities with house prices increasing astronomically the higher that the home was situated. Yet there were still older barrios like this one, where some streets were unpaved and rutted from the rushing waters of heavy rains. Gang graffiti marred almost all the commercial buildings and many of the homes. Corvette realized instantly that Ignacio had educated himself and pulled himself out of poverty, probably with the loving support of his mother and sister. Inside the house where he grew up were furnishings and décor of simple elegance.

Ignacio has been helping his family, Corvette concluded.

Enrique spoke in Spanish to the woman and the girl. Ignacio's sister was plain and a little overweight, but she had intelligent, sensitive eyes. She spoke English fluently, and out of respect for Corvette, she remembered to translate for him much of the conversation as it occurred.

When Enrique broke the news that Ignacio was alive, his mother began crying and his sister came behind her and put her arm around her shoulder.

"Please, can you save my son?" the mother asked, and Corvette knew from the tone what she was begging even before it was translated.

"Sí, Señora, there are many people who wish to do this, including even some very important people in the United States government," Enrique answered. "We'll all try. Your son is a friend of mine whom I respect very much. But I have to tell you that he'll refuse to let us know where he is until he knows that you and your daughter are safe. He doesn't think you're safe in México. He wants you in the United States immediately. He's there and in grave danger, and we have not a minute to spare."

"He's in the United States?"

"Sí," Enrique answered. Corvette noticed that Enrique didn't say which city.

"I want to see my son!"

"We'll go," added Ignacio's sister, as if she were reading her mother's mind and wanted to communicate her own feelings at the same time to her mother. "Is this for a long time?"

"Probably," Enrique told them. "You will have to leave your lives here behind. You will need new identities. Ignacio is insisting on this. He wants to be sure you're safe before he'll take any action for his own rescue."

"He has information for you, doesn't he?" asked the girl.

"Sí" Enrique responded without hesitation. "That's why he'll command the attention and efforts of very important people in México and the United States. But I want to find him because he's my friend."

297

The mother continued crying, but Corvette understood that hers were tears of relief. She was overcome with emotion, and although Ignacio's sister also was happy that her brother was alive, Corvette observed that the girl was calculating things quickly. She looked briefly into Corvette's eyes as if to judge the sincerity of his heart while she was making decisions.

"Why are you here?" she asked Corvette.

The answer came out of him fast, and it surprised him:

"I came to Mexico to look for a girl, but I'm here now with Enrique because he's my friend and this is important to him, to find Ignacio."

"My brother means everything to us," the girl told him. "He has always been the heart of our family and very much the man after our father died."

She looked at her mother. "So we'll go, mama?"

The woman nodded with a fresh round of crying.

"We have passports," the girl told them. "We shop in the United States during the holidays like many people from Monterrey. Ignacio used to take us on those trips. Usually we went to Mcallen, Texas." She emphasized this as if it were a guess that Mcallen was where her brother was.

"He's not there now," Enrique told her.

They spent another fifteen minutes or so discussing some of the things that the women might have to do to prepare for a quick exit from Mexico, including the fact that no one could know or suspect what was about to happen. Ignacio's mother only had one living close relative, a brother who lived in León, and he became identified as possibly someone who might be informed in the future what had happened to his sister and niece. Apparently Ignacio's mother and her brother didn't converse that often. Enrique got on the phone with some Zs and requested that they be on standby to help him and to watch the house in the meantime. Ignacio's mother and sister had strong, tearful farewell hugs for both of them.

Corvette and Enrique rode in an emotional silence for a while back toward the heart of the city. Finally, Corvette spoke:

"Enrique, there's something I need to do. I have to call Raymundo and prepare him to meet my mum, and also I want to discuss with him letting everyone in Vegas know that I'm coming to play in the poker tournament. I want a big deal made out of it, so that the Zetas will know to contact me there."

Enrique nodded, but he looked glum. "There are dangerous times ahead. We need to get with David and talk to him about this. If you really want to do this, we have a lot of planning."

"Yeah, well, I've seen and learned a lot here. I want to find Valentina. I want to help catch the bad guys. I don't want to die or anything, but I can't just stand on the sidelines," Corvette replied. He hoped that the genuineness of his emotion overcame the lack of elegance in how he expressed it.

Then he remembered something. "I wonder if Ana has a good picture of Valentina. Raymundo has so many contacts and eyes all over Vegas. I already mentioned to him that I was looking for a girl. I would like to send him a picture. No one else has found her yet. If anyone could find a person, it would be Raymundo. He already had the Corvette everyone was looking for."

"Don't remind me," Enrique said, almost smiling in spite of himself. "Well, you're in luck. I have a picture of Valentina on my phone."

"Damn!" Corvette answered.

This time Enrique laughed. "Don't worry," he said. "She didn't give it to me. I just got it once when I had a fantasy."

Z-30, the Zeta
Las Vegas, Nevada
Thursday Morning

Santi arrived at the house with news and lots of opinions, the Zeta thought, like a man who wanted to move up in the ranks and get close to him. He remembered how Horacio had been the same way in the early days. The young guys did bold things to impress the boss. Santi was seated in a wicker love

299

seat opposite the Zeta, who was in what had become his customary place on the sofa in the solarium, the room which was his favorite in the house.

The first matter was that of Corvette Nightfire. "He isn't in Barbados," Santi reported. "The men followed his mother, and they turned the house upside down when she was out. No cash lying around the place. No sign of him there. They're now asking around the island, and we have guys who are now talking to associates of his in the poker world to see if anyone knows anything. No one talked to the mother. Figured she would never give him up unless it got rough, and you didn't want that. I'm hearing that there are rumors in Vegas, though, that he's going to play here."

"He's in the Final Table," responded the Zeta. "It would be huge news if he weren't going to play. If he comes to town, I want to be the first to talk to him."

"Don't you think he'll stay away because he took our money? What about the Feds wanting him?"

"They want me," the Zeta replied. "The kid took a bag from a woman who gave it to him and then left town with money in it. He has had time to think about things. That money is nothing compared to what he can make in the future. If he wins this tournament alone, he walks off with eight or nine million dollars. Even if he loses, he has won close to a million. He has a calculator in his head. I have one in mine that puts him in a big asset column for me. Besides, I have what he wants. He'll figure out that he needs to talk to me."

"What do you have that he wants?" Santi asked.

"The woman who gave him the bag. She might be what I want too. I haven't decided. She doesn't know it yet, but she's about to help me decide."

The Zeta saw that Santi let the last comment pass so he could bring up another topic that was truly a bombshell:

"Jefe, there's news in Monterrey. You know that on Saturday there's a kick-off rally for the anti-violence march being led by Ana Valdez and the poet, Carlos Limas. Before then, tomorrow night, there's a private party for many dignitaries of Monterrey and Mexico who are going to attend on Saturday. It is very high profile in terms of the guest list, but la fiesta itself hasn't been talked about much. There was a last-minute change in the entertainment. Now Los Zapata are the ones providing the music at the event."

"Madre de puta!"

"Sí, jefe, it's true. The guys didn't put it together until one of the musicians mentioned the name of Ana Valdez as attending."

"So, she's in Monterrey tomorrow night," the Zeta thought out loud. "And probably she's there even tonight. Usually, wherever she is, David James is there. So those two are probably in Monterrey right now."

Santi looked proud that he had been able to tell the Zeta something that he didn't already know. The Zeta stared out the glass windows of the solarium. He thought of Valentina and Corvette.

"I need to cut off the woman I mentioned to you from her aunt, who is Ana Valdez. For that matter, I want to cut off Corvette Nightfire from anyone other than me or the woman. The niece of Ana Valdez is Valentina Garza. I want her and Corvette to become completely dependent upon me. I had wanted to avoid killing Ana Valdez because she's an emotion for Mexico, but now I think this is the best thing."

"You should do David James at the same time," Santi replied. "It's not good if he's in Las Vegas when you are. He'll never stop tracking you, especially if you kill his wife."

The Zeta nodded. "He's already on me. Killing his wife will really make him crazy, and he would cause me unfathomable problems until I end it. I thought crippling The Z Foundation would slow him up, but the man doesn't think in traditional ways, I've discovered. He found me by following money and my enemies."

"You have to kill both Ana Valdez and her husband."

"It can't be murder. Their assassination would become an international concern with demands for justice. They have to die in an accident. I'll have someone in Monterrey find out their plans and itineraries the next few days."

The Zeta
Thursday Night

That night a black Chevrolet Suburban pulled up in front of the house to take the Zeta and Valentina to a private party in Henderson to celebrate the successful execution of El Asesino. Valentina looked stunning in a short white dress with a scandalous bodice and in silver high heels that caused the muscles of her toned calves to flex. She took the Zeta's arm and performed perfectly the role of narco-first-lady with the grace and sexiness that the Zeta desired in a woman who would be his wife. He received the envious looks that he wanted from his men. He was proud that his judgment of Valentina had been correct: She knew exactly how to act.

Yet much of the evening he spent reflecting on the visit that he had paid Ignacio on the way to the party. Something wasn't quite right.

He had taken Valentina inside with him. The three of them had drinks while they talked. He and Ignacio had drunk Modelo beer while Valentina sipped a red wine. The Zeta hadn't exactly introduced her other than to present her casually to Ignacio by saying, "This is Valentina." They had some initial conversation, and then the Zeta pulled out the ledger book which he had been consulting for days while he made phone calls.

When he handed Ignacio the book, he began speaking to him about it in English. As he handed it to him, Ignacio said, "Oh, this is the one...," and then he stopped.

"The one what?" asked the Zeta.

"Nothing, really. Someone said, I forget who, that you had a book that you would bring personally to me."

But he seemed nervous when he made that explanation to me, the Zeta thought.

The other thing was that from the moment in which they had entered the room, Ignacio kept glancing at Valentina. It wasn't like the looks of the other men who were admiring her, the Zeta thought.

Was it one of recognition?

As the evening at the party wore on, from time to time the Zeta returned to thinking about Ignacio and the way he looked at Valentina. His glances came nervously and quickly, as if he were both trying to focus on the conversation he was having with the Zeta and...and what?

...and memorizing her features. Why? To report this to someone?

Suddenly the Zeta remembered the look on Ignacio's face when they had first entered the room and Ignacio had seen Valentina. It was almost as if he had been told something about her beforehand. It wasn't exactly a look of recognition on Ignacio's face as much as it had been a revelation. He had not only been told about a ledger book, but he had been told about a woman! The Zeta was now sure of this.

And so, in the middle of the party celebrating the assassination of El Asesino, the Zeta summoned Santi from across the room to join him in a corner.

"I've been thinking about my conversation with Ignacio Lopez," he told Santi. "The man has been talking to someone outside the Zetas. Tomorrow, find out who it is."

David James
Monterrey, Mexico
Late Thursday Night

David easily spotted Ana as she emerged from the baggage pick-up area of the airport in Monterrey. She was walking big as always, big and proud, even though she stood only five foot two inches in bare feet. She wore the smile that melted his heart every time he saw her. He knew that she loved dazzling him. No matter how fatigued she might have been from her trip and long recent days, Ana would want to come to him looking Mexican-hot, the way he liked her.

So he was surprised by the big hug from Paula, who had run up to him without his registering her approach because he was looking at Ana.

"Dad!" she squealed in delight. She had stopped calling him "David" a couple of years earlier. She was taller than her mother. Her momentum from running actually knocked him back a step, and he laughed as he acknowledged her.

"Bienvenido, Angel!" he told her. "I'm so happy that you came!"

She kissed him on the cheek and then asked him excitedly, "Did you bring Enrique? I don't see him anywhere."

"Dios!" said Ana as she finally made it to David. "I think she has a one-track mind about Enrique now."

"Oh really?" David asked, but Ana cut his conversation off with a welcomed kiss. He hugged her closely afterwards as he told Paula, "Honey, he's with Corvette tonight, but you will see him tomorrow."

An airport attendant came up with a dolly loaded with luggage.

"We're women going to a gala," Ana said in response to David's bewildered look. "We have bags. Please tell me that you didn't bring the Camaro."

"No," David laughed. "I brought the SUV. Let's go home. We have some big days ahead."

Chapter 22: The Devil around Midnight

Corvette Nightfire
Monterrey, Mexico
Friday

Ana appeared on the scene early Friday morning with David and Paula at Enrique's condo while Enrique and Corvette were still chomping down omelets that Enrique had prepared again with hot coffee. Corvette saw that Ana was more stunning in person even than she appeared on television and internet clips where he had seen her before. She gave a warm and affectionate greeting to Corvette, and then, he noted, she took command. After being the past days in San Antonio, she had flown into Monterrey with her daughter determined to become involved in the last-minute details of the party that would be taking place that night at a private club called Noches Calientes. The name meant "Hot Nights," Enrique had explained.

"It's downtown near the old historic Monterrey district," he had added. "It's a very media-centered, high-tech building leased for lavish society parties, award programs, and corporate functions. They have a staff and events manager, but somehow Ana will become the boss even in the last few hours before the party," he had laughed.

That turned out to be true. Corvette and Enrique had spent the day and afternoon running errands to pick up items for the party, things "not thought of by the staff of the club," as Ana had put it.

"Although this party will be fun, the program tomorrow will focus on serious and very sad things that have happened to people in Mexico," Ana had said. "So I would like the festivities to wind down in a dignified way that commemorates and honors the guests."

So there were last-minute printings of poetry by Carlos Limas to be laminated and to be given to the guests, preparations for special toasts in glasses that Ana wanted, and numerous other things that she dispensed as duties for Enrique and Corvette as a team, David, and even Paula. On top of that, she pointed out that no one had made arrangements for Corvette's tuxedo. She made a call and received an appointment for a morning fitting of the gringo.

"Let me guess," Corvette had said to Enrique. "You and David own tuxedos."

"We're with Ana," Enrique had replied. "Of course we have tuxedos! We have them in several colors. There are always galas to go to when you're with Ana."

He did find an hour in the early afternoon to make phone calls, just after he and Enrique had gulped down some tacos from a sidewalk stand. Corvette sat on a bench in a small grassy park near Noches Calientes while Enrique went inside the building to confer about something with David. He had suddenly realized that it was about time for his mother's flight to arrive in Las Vegas, and he tried to call her. He was about to become frustrated by several attempts which went to her voice mail, when a text popped up from Raymundo:

"Your mom and I have met. She's lovely. We're on the way to my house."

"Tell her to cut on her phone," Corvette texted back.

She answered his call moments later.

"Is everything okay, Mum?"

His mother sounded exuberant. She seemed to *sing* her responses. "Yes, I'm fine, Luv. Everything went so well. I transferred from a Miami flight. No problems of bad men following me in Barbados or in Miami. Raymundo is so charming. You didn't tell me that he would be so funny. He's taking me to his home to meet his girlfriend. His cousin is in the van with us, and after I settle in the house, apparently we're all going out to have a seafood dinner. I'm having a lovely time."

That didn't take long, Corvette thought, grinning as he remembered what times could be like with Raymundo.

"You're on posters everywhere in the airport, Corvette! There are so many advertisements about the Final Table next week at The Rio with pictures of the nine of you. It's so exciting to see you on those! I'm so proud of you, son!"

"Aww, thanks, Mum. Listen, would you mind handing the phone to Raymundo for a moment so I can talk to him?"

When Raymundo got on the phone, he said to Corvette, "Hola, mi amigo méxicano! Your mom is tall, blonde, and beautiful. What happened to you?"

"A recessive Mexican gene, I guess," Corvette answered. But the fast pace of his day had Corvette hyped, so he pressed forward with business.

"Ok, Raymundo, thanks for getting my mother and taking care of her. Listen, I'm landing in Las Vegas Sunday evening on flight 4254 from Monterrey at 5:45 p.m. Can you get the word out to the press; the hotels, especially The Rio; and to some of my poker buddies whom you know? Well, you know how to do this stuff. I just want to be sure that people know that I'm coming to play. Don't say from where I am coming. The flight I will be on will be a connection from Los Angeles."

"Already working on that. Just needed to know when you would arrive. Gracias!"

"And you received the picture of Valentina that I sent you..."

"And the search is on, sí. Ella es muy hermosa. She's so beautiful. No wonder you're looking for her!" Raymundo interrupted.

"Sí, I'm very worried about her," Corvette said. "And the other item: the bodyguards, Jupiter and Mars."

Raymundo laughed. "Jupiter and Pluto," he corrected. "You're thinking of the song, 'Fly Me to the Moon.' You're wondering what life is like on Jupiter and Mars. It's a very Vegas song."

"God, yes, Pluto, I mean."

"He's the god of the Underworld."

Corvette sighed. "I hope he's on our side," he said.

"The gods will be there when you land Sunday night."

The day passed in a quick succession of errands, stops, deliveries, and tuxedo fitting. It was Friday night at the gala when Corvette found himself alone sometimes, smiling and nodding to the dignitaries passing by him in the entranceway. He felt unaccustomed emotions, a mixture of sadness and wistfulness as he stood there, an English observer of a Spanish world. The Mexicans coming in were educators, philosophers, editorialists, television commentators, historians, manufacturers, artists, poets, novelists, recording artists, actors and actresses of the theater and cinema, and, of course, politicians. Enrique pointed out the governor and his wife, and even some Senators and Deputies from the Distrito Federal. It seemed a small world, Corvette noticed, as if these people all knew one another. They were animated and physical, hugging and kissing one another, and being overly complimentary on how well everyone looked. The women wore curve-hugging gowns and much jewelry. Corvette soon concluded that the people at the party weren't necessarily ones who had lost children, brothers, sisters, or parents to the pervasive, cruel violence of México. These were influential people who wanted to support the ones who had and who wanted to carry the agenda of change across their country and over the border into the United States.

Outside in the city streets, the scene starkly contrasted with the elegance inside the building. Corvette had been on the sidewalk with Enrique just before it had grown dark. He had seen the arrival of the Army units. The soldiers posted themselves in full uniform and weaponry in front of the building and throughout the surrounding blocks. He found it shocking to see them. It wasn't anything normally witnessed in the United States. The military jeeps, pick-up trucks, and flat-bed troop carriers parked alongside the police cars that bore the notations, "Federal," "Estado," and "Civil Fuerza," representing the federal, state, and city police units who were on hand to manage the arrival of the dignitaries. In addition to these, young people in black pants and shirts, the Zs, also posted themselves

308

in small groups for blocks around Noches Calientes. They were equipped with radios and data phones and were constantly texting or speaking on them. Corvette had accompanied Enrique in the late afternoon as he went from one Z group to another and offered each suggestions on what to be observing and communicating.

Downtown Monterrey was even more of a mess with traffic than usual. It wasn't only because of the gala, but also because tens of thousands of people were arriving in the city from all over the country to jam the streets surrounding the Macroplaza in the morning. Work crews were in that plaza, about a mile away, still preparing stages for the programs that would begin Saturday morning.

The road crew for the musicians, Los Zapata, had arrived in the early afternoon, and Corvette had watched them for a while preparing the stage in the events building. Just as darkness extinguished the last orange hints of the day in the western sky, the musicians arrived and filed into the entrance as Corvette and Enrique nodded greetings to them. There were twelve in the band, Corvette saw, and later a group of male dancers dressed as Mexican cowboys arrived. Inside, they put on the colorful "pointy boots" with exaggerated toes that extended in front of the shoes up to five feet and then curled upward. These muchachos practiced their dancing in the boots to tribal guarachero music, and when they came out to dance later at the event, the guests pushed to crowd around them and gave them raucous applause.

Corvette's heart stirred in an unfamiliar way when he saw them. They appeared so proud, so macho, and so elegant in their style. He was surprised suddenly to feel tears in his eyes.

He wondered, *Why am I so emotional?*

He turned and looked around, seeking Enrique. Enrique wasn't far away, watching the dancers with Paula. Corvette felt that he needed to be beside them. He went to stand with Enrique, and the dancing ended at that moment. Corvette pulled at Enrique's arm.

"Enrique, I..." But the words caught in his throat. He waited a few seconds, and then he said. "I guess I want to tell you that from now on, I'm going to give half of my future earnings in poker to The Z Foundation. That includes whatever winnings I have next week in Las Vegas."

Paula, who had attended bilingual schools all her life, understood Corvette's English, and her eyes went wide. Enrique stared intently into Corvette's eyes. Nodding with his usual serious expression, he thumped twice on Corvette's chest.

"Your heart is good, Corvette," he told him. "Your life is going to make a big difference to many people." Then, to Corvette's surprise, Enrique hugged him. Paula came forward and did the same.

Corvette didn't know what else to say. The lump in his throat hurt a little. The other two apparently didn't know what to say either. The dancers left the floor to the loud cheers and whistles of the crowd, and then the musicians began to play so that the gala guests would dance. To Corvette, the silence of the three of them began to feel awkward. He turned to Enrique, and in a low voice, suggested, "Amigo, perhaps you should ask Paula to dance. I think she wants that."

Enrique's whispered response had to be loud because of the music: "I'm not such a good dancer, Corvette." But Paula heard.

She said, "Enrique, I've seen you dance before. You show real promise. You're in luck because tonight you're with me, and I'm going to show you some steps. They're easy."

When she led Enrique away to the dance floor, Corvette thought that Paula looked just like Ana. She walked big. When she got into Enrique's arms, she looked up at him with a smile that made Corvette know that Enrique was a goner. He watched long enough to see that Enrique wasn't going to be able to take his eyes off her. Then he went outside. He wanted to talk to some Zs. Some of them knew English.

He was in the "family room" of the small ranch house when he heard the two vehicles drive up. The whole day had been non-routine. In fact, ever since the Zeta's visit the previous day, there had been numbers of hushed private cell phone calls to the men in the house. They left his presence when they received the calls. That was different from all the other days since he had arrived in Las Vegas and had lived and had worked in this house.

He knew why. The Zeta had noticed his mistake when he commented about the ledger book. The Zeta had sensed his nervousness. Since yesterday, Ignacio knew that his time was soon coming to an end. He had hoped to give Enrique enough time to develop the plan to move his mom and sister out of Mexico. When the vehicles arrived and Ignacio saw through the window the men get out of the two SUVs, he realized that he was out of time. These weren't men he had seen before. It was late. There was no reason for them to be there except for him. It wasn't a house, a location, visited by many. They were there for him.

He had had a guard for the evening. The man's presence was supposed to be subtle, Ignacio understood. The guy lived in the house off and on, but he had never spent time with him in the evening before. Suddenly tonight he was friendly and interested in conversation, interested in everything that Ignacio was doing.

The man made the mistake of standing beside Ignacio to look out the window with him through the partially opened blinds to watch the men getting out of the SUVs. Without hesitation, Ignacio grabbed a table lamp beside them. It was heavy and metal, and the light went out when Ignacio jerked it and the cord ripped from the wall. Because of the lamp's heft, Ignacio held it with both hands. Rotating his body, he swung it with a powerful blow against his guard's cranium and sent the

311

man crashing to the floor. There was another lamp on in the room. It provided enough light for Ignacio to see. He grabbed the man's pistol from his holster. When he raised up, Ignacio saw through the window that the men were apparently conferencing briefly. He wasn't going to wait to see if they had noticed a change in light in the room. He picked up the lamp, and, holding both it and the pistol clumsily, he ran to his bedroom, which looked out from the rear of the house.

His bed was parallel to a wall that had a single window. He put the lamp and pistol on his bed and then hurried to his closet and retrieved a cell phone which he had hidden in a shoe on the floor. Hoping it still had battery charge, he powered it on. Hearing it come alive, he thrust it into his pants pocket. He looked in the corner of the closet floor and observed the laptop and the desktop computers he had moved there a couple of hours earlier. The Zeta had brought him the laptop to replace the one taken away when he had come to visit him with the woman, Valentina. It had been taken away along with all storage media to be analyzed, he knew. They had replaced the hard drive in the desktop computer. This confirmed to him that he was under suspicion.

I was right that they would come for me soon, he thought. *But when I'm gone, they won't find anything on any hard storage that would help them. I've made sure of that!*

The anxiety motivating him right now to escape had to do with his mother and sister. He must talk with Enrique!

He already knew that the small bedroom window wouldn't open because he had tried it before. He knelt on top of the bed in front of the window. He stuck the pistol in his pocket, picked up the lamp near its top, and then swung the base of it with all his might against the glass of the window. Shards went flying both inside the room and outdoors. Ignacio used the lamp to knock out remaining jags of glass in the window until he had enough room to put his body through. He backed his way out and dropped to the ground.

The back yard was fenced by an adobe wall that matched the house. He already heard shouting and cursing coming from the front yard. They knew that he was escaping. He judged that the wall and the gate to the front would slow them a moment. He ran to the rear wall grabbing as he went a lightweight plastic chair that was beside the home's small swimming pool. He used the chair to give him enough height to put his hands on top of the wall. He was able to raise himself by locking his arms straight, and then he got a leg on top of the wall, went over the top, and dropped to the other side.

He was young. He had played fútbol at the university in Monterrey, and although he was nowhere near in shape like he was in those years, he could still run fast. He remembered that he was in a community of homes in a still somewhat desert area on the outskirts of Las Vegas. He managed to climb walls, cross streets, and get a few blocks away from the house where he had been staying. He could hear his pursuers. They spotted him from time to time, and they paused to make radio calls to others to report his location. In the quiet community, he easily heard the sounds of the approaching SUVs guided by the directions of the men who were running after him.

Ignacio got into the back yard of a home with a storage shed. He only needed a little bit of time, and with hope, he tried to open the double doors. They opened! He hid inside. By the light of the phone he could see, and he dialed Enrique's number. He let it ring what felt like twenty times, but there was no answer.

He screamed in his mind, *God, Enrique, please!*

He cut the call and redialed.

This time Enrique answered on the fourth ring.

"Enrique, it's Ignacio," he whispered. He heard a lot of background noise on the other end of the line.

"Ignacio? Louder..."

"I can't!"

"One moment," Enrique told him. Ignacio heard less noise on the line as precious time ticked by.

"Okay," Enrique said at last.

"They're here for me! They're almost on top of me. Listen to me carefully! Have you made arrangements for my mom and sister?"

"Sí, sí!" Enrique responded. Ignacio could hear the tone of alarm that had rushed into Enrique's voice. "They're leaving, Ignacio! They're being moved in the morning. The FBI is helping us with this. David got the right people involved. Your mom is so happy that you're alive! She wants to come to the United States because you're there."

"Listen to me! Move them tonight! Get them out of Mexico! The cartel guys are here for me now. I only have moments! Promise!"

"I promise! Please, where are you?"

"Shut up and listen! Remember this information. Listen to me!"

"Okay, Ignacio, I'm listening!"

"What I told you before about the Deep Web: You have to find El Camino Oscuro. It might be called The Dark Way. You have to remember these important numbers: Seven, forty-two, three, twenty-one, three, eighty-four. Repeat them!"

Enrique repeated but missed one of the numbers.

"No! Listen! Seven, forty-two, three, twenty-one, three, eighty-four. Repeat!"

Enrique did, and he spoke them correctly.

"Sí! Keep repeating them in your mind until you write them down. That's the start of the sequence. You have to get the rest."

"Please, Ignacio, where are you?"

Ignacio could hear men in the yard outside. He knew he had just seconds before they would open the door.

"I can't let them torture me and learn what I have done, Enrique. You have to find El Camino and use the numbers." He spoke even faster now, knowing that he needed time to fire two shots with the pistol. He thought he heard them just outside the doors of the shed. "They're here! Keep your promises! These

314

guys won't stop. You've been a good friend to me. Please understand what I have to do."

He heard Enrique screaming, "Ignacio! Please tell me where you are!"

But the men were at the door. He heard one call out, "Santi, over here!"

He threw the phone down in front of him and pulled the pistol from his pocket. He shot the phone, and then he thrust the nozzle to the roof of his mouth and pulled the trigger.

Ricardo, "La Luz"
Saturday, 1:30 a.m.
A Ranch, eighteen miles from Monterrey, Mexico

Jesús! Jesús! Ricardo screamed in his mind. He wanted to cry. He had stopped going to mass with his mama, but in all the years of his life, he had never said prayers with such feeling as this: desperate beyond what anyone should feel in life. He couldn't even think a longer prayer, like, *God, please help me!*

Just *Jesús!*

Again and again he heard the man leading the executioners say, "Tell me who you work for." But, one by one, each of Ricardo's associates in the band just cried for mercy or insisted that he was simply a musician.

"We're not in a cartel!" one cried pleadingly.

Then, from under the truck, Ricardo could see the executioners put a pistol to the head of his wrist-tied companions and pull the trigger. Each of Ricardo's friends rolled over with a sickening thud. Then the men from the cartel picked up the body and threw it into the well.

They were going to kill all fourteen of the others, Ricardo realized. The musicians and three crew members. It wouldn't matter what the answers would be to the executioner's question. Los Zapata and the crew members had already been condemned as working for the Zetas.

"Just so you know," one of the executioners had said before pulling the trigger. "You die at the hands of the proud men of Sinaloa!"

Ricardo, "La Luz," so nicknamed because his voice was like light (said his friends), was diminutive. After the band had left the gala at Noches Calientes and were traveling in their van, the pickup trucks and SUVs of the executioners had stopped them. The kidnappers had AK-47s and had transferred the musicians into the rear beds of three pickups with camper shells. Before pushing them inside the trucks, the armed men had slapped cuffs on them and then locked them inside. The musicians reclined in the beds of the trucks as they sped from the city into the moonless night of the country. They heard the engines of the vehicles slow as they turned into the entrance of a ranch, and then they bumped across scrubland until they came to this ancient-looking stone well.

When the trucks were being unloaded, Ricardo simply lay on the floor against the length of the truck cabin. It was the darkest spot. He thought it was a miracle that the man who got the others out didn't see him. The Sinaloans seemed hyped-up and anxious to get to the work at hand. Ricardo thought that this might be a reason why he had been unnoticed in the dark shadows of the pickup bed. His prayer began as soon as he realized that the man wasn't seeing him and telling him to get out.

Jesús!

As silently as he could, Ricardo had inched his way to the edge of the open bed door and had dropped to the ground. He then rolled under the truck to hide, and from there he had a perfect view of what was happening. But when he saw that all his friends were going to be murdered, he understood that his fate would be the same if he remained where he was. It seemed like a complete impossibility to escape, but he had no options other than to try.

He emerged from under the rear of the truck. He saw that the vehicle was the one most at the rear of the haphazardly parked SUVs and trucks. All the men and his friends were forward of the vehicles and in the headlight beams. Those were blinding anyone who might have been looking in his direction. What Ricardo saw behind him was completely dark flat scrubland. He crouched and ran silently through it.

Jesús! They weren't noticing him!

When the sounds of their voices grew very distant, Ricardo straightened and ran as fast as he could. He was still in his musician suit and dress boots, not clothing designed for running in wilderness. But tonight he didn't feel the scratches and tears of his clothing and skin as he ran, and he didn't care about the occasional stumbles. With every second his chances of surviving increased. He came to a wire cattle fence. He cut his cheek and arm getting through it. There was a dirt road on the other side, and he followed it, running as fast as he could. Just when he began to gasp in the cold night air and his side ached from breathlessness, he saw ahead the dark shadow of the ranch house.

He needed help. In the house, were there people who would help him, or would they be aligned with the executioners, he wondered.

He heard a voice inside tell him to run and pound on the door of the house and to shout for help. He took this to be the voice of Jesus, who was answering his prayer. When the concerned and anxious man and wife answered his calls for help by opening the door and immediately phoning state police, he saw that the complete miracle of his escape had come to pass.

Now he was the sole witness of a heinous mass murder, and he would need all God's angels on earth to protect him.

Chapter 23: Explosions

The Zeta, Z-30
Las Vegas, Nevada
Saturday Morning

The mental storm struck first in English, maybe because he was in the United States.

No fucking way! No fucking way! This did not happen! No fucking way!

Then in Spanish:

Madre de puta!

It was a hurricane of rage, and the Zeta, so skilled in controlling his emotions, almost became uprooted. He saw Santi revolving in and out of view, but it was because he was turning himself around, trying not to smash his fists into anything, just trying to spin off feelings that he felt were beating him to a pulp. His heart was racing. He had to do something or he would explode.

So he screamed, "Fuck!" He screamed it again and again, and Santi backed away. The Zeta felt his face become beet red. The bodyguards in the room looked at each other nervously. The Zeta kept cursing until he could hear his own voice cracking, and then he quit because he was breathing too fast. He put his hand on the back of the wicker sofa so that he would stop turning. When he felt steady enough, he turned his gaze toward Santi.

"All of them, Santi? All but one?"

He asked the questions only to reassure Santi that he was going to calm himself and that it would be safe for Santi to continue talking.

"Sí, jefe," Santi responded, verifying what he had already reported. "All the musicians and the road crew except one. The police announcement to the news reporters this morning said that one of Los Zapata had escaped and had gone to the ranch house of the property and had contacted authorities. He showed the police the well where the bodies had been thrown. He told them that they had been executed by the Cartel of Sinaloa because they believed that Los Zapata worked only for the Zetas."

"Who escaped?"

"They wouldn't say, jefe. In fact, they said that the Federales already had moved him outside the country for his protection. They said that he was terrified of retributions for escaping and reporting what had happened."

"So we don't know which one it was?"

"No, jefe, not yet."

The Zeta looked down at the floor, but he knew that the others could see what he was feeling: his face flushing red again. He waited a minute more until the heat that he was feeling passed.

Then he said, "This is a fucked up morning, Santi. First of all, we know why those dogs from Sinaloa murdered our boys. That was retaliation for El Asesino, pure and simple. I admit, I'm surprised, not by the retaliation, but by how they chose to do it. I thought they might make attempts directly on us. They're cowards, but very clever. They murder the musicians right before the rally for stopping violence! How is that for a big up-your-ass to the politicians and do-gooders of our country, many there in Monterrey this morning? A big 'Fuck-you!' to us. A big 'Fuck-you' to Ana Valdez and the President of México who are trying to reduce violence in the country. We had a change in government because of this shit before, and now Sinaloa is saying, 'You changed nothing! In fact, we're bringing our war into the United States now.'"

In fact, he was thinking, *Sinaloa just did to me what I did to them when I executed the former President of Mexico and his family.*

He got quiet again. He saw that Santi knew what would be coming next.

"You let Ignacio kill himself, Santi."

Santi nodded. "We were seconds too late."

319

"What has that mistake cost us?" The Zeta asked the question knowing that it couldn't be answered. He didn't intend for Santi to try, but Santi spoke anyway, clearly trying to make Ignacio's death seem less of a screw-up.

"We didn't find anything on the hard drive or the storage media. There's no evidence that he reported any information to anyone."

"He did," the Zeta answered. "I would bet my life on it. Or yours." He observed Santi looking through the sides of his eyes at the bodyguards to see if they were moving toward him or not. He wanted Santi to sweat because of his carelessness, but he knew that he still needed him.

I have to use him on the other mission, the Zeta thought. *Ignacio fooled me. I waited too long to give Santi his instructions. I've been too fucking distracted. This is as much my fault as his. He has done okay up to now.*

But a small wave of anger snuck up on him, an aftershock. *Mierda! Shit!*

He kicked the back of the wicker sofa. It helped. He calmed.

"Santi." He pulled out his pistol with the gold handle and walked up to him. He put the pistol to Santi's temple. The man's pleasant face constricted with the expectation of the gunshot. The bodyguards tensed.

"This isn't for you," the Zeta said. "You fucked up, but I underestimated Ignacio. I got a lot from him, but he fooled me into thinking that his usefulness to me could continue. I want you to remember this gun to the brain. Ask me why."

"Why, jefe?" Santi said without hesitation.

"This is what I want you to do with every Sinaloan pig in Las Vegas. A gun to the head. I want them all, Santi. You understand me? I'll give you the men you need for the job. Don't shoot the Sinaloans in the streets. You find them quietly. With the guns to their heads you lead them out to the desert; you pull the triggers; and you pile them in a big hole like that well in México. This is your job. You do this over the next days as quietly as possible. While you do that job, I'm going to do mine."

The Zeta returned the pistol to its holster. He stepped in front of Santi and spoke to him face to face.

"I'm going to call in favors to get information where these dogs of Sinaloa are. You will talk to me before each strike. I'll authorize the hits. I have a man in Monterrey who I'll put into action to do the same there. I'll coordinate the timing of his strikes with yours. While we do this work, I'll also manage what needs to happen at the big card game, The World Series of Poker. But I want what you do to be a surgical operation, not a public butchery of these putas. Me comprendes?"

"I understand you perfectly, Jefe," Santi said without hesitation. "Gracias for this opportunity to do this for you."

The Zeta stepped back. He let out a long exhale. "Bien," he said. "Bien."

He thought for a moment that Santi might slump to the floor from relief that he wasn't going to be executed, but the man quickly regained his composure. The Zeta suspected that Santi was looking at him now with a huge increase in respect. He nodded to the bodyguards to leave the room so that he could be alone with him.

When they closed the door behind them, the Zeta told Santi, "Word is that Corvette Nightfire is arriving in Las Vegas tomorrow night. Suddenly everybody in town knows this. I'll meet with him. This morning I'll help you prepare things for the work you'll do. We'll find out what facts we have and we'll plan. We'll call in men."

"Good," Santi said.

"This thing we discussed before: the accident for Ana Valdez and David James. I have put the man in Monterrey in charge of that. You need to forget it."

"Forgotten, Jefe."

"Then, vámonos," answered the Zeta. "Let's get to work."

He grabbed his jacket from the sofa and led Santi from the room.

Corvette Nightfire
Saturday Night
Los Angeles, California

He felt so upset that he wished he had a psychiatrist to talk to right then. He had never been to one before. He could have a conversation with one; and she (he envisioned a woman doctor) would order him some medicine for anxiety, maybe reassure him that he would be fine; and then he would relax enough to be able to focus on the strategies for the poker hands that were coming in the next days. Without this, how was he ever going to be able to settle down enough to play?

The jet was about to land in Los Angeles. He had spent the entire flight with his eyes closed, trying to sleep; but fragments of conversations and memories coming in random order tortured him.

"We have to get you out of Monterrey," David had said. "Things are unpredictable right now. This murder of Los Zapata has thrown the city into turmoil. The whole country is upset about it. The Zetas and the Cartel of Sinaloa are escalating a war of retribution. I would feel better if we already have you at the airport for your flight to LA, even if it is a couple of hours early. A couple of General Alvarez's soldiers will sit with you until you board."

David had told him this in the early afternoon, just after the President of Mexico had made his emotional speech at the rally in the Macroplaza. All day the crowds had been crying as the speakers, who had come with speeches already prepared to play on emotions, became overwhelmed themselves as information about what had happened to the musicians the night before flowed in throughout the morning. It had been difficult for Corvette to understand what people were saying, but he understood the cracking voices and the crying. He saw the grief and the alarm on their faces.

Ana had been one with power in her speech. She had delivered her words laden with courage. Corvette could feel it

322

even as she spoke in Spanish. Then she had surprised him with portions of her speech in English, and, clearly, many in the large crowd had understood her. When she was done, Corvette almost envisioned everyone turning to march north to the border behind flag bearers with the flags of Mexico and the United States and Ana leading them. She had done something similarly symbolic at the International Bridge during her brief stint as the Interim President of Mexico. On that occasion, she had met President Donald Austin Blair halfway to celebrate the reopening of the border after the military coup had overthrown the government of Mexico.

And one of the leaders of that coup, General Alfonso Alvarez, highly regarded as a hero in Mexico, had just ridden with him, David, and some other man, who apparently was in military intelligence in the United States Army, to drop Corvette off at the airport!

What a crazy day, Corvette thought, reflecting on everything as the jet touched down in Los Angeles. He guessed that the men had ridden with him to have an opportunity to meet and plan and discuss all sorts of things that Corvette couldn't know because they spoke to each other in Spanish the whole way to the airport. Corvette had largely been ignored. They had had plenty of time for discussions. Because of the crowds and the traffic gridlock in the city, even their small military convoy with special privileges had to claw its way through, and it had taken nearly two hours to arrive at the airport. On the way, Corvette had been able to discern that the men were deeply concerned about some information that the intelligence man had shared.

But even before they had left to go to the airport in Monterrey, David had told him that it was a good idea that Corvette was arriving in Las Vegas from Los Angeles on the next day, Sunday.

"The Zetas have been looking for you," he had said. "If they find you, they'll want to know where you've been. You can tell them you've been in Los Angeles."

"Yeah," Corvette had answered, "that's what I had planned to say." But he could hear what was in his voice. He was a little afraid.

David had put his hands on Corvette's shoulders and had looked him in the eyes.

"Listen to me, Corvette. You're going to hear all sorts of rumors and crazy things leading up to the tournament. Only believe what you see. Nothing else. You're going to have all kinds of protection around you that's invisible. Trust me, it'll be there. Enrique will be in Las Vegas already when you arrive."

That had surprised him. Enrique had told him that he would come to Las Vegas, but he didn't know that it was already arranged for him to be there ahead of him.

"I guess there will be Zs around," Corvette offered.

"Yes, and undercover protection too. So I want you to focus on the tournament and do your best."

"God, David, I'll try, but you know I'm desperate to find Valentina. I have my mind on so many things."

"We all want to find her, and we will. I promise you. Keep your mind on the probabilities of the cards."

"And the bluffing. It's what I do in life now," Corvette responded. He had then remembered something:

"You know that Raymundo has hired bodyguards for me and that he has been looking out for my mum."

"Yes, we're taking all of that into consideration."

Then David had sighed and had been silent a couple of moments, apparently reflecting on what he was about to say next:

"Ana and I had a big argument, but we got things straight. When Enrique told us that he was going to be in Las Vegas with you, and that both of you believe Valentina is there, I wanted also to come. Immediately Ana said that she was coming. I thought it might be a good idea for her to stay away from Vegas, but there is never any way to change her mind once she has decided something. We all have the same hunch as you: that Valentina is in Vegas and that the next part of all this will play out there. We haven't made final plans yet, but we're coming to Las Vegas either Sunday night or Monday morning. We have to get Paula back to San Antonio, and we have to make arrangements for someone to watch over the kids." When he said the last thing, Corvette saw David's face darken even more with worry.

In Los Angeles he had to get his bags and go through customs, and that activity gave him a few moments of relief from the barrage of anxious thoughts that kept besieging him. But when he stood in the customs line, he remembered the surreal scene at the Monterrey airport when they had finally arrived and soldiers had accompanied him into the terminal with the General and David. The fourth man who had ridden with them had disappeared. The airport was swamped with fully-geared soldiers. Corvette deduced that it was protection for the dignitaries who were traveling as a result of attending the rally.

And also because of Mexico's edginess after the murders of Los Zapata, he had thought. He had remembered the bright and happy faces of the musicians as they had played for the appreciative crowd the night before. A shiver of sadness had shaken him.

In the Monterrey terminal, it had been so crowded that people had been bumping into them. When David had given a farewell hug and was leaving him, Corvette had worked up the courage to ask a question that had been nagging him since the ride in the car.

"David!" he had called out, and David had returned to him. The General had hung in the distance talking to soldiers.

"I want to ask you what you guys were discussing on the way here. It looked really serious. Can you tell me?"

David had nodded and had lowered his voice. "Okay," he said, "It's just that there's a lot of intelligence that there will be an attempt on our lives. Mine and Ana's. That's nothing really new, Corvette. Ana and I live with that possibility daily. But the man riding with us wanted to talk with me and the General specifically about a flurry of new intelligence information that an attack on us could be imminent. Sources here in Mexico and in the United States have been reporting it. None of it has been very verifiable yet. But Ana and I have Paula here, so you can imagine how we want to get her home and make sure that she and her brother are safe. The discussions in the car all had to do with what precautions and actions we should be taking now."

"I wish there was something I could do to help."

David had then smiled and had given him a second goodbye hug. "You just kick ass in Vegas and keep your eyes and ears open for Valentina," David had answered. Then he and the General exited the Monterrey terminal, and Corvette went to find the gate of his flight.

Accompanied by two soldiers, he thought. *How my life has changed in Mexico!*

But in Los Angeles, now alone, Corvette remembered the names of his new friends as he stood in line to go through customs.

David, Ana, Paula, and Enrique.

He already cared deeply about them. The week he had spent with them had been the most dramatically intense week of his life. It had been life in a Spanish world, and he wanted to understand it more: the language and the culture. Now, as he looked around, he saw English signs once again, but with Spanish language also included. This was symbolic to him of the person he had discovered within himself. He was both gringo and Mexican. He felt like he was awakening from a dream, but what lay ahead of him to do was real. The future seemed daunting.

Welcome home, Corvette thought. *Why didn't I just become a CPA? Maybe I would be just be going to work in a cubicle every morning.*

But he knew that he was too deep in the game for that kind of placid life now.

From sheer nervous exhaustion, Corvette slept in the room of his motel, located right beside the airport in Los Angeles, until time for him to prepare for the second leg of his journey. The flight to Las Vegas was quick. It was amazing to him the difference that sleep had made. He felt calmer. When he looked out the plane window to the lights of Las Vegas as they descended, he felt back in his element. He was convinced that in the lights below somewhere was Valentina, and this made him feel braver.

When he arrived in the baggage-pickup area in McCarran International Airport, he immediately spotted Raymundo; his mum; an absolutely gigantic, mean-looking young white guy; and a black-skinned, short, fire-plug of a man, all of whom suddenly noticed him. His mum clapped her hands together and ran forward; Raymundo broke into a smile; the white giant relaxed his face and became dopey-looking; and the short black guy maintained a stare that looked murderous.

After the greetings, Corvette told them that he was ravenous. They all piled into Raymundo's van and, upon Corvette's choice, stopped at a diner so that Corvette could satisfy his craving for a late steak-and-eggs breakfast. Some young guys sitting at a table in the restaurant greeted him as he passed:

"Hey, Corvette! Good luck this week, man!"

The greeting caught Corvette off guard. *I should get used to being recognized a little more frequently than before*, he thought.

Being with his mum and Raymundo cheered him. Jupiter and Pluto sat on the ends of the booth seats and watched the room of people as they ate. Jupiter spoke a little and seemed affable, but Pluto was silent. Corvette felt something disquieting about the way the man looked at him.

That's probably what makes him an excellent bodyguard, Corvette reassured himself. *He's short but manages to be intimidating just from his stare.*

It turned out that the plan was for Corvette to stay at the home of one of Raymundo's cousins for the night, even though he was booked at The Rio. He would go to The Rio the next morning and would stay there during the tournament. Raymundo had clarified this with administrative staff of the hotel and the tournament. Madeline would continue to stay in the home of Raymundo and his girlfriend. Pluto was going to have the night shift watching Corvette, catching a nap in the morning, and then joining Jupiter to attend Corvette backstage at The Rio during the tournament.

"Just wanted to keep you away from The Rio until the last minute, hermano," Raymundo explained. "A whole lot of people know that you're in town now. Trying to hide you from the public until it is necessary for you to show. You wanted everyone to know you would be at the tournament to play. Well, they know."

"Gracias, Raymundo," Corvette said. He signed off on the plan for the sleeping quarters and the bodyguards. But he was wishing that Jupiter was the one who had first duty with him. He also wanted to talk to Raymundo about Enrique, that he was someone he should meet and know, and that Enrique probably was already in Las Vegas. However, there was no opportunity to explain this while they were all together. For some reason, probably because of his discomfort with Pluto, Corvette didn't want to talk about Enrique in front of the bodyguards just yet. In all the franticness of the last couple of days, Corvette had forgotten to fill Raymundo in on the fact that David, Ana, and Enrique were all coming to town and that there would be other protection for him in Las Vegas in addition to Jupiter and Pluto.

But while they ate in the diner, Corvette decided to text Enrique to let him know the plans for him for the night. He tried to do it surreptitiously, but he saw that both bodyguards noticed him typing on the phone. Enrique didn't answer the message.

Then Corvette had a revelation. He texted Raymundo and told him not to show a reaction to what he was about to read. He wrote that he needed to inform him about other protection he might have, including Enrique and the Zs, but that he wasn't comfortable with the bodyguards knowing about this until after he and Raymundo had an opportunity to talk. He saw Raymundo read his message with a completely impassive expression and then put the phone back in his pocket. He gave a slight nod to Corvette that he understood.

Maybe it was the coffee and the breakfast, but suddenly Corvette felt very alert. He remembered what David had said:

You're going to have all sorts of protection around you that is invisible.

He looked at the table of young men who had greeted him. They were Hispanic and athletic looking.

Zs? he wondered.

Then he felt foolish. *God, Corvette, get a grip. How could Zs have been in here ahead of you? No one knew that you would want to come to this diner.*

Now he looked around because he hadn't paid attention to the customers who had entered the diner after him. The place was crowded, and several of the patrons looked like they could be candidates as his invisible protectors.

Okay, settle down. Let's just assume that I have guardian angels out there and not worry. Also, don't forget St. Rogelio! he remembered. He said his little prayer to his father silently.

Raymundo's cousin lived in a tidy neighborhood of very small single-story homes in one of the infinite number of similar suburban developments that had spread like wildfire throughout the desert surrounding Las Vegas. It was about ten p.m. when they arrived. Raymundo insisted that Corvette should go to bed early before the tournament, although Corvette now felt wide awake from all the sleep he had had. So while Madeline and Jupiter waited in the van, Raymundo and Pluto accompanied Corvette for a quick introduction to the cousin.

A figure sitting on the front stoop started to make his way in the darkness toward them as Raymundo and Corvette got Corvette's bags from the rear of the van. While Corvette lugged a heavy bag down to the ground, Raymundo said, "This is Cool."

"What's cool?" Corvette asked, turning and suddenly seeing the man beside them.

"My cousin," Raymundo answered. "His name is Cool."

Corvette started laughing. "Of course it is. Jupiter, Pluto, and Cool. Life with Raymundo!"

Raymundo and Cool laughed as the cousin shook hands with Corvette, but Pluto didn't.

In fact, it wasn't until after he had settled in his bedroom and had exchanged a couple of stories with Cool about Raymundo that Corvette realized that Pluto had never uttered a single word since meeting him.

There were two single beds in the tiny bedroom assigned to Corvette, and apparently Pluto was going to be his roommate in there as well. Cool had to be up early for work the next morning so he said his goodnight and closed himself in the adjoining bedroom. Corvette and Pluto heard him snoring almost immediately.

Then Pluto spoke for the first time.

"I need a smoke before bed. Come outside with me. It'll only take a minute."

"Oh, go ahead, Pluto. I'll stay here. I'm sure I'm safe long enough for you to do that." Corvette made a small laugh to try to relax the man.

"Look," Pluto said, "I do need a smoke, but also someone wants to meet you. You'll be safe. Come with me." He said this in a very authoritative tone.

What the hell? Corvette thought. But then he had a premonition of who it might be that he should meet. He decided to go.

"Leave your phone in the room. You don't want to mess this up."

Corvette was uneasy, but he put his phone on the nightstand and followed Pluto out the front door of the house. They walked half a block down the dark street. Most of the people in the neighborhood had already gone to bed at the end of their Sunday evening in preparation for their new work week. Corvette actually thought about that as he followed the man named after the dark god of the underworld to two black SUVs parked along the curb. Leaning against the first one was a muscular, compact man, not very tall, but exuding powerful physical presence. Corvette saw that he was wearing a casual suit, and he guessed that the jacket was probably light colored. He remained leaning against the vehicle until Pluto and Corvette arrived. Then he straightened and greeted Corvette with an extended hand.

Up close, even in the darkness, Corvette recognized him. He was the man who had taken Valentina away the night Corvette had danced with her.

"Good evening, Corvette," the man said, "My name is Raúl Jesús Espinoza. You might know of me as the Zeta, or, perhaps, Z-30."

"Evening," Corvette acknowledged solemnly. His heart pounded in his chest. He thought the whole neighborhood might hear it. Instantly he wondered about the SUVs: who might be inside? He had a feeling about the second one. He thought she might be in there.

Valentina.

The Zeta said, "It appears that we're being observed from the small pickup down the street. We noticed two men sitting in it when we arrived, and they have not emerged from the truck. They have a good view of the house in which you're staying. So this conversation needs to be a short one."

"Okay," Corvette answered uncertainly, shooting a quick glance at the mentioned truck.

"I'll come straight to the point. You have something of mine that I want, and I believe I have someone that you would be interested in seeing. Now I understand that you accepted a bag from this young woman without knowing who she was or what was in the bag. Nevertheless, the money in the bag belonged to me, and I know how much money was in it.

"That's it?" Corvette asked. "You want the money for Valentina?"

"I have come to know Valentina," the Zeta answered, "and I think you will agree with me that she's worth much more than the currency in that small bag. No, Corvette, we have something bigger to do together. I'm here to give you the opportunity to lease Valentina from me."

"Lease her? What are you talking about?"

"The lease I have in mind has an upfront payment that keeps Valentina alive. Basically, that amount is about eight million dollars. You have to win the tournament next week. The World Series of Poker. You have to win it. Then you have to pay me the prize money. That's my fee for the trouble you've caused me in taking the money, the costs I have had to bear trying to find you, and the emotional distress of knowing that you're interested in the woman who's considering marrying me."

What the fuck? Corvette thought. In his brain alarm bells were ringing everywhere. *Is he messing with my mind? This man is certified whacko! What is he talking about? I have to keep him calm!*

He desperately searched for the right words. He responded, "Sr. Espinoza, honestly, I don't know Valentina that well. We danced one evening. You saw us. I liked her a lot, I admit. But she doesn't even speak English, so we really didn't have time to know each other very well."

Good one, Corvette, he told himself. *Maybe the Zeta doesn't know that Valentina speaks English. If he thinks I believe that she doesn't, it supports her cover.*

Corvette continued, "Listen, please, don't get me wrong. I don't know why you're putting the burden on me to keep

332

Valentina alive, but that worries me to death. I'll gladly return the money to you. I'll be happy to pay you interest and try to compensate you for all costs. Just, please, don't put Valentina's life on my ability to win this tournament. There are nine players, and I'm going in as one of the least advantaged. Please don't hurt her. If you're thinking of marrying her, why would you hurt her?"

The Zeta answered levelly, logically, as if in a conversation discussing the clauses of a business lease. "Actually, Corvette, it's a three-party lease, because Valentina also has to do her part to keep *you* alive. Maybe you could think of this as a life insurance policy, if that helps you understand things. It would be a tremendous disappointment to me to lose the two of you. To be honest, I need the services of you both. You and Valentina would be huge assets in the operations of my businesses. In the case of Valentina, she's perfect to manage the households that she and I would have together. No one comes closer than her to the vision I had for a wife and the role a wife would play in making my life easier. As for you, what I'm offering you is employment. I can bankroll the ups and downs of a poker tournament career. Your special skills would be very useful to me in my casino operations. I'll explain that to you later. The financial compensation for you would be far more than you've ever imagined, I assure you. The benefits you would receive include the satisfaction of knowing that as long as you're employed by me, I'll honor the terms of the contract that says I'll keep you and Valentina alive. The lease has a term, and both of you have to provide satisfaction under it."

Oh my God, he's serious! Corvette thought. *Stay calm. Keep him talking. He's dangerous. This man has killed many people.* He risked a surreptitious glance at the truck down the street. He wondered, *Who's in the pickup truck? Could they help me?*

"What is the term?" Corvette asked, as if he and the Zeta were having a sensible conversation. He wanted to buy time in case a rescue could come into play.

"Fifteen years," the Zeta answered.

"Why fifteen?" He was surprised by the Zeta's specific number.

"By then either I'll be dead or in prison, most likely," answered the Zeta. "And if not, then those fates won't be far away. By then, both you and Valentina will have peaked in what you can do for me, and the two of you would have earned your release from the contract."

"Sr. Espinoza, I mean this respectfully. You could have us simply killed at any time you don't think we're doing any good for you. I don't understand..."

The Zeta interrupted him. "When you do your research on me, Corvette, you're going to find that I'm known as a man who always does what he says he's going to do. I, therefore, speak carefully and am sure about everything that I say. I'm aware that this lease we're talking about is offered under duress, of course, and isn't legally enforceable. But it is illegally enforceable because I run the justice department of my world. The duress that applies to you is the condition of entry into the lease: your life and the life of Valentina. The entry requirement is your victory Tuesday night in the World Series of Poker. Your defeat at any time before the end of the tournament then results in Valentina's instant execution. Would you like an opportunity to speak to her before we enter into the contract?"

What?

To Corvette, it felt like the earth had started trembling. It was shock, he knew. Probably his legs were trembling. Feeling that he had to steady himself, he stepped up to the hood of the SUV and leaned against it. The Zeta had caught him completely off guard. The surge of adrenalin gunned his heart so fast that he feared that he would become short of breath. He glanced quickly around. Pluto stood across the street. Cool's house was across the street and behind him. The small pickup truck was on the same side of the road as the two black SUVs of the Zetas. It was parked approximately seven car spaces away. Corvette looked over to the second SUV. Was Valentina in there looking

334

at him now? It was dark, and it was impossible to see inside it also because the windows had been darkened.

"Y-yes," Corvette stuttered in reply to the Zeta's question.

"Good," answered the Zeta. "Remain quiet please while we make a small preparation."

The Zeta made two taps on the rear side window of the SUV beside him. Two men emerged from the rear and began walking casually in the dark along the sidewalk toward the pickup truck. Corvette was facing the Zeta but could see the men beyond him.

The neighborhood was completely quiet, except that suddenly there was the sound of a distant car apparently moving at high speed.

When the two men got near the pickup, one split off and stepped from the curb in an approach to the driver's side. The Zeta remained staring at Corvette. Just as the men were almost on both sides of the truck, the passenger side door began to open. Immediately the men reached inside their jackets and pulled out pistols. They rushed to the sides of the truck and pointed their arms.

Pfffft. Pfffft.

Two small sounds.

Corvette realized with horror: *Silencers!*

He saw the men returning quickly. The noise of the distant speeding vehicle was becoming louder.

"We have to make this fast," the Zeta said. "Follow me."

Corvette felt terrified, but the Zeta's tone was so commanding that Corvette automatically walked behind him. His senses were heightened. The air was cool and sharp. He noticed that his neck muscles had contracted so much with tension that a bad headache was rapidly developing. He smelled garbage cans that had been taken to the sidewalks for morning collection on both sides of the street. The Zeta strode to the second SUV and tapped on the window of the rear seat. He turned and motioned Corvette to approach, and then the Zeta stepped aside.

The window rolled down. Corvette saw two heads. It took a moment for his eyes to adjust, but then he saw that Valentina was sitting beside the window while a man stretched forward and looked out the window at him.

"Hola, Corvette," Valentina said in a voice one level above a whisper. She then spoke a few English words in a thick Mexican accent: "Glad to see you. Pleez, pleeez try to help us." The words sounded as if they had been memorized. The Zeta was listening.

"Valentina! Are you okay?" Corvette asked, very afraid, but trying to keep his voice controlled and calm.

The window began to roll up, but he saw Valentina force a small smile and nod her head. "Okay!" she answered.

In spite of his fear, in spite of feeling he was in the middle of calamity, Corvette had a coherent thought: *She's acting! She just let me know something important. The Zeta doesn't know she speaks English!*

The approach of the speeding car was now threatening to wreck the peace of the neighborhood. Headlights were silhouetting the roofs of two houses a couple of streets over. The Zeta moved forward and pulled Corvette by his arm.

"We've run out of time, I'm afraid. Do we have a contract?"

"Yes," Corvette answered quickly.

"Get back into the house. Your bodyguard is riding with us. You don't really need bodyguards now, unless you cross me, in which case you can't hire enough on earth to help you."

The two men who had fired the silenced pistols had already returned to their SUV. The Zeta gave Corvette a small push toward Cool's house. "Get in there fast. You don't want to be on the street when this car arrives."

The Zeta strode to the front passenger door of the first SUV and opened it. He gave Corvette one last piece of information:

"I'll be watching the tournament with Valentina. We'll hope for your victory. Now, run!"

Pluto had already gotten inside the second SUV. The drivers of the vehicles started them. As Corvette darted to the house, he saw the SUVs rush to the corner ahead. One sped to the left. The other made a U-turn and began to race back in his direction.

And in the direction of the coming car! Corvette realized. He might have frozen to watch what would happen, in spite of the Zeta's warning, except that he remembered his phone in the bedroom of Cool's house. He had to try to reach Enrique, David, Raymundo...somebody!

And when he thought of Raymundo, Corvette had another horrifying realization:

Oh my God! They know where my mum is! Pluto would have told them everything!

He got inside the front door of the house. Some instinct made him push the door hard behind him as he darted to the bedroom, but before the door shut, Corvette heard the black SUV pause in front of Cool's house. He heard the car racing toward it, now on the same block. Men in the SUV were shouting instructions to someone who had apparently gotten out of the vehicle. Then he heard the rapid cracks of an automatic weapon. He got to the bedroom and couldn't resist looking out the window. The headlights of the car illuminated two figures in front of the SUV. One was pointing an automatic rifle. The other had removed a tube from the rear and had rushed forward with it. He hoisted it to his shoulder and pointed it at the car. There followed a loud noise that Corvette hadn't heard before, and then...

Boom!

The explosion of the car lit up the entire block. The percussion knocked over a garbage can nearby on the sidewalk. For an instant it was like daylight, and Corvette saw clearly the men rushing to get back inside the SUV. The man with the tube jumped inside the back and pulled the tail door down. Then the SUV raced backwards to the street corner. It screeched off in the direction that the other had gone earlier.

The car was in flames, casting a ghastly light over rubble in the street. People were rushing outside their houses.

In the doorway to his bedroom, Cool appeared, his eyes wide with terror.

"What the fuck was that?"

"A terrible mess, amigo!" Corvette responded. "Call Raymundo! Pluto betrayed us! We're all in trouble." Corvette got his cell phone from the nightstand. "I'm calling nine-one-one while you do that; then I'm going to call some friends for help."

Cool was already running to his bedroom to get his phone, and he yelled as he went, "Is that a car on fire outside?"

"Yes, and before that, a couple of people were murdered out there!" Corvette answered.

And then the emergency dispatcher came on his line.

David James
Monterrey, Mexico
Sunday Night

It seemed so unfair, a cruel trick of fate. But he got it. It was a horrible detail that would make sense in the kind of world in which he had spent his life.

A little over forty years earlier, an eighteen-wheel truck had snatched from him the life of the woman he had adored since he was ten years old. Like his beloved wife next to him, her name had...coincidentally...been Ana Maria. She had called herself Annie. They had been driving in Virginia just days after her college graduation and had pulled over to the shoulder so that they could change drivers. The eighteen-wheeler had blown by them with a gush of wind, but the car hidden close behind it in its trail had driven close to the shoulder and had struck the old convertible that David had recently bought. He had seen his love get killed, and for years after that he had re-lived in nightmares that moment in which his spirit had died with Annie.

So what kind of spiritual author had dreamed up this demise? he wondered. This time he was driving, and Ana...she was his vida, his life, his heart, his soothing...was humming softly

338

in the seat beside him. They were on the way to the airport, on a two-lane road leading to the toll road that went by it.

He saw the outline lights of the approaching eighteen-wheeler. There was considerable traffic on the road despite the lateness of the evening, as there always was in Monterrey on certain roads. Ever since that accident of his youth, David tensed when he saw these trucks, not so much nervous tension in recent years as it was an alert kind of tension. The truck was almost to his car when David saw some large animal, he thought a dog, dart into his headlight beams. The animal raced across the road in a hysteria of confusion. It had emerged on David's side of the road, so he swerved a bit to the center to avoid it while he jammed the brake pedal of the Ford Explorer. At the same time, the eighteen-wheeler's driver slammed his brakes to avoid hitting the animal.

There was a truck following closely behind the eighteen-wheeler. To evade collision, the second truck swerved out into the center of the highway. David only had a second to see what was about to strike them head-on: It was a truck carrying natural gas cylinders. It looked like the driver of that truck was jumping out.

There would be a big explosion.

It was all very sick, David thought. He had wanted his life to end differently.

Joyfully.

He would have written his life story to protect Ana until the very end.

Chapter 24: Ghosts in Vegas

Enrique Santos
Las Vegas Nevada
Early Monday Morning

David and Enrique sat red-eyed and glum at the kitchen table in a time-share condominium just ten minutes from McCarran International Airport. Three cups of coffee steamed in front of them. They heard Ana talking on a cell phone in one of the bedrooms. David had poured her waiting cup.

"Corvette just texted," Enrique told David. "He's in front of TV and internet news cameras for interviews this morning with the other tournament players. The poor muchacho is trying to keep his head straight. Here, I'll let you read what he wrote. The first messages are from the middle of the night, and the last one is what he just said." He handed David the phone.

CORVETTE: They made contact. They have V. I saw her. People dead! Police are everywhere here. Are you ok? Where are you?

ENRIQUE: Am ok, amigo. I escaped from the burning car on your street with one other, an agent of DEA. Was that the Zeta?

CORVETTE: God! Sí, and he told me I have to win the tournament as ransom for V's life or we both are executed. Who died?

ENRIQUE: Two Zs! Awful! So the Zeta got away. We'll find him! Don't worry what Zeta told you. Concentrate on play. We have mucho resources closing in. Don't call me. Text. Stay focused no matter happens. Your phone tells us where you are. If you see Zeta again, text "Zeta." If you see Valentina, text "V." Describe the Zeta.

CORVETTE: Short, powerful looking. Body builder maybe. Age late forties.

ENRIQUE: Gracias. Try to rest now.

CORVETTE (Monday morning): Enrique! Arrived for interviews at The Rio. My mum and reporters here say Ana and David were in terrible car accident last night in Monterrey! Is this true? Are they okay?

"How should I answer him?" Enrique asked David.

David shook his head sadly. "I'm sorry, Enrique. I really hate this. We have to tell him what the news reports are saying, that the bodies in the car are too badly burned for immediate identification but that they're checking DNA and dental records to determine if they're Ana Valdez and David James. We need this time for people to think we're dead. Corvette needs to believe we're not around so he feels somewhat cut off. He needs to feel the pressure to do what the Zeta wants him to do: to win the tournament. He has to play well today to be in the finals tomorrow. We need every second. We have enough to do to find these guys. We can't take time being distracted with Corvette either. He's your assignment. It's simpler for him to only have one contact if he needs to share anything. He trusts you. He believes in you. Once he starts playing, he won't have a phone. No one in that tournament room will be allowed to have their phones because of the heightened security with all that has happened in Las Vegas this past week."

"Corvette might get too shocked by your accident to play well."

"It also might make him angry and give him the fire he needs. He'll feel even more desperate to save Valentina. Besides, if he knows that we're really okay, he might unintentionally let this slip."

David handed Enrique back the phone. Enrique sighed. He texted Corvette.

"I know it's a done deed," Enrique said, "but are you sure staging your deaths was the right thing to do?"

"Possible deaths," David corrected. "It was an intelligence recommendation. Bodies are piling up in two countries. I didn't like the idea, but the fact of the matter is that the secret joint mission of Mexico and the United States needs my help right now, and if the cartels were going to take out me and Ana, it would be a serious blow to the mission. We already had a setback with the death of Ignacio. Ignacio's work might have really helped us if we could have saved him for our team. At least we have some clues from those numbers he gave you. If the Zetas think that Ana and I are already dead, then they will be a little less vigilant with their next moves over the next couple of days. I'm sure the Zeta has been worrying about what I'm doing in particular. He knows I work with the DEA and all the executive agencies."

"Okay," Enrique said. Then he asked, "Did Paula get home okay?"

"Yes, she was taken care of. That was another reason that Ana and I went along with the plan to stage our accident. We didn't want Paula with us if there would be an attempt on our lives. A DEA agent whom I trust flew back to San Diego with her."

"Dios," Enrique said, "Paula and her brother..."

"They know we're okay. They're staying in the house a few days. We have protection for them. We have a spokesperson to ask for privacy for the family while the identities of the victims in the car are being confirmed. When we surface later, we'll come clean that Ana and I were involved in an undercover, joint-nation police operation."

Enrique paused and sipped his coffee, and then he told David, "I feel sick about these guys last night getting killed. I can hardly stand it."

He heard the anger in David's voice when he responded. "You didn't murder them, Enrique! The cartel did it. You're fighting those guys. So are all the Zs. You did everything you could to get there when they called you. You almost got killed yourself. If anything had happened to you, I'm not sure I could take it anymore. I've lost too many close people in this life. Thank God you're okay! Thank God you're helping me."

He knew David's anger was with the Zeta. The coffee started to kick in. He remembered something else.

"David! What about Valentina? Certainly she's going to hear the news! She's going to think that you and her aunt are dead! This is so cruel..."

But David held up his hand to interrupt him as Ana entered the room. It was actually Ana who addressed Enrique's remark. "Valentina is going to know we weren't in an accident. We can explain this to you, Enrique, but first we have to take this call."

She walked over to the table and retrieved her cup of coffee as she handed David his cell phone. She said, "David, Donnie is calling you in just a minute. The White House assistant was talking to me on your cell. I answered back there in the bedroom."

She handed David his phone.

"Good morning, Mr. President."

Noting David's formal address, the President said, "You must be there with people, David. Good morning."

"I have Enrique Santos and Ana here."

"Good, put on speaker if no one else can hear. You can call me by name."

Enrique listened intently as David set the phone on the table and punched the speaker icon. The group exchanged greetings.

"How was your flight?" the President asked.

"It has been a couple of years since Ana and I flew in a Black Hawk helicopter," David answered. "It brought back old memories of the military coup in Mexico. The flight was good. One fueling stop. Ana and I appreciate the support we got from the Mexican Army and the United States. It was the Mexican-owned copter that had been bought by the state of Jalisco back in the days before the coup. The Mexican Army owns it now."

"Quite a world we live in! Glad the trip to Vegas was uneventful for you. Everyone appreciates your service, Ana and David. Listen, I thought it would save time since I had a briefing this morning from FBI and DEA if I gave you a call to bring you up to speed. The Directors are getting used to our informality, sort of." The President let out a small chuckle, then he continued, "I really wanted the opportunity to talk to you personally once you two were back safely in the States. So let me do this quickly. David, FBI agents will be coming within the hour to make you and Ana up with disguises. Update them with any new information you might have that can help with the Vegas operation. There's a combined FBI and DEA undercover unit inside The Rio watching for cartel activity and any attempted contact by them with Corvette Nightfire. Both agencies are looking at the numbering sequences that Ignacio Lopez gave to Enrique to try to make sense out of those. David, I know that you're good with that kind of thing. Follow their progress and advise them as appropriate. Today if you would like to work from inside The Rio, FBI will get you in there with their people. The Rio is nervous about security with all the violence of the past couple of weeks in Vegas so they're being very cooperative with the agents and the police. They and the broadcasting network are permitting agents in the booth where the revelations of the poker hands during the tournament on television are delayed by fifteen minutes. That permits first-look knowledge of Corvette's hands and level of play before the public knows."

"I would like being in there," David said. "Z-30 has told Corvette that he has to win the tournament as a ransom for Valentina Garza's life and his. The Zeta is going to be watching, presumably from somewhere in Las Vegas, but certainly he won't be in the poker room. He'll see it on television. So this gives us a fifteen-minute advantage if we need it. For example, if Corvette gets eliminated."

"I hope we don't require that advantage. We do think for certain that Z-30 is in Las Vegas and that Valentina is with him."

Enrique looked at David questioningly. *How would he know that?* Enrique wondered. *Corvette texted me that he saw*

Valentina during the night, and I just showed it to David. Has Corvette spoken to someone in the DEA or the FBI?

David understood the question in Enrique's face.

"Donnie, how do you know this? Corvette saw Valentina last night when he was contacted by the Zeta. He passed this information to Enrique last night."

"Interesting," answered the President. "The FBI has a source who swears he saw Valentina at a private party Thursday night in Henderson when Z-30 was celebrating the murder of the leader from the Cartel of Sinaloa. Up to now that has been the only reported sighting of Z-30 in or near Las Vegas. The source isn't known well, but the FBI regards him as credible. One problem we might have, if he's credible, is that he says that the woman who matches Valentina's description was presented as his companion or date and that she was cooperative with him."

"Of course," Ana spoke up, trying to keep a tone of irritation out of her voice. "She's undercover DEA. The DEA has put her in a very dangerous situation with that man. I know my niece well. She'll maintain her cover until she finds the opportunity to bring him down. She needs help."

"We're going to get her help, Ana," the President said quickly. "I agree."

But Enrique saw the fire in Ana's eyes.

"The Zetas did take her from the interstate, Donnie," David said. "The three of us do have an emotional commitment to getting her safely from them. Corvette Nightfire is another one who's putting his life on the line for her. From the Zeta's point of view, Corvette is the one who can save her. That is, if he wins the tournament."

Ana sighed. She scribbled a quick note to David and passed it to him. Enrique saw that she had written a question for David to ask.

David said, "Donnie, the accident went as planned? No hiccups?"

"Yes," the President answered, "as far as the reports go, the field and the supervisors in both the Mexican unit and the USA are happy with the execution. We have the car company to thank for the remote satellite operation of the SUV that looks like yours, David. They cooperated completely and worked well with the Mexican Special Forces Intelligence. The highway was loaded up with professional drivers behind the trucks, and the explosions from the gas truck were scaled to consume the car and not create much other damage. There were some actual witnesses who saw the accident, which is good in case there are genuine interrogations, like from cartel members. The stunt driver of the gas truck got out safely. The SUV burned to a crisp, and the victims could never be identified visually."

Enrique saw David staring at the note that Ana had written. David seemed to hesitate, but then he addressed the President in a formal way:

"Mr. President, who were you told was riding in the Explorer? Dummies or mannequins?"

Enrique thought that there was just a slight hesitation, as if the President were weighing how to answer, but he answered in a direct manner.

"David, it was presented to me that there had to be human occupants because any artificial representations of you or Ana in the heat of the fire would melt and obviously not be human and that first responders would notice. I was told that unidentified cadavers were used."

Ana emitted a huge sigh and put her face in her hands. The President heard her.

Enrique was amazed at what the President said next:

"I hear you, Ana. I'm very sorry. I know that there are many unknown victims of the drug wars in your country and that you work so hard with many good people to try to get respect for the victims and their families. I can tell that this is very sorrowful news for you. It might be small consolation to understand that the victims in the automobile were used for the same reasons that you do your work: to make a better future for your country."

Ana raised her head, and Enrique saw the tears in her eyes. "Thank you, Donnie," she said softly.

Valentina Garza
Las Vegas, Nevada
Monday

Raúl was edgy, Valentina decided. He maintained his external expression of control and stoniness, but since the escape-with-victims from the meeting with Corvette the previous night, Raúl had worked non-stop with calls and hushed meetings in rooms away from her. The property was filling with different vehicles. Men were arriving and taking away the SUVs and were leaving older-model four-door compact cars. The guards were staying indoors. Weapons of all types lay everywhere in the house. The men carried radios. They talked constantly on the cell phones. A man brought in a cardboard box full of obviously used phones and credit cards. *Someone was going to get careless,* she thought. She watched in the house for the mistake of a phone that might be temporarily forgotten on a sofa or table.

From the rooms with televisions blared the news reports, in English, about the possible deaths of her aunt and David James in the automobile accident as they were traveling to the airport in Monterrey. When she first heard this, she felt shock. At the time, Raúl was standing beside her so she had the difficult task of pretending that she couldn't understand the news report that was in English, but she wanted to scream. Raúl turned to see if she had a reaction to the report. At the bottom of the television screen the names of Ana Valdez and David James were in a caption that stated they might have died in a fiery accident that had consumed Ana's Ford Explorer. Valentina demanded that Raúl explain what was going on. As he told her, the images of the burned vehicle in early morning light appeared on the screen showing the highway blocked off and dozens of police and military vehicles pulled up around the accident site. Valentina threw her hand to her mouth and said, "No puede ser! No lo creo!" (It can't be! I don't believe it!)

At first Raúl didn't believe it, Valentina thought. Either that or he was very confused by the news report. He whipped out his phone and called someone whom he addressed as "Leo," a man evidently in Monterrey. Raúl was distracted enough that he talked to Leo near Valentina. He didn't take the normal precautions to try to keep her from hearing, other than speaking in English.

What she learned was that Raúl apparently had had discussions with Leo about the possibility of Ana and David being murdered in an assassination made to look like an accident. What Raúl found out was that Leo hadn't done it! Apparently, Ana and David might have had an accident by coincidence, if the people found in the vehicle were they. David and Ana hadn't come forward as alive, so the general conclusion was that they were, in fact, dead. It took several minutes of conversation for Raúl to wrap his head around this amazing turn of fate to his benefit. He had been plainly confused at first, but once he comprehended that Leo truly had nothing to do with the accident, Raúl did a good job of containing his glee. But Valentina saw it in his eyes. He tried to feign sadness when he consoled her.

Valentina pretended grief.

She pretended because she didn't believe that her aunt and David were dead.

The reason was that her aunt had sold her Ford Explorer to Valentina the month before. That vehicle should be parked in its space in the parking deck of the condominium where Valentina lived.

David James is on top of his game, Valentina thought. *He and Ana wanted me to figure this out. I would bet anything that right now David and my tía Ana are in Las Vegas. Certainly they know that Corvette is here.*

348

Raúl drew her into the entertainment room and sat beside her on the sofa. He put his arm around her shoulder, and Valentina put her head against him. To make herself sad, she thought about the possibility of her aunt dying, and she became teary eyed. She showed Raúl her eyes. She told him, "This is a very sad day for México, Raúl. The country will pass several days of mourning, and the world will send its condolences. I know you didn't like her, but in the early days she was like a mom to me. We went different paths. I'm going to need you more now, you know."

"I'm sorry for you, angel," he answered. "I know loss such as this. Look, if this is your aunt, we'll find some way for you to make an appropriate farewell visit to her site just as soon as possible, so you can pay respects. That's an important thing to do. It helps you to move on in life."

Valentina feigned a sob and thanked him. Then, knowing that he was trying to fake tenderness, she took a shot at finding out what was going on in the house by taking advantage of this opportunity that he might share information. She sat up and turned her head to look at the door of the room as men passed by.

"There's so much activity, Raúl. What's going on?"

"We're going to leave here soon, amor. Last night someone was watching Corvette when we met him. I have been too many days in Las Vegas, and it is getting too hot here with shootings that they're holding the cartels responsible for. They know I'm in Las Vegas now. I want to create a scene somewhere else to draw attention away from this city. This isn't good for my businesses here. As I told you last night, Corvette has agreed to come work for me. His skills apply anywhere in the world. I began new kinds of businesses in Las Vegas, and what I have learned from experience here can be taken to other cities. I need more people like Corvette Nightfire. There's so much turnover in this work. You remember meeting Santiago the other day? Santi?"

"Sí."

349

"There was other bad news this morning for me. It has been on the news, but it has been overshadowed by the reports of your aunt's possible accident. He and two other employees were shot at, and Santi was killed. This happened about eleven kilometers from here. The news reports say that the assailants are unknown, but I'm sure they were attacked by men from Sinaloa."

Ah! Valentina thought. She remembered one fragment of a phone call that she had overheard early that morning when Raúl had become agitated by the information that he was receiving. He had started walking away from her as he usually did when he got a call, but she heard him say, "It wasn't the police who killed him. It was Sinaloa. Get his body. I don't want them to have his body."

"There's too much blood, Raúl!" Valentina told him. "I'm sorry to hear this about Santi, but you need to protect yourself. You do need to get out of this place. You need to take me! I told you the other night that I didn't want to die in some bloody shootout with police or federales from the USA!"

She wanted to heighten the sense of danger. She wanted there to be the chaos of a sudden move. Someone would make a mistake, and she would have an opportunity to send out a call for help. But she knew that the Zeta usually kept calm and calculating and that he would try to plan things for zero mistakes.

"Sí, that's what I'm doing, mi vida. El camino de aquí, the road from here, takes us to an interesting place which will be a surprise for you. You will like it, and, sí, it is a place where you will have a lot of protection and can make many friends. This is why you're seeing this activity. I'm making arrangements for our exit."

"Dios, Raúl, tell me where we're going!" Valentina tried to sound like a young girl excited about a trip.

He laughed and hugged her close. "You'll know soon enough. Right now I'm mainly interested in how Corvette is going to do in this tournament today and tomorrow. I think that there's so much interest in security in that area of The Rio by the police and the federales, as you call them, that we can safely remain inside the house here and leave when the tournament ends or when Corvette finishes his playing, whichever comes first. But I'm expecting him to win. That would be late tomorrow night."

While he was hugging her closely, Valentina rubbed his hip and thigh as if affectionately. She could feel the bulge of his phone in his pants pocket. For some reason, she thought about the mess throughout the house, and she wondered what Yandel Sandoval would think if he knew that one of his houses was being trashed like this.

She wondered, *How would Yandel like seeing the weapons, boxes of stolen items, phones, and men everywhere in his home?*

Suddenly Corvette appeared on the television! He was at The Rio, and a reporter from ESPN was preparing to interview him before the tournament. There were fans holding signs and shouting his name behind them. Mostly young women. He looked preoccupied and distant as the woman interviewer approached, but when the questions began, he transformed into someone focused and confident. Beside Valentina, Raúl suddenly sat up, attentive.

"Corvette Nightfire!" the reporter began. Valentina noted that the reporter herself looked excited to see him.

God, he's handsome, Valentina thought. She was surprised to feel a slight jealousy about the pretty female interviewer.

"This is the big day! The first question on everybody's mind is, 'Where have you been in the past week?' Your fans have been dying to hear from you and know how you feel coming into the Final Table with players such as the Legend, the Knave, and the Ambusher."

The camera zoomed in on Corvette's face. "Well, I wanted to have some time away from the lights to get ready for the tournament in a more relaxed environment," Corvette answered. "So I was in Los Angeles at a friend's house. He's a good poker player, so I prepared there in the quiet."

He continued talking, but Valentina saw in his eyes that mentally he was looking off to a different place than Los Angeles. It was some other landscape. She had seen that expression in his eyes once before, the night that she had danced México for him in El Magnifico. She had become the black jaguar, and at that moment Corvette had surrendered to her completely. She suddenly realized that he had come back to Las Vegas for her.

He's here for me!

He came back knowing that he would confront the Zeta.

Oh my God! He's riding the black jaguar!

Chapter 25: Of Knaves and Men

Corvette Nightfire
Las Vegas, Nevada
The World Series of Poker
Monday

Just before the ESPN reporter had thrust the microphone into his face, Corvette was trying to collect himself from a triple blow of disturbing distractions. The Rio itself was one. In The Rio there was the madness of mayhem: the crowds to see the tournament, the staffs of the hotel and the WSOP, the security personnel, the news media staffs, Corvette's fans, and the fans of the other players, all hustling and jostling one another, created a loud roar of confusion. That would have been hard enough to deal with, but on the trip to The Rio, Corvette's mum had broken the news that Ana and David had possibly been in a fatal car crash just outside Monterrey. While Corvette was reeling from the shock of that, Raymundo was dealing a drama of his own: He was beside himself because Pluto had betrayed them to the Zeta. Raymundo was taking it as a great personal failure.

"Amigo, it is the one time I didn't carefully screen a candidate coming to work for me with my usual obsessive fanaticism to provide good service. I made an impulsive decision to hire him because he had said something clever to me. I can't believe I did this! It's a lesson for me. I'm so sorry."

Corvette had told him, "It's okay, Raymundo, I actually wanted to meet the Zeta and didn't know how it would happen. Remember, I asked you to let everyone in town know that I was arriving. I wanted the Zeta to be able to contact me."

"Sí, but there were two men shot. You could have been killed too, and I believed that I had a man there to protect you."

"It's all right, Raymundo," Corvette had replied. "You're here with me now; my mum is here; and Jupiter. I'll feel fine knowing you're sitting behind me in the poker room."

However, the truth was that Corvette did feel very unsettled about things while they were en route to The Rio. Once he arrived in The Rio, there was so much frenetic activity that the knot of anxiety in his chest tightened even more. He was still getting his bearings when the ESPN reporter put the microphone in front of him and asked her first question about where he had been.

He heard the words coming from his mouth about Los Angeles, but he fled in his mind back to Monterrey where David, Ana, and Enrique had made him feel at home. A montage of memories of the city sped through his mind. He recalled its mountains, the stunning architecture of many of its prominent buildings, the challenges of its mad urban traffic, the creativity of its energetic people, the commitment of the young people who had joined the Zs, and, in the last moment, Valentina. It was as if to him she embodied the city. She was like Monterrey: rich in her cultural history and seductive in her modernism. The flash of her image in his mind had an immediate calming effect upon him. The madness around him disappeared. He remembered his purpose. He felt suddenly that he had control of his emotions.

"And how do you feel coming into the Final Table with players such as the Legend, the Knave, and the Ambusher?" he heard the reporter asking.

The question snapped Corvette back to the moment.

"I admire the style of play of those men very much," Corvette told her. "In particular, I look forward to the competition with the Legend and the Knave. I have watched them win many televised tournaments. They play super-aggressively."

"That's what the analysts say about you," the interviewer responded.

Corvette chuckled. "Yes, I usually do; that's true!"

The rest of the ESPN interview went exceptionally well. Corvette surprised the young lady interviewing him with his knowledge of poker history and his fascination with men like

354

Doyle Brunson and Amarillo Slim, two giants during the "Rounder" days of poker. He listed facts and figures about Phil Hellmuth, Johnny Chan, Phil Ivey, Daniel Negreanu, and others whose personalities and style of play had helped catapult Texas Hold'em onto the international stage. He spoke with special enthusiasm about Chris Moneymaker, whose 2003 victory at the WSOP had inspired Corvette and thousands of others because he proved that an on-line player--an outsider--could win the grand prize.

"I tell you," Corvette said, "playing in the same tournament as these men have done not only makes me feel connected to great tradition, but it makes me want to do my best so that others in the future, anyone who loves the game, will be inspired to try and go for the ultimate like me."

The crowd erupted into applause and cheers when they heard that, and Corvette's boyish grin spread over his face. Their approval helped him relax even more, and as the interview went on, Corvette's natural charm bubbled to the surface. His love and fervor for the game were obvious. He received applause at several points of the interview, and by the time it was wrapping up, the people had begun chanting his name again.

Looking at them, the ESPN reporter began to laugh. She said, "It's interesting, Corvette. In the case of the other players, the people like to shout their nicknames. But you're just 'Corvette,' the name for you that everyone loves. Judging by the enthusiasm here," and she waved the microphone toward the crowd, "I would say that you're definitely a star and a favorite personality here at the Final Table. The best of luck to you, Corvette Nightfire!"

He didn't have much time after that until the "live" (but fifteen-minute delayed) television broadcast began. Corvette was one of the first of the nine players to be called out into the poker room for his introduction to the vociferous, adoring fans seated to watch the tournament and, of course, to the tens of millions watching on television throughout the world. He took his assigned seat. He turned to locate his mum, Raymundo, and

355

Jupiter, who were standing and cheering behind him. He smiled his appreciation. He acknowledged his other fans with a wave, and then he gave a nod of greeting to the other player who had already been introduced and had taken seat.

Now he really felt in his element. He surveyed the environment around him. Beyond the poker table were the cameras and the ESPN crew, some broadcast producers and staff, executives of The Rio, and a couple of other people whose function he couldn't guess. He saw the booth where the screens for the players' hands were captured by the cameras in front of each player at the table. The operator in there would know the hands before these were revealed fifteen minutes later on television. No one in the poker room had been allowed to enter with cellphones. All of this was so that the players couldn't know immediately if the others had bluffed and had taken the hand with poor cards. The television viewers were seeing the hands of cards of the players fifteen minutes later.

While Corvette was looking at the booth, he remembered how incredibly tight the security was just to enter The Rio. At all of the entrances to the hotel, metal detectors and screening personnel were there to make sure that no one was entering with weapons. These were present again at the entrances to the poker room so that no one could bring in phones.

Las Vegas is truly on edge because of all the shootings here the past week, Corvette observed. But when he thought more about it, he realized that the whole country was jittery. He had heard on the news that there had been sensational cartel-related shootings in other major cities in the United States. In the uproar of alarm that had ensued in the country, the President of the United States had made a couple of statements of reassurance that public safety would be paramount and that perpetrators of organized crime would find a harsh justice awaiting.

It was at this moment while Corvette was observing the television booth that an odd thing happened: A man in a dark blue business suit led a casually dressed couple into the booth.

They were not anyone whom Corvette recognized, but their body shapes reminded him of David and Ana. It was just a moment, but a pang of longing to see his two friends safe and alive almost brought tears to his eyes; however, when he heard the Legend being introduced, Corvette's focus returned to the table. There it remained for the introduction of the other players and the duration of the game.

Soon all nine players had taken seats at the table. The crowd was raucous. Each player had sections of fans dressed in costumes and holding placards supporting them. The spectators applauded and cheered wildly after each hand. But once Corvette saw the other players at the table with him, he tuned out all noise and mental static. The familiar calm that settled him down when he focused came over him. To maintain this focus, he reminded himself of Valentina from time to time because he was playing for her life. He discovered that thinking of her between hands helped keep him undistracted by anything going on in the audience or by the attempts of other players to psyche him out. He also believed in his ability, and, just before play began, he said a prayer that God would keep Valentina safe. He then sent up a request to his father:

St. Rogelio, stand over my shoulder and watch my hands. Don't let me miss anything! You went crazy over Mum when you first danced with her. Well, I'm this way with Valentina. You would love her. Let's keep her alive!

The tournament began. Instead of playing in his usual aggressive manner, Corvette tightened his play for the first few hours. It appeared that all nine players did the same. No one wanted to be the first sent home, and so all of the players seemed unwilling to take major risks. Especially in Corvette's case, with Valentina's life hanging in the balance, he would have to pick his opportunities with care.

Fortunately, during the first few hours Corvette was dealt good cards, and he could play the hands with a minimum of risk. He won several small pots, and, despite the pressure, Corvette became amused when he was dealt a 10-2, a hand which he ordinarily would have folded. But since he was the big blind and no one had raised, he was able to see the flop. He knew that the 10-2 was called a "Doyle Brunson" because Doyle had won both the '76 and '77 WSOP with that hand. Corvette had briefly sat at Brunson's table during the main draw at this year's tournament months ago, and he marveled that the old man still had game. He almost laughed when the flop was 10-3-2. The turn had been another 10, but both men checked. The river was a 5, and when his opponent (holding Ace-4) had gone all in, Corvette won a huge pot when his full house (tens over twos) beat his opponent's straight (Ace through 5).

The tournament continued, ten hands, twenty, forty, eighty, and on. There were brief breaks when Corvette walked over to chat with his mum and Raymundo while Jupiter kept his stony surveillance of the room. But despite the conservative play of the nine at the table, inevitably the eliminations came, and the remaining players gradually felt more tense and tired. Corvette was holding up. Mostly he remembered Valentina. He recalled that the Zeta had said that he would be watching, and he assumed that he would have her beside him when he did. David had told him that there would be lots of invisible protection for him in Las Vegas, but now, perhaps, David was gone. And Ana. So he wondered who was out there, beyond the poker room, working to help him save Valentina. He felt alone, and then he remembered Enrique.

"Don't worry," Enrique had told him once. "I'll look out for you."

Enrique Santos
Las Vegas, Nevada
Monday

David and Ana were with the FBI, but David had asked Special Agent-in-Charge Zolinsky to assign a DEA agent to help Enrique. That agent's name was Eddie Ricotto, a Las Vegas native the same age as Enrique and a man who had a photographic memory for the map of the city streets.

"Okay, we're a good team," Enrique said when he welcomed him. "You know the city and I have the Zs. Do you speak Spanish?"

"Not much," Eddie replied. "My family is Italian. Some of my relatives date to the seventies in Vegas when the Mob ran everything."

"Perfecto," said Enrique. "Then we have all the criminal types covered: the Mafia, the corporations, and the cartels."

The way Eddie laughed, Enrique knew that he had won him over. Trust would be paramount in what might come next.

And I actually made a joke, he marveled.

What Eddie marveled at was the way Enrique could use his phone with internet to call in a conference of Zs quickly. Within an hour some fifty-plus young men and women dressed in black met them at the entrance to a park used by them for parkour exercises and outdoor group meetings of the Zs.

"What you're going to do is to drive in pairs to assigned sections of the city and environs which Agent Ricotto and I'll give you," Enrique explained to them. "Agent Ricotto has been making sheets of paper with addresses and sections of the city to distribute to you. These are just in pen on sheets of paper which he has done quickly, but you can use your maps and navigation features on your phones to help you in those sections. You guys know what the cartel guys look like, what they drive, how they dress, where they like to go. Don't waste time with high-rise buildings or office buildings. We're looking for houses with SUVs and those that have three or more vehicles. Look especially for houses set back, that have some land, and that might be easily defended, like those on the edge of neighborhoods with access to the desert. Get out and talk to neighbors of suspicious places and ask if those houses see a high number of comings and goings. You know the drill.

He continued, "We have an old, not-so-good photocopy for you also of the Zeta, Z-30, when he was younger. This might not be so helpful because he's now about forty-eight years old and is a bodybuilder sort. We also have a picture for you of Valentina Garza, the young woman whom he has kidnapped. This woman may appear with him in a cooperative way. Don't be fooled by this if you see a couple fitting this description. Valentina Garza is trained in martial arts and knows how to fire weapons. She isn't a Z, but she's fit.

"Finally, remember your Rules of Life. That's the point: to live. Pull out your Rules-of-Life cards and read them again before you start this work if you need a reminder. The men you're looking for are loaded with weaponry. They kill without remorse. Your job today is to find them and report their location. Only engage if this can't be avoided. In any engagement scenario, disarm them as you've been trained, incapacitate, and get out. There are literally hundreds of police, FBI, and DEA agents who are ready to move in and make a capture. These professional law enforcers are also working hard checking with their sources to find the Zeta. So report to me anything suspicious, and we'll try to leave the most dangerous work to them. Any questions?"

There were a few, but within a half hour the Zs had paired up and headed out to their assigned sectors to reconnoiter.

"Could I see one of those cards that you mentioned?" Agent Ricotto asked.

"Here, take this one," Enrique said, reaching for his wallet. He gave him a card.

"What do we do now?" Ricotto asked.

"I want you to take me to areas around here with large houses where men might hide in broad daylight and no one would notice anything weird to report them...or where the neighbors might be afraid to report them," was Enrique's answer.

"That would be where the neighbors have something to hide," Ricotto answered. "Well, there are places like that in Vegas. Let's go."

The eliminations continued. Corvette was now feeling tired from the effects of sleep deprivation and the roller coaster emotions of the past days. During long pauses when some of the players seemed to be taking forever to decide their move, Corvette began to think of the Zeta watching him with Valentina.

"He's still in," he could imagine the Zeta telling Valentina after every elimination. Maybe the Zeta would explain the game as it progressed because he believed that she only spoke Spanish. How strange this experience must be for her, Corvette mused.

On the one hundred seventy-second hand, the table was down to the final three players: Corvette, the Knave, and the Legend. On the next elimination, Day One of the Final Table would end. The two remaining players would have until the next night to recover before going "Heads Up" for the title, the trophy, and the coveted World Series of Poker bracelet. It was on this hand that Corvette's sleep deprivation led to a fatal mistake!

Corvette was dealt the King-9 of hearts and raised pre-flop. Both the Knave and the Legend stayed in the hand, but when the flop showed the Queen of clubs, 10 of hearts, and 3 of hearts, the Legend folded. It was now heads up between Corvette and the Knave. When the turn was the Jack of clubs, Corvette went all in to protect his straight against the possible club flush of the Knave. He was shocked when the Knave called the all-in bet and turned over his cards: the Ace and King of clubs! The Knave's straight was higher than his!

Corvette felt the blood drain from his face. He couldn't believe it! He always allowed for the possibility of a higher straight, but thinking that his opponent was on a flush draw in clubs and with the excitement of hitting his straight, Corvette had acted too quickly. Valentina's life hung in the balance, and Corvette had made a rookie mistake! He needed a flush to win, and only a heart on the river could save him! With just seconds before the final card was revealed, Corvette instinctively said a desperate prayer. But this one wasn't to God; it was to St. Rogelio:

I beg you, St. Rogelio, to help me! If you're here watching over me, please answer my plea! If not for me, then for Valentina!

When the river card was revealed, the crowd erupted in a turmoil of cheers and screams. Corvette could hardly believe his eyes. The river card was the Queen of hearts!

THE QUEEN OF HEARTS!

The Queen gave Corvette the flush that he needed to win the hand. Corvette looked at the cheering crowd. He knew that they thought it was a miracle of luck, but Corvette understood that he had been sent a sign: Valentina was his Queen of hearts, and the Queen had saved him.

Corvette was more than just "still alive" in the tournament. He had reduced the field to the final two. Tomorrow night he and the Legend would square off for the title!

His mum and Raymundo rushed to him and crushed him with hugs.

Chapter 26: "Off With His Head!" Said the Queen

Corvette Nightfire
The Rio, Las Vegas
Late Monday Night

He didn't remember falling asleep. He didn't even remember how he got to his room at The Rio at the conclusion of Day One at the Final Table. There had been so many people rushing him, so many microphones, and so many invitations to parties. He had felt euphoria but had declined the parties so that he could be ready for the next day. He wanted badly to talk to Enrique to find out if there was any update about Valentina or David and Ana's accident. Some instinct instructed him not to turn on the television so that he would not be upset by anything he would see regarding the latter. He remembered again what David had told him:

Only believe what you see. Nothing else.

It had been a mad but ultimately triumphant day. He had kept Valentina alive, and that was his last coherent memory of the day. He had exited the poker room, and, after that, everything had seemed a blur. Time had spun out of control, and suddenly it was Day Two at the Final Table:

Four Sevens!

When Corvette saw the fourth seven on the turn, his heart nearly leapt out of his chest!

Stay calm! Don't react! Breathe!

He had the surreal feeling that time had collapsed into a singularity. He was playing Heads-Up against his only opponent now, the Legend, and the blinds were a half million and one million dollars. This was the second time he had been dealt pocket sevens (this time the 7 of hearts and the 7 of spades), and Corvette, trailing slightly in the chip count, merely called when the Legend raised to five million.

The flop had been the Queen of spades, Jack of spades, and 7 of diamonds.

OK, Corvette, you've flopped a set, but you might still be behind. Slow down and think. The Legend probably has ace-king or king-queen, and he might also be on the flush draw. Watch out for pocket queens or jacks.

Corvette tried to get a read on his opponent, but the man's face was oddly blank, as if he had no facial features. When Corvette checked, his opponent bet eight million.

Corvette paused to contemplate his bet, and then he called.

The turn was the 7 of spades.

Corvette worried that he had visibly reacted and that the Legend had seen, but when Corvette bet eight million, the Legend raised to forty million!

Corvette stared at his opponent as if he were struggling with his decision. When he thought he had waited long enough, he went all in.

But the Legend called!

Both players turned up their cards to show that each had pocket pairs: sevens for Corvette and Queens (clubs and diamonds) for the Legend. The Legend had a full house: Queens over sevens, but now Corvette's four sevens ruled.

He was actually going to win!

Thank you, Saint Rogelio! I honor you with this hand! Bless You! I'll have your name inscribed on the WSOP bracelet which symbolizes the best player in Texas Hold'em!

Then came the final card, and it stunned everyone at the table and in the audience: The Queen of hearts!

The Legend would receive the bracelet. He had four Queens. He had captured the Queen of hearts!

Corvette felt the room spinning, and, as he fell to the floor, he let out a mournful scream.

This jolted him from his nightmare. Cold and covered with sweat, he sat up in his bed.

Chapter 27: Hope Is Alive

Valentina Garza
Las Vegas, Nevada
Early Tuesday Morning

As she liked to do, as she had done every day since being in the house of Yandel Sandoval, Valentina lay in bed in the early morning darkness to listen to the sounds of the house and the property and the street outside. While the "grosero" (as she thought of the Zeta) snored beside her, she ran the inventory of memorizations on the screen of her closed eyes: the map of the house, the articles in each room, the ever-shifting numbers and locations of men, their weapons, the vehicles coming and leaving, the radios and phones, the stolen credit cards, the fragments of plots and schemes inadvertently revealed in her presence when it was believed that she didn't speak English, and the location of Yandel's home. She had accumulated much useful information about the Zetas for the DEA and Justice departments if she got out alive.

She didn't know the street number of Yandel's home because it wasn't on the house, the entrance gate, or the wall surrounding the property. But when they had driven out, Valentina saw at an intersection about a mile from the home that the road was named Fortunada Avenue.

So Vegas, she thought, *to use a Spanish word that means "Fortune."* The avenue dotted with palms was one of those long roads with expensive homes set back in large lots. It marked the current frontier before the desert surrendered new borders to the ever-expanding suburban encroachment. The few visible street numbers marking addresses had five or six numerals and seemed non-sequential and lofty as if a more mundane numbering system with fewer numbers would somehow devalue the properties.

When they had left the house, Valentina could see the skyline of the hotels and casinos of Las Vegas Boulevard in the distance. She knew the airport location along that skyline. The home was located in the southeast part of the city.

Things were changing rapidly in the house in preparation to leave for the next location, she realized. She wished that she could talk the Zeta into taking her out so that she could have an updated view of the outside of the property. Vehicles were arriving and leaving quickly. Men came inside the house for quick conferences and left. She had lost track of how many men remained and what vehicles were around. She knew that there would be zero chance that the Zeta would go out now because he was apparently not going to risk another public showing before the poker tournament. He was obsessed about it and how Corvette would do. She knew that once it began, she would again be his prisoner in front of the television. He got thrills from touching her during the tense moments, touching her in ways that made her nauseated. Today the tournament was going to begin about five p.m.

It's going to be a long day, she despaired, *and a disgusting evening. I have to find an end to this!*

But she was worried about the numbers of men and weapons in the house. She suspected that the Zeta's small regiment of troops were positioning to protect him when they would leave. She did know that scouts were observing the roads and updating reports to him. She had heard the Zeta once on the phone talking to someone about where a helicopter might land. They were formulating escape and exit plans, but she could overhear only snatches of conversations when she happened to be nearby.

She had hoped to find an ally in the house during the week. Sometimes she had found the female servant and the two young girls alone in the kitchen and had tried to engage conversation. The older woman was very reserved at first, as if scared to talk. Later in the week, she displayed a growing attitude of deference. It took a couple of days, but Valentina figured out why:

The word is out that I might become the Zeta's wife.

366

The previous day Valentina had had an awkward conversation with the woman whose name, the lady had revealed, was Florencia.

"I see that you've become busier day by day, Florencia," Valentina had said, smiling. "I suppose that you will be glad to see us all leave so you can have peace and quiet here."

A severe look of worry had drawn on Florencia's face. She responded, "Why, señora, have I done something wrong?"

Valentina had been taken aback. "Oh my goodness, I'm not saying anything like that! I just meant that you might be glad to see all of us leave so that you can work just for señor Sandoval again. We have become so many guests. With everyone coming and going, it must be nerve-wracking."

But Florencia had still look confused. "I don't work for señor Sandoval, señora Valentina. I work for señor Espinoza. I go to his properties. He sends me and my nieces to them, sometimes with other staff. This is the first time I have come here, to señor Sandoval's home. So I have been a little unfamiliar with this place. I hope I have not disappointed señor Espinoza."

"Not at all," Valentina had reassured her. "I'm sorry for the misunderstanding. I thought that you worked for señor Sandoval. Then perhaps you will be coming with us when we move. I'm glad, Florencia!"

I'm also glad that I didn't try to press her into a conspiracy with me, Valentina thought as she lay in the bed. *I truly am in this alone.*

She had committed three phone numbers to memory: those of Enrique, David, and Ana. She didn't believe for a minute that David and Ana had been in an accident, but if pressed for time in an escape emergency, she wondered if that charade might complicate their responding to a call or text message. She decided that she would send her SOS to Enrique first, and if time would permit a voice call, she definitely would phone the DEA and 911.

Dios, I have to avoid drawing my rescuers into a hellfire of gunfire and grenade launches, she realized. *My best opportunity might come if we're moving and the Zeta's men don't have the house to use as a fortress!*

As it happened later, things took a different turn.

Enrique Santos
Las Vegas, Nevada
Tuesday Morning

They were repeating the routine of the previous day, driving the streets in agent Eddie Ricotto's government-owned Ford Fusion. In the two days of their work and that of the Zs who were canvassing neighborhoods, there had been a handful of exciting moments when a possibility had been raised of a discovery of the Zeta's location, but each had turned out to have other explanations for gatherings of people and cars.

"This is Vegas," Eddie had said. "Lots of parties."

He had driven them to wealthy neighborhoods where people lived who had seen all kinds of problems, according to Eddie: people who had filed bankruptcy, who had defrauded the IRS, who had committed mail fraud running phony investment schemes; and who had been disgraced by scandalous high-profile affairs, among other problems. All fit Eddie's description of "places where neighbors have something to hide." These would be areas where people would be less likely to report suspicious activities around them, he thought. To Enrique, there seemed to be no end to such communities. They had spent the entire previous day in them.

Enrique had a wi-fi hotspot device to provide internet access in the car. On his lap in the front passenger seat was a tablet computer that had telephone capability and a special GPS application that David had loaded previously.

Enrique had explained it to Eddie:

"As we drive along the road here, the application tells us who owns each of the residential or commercial properties. The data comes from public records, and it gives us the street number, names of owners, and phone numbers of land lines inside each. Sometimes the data even includes e-mail addresses of the property owners and their social media sites! Updates are continuous via the satellite that's tracking the phone inside the notebook computer."

"Whoa! That's very useful!" responded Eddie. "Who's updating the information?"

"A civilian company contracted by the intelligence agencies of the military. I'm sure that this is used also by the FBI, CIA, and probably even your employer, the DEA," Enrique said, smiling. "David James provides services to all these agencies. He spent a lot of his career with the CIA. I guess he has access to special things."

As during the previous day, Eddie did the driving while Enrique watched the screen that showed their car moving along a roadmap. A box in the bottom left corner of the screen displayed ownership information of the houses as they passed. This monitoring got occasional interruptions when Enrique received a message or a call from one of the Z teams to report something unusual, in which case he supervised from the car the resolution of each lead with the Z on the phone. So far, none of the investigations had produced results leading to the Zeta.

Enrique was feeling a bit bored and was chatting casually with Eddie when a name that he recognized suddenly appeared on the screen: *Yandel Sandoval.*

"Hey, slow down," Enrique commanded. "This property here belongs to a famous Mexican film producer."

"Really?" Eddie asked. "I don't know this house."

Enrique felt a sudden elevation of excitement. "Sí, the thing is, this man is rumored to be linked to the cartels. Well, that by itself is nothing unusual. Everyone in the entertainment industry in Mexico is rumored to have such connections. I knew that Sandoval has properties throughout the world, but I didn't know he had one in Las Vegas. Hmmm, the application says that this house was purchased two years ago by him."

Enrique looked out the window to the property. It was on his side of the road. It had an adobe wall with a double-door entrance gate. The gate doors were grill-style with an ornate curved arch above them.

"Pull over."

Eddie stopped the car on the street just at the entrance. Enrique got out of the car, and Eddie followed him to peer through the gate.

"I don't see cars or a sign of anyone," Enrique said.

Eddie rattled the gate. There was an intercom box beside it on the wall. Mounted above was a security camera.

"Don't push the speak button. Let's go take a look. There's a three-car garage. There could be cars inside it, so someone might be in the house," Enrique said. "If anyone is inside, that camera there has announced our presence. No one is talking to us, though. Seems like the place is empty. Let's go take a look."

"Yeah?" Eddie responded. "Look at that wall, buddy. Gotta be twelve feet high and nothing to grab onto. How are we going to get over that thing?"

Enrique was already backing up. "Like this," he answered. He went running, jumped high against the wall, walked his feet up with the momentum, stretched his arms upward, and with his fingertips grasped the top of the wall. Then, in one flowing movement, he did a pull-up while throwing his legs sideways to anchor his body on top. He then let himself hang on the other side of the wall for a second before dropping to the ground. He reappeared on the other side of the gate.

"Um, I can't do that," Eddie said to Enrique in a tone of understatement.

"You can! You just don't know it yet," Enrique said. "Wait here and watch. If I get in any trouble, call for backup. The place looks zipped-up and locked for the winter from what I can see from here. I don't think this is going to turn up anything."

"I don't like this too much," Eddie responded. "You don't have a weapon. There could be someone in there. You wouldn't have a chance."

"I'm a weapon. I have skills," Enrique answered, half joking. "I'll do this fast. Besides, if someone were there, they would have discouraged us by now."

He jogged to the front entrance of the house and peered through the glass panes that were on both sides of the front door. Then he went to the living room window for a glimpse. He walked around the house, and within four or five minutes, he was back at the gate.

"There's absolutely no one here," he told Eddie. He stepped back and repeated the maneuvers over the wall which he had made before. He dropped beside Eddie and gestured that they return to the car.

When they were back inside the Ford Fusion, Enrique checked his notebook screen again.

"Okay, this is 906 Astrid Drive, the home of Yandel Sandoval. We can rule this one out," Enrique reported.

David James
Las Vegas, Nevada
Tuesday Morning

David was in a conference room with Sheriff Paul Robertson and Special Agent Nick Easter in a Las Vegas Police Department building. He felt frustrated and irritable from the discouraging reports of the previous day.

"Corvette Nightfire was lucky," an analyst of the tournament had told him. "He survived the eliminations by playing conservatively during a run of good cards. He absolutely lucked out in the final hand of the day. He'll have to play much better and more aggressively in a heads-up with the Legend."

That was on his mind as he listened to the Sheriff and the FBI agent discussing the possibility that the Zeta had already left Las Vegas. He listened, but as he did, he scrolled his phone for e-mail, texts, and social media messages to see if there were any unusual reports from Enrique or the Zs in the streets. He came to an interesting text message from Enrique about checking out the home in Las Vegas of Yandel Sandoval with a negative result. Then, out of habit, he looked at Twitter.

God! Some of Enrique's Zs are reporting about their searches for the Zeta on a Twitter hashtag! Anyone can see what they're up to!

David fired off a text asking Enrique to clarify to the Zs that they should report only unusual items directly to Enrique's phone.

The Sheriff's report to him and the FBI agent basically boiled down to the fact that there hadn't been success in finding the Zeta. David was frustrated.

"If he makes a move en-mass, we'll find him," the Sheriff stated. "We're watching everything: the roads, the airports, the public transits, trains, buses, taxi and car leasing companies...it's just a question of time."

"We don't have time," said David. "This is personal with the Zeta. He wanted me and Ana dead. He'll kill Valentina Garza, just as he says, if Corvette Nightfire doesn't win this tournament. Corvette took his money. He'll kill him. You have to understand the way the cartel leaders think. They don't have life expectancies. They make bold moves. In the ambush of El Asesino, the Zeta had three of your police officers murdered. He set that up with those men and then double-crossed them. It was because getting back at the other cartel trumps everything. He has more of your policemen on his payroll, whether you believe this or not, by the way. When the Cartel of Sinaloa executed the entire band of musicians in Monterrey, it was a personal message to the Zeta. Now you can bet that the Zeta is retaliating for that even as we meet here."

"David, is there something you think we can do now that we have not been doing?" Special Agent Easter asked.

"I doubt it, Nick," David answered, clearly flustered. "We're watching aircraft from the satellites also, right?"

The FBI agent nodded. "But even so, we can't see everything. The Vegas skies are filled with craft day and night."

"There are two possibilities," David said. "As you were just discussing, one is that Z-30 has already left Las Vegas. He might have been spooked by the confrontation outside the house where Corvette stayed Sunday night. He might have left the city before our net was as tight as it is right now. He can watch the poker tournament from anywhere. The other possibility is that he's still in Las Vegas, in which case he has plenty of financial resources and people in his pocket to find a clever way to defeat our efforts to catch him."

Easter sighed. "There's a third possibility, and, although not likely, we can't rule it out yet."

"What's that?" the Sheriff asked.

"That the man who's with Valentina Garza is not the Zeta."

He saw the "get-out-of-here" looks on the faces of David and the Sheriff.

"I know, I know," commented the special agent. "The problem of identification lies with bureaucracy and inefficiency in Mexico. Some noisy relatives of the Zeta in his home state of Puebla continue to insist that the Zeta isn't dead. Meanwhile those in Puebla who believe that the body we have from The Oasis is, in fact, the Zeta are clamoring for the return home of their native son's body. We rushed DNA samples taken from the corpse in The Oasis to the state forensic lab in Puebla. The Federal Government in Mexico is under the gun about the controversy, so they're being very cooperative and have helped expedite the testing. This morning the call came from the Puebla lab that the DNA didn't match the DNA of blood samples allegedly from Horacio Vazquez at a crime scene in Mexico a few years back. They sent us digital images of the report and a description of the care taken in their testing. The report states that the DNA in the samples taken from the body in The Oasis has a close correlation to samples taken from relatives of Raúl Espinoza!"

"Damn!" exclaimed the sheriff.

"I know, Paul, but this kind of thing has happened before in Mexico. There's often complete chaos when it comes to getting accurate identification of people there. There are mistakes in testing, mis-filings of reports, lost evidence...much of this depends on the strengths of cartels in the local area. Sometimes the problems are due to inefficiency and sometimes due to corruption. The cartels like for their leaders to live on in stories and songs, and mystery often surrounds their deaths. So big money goes toward falsifying reports, stealing bodies from morgues, and making things look like the dead leader is alive and in hiding."

David was too stressed to hide his bad mood. "Okay, Nick, all of that's true. But someone has Valentina, and he's sure acting like the Zeta! So let's assume that he's the Zeta. We have to get him."

"Agreed."

"So the puzzle we need to resolve is this," said the Sheriff. "If he's in Las Vegas, how will he try to escape? How can we find him?"

"Every minute that goes by, we're eliminating where he's not. So that's some progress." Agent Easter observed.

"We only have until the tournament ends tonight," David added pointedly.

"If we have the city and the air covered, what is left?" asked Sheriff Robertson.

"The desert," answered David.

Valentina Garza
Las Vegas, Nevada
Early Tuesday Afternoon

She thought it was weird, but Raúl insisted that they eat lunch together in the bedroom. She worried what he might have in mind, but he had a table brought in and set up. When he came into the room, he cut on the television to watch analyses and pre-game shows on ESPN about the World Series of Poker. Florencia and her nieces came in behind him and served a hot lunch of barbecued chicken legs, mashed potatoes, green beans, a garden salad, and iced tea. The Zeta did seem more interested in the food than he did in trying to sample her body, at least for now.

"It's a Southern lunch," the Zeta told her. He laughed and explained that he was trying to learn about regional cuisine and culture in the United States. Valentina took it as a hint that their next stop was going to be somewhere in the deep south of the USA. Thinking about money centers for the cartel, she ventured to guess New Orleans or Memphis.

It was while they were dining at the folding table with the fancy table cloth that Valentina heard the arrival of a big truck outside in the driveway. To her it sounded huge, like an eighteen-wheeler. Raúl acted as if he didn't notice. Valentina could tell that the truck had pulled up close to the house on the side that had the garage. During the next few minutes she heard seven engines start up, run briefly, and then silence. She guessed that motorcycles were being driven down an unloading ramp from the truck's enclosed trailer and were being parked beside the house. On one of the outings, she had noticed a carport constructed behind the garage to shelter more vehicles. That sounded like where the motorcycles were going. If they were there, it wouldn't be possible to see them from the road, she remembered.

Then she understood the reason for the bedroom lunch:

Raúl didn't want me to see the truck. The television is on to help hide the noises and the voices of the men out there right now.

She noted that the truck stayed about half an hour. Later, when she finally was able go to the front part of the house, she saw that there were two SUVs parked in the circular entrance drive: a black GMC and a silver BMW. The small cars that had arrived in the morning weren't there.

So how many men are in the house? Valentina wondered. She walked casually through the house to find and count them. She hoped also for an opportunity to see inside the garage. However, she didn't get the opportunity because Raúl emerged from the bedroom to join her. Nor did she have a chance to visit the north wing of the house that had a second story with a couple of bedrooms. She couldn't go up there without it looking suspicious.

But from her visual tour and the sounds in the house, she concluded that there were only seven men inside the home, plus Raúl, Florencia, and her nieces.

Z-30, The Zeta
Las Vegas, Nevada
Tuesday Afternoon

After Valentina left the bedroom, the Zeta got up and went to the door and observed her as she went down the hall. He saw that, as he had thought, she was going to go look out the living room window to see if she could find out what the truck had delivered.

I don't blame her, he reasoned. *I would do the same.*

He really liked her, and he hoped that he would be able to be with her for a long time. Still, he was glad that he had taken precautions.

In the end, one can be betrayed by the closest people, he mused.

As she passed the entertainment room, he thought about Yandel, and a slight smile came to his face. When he had asked Yandel if he could borrow some framed photos of his family to use "for a special private purpose" while Yandel would be in Hollywood, Yandel had regarded him uncertainly; but then he had agreed when Raúl told him that he would return them in a couple of weeks. Raúl knew that Yandel had learned not to ask him many questions. In that way he wouldn't be incriminated in activities which he didn't want to know anything about. Yandel also knew how careful the Zeta was about everything. Yandel had lent the photographs to him because he had trusted that the Zeta would have good use for them. Besides, Yandel had a family, a beautiful one as shown in the photos, and he knew that it was always much safer for them if he granted any small favor the Zeta wanted. In addition, the Zeta was a good financial supporter for some of the cinema projects for which Yandel hadn't been able to find financial backing.

The Zeta had placed the photographs in the entertainment room to make Valentina think that she was in the home of Yandel Sandoval. That was important the first couple of days before they went out together when the Zeta was establishing how much he could trust her. Trust had always been paramount with the Zeta. Later in the week, Valentina rode with him through Las Vegas, so she had the opportunity to know where she was in the city. But the addresses marking Fortunada Avenue were notoriously scattered, and the Zeta had been careful not to have any numbers hanging on his house, wall or gate. He wasn't in this home often. Owning the home was as much a way of laundering money as it was being a place to stay. The Zeta had bought the house through a straw purchaser and had titled it in one of his aliases. Most of the time in Las Vegas he preferred to stay in hotels on The Strip. After the incident in The Oasis, he thought that the house would help provide him a low profile, so he retreated there. He had led Valentina to believe that the home belonged to Sandoval to create confusion. He liked confusion.

The more confusing things are, the better, the Zeta mused. *Confusion always buys me time.*

Days before, he had heard from the laboratory in Puebla. As he expected, the gringo police forces were trying to use DNA testing to identify the body in The Oasis. It had cost him a lot of money, but he had arranged that the resulting report would inform the gringos that the body wasn't that of Horacio Vazquez. Instead, it would suggest that the body was that of the Zeta! The police, FBI, and DEA of the gringos might not believe it, but he counted on the confusion of that report to provide him time to formulate his plans for exiting Las Vegas to his next destination. He really wanted to be in Vegas while Corvette was playing. If the gringos were uncertain who they were really after, their uncertainty could lead to mistakes that would favor him.

Even Valentina could get confused on this issue! She had met him at a party, and slowly she had come to know him as the Zeta. But what if he had lied to her? What if she had really been dancing with Horacio? There were so many ways to produce smoke.

He went back to the table in the bedroom to finish a chicken leg. He thought about his childhood in Puebla.

Well, I know who I am, he told himself. *I know the truth. And the Zeta needs to live a little longer.*

When he looked up at the television screen, he saw Corvette Nightfire in a pre-tournament interview.

Home stretch, he thought. *Corvette, you Mexican gringo, you better fucking win.*

Enrique Santos
Late Tuesday Afternoon

Since checking out the home of Yandel Sandoval on Astrid Lane, Enrique and Eddie had spent time looking at several houses that Zs had reported during their rounds. A double-check with the police or a conversation with neighbors led to explanations about visitors or numerous cars at the residences. Some of the occupants ran businesses from home, and delivery trucks were common sights coming and going. Enrique felt that it was important to conference with the Zs about each questionable site, but these were piling up. He didn't want to let himself fall into a landslide of possibilities. He needed to keep organized.

So at one point, he asked Eddie to pull over so that he could quickly type some mass messages to all Zs in the area.

"I'm getting a little car sick," he explained. "I want to stop long enough to do this to make sure we have lots of Zs on call tonight during and after the tournament. Some of the guys working with us the past couple of days are getting tired and bored. I need to check the state of our human resources and have us ready if we need to move quickly tonight. Also, I need to get a call in to David."

He saw that daylight was fading fast. He checked his watch.

"Damn, it's five p.m. The tournament should be starting now."

As he phoned David to update him on what he was doing with the Zs and to hear if David had made any progress with the FBI and the police, Enrique noticed a text message from a Z named Eugenio:

"Report of 18 wheeler in driveway of home on Fortunada Avenue for short-stay delivery. House is walled with gate. Many vehicles coming and going for two days. Neighbors say home is usually empty."

We're running out of time, Enrique thought. *Eddie and I are going to have to start deciding which of these reports to check out and which not. This definitely will be one.*

Then David answered the phone.

"Hang on one second, David," Enrique requested. He typed a response to Eugenio's message:

"Stay posted with your partner from safe position and watch the house. Report back the number address on Fortunada Avenue please." He thought of the setup at the home of Yandel Sandoval, and he added, "Stay out of view of security cameras on gate or wall."

Then he returned to talk with David.

"We're nowhere," David told him. "This afternoon I have been learning what kinds of planes can land in the desert. The sand makes for unstable landings, and it's hell on engines. But bush planes with big fat soft tires can do it, like a Cessna 206, for example."

"Why are you telling me this?"

"Because I think this is how the Zeta will try to make his escape."

Security was tight but The Rio was mobbed. Madeline stood in a crush of people at the entrance to the poker room with Raymundo and Jupiter waiting to be screened for admittance to the audience section. There were only two players now, so the audience would be smaller; but the supporters took up space with costumes and placards. They were noisy and excited. She saw an area where Corvette and the Legend were being kept "back stage," and once she caught a glimpse of her son being directed to a spot to stand for a television interview.

She had only been able to see him briefly in the casino a couple of hours earlier. She didn't like the way he looked. She searched for words as she watched Raymundo try to bandy with him, and "discouraged" and "scared" came to her. She herself could hardly stand the pressure. She actually had considered not sitting in the audience so that she could just learn the result of the final after it was over.

That had changed when she finally got a private moment with her son.

"Mum, I had a horrible nightmare about the tournament last night," Corvette told her. "I dreamed I lost because the Legend won with the Queen of hearts. It has really psyched me out. It's just that the Queen of hearts symbolizes Valentina to me. I wish I had never taken that money. Now somehow her life depends on my play today. Under ordinary circumstances, coming in second and winning millions of dollars would have been a good consolation prize. But not now!" He shook his head, and Madeline noticed his red eyes. He had been crying, and he looked like he might do it again.

Seeing her son like that gave Madeline some steel. "Listen to me, Corvette," she told him. "You didn't put Valentina in this situation. Someone else is doing this to her. You're not the only one trying to save her. There are literally hundreds out there trying to do it. In fact, you've been prolonging the time they have to find her. So just keep up the good work. Try to focus only on the game and don't think of outcomes. Play each hand well. Take it hand by hand. In the past, that's what you've told me that you do. I'll be in there praying for you. Trust in yourself. Trust in the people trying to find Valentina also. Who do you believe in the most?"

"Enrique," Corvette answered.

"Okay," Madeline said. "I believe in him too. I also believe in you."

When he left, she had felt heartbroken for him. She knew that she had to be in the room for him.

As best they could, the staff at The Rio tried to decide admittance based on family and close friendships. They had some names given to them by the two players listing people whom they would like to have in the audience. Madeline knew that, as his mother, she would be in the front row behind Corvette and that also Raymundo and Jupiter would be beside her. As she got closer to the metal detectors and the tables where staff examined bags to make sure no cell phones were being brought in, she noticed a woman in a Rio uniform staring at her from just inside the door to the poker room. The woman had blonde hair pulled back severely; her dark eyebrows needed serious attention; and she wore ugly thick black-rimmed glasses. The woman's stare did not abate as Madeline got closer to the entrance. Madeline had never seen her before, but her eyes did remind her of someone whom she couldn't place.

Madeline hadn't brought her phone. The bag search went fine. She passed through the metal detector, entered the poker room, and paused to wait for Jupiter and Raymundo to pass. When she did, the woman who had been staring at her came forward and said to her, "Madam, please step just over here to the side with me and let me look one more time inside your bag. We do random checks in the room. Thank you for your cooperation."

The woman had a Hispanic accent, Madeline noticed, as she moved aside with the lady. She took Madeline's cloth bag and opened it wide. When she did this, she produced a small brown box from her pocket and quickly set it in the bag. It had a note pasted on the top of the box. The woman held the bag open and motioned for Madeline to inspect the contents of the bag with her.

"What is this in here? Just cosmetics?" the woman asked in a voice a little louder than normal.

Madeline felt confused, but she peered inside the bag. She saw the box and read the note on top:

"I'm Ana Valdez. Don't react. Cell phone is in box and is turned on. Take out in emergency only. Answer all rings even in poker room; might be emergency. Speed dial 1 for Ana, 2 for David. 3 for Enrique. Don't reveal this phone to anyone."

Madeline felt shocked, but she kept outward composure. She looked into the woman's eyes and at that moment recognized Ana.

"Yes," Madeline answered, "that's just my makeup in there. Please feel free to look at it. I understand what you have to do. Be my guest."

"Thank you, madam, that's all," Ana answered, handing back Madeline's bag. "I believe that's your party entering the room now." She gestured toward Raymundo and Jupiter, who hadn't noticed the intervention by Ana. "Please enjoy the tournament."

Madeline left and took her seat beside Raymundo and Jupiter. When she looked again, Ana was gone.

Corvette Nightfire
Seated, Day Two, World Series of Poker
Tuesday Night

He tried to remember his mother's words to focus, play hand by hand, and not think of anything else; but he couldn't put aside the thought of Valentina. He imagined her watching him on television, probably with the Zeta. For that reason the television cameras, which had never bothered him before, now seemed like the eyes of Valentina.

If I can just prolong this as long as possible, he kept thinking, *maybe Enrique, David, the police, or someone can find her! Why is it so hard to find her?*

But after thinking that, he felt that he was just trying to share the burden of Valentina's life with anyone else. *Her life really is on my shoulders,* he sighed. This made him realize anxiously that he wasn't, in fact, focusing on the game.

During the first hands, Corvette limped in, either calling or making minimum bets. Any time his opponent made a significant bet, Corvette folded the hand. After two hours of this, the Legend had one hundred and twenty-seven million chips and had built a nearly two-to-one chip lead. Fortunately, the network had scheduled a break, and the players were given fifteen minutes. Raymundo pulled Corvette aside.

When they were alone, Raymundo spoke. "Hombre, what's going on? Keep this up and you won't last long. Talk to me!"

Corvette broke down. "I can't do it, Raymundo! It's too much! Everyone talks about how great I played yesterday, but I almost blew it! Valentina's life was in the balance, and I screwed up! The only reason I'm here is because I got lucky on the river. Every hand I get, all I can think of is how his hand might be better! I swear to God, the fear is paralyzing!"

"Screw that! Get angry, amigo! That's what you need to do. Anger destroys fear! This game is threatening your love, your life! Get pissed! If you give in to the fear, you'll definitely lose. You know the game! You know the odds. Trust yourself and trust in God. Didn't you tell me that when it came down to the final two, it was more about the cards than the men?"

"It is, Raymundo. The best players can pull off the occasional bluff, and the Legend is one of the best, but it's really about the cards. Everything is relative. It's not about getting good cards; it's about getting great cards when your opponent gets good cards. The player has to think he has the winning hand or he'll simply fold. It's all about timing and luck."

"Well, you can bluff as well as he can. I've seen you do it, hermano. And remember, the odds for you are the same as the odds for him. In the long run, the cards treat every player fairly. So trust yourself and your luck, and do what must be done."

The signal came for the end of the break, and Corvette had to return to the table. He looked over to his mother. She must have overheard the conversation which he had with Raymundo despite the background noise of the room because she stared into his eyes and nodded meaningfully, as if in agreement.

The first two hands repeated the pattern of the previous two hours. Corvette called pre-flop and then folded when the Legend bet the flop. But in his heart, Corvette knew that under ordinary conditions he would have done the same thing. On those two hands he was trusting his instincts.

On the third hand, the Legend bet two million pre-flop, and Corvette called it. The dealer dealt the flop. It was the Ace of clubs, King of spades, and 9 of diamonds. The Legend bet five million. Corvette paused for a long time before finally calling his bet. The dealer dealt the turn: the 6 of clubs. Both the Legend and Corvette checked. Then came the final card of the hand. The river was the 2 of hearts, and Corvette checked.

Next, when the Legend bet twenty-three million, Corvette, without hesitation, pushed all in! A gasp came from the crowd!

The Legend stared into Corvette's eyes several minutes.

He said, "It's finally starting to become fun, isn't it, Corvette?"

But Corvette just looked back stone-faced at him.

The Legend grinned and folded. He looked to his fans behind him and shrugged with a smile. His bluff had been exposed.

Corvette Nightfire was back in contention!

Chapter 28: End of Game, New Game

Enrique Santos
Las Vegas, Nevada
Tuesday Night

When Eugenio, the Z who was on Fortunada Avenue, responded to Enrique with a text message that the street address of the suspicious house was unknown even by the neighbor, Enrique asked Eddie to have someone in the DEA get the exact address. Enrique's intention after he had talked to David on the phone was to go directly to Eugenio, but a new report came in of a house that had received numerous cars throughout the day from which single persons had emerged for short visits. It was closer to them, so Enrique and Eddie went there first. When they checked that location out with the Z on the scene and, subsequently, with the police, it was revealed that the house had been the location of a drug bust two months earlier. Enrique's investigation of the site ultimately turned up a small-time drug point-of-sale back in business, but no Zeta or Valentina. This had eaten up time.

When they arrived on Fortunada Avenue, they parked on the street about an eighth of a mile from the house. They had obtained the street number, and Enrique's GPS application had guided them there. Eddie and Enrique walked a little way in the darkness until they saw the forms of two young men in black clothing. One of them was Eugenio. He reported that the house had been quiet the past couple of hours, but before then, several men had left in small cars that had been in front of the home. Also, a small rental truck had backed up to the garage and was quickly loaded, but the Zs hadn't been able to see what the men were loading.

"Maybe someone is moving," Eddie suggested sarcastically.

They walked along the sidewalk to get a closer view of the property. Enrique saw that the house, like many of the more expensive homes along this street, had a wall and an entrance gate operated remotely. There was a long driveway to the house, which had a three-car garage on the side. Near the front entrance, in a circular driveway for receiving guests, were parked two SUVs. Neither the entrance lights nor the outside garage lights were lit.

Along the sidewalk where the group of four stood were streetlights, but these were spaced so far apart that big splashes of darkness between them provided cover for the men.

"As you can see, it's pretty dark here, but earlier in the daylight Martin and I saw something strange about the house's wall on the far side of the house over there," commented Eugenio, pointing. Martin was the name of his partner. "It has two straight thin vertical cracks running top to bottom, spaced about ten feet apart. It looks like it was a segment of the wall, as if it had been added in later. We couldn't get a better look because we were afraid of being seen, so we don't know what is on the inside of that segment."

"That is strange," Eddie agreed.

"No sight of any women at all here today?" Enrique asked.

"Nada," replied Eugenio.

Suddenly the vibration of Enrique's phone startled him. He checked caller ID and recognized the number as being Ana's. He answered, walking a short distance from the others.

Ana spoke in a hushed tone, but loud enough to overcome a lot of background noise. "Corvette almost got played out early," she reported, "but he just made a good move and he's back in the game with the Legend. Are you and Eddie having any luck?"

"Not sure," Enrique responded. "Let me give you this location on Fortunada Avenue where we are now. We had to research the street address because the homes on this road don't always their street numbers. It is 111077. Pass this to David as a suspicious location. To be accurate, right now this is the only suspicious location that hasn't checked out. We're working on it. We received ownership information that it belongs to someone named David Gonzales, but not much else about that name. This is a road on the outskirts of the city. Across the street from the house is the desert. The road borders a number of suburban communities that front along the desert. David is suspicious of the desert. That's why I mention this. Where is he?"

"All over Las Vegas with the FBI and the police," Ana answered. "He's very frustrated. He's in his Corvette somewhere with Special Agent Nick Easter."

"Okay, maybe the FBI could get more information on this David Gonzales. The DEA drew a dead end from their search of records. Not much there. Ask David to have this checked out."

When the call was over, Enrique returned to the other three. He asked Eugenio and Martin, "Are you guys holding up okay?"

"Sí, but we're a little hungry," Eugenio answered.

"I'm going to call in some more Zs to join you here. This is the most suspicious location that we have right now. I'll have them bring you some food. Stay hidden, but watch the house."

He turned to Eddie. "Let's drive the road a little way."

They drove a couple of miles north. Lost in thought, Enrique stared at the dark desert. The wall that Eugenio had described bothered him. Deciding that he wanted to ride past it, he instructed Eddie to turn around and return to the house. Eddie slowed the car as they approached it, and Enrique strained to see in the darkness. Enrique saw that nothing was outside the wall along the ten-foot section that Eugenio had described as a "segment" other than land that was probably part of the property of the house. The next neighbor's home was about one eighth of a mile behind them, and that house also had a wall enclosing it. Somewhere between the two homes would be a property line. Except for some planted islands of trees and shrubs, the land between the houses was pretty much like the desert across the street.

They continued about a mile when they finally arrived at an intersection where there was a Baptist church. Enrique had noticed it earlier and thought something odd about it.

"Pull in and park in the church lot," he instructed Eddie. "I want to call in the Z reinforcements from here and have a few moments to think."

The church building was dark, but the parking lot had about ten compact cars parked in random spaces. Eddie apparently had the same feeling as Enrique.

"Kind of weird, isn't it? A dark church with this many cars parked in front," Eddie commented.

"Eyyy," Enrique agreed. "I suppose it is possible that church members met here and then took a van or something to some event in the area. Church people do those sorts of things."

"Let's call in the license plate numbers of the cars," Eddie said.

"Good idea."

They got out of the car with a flashlight and were writing the plate numbers on a piece of paper when a distant droning sound became suddenly near and loud. To Enrique, it sounded like a small plane. The engine noise seemed to be in the direction up the street where they had just been. He looked all over the sky, but he couldn't see anything. He observed Eddie doing the same thing.

"That sound like a low plane to you?" Eddie asked him.

"Sí, let's hurry and get the rest of these numbers and then get back up the street."

But less than a minute later, Enrique received a text message from Eugenio:

"Not certain, but I think a plane just landed in the desert. We thought we saw a shadow in the sky, then engine cut suddenly."

The Zeta, Z-30
Las Vegas, Nevada
Tuesday Night

Earlier the Zeta had sent Florencia to help Valentina pack a bag for the trip that would take place after the tournament. A

388

truck had arrived to pick up the belongings that they would need, plus much of the weaponry, ammunition, and stolen items that were excessive now that so many of the men had headed on toward their destination. The bland stolen cars from other Nevada cities had served their purposes of transport as the Zeta's men drove freely through Las Vegas without the ostentation that they usually enjoyed in their vehicles. It was surprising the number of automatic rifles that could fit in the trunk of an older model Honda Accord. The cars were now parked in the church lot up the street. In groups departing at different times, the men of the Zeta's troop loaded their weapons into the SUVs and trucks which they favored and began the journey which the Zeta would make later. It was unlikely that Z-30 would ever return to the house. Soon there would be a "For Sale" sign in front.

Before leaving, the men had rolled the four-wheelers into the garage. The Zeta smiled, thinking about how Valentina might (or might not) like riding, holding on to him from behind. He loved the all-terrain-vehicles. At the fiestas of his favorite ranch near Santiago in Mexico, his festive parties always featured exuberant group rides and races through the mountains on ATVs. He had driving experience in the desert too, but he preferred the challenges of mountain crevices.

He had asked Valentina to lie beside him in the bed to watch the tournament. He had undressed her down to her panties and had pulled her close to him so he could fondle her while Corvette sat at the table in The Rio and played for her life. He expected this to thrill him, but for the first two hours of the tournament, as Corvette's pot dwindled, the Zeta's body tensed from his increasing frustration and anger. He didn't want Corvette to lose. He wanted the satisfaction of taking his money. He wanted to keep him on a tether in the future, to have him at his beck and call. He wanted to taunt him by having Valentina.

He truly hoped that the tournament would result in that Valentina could live. Her body drove him frigging nuts, but, equally important to him, she was a woman whom he really liked and tolerated being around. She held her own with him. For the future that he envisioned, he was convinced that Valentina would make the perfect wife for him. She would provide him beautiful, smart children. But if Corvette lost the tournament, the Zeta would have to lose Valentina.

I can't be the Zeta unless I do what I say. The Zeta always does what he says he'll do.

Just before Corvette made the play that put him back in the game, the Zeta, anxious that Corvette was about to lose, picked up the phone beside him in the bed and went into the bathroom. He made a call to el Amarillo, the jaundiced aide who was at The Rio just outside the entrance to the poker room. The Zeta was aware of the fifteen-minute delay of the televised transmission of the match. Nevertheless, people in The Rio were learning what was happening in the poker room. There was confusion: this-guy-saw-this, this-guy-heard-that, but the real-time events of the game were leaking from the room just moments after they occurred.

"Did he lose?" the Zeta asked el Amarillo irritably.

"No! He's back in! He just won a huge pot!"

The Zeta felt relief surge through his body. "Call me right away if he loses. If he wins, don't call. I want to watch and savor every moment of that."

Before returning to the bed, the Zeta went to the living room to conference with his remaining men on last-minute details of their exit. They would move as soon as the tournament ended. Everything was ready, even the preparation for moving the corpse of Valentina if necessary.

The Zeta now felt exhilarated. Everything was going well, and Corvette was back in the game!

He returned to the bedroom. He saw Valentina's robe on the floor on her side of the bed. His clothes and hers were on a chair nearby. She was sitting up against the headboard on his side of the bed, her eyes glued to the TV.

When she noticed him, Valentina shouted, "Oh my God, come here and look at this, Raúl! The Legend bet twenty-three million and Corvette has just gone all-in!"

But the Zeta knew what the outcome of that bet would be. He was more interested in Valentina's breasts, calling to him now like two promising mounds of high-dollar poker chips. He got beside her in the bed and set his phone between them for the call that he hoped wouldn't come.

Later he felt sure that he heard the plane pass overhead.

Corvette Nightfire
End of Game
Tuesday Night

Winning the big pot and calling the Legend's bluff gave Corvette footing. He didn't want to become euphoric. He was so relieved to still be in the game. Now he wanted to rely on the feeling of being on solid ground so that he could truly focus hand by hand. That pivotal play had done the trick.

For the next two hours, he and the Legend played neck and neck, and the lead changed twice. Once again, the network had scheduled a break, but it was a different Corvette who spoke to Raymundo and his mother.

"So happy for you, son!" Madeline exclaimed. "You're showing the kind of steel your father had! He would be so proud of the way you are playing."

Raymundo grabbed him and ruffled Corvette's hair with his knuckles. "La Leyenda tiene respeto ahora, cabrón," Raymundo laughed in a fit of glee. "The Legend has respect now, you bastard," he translated. "Respeto por el Méxicano."

Corvette understood the last part and grinned. "I still have to win," he pointed out. "Any news out there? Is anything happening?"

"I've gone out a couple of times, amigo, but not hearing anything yet. It's so hard for me to leave the room with this level of play going on. Don't worry about out there. Just keep doing what you're doing. All of this is in the hands of God, not yours."

"Yes!" Madeline chimed in. "Corvette, trust me, I think it's all going to turn out okay."

"Damn," Corvette sighed.

His fans were cheering loudly for his attention. Corvette collected himself to speak to them a few moments, and then the match resumed. He was relieved to find that he still had his focus. When dealt the cards, he was able to forget his anxiety about Valentina.

The end came on hand number 283:

Corvette trailed the Legend by a mere five million chips. When he was dealt pocket-Aces, he knew that this could be just what he needed to finish off his opponent. The Legend raised to five million, and Corvette re-raised to twenty million. The Legend countered with an all-in bet!

Corvette immediately called it. He confidently turned over his cards. Revealed on the table was Corvette's two red Aces against the Legend's Ace and Queen of spades.

Corvette quickly calculated the odds in his head: He realized that he had an 87% chance of winning. His heart nearly beat out of his chest. The energized crowd felt the electricity of the moment. Corvette could no longer sit. He went by his cheering section and stood in front of Raymundo and his mother and Jupiter. The Legend also stood in front of his fans. They awaited the next card at the table.

The dealer burned a card and then turned up the flop: the 10 of spades, King of hearts, and 3 of spades.

Shit! Corvette heard in his mind. He calculated that his chances had now dropped to 53%, but he still had the advantage.

The dealer burned another card and then dealt the turn. It was the Jack of diamonds!

No, no, no! Corvette's mind screamed. *The Legend has filled a straight!*

The crowd erupted, and Corvette saw the Legend dancing with uncontained joy. Both men now realized that it was impossible for Corvette to win. The odds were 93% in favor of the Legend with a 7% chance of a split pot. Corvette's only hope to stay alive lay in the river: a Queen had to appear!

This is too crazy! Corvette thought. *God, please help me! Dios!* He felt on the verge of panic. He thought of his nightmare. He remembered his father. His mother reached down from her place and took his hand and held it tightly.

St. Rogelio, please be here...dad, please help!

It seemed like the dealer's hand moved in slow motion as he dealt the river card: the Jack of Hearts.

A knave had done Corvette in!

Corvette wheezed an inhalation of horror. He turned to look up at his mother, and she was doing something strange. Inexplicably, she pulled out a phone from a brown box in her purse and punched a number. Raymundo leaped down to the floor from his seat and grabbed Corvette.

"He's going to kill her; he's going to kill her!" Corvette began muttering almost incoherently.

"Steady, amigo, we got this! Get control! We'll find out what to do. Steady, hombre..."

Corvette felt the panic take him over. He started to shout about the Zeta killing Valentina, but then Raymundo slapped his cheek and pointed to Madeline.

"Listen to your mom! She's talking to someone about Valentina!"

"What?" Corvette asked, dazed.

A blonde woman wearing thick glasses and a Rio staff uniform rushed up and waved a phone in the air so Madeline would notice. Madeline nodded and cut her call. The blonde woman pulled Corvette down to her and put her lips to Corvette's ear.

"Corvette!" she told him. "I'm Ana Valdez. Don't say anything else. Come! We have to get out of here. Come with me quickly! Hurry!"

Corvette looked with skepticism at the woman, but then he saw the familiarity of Ana's eyes. His mother rushed up and took Corvette's arm. She told him, "Corvette, this woman is Ana. Enrique might have found out where Valentina is!"

"Follow me," Ana commanded, and then Jupiter, Raymundo, and Madeline started pushing Corvette to follow Ana as they fought through the mayhem in the room to the nearest exit door. Along the way people were screaming Corvette's name, confused by his departing.

Valentina Garza
The bedroom with the Zeta
Tuesday Night

The match was tense, back-and-forth, and truly she could see that Corvette was playing courageously. She was disgusted by the Zeta's touching her, but he was absorbed in watching the match, and this was saving her from anything worse that he would do to her. She couldn't put her finger on it, but there was something about the Zeta's tension that made her think that more was riding on the tournament than she had been told. At one point, he got up and went to the bedroom door in his undershorts, opened it, and yelled a summons to one of the men, who quickly appeared in the hallway.

"The keys to the GMC are on the kitchen table," the Zeta told him. "Drive around and do a reconnaissance to make sure things are quiet around here. Stop at the Seven-Eleven up the road like you're going for cigarettes or something in case anyone is watching you. Report to me when you get back. We'll be leaving soon. Oh, and look to make sure that nothing can be seen in the desert across from the house."

Valentina had seen the Seven-Eleven and knew that it was on a main commercial road about a mile and a half away. She was puzzled by the desert comment, but then she remembered thinking that she had heard a plane pass overhead earlier.

Is that what's in the desert? She thought.

She noticed that the Zeta didn't pick up his cell phone when he went to the door. After instructing the man in the hallway, he returned immediately to the bed.

She had a bad feeling. His last sentence in particular had alarmed her.

I need to make a move soon, she decided.

She did it when she heard the Zeta's scout return to the house. As the Zeta got up to go to the doorway again, she did also, telling him, "Raúl, I'm going to the bathroom. I have a bad stomach cramp."

He only half looked behind him, nodding in a distracted way that he understood as he opened the door and began speaking to his man again. She saw him make several steps into the hallway. She scooped up the cellphone from the bed and pocketed it inside the bathrobe which she threw on as she hurried. Inside the bathroom, she locked the door. Trembling, she tapped a phone number and a text message:

"Enrique, this is Valentina. I'm captive at Yandel Sandoval's home on Fortunada Avenue. Seven men plus the Zeta, many weapons. Emergency!"

Steadying her nerves, she concentrated to see if she had entered Enrique's number correctly. After satisfying herself, she tapped "Send."

She was preparing to delete the message when the phone suddenly began to sound a musical ringtone. A call was coming in! Startled, she dropped the phone. Never had she thought a ringtone sounded as loud as this one! She nervously picked up the phone and quickly unlocked the door. She wanted to delete her text message to Enrique.

I have to get out there and act like I heard the phone in the bed and hand it to Raúl, she thought. Then she hoped, *If only he's still talking and ignores the ring...*

But before she could delete the text, the door to the bathroom swung open with force, and Raúl imposed himself in the doorway. His eyes were wide with accusation. His body filled the frame of the door. She handed him the phone and said,

"Raúl, your phone is ringing," trying to sound innocent of wrongdoing. Not moving from the doorway, he snatched it from her and answered it, glancing at the caller ID as he did. She could see that he was furious. He was also completely blocking her escape.

It was the weird way in which he answered without making any type of greeting to his caller that told her she would have to fight for her life. With his eyes glued on her, the Zeta said into the phone, "He lost."

She could hear the caller answering, "Sí," and beginning to elaborate, but the eyes of the Zeta bearing on her now were the eyes of a murderer.

She was half his size, barefoot, and wearing only a pair of panties and the bathrobe. With all the strength that she could summon, she delivered a kick directly to his balls. He dropped the phone and doubled over. When he did, she clasped her hands around the back of his head and slammed his face into her right knee as she thrust it upward to his nose. She repeated this three more times, swinging her knee forcefully in an upward arch while pulling his head down to meet it. She had learned the maneuver in a Krav Maga class. The Zeta's pain caused the mountain of his body to crumble enough that she could get by him. Yelling a half-scream, half-grunt, he pitched farther into the bathroom while she rushed from the bedroom to the hallway. Two men were in the hall. One of them, she supposed, was the man who had returned to report the results of his reconnaissance.

"Help me!" Valentina screamed. "I think Raúl is having a heart attack in the bathroom!" She ran back into the bedroom, and they followed. She let them rush past to the bathroom, and then she bounded into the hall. Behind her she heard the confused men asking the Zeta what was happening. He was struggling to answer, but he still had the breath knocked out of him and could only rasp sounds. She knew that she only had moments to escape.

She flew into the kitchen and went straight for the block of knives. She grabbed a large butcher knife. When she returned to the door, one of the men who had been elsewhere in the house appeared and lunged at her. She plunged the knife into his abdomen, extracted it, and shoved him aside. Sprinting past the washer and dryer, she opened the door to the garage, found the light switch, and punched the button that would open the large garage door to the driveway. She pulled the door to the house behind her shut, but she could hear men shouting and cursing inside, including now the voice of Raúl.

The fluorescent lights of the garage flickered on, and, to Valentina's astonishment, she didn't see any cars, trucks or motorcycles. The garage was filled with four-wheel ATVs! They were different brands and shapes. Names came into view - Arctic Cat, Polaris, and Suzuki - but she had no time to consider the meaning of her discovery.

The electrical switch panel was on the wall to her left. She had to make a decision: throw the main switch to cut power to the house, or keep electricity so that she could lower the garage door behind her when she ran out.

Damn! she thought. *I don't know if the switch box would cut the lights outside along the driveway...plus there are street lights out there*, she remembered.

She decided to hit the garage door button. As it began lowering, she heard men at the door behind her. She darted across the garage and bent down low enough to get outside, just seconds before the door touched the floor behind her.

But in a moment the garage door began to raise again. One of the men behind her had hit the door-opening button on the wall. Valentina observed the long, well-lit driveway to the gate. She didn't believe that she would have enough time to learn how to open the gate even if she made it there. Someone had always done that from the house.

They can see me for a clear shot if I'm in the open in the driveway.

She remembered that the privacy wall enclosed the property. She only knew what was in the back of the house from what she had been able to see from windows, and that had been a partial view. But she thought that her only hope might be to run in the back and find a place to hide long enough for help to arrive. That hope rested in the text message which she had sent to Enrique earlier. Therefore, she decided to head to the rear of the house.

And that was when she tripped!

A concrete drainage slab located at the corner of the garage caused her to stumble to the ground. While falling, she felt the possibility of her escape smash to pieces on the ground. She also thought that she heard an animal thudding across the roof above her.

What the hell is that? she wondered.

A group of three of the Zeta's men ran from the garage and appeared over her, one with his extended arm pointing a pistol.

"Shoot her!" she heard Raúl commanding from inside the garage. At the same moment, engines of the four-wheelers began to fire up.

The man took a shot, but Valentina instinctively rolled to the side when she heard Raúl give his command. The shot missed her.

But something else had thrown off the shooter's aim: It looked like a long black animal had dropped from the roof of the garage onto the shoulders of the three men who had bunched together in front of Valentina. The animal's weight and momentum pushed the men to the ground. The man who had shot at Valentina fell close to her. Moving quickly, she slashed his arm with the knife that she was still holding. Screaming in pain, the man released his pistol and Valentina snatched it. She knew this weapon from the feel of it, plus she had seen some of Raúl's men with these. It was a Glock 20. She had practiced target shooting with this and many other types of pistols, but she liked the Glock. The weapon gave her an immediate feeling of control over her life for the first time in a week. She threw the knife into the darkness. She no longer needed it.

She got up and put her back to the wall of the garage. The black animal that had jumped on the men raised up to its full tall form, and she recognized him.

Enrique! Dios! It's Enrique!

But she didn't have time to shout his name.

The first of the three fallen men to recover his stance raised to fire at Enrique, but the leader of the Zs was ready. He did a trademark Z maneuver: He jumped into the air with a spin and knocked the man insensible with a kick to his head.

Now the man from whom Valentina had wrested the Glock was trying to encircle his uninjured arm around her legs to pull her to the ground. Losing balance, Valentina fired the pistol, and the shot went through the man's neck. The reactive jerk of his body brought Valentina down underneath him. The main weight of his body pinned her pistol arm to the ground.

So Valentina was helpless to save Enrique when she saw that the third Zeta was now up and preparing to fire his gun at Enrique. She wasn't going to have enough time to get her arm free for a shot at him!

All around Valentina there was total confusion of lights and engine noise. From the garage came the revving sounds of the four-wheelers and the beams of headlights. In the street were the insistent sirens of vehicles approaching rapidly and shouts of people at the entrance gate.

She decided to scream, hoping to distract the shooter from a good shot at Enrique. As loudly as she could, she called out, "Enrique!"

She squirmed from underneath the body on top of her. Just as she stood, she was astonished to see another young man in black drop down from the garage roof onto the back of Enrique's would-be shooter. This gave Enrique the opportunity to rush forward and disable the assailant with blows to his wrist and neck. When the man dropped his pistol, Enrique scooped it up.

But he wasn't fast enough to save the friend who had jumped down to rescue him. Firing his pistol repeatedly, another of the Zeta's men rushed from the garage with the gunshots that took down the young Z. When Valentina realized what was happening, she whirled around and without hesitation blasted the Z's attacker. The force of her shots caused the Zeta's man to fall backwards into the garage.

Raúl and the two remaining Zetas weren't going to wait longer. Three four-wheelers revved loudly and pitched into the driveway. The first one turned sharply just after emerging, and its headlight bore into Valentina's eyes. Raúl was driving it. Valentina wasn't expecting the turn of the ATV in her direction. She froze in the light. Raúl raised his pistol and shot her. She felt the bullet hit her left shoulder, and she collapsed beside the body of the man she had cut and shot. But instinctively, she tugged his arm to pull him up enough to make a partial shield. This move made a second shot at her more difficult, but Raúl attempted to find his mark anyway. When Valentina realized that he was aiming at her head, she ducked to the side enough for the bullet to miss her, but the ricochet fragmented pieces of the garage wall behind her head. One struck her hard. The potent blow left her stunned for a moment.

Apparently determining that he had no more time to lose, Raúl roared past, and the two other four-wheelers began to follow. It was odd, but Valentina noticed even in her dazed moments that Raúl had grabbed a jacket and loafers, but he was still in his undershorts.

Suddenly she heard Enrique yell a command to a dark-haired gringo who had appeared: "Eddie, tend to Valentina! Call an ambulance!"

She was feeling physically unsteady, and her shoulder was bleeding, but she collected herself enough to focus her attention. She saw Enrique jump on the small rear seat of the last four-wheeler as its driver was beginning to follow El Zeta and the other companion. Enrique struck the driver on the back of his head with the butt of the pistol he had taken and pushed the man off the ATV. As Enrique slipped into the driver's seat, Eddie ran to the fallen Zeta and beat him until he stopped moving. Then quickly he began rummaging the man's clothing for weapons.

Valentina mustered all her strength to stand. She kept her eyes on Enrique. He was fiddling with buttons and the gear shifter as if learning the controls of the ATV. Then suddenly he lurched it forward and sped toward the back of the house in pursuit of the Zeta and the other man.

At that moment, Eddie approached her. Valentina told him authoritatively, "I'm all right! Come with me!" She slid her hand along the side of the house for support her as she moved to the back as Eddie followed. Valentina hoped that she and Eddie might get to see where the ATVs had gone.

What she saw when she got to the rear of the house was astonishing: A straight section of the privacy wall that secluded the opposite side of the house was missing! The gap was clearly large enough for cars and pick-up trucks to pass through.

And four-wheelers! Valentina noted with wonder.

By then she heard voices and vehicles in the entrance drive of the home, and she realized that people had managed to open the gate to the driveway. A few young men in black clothing rushed up to her. Eddie had put his arm behind her back to support her, which was good because Valentina was feeling warm and dim. She watched as two of the Zs ran to the hole in the wall.

Before she lost consciousness in the swirl of dizziness and heat, she heard one of them yell, "Incredible! The wall lowered into the ground!"

Enrique Santos
Las Vegas, Nevada
Tuesday Night

401

When the report came to Agent Ricotto that all the cars in the church parking lot had been reported stolen, Enrique and he had let out the same expletive together:

"Shit!"

"Then that has to be the house where El Zeta is!" Enrique had said. "We've got to get a closer look and find a way in! There must be security cameras and alarms around the place, so we need to locate those."

He had decided to call David to discuss everything: the eighteen-wheeler that had arrived earlier, the loading of the truck, the neighbor's observations, the strange wall, the low-flying plane, and, now, the stolen cars just down the street.

"I'm with Nick Easter from the FBI," David had responded. "We're across town, but we'll be on our way. I think this is interesting enough to give a heads up to the Bureau and the DEA. Eddie can handle the DEA."

"Sí! Some police are on the way to look at the cars already. As for the DEA, we have been talking to them throughout the day."

"Okay, make sure Agent-in-Charge Zolinsky is aware there. I'll give Ana a call too. She's still at The Rio keeping an eye on Corvette."

Enrique, Eugenio and Martin had helped Eddie climb over the privacy wall in a shadowy area, and then the four had made their way unseen to the house. The home was mainly ranch style, but there was a partial second story on the end of the house opposite the garage. That story, with its rear windows, held promise for entry into the home. On that end of the house, the four had silently climbed to the A-frame roof when a man came out of the front door and drove off in the GMC parked in front. They had lain out of view on the other side of the roof and had listened to him drive away. They didn't hear noise in the house except for a muffled murmur of a television. They had tried to figure out the configuration of the rooms below them. They hadn't had much time to determine that plus find exhaust vents and learn the topography of the roof, about ten minutes

402

or so, when the GMC returned through the gate. They had watched the man re-enter the house. It was just a minute or two later when Enrique had received the text message from Valentina. By that moment the four had spread out to different sections of the roof.

Enrique's heart nearly arrested when his phone vibrated with her message. In his excitement after reading it, he immediately forwarded it in a broadcast mail that went to David, Ana, the DEA, the FBI, the Sheriff's department, and the state police.

But immediately after sending it, he realized that he had made an error:

Santa Madre! Valentina wrote, "Yandel Sandoval's home on Fortunada Avenue." He doesn't live on Fortunada Avenue! That's going to confuse everyone! How many law-enforcement people will go to the wrong place?

He didn't have time for a correction message to be sent. He had seen Valentina emerge from the garage and then trip to the ground as men came out and stood before her! One was pointing a pistol at her. He had instinctively run to jump them. The split-second decisions made during the fight and gunfire that ensued amazed him. Even Valentina had shot two people!

Now he was driving the four wheeler in pursuit of the Zeta and an accomplice. He had a problem. He had only driven an ATV a couple of times before in his life for brief periods, and that had been a while back. Fortunately, this one that he was driving was automatic, but there were still choices like two-wheel drive, four-wheel drive, high gear, low gear, and reverse boost. Plus, there were skills in turning and leaning and rising from the seat that came with practice. The latter he didn't have.

But he had started off after them thinking that they would become trapped in the back yard or that there might be a race around the house and to the front gate, and he knew that help was probably on the way. But when he rounded the corner of the house in the rear, he arrived in time to see the second four-wheeler drive through the hole in the wall.

403

Mierda! he thought. *Shit!*

He managed to maneuver through the hole and take his turn in the direction they had gone. When he had jumped the driver, the man had already turned on the headlight of the vehicle. But the Zeta and companion had killed their lights and were bumping their way as silhouettes toward the street. Enrique knew where they were heading: the desert. The two ahead of him obviously knew how to drive the things. They were leaving him behind. He saw them shoot across Fortunada Avenue and go straight into the desert. He felt despair.

Enrique slowed out of caution when he arrived at the road. Looking right toward the gate, he saw a couple of unmarked cars of law enforcement screech to a stop at the entrance. Some of the Zs who had come at his request earlier started running to them and pointing in his direction. No doubt they were telling the arrivals about the men escaping on four-wheelers into the desert. But when Enrique looked to the left, his heart leapt with joy. David's Corvette was barreling toward him at full speed, its pipes roaring full-throated!

He eased the four wheeler across the street and stopped as David braked the Corvette to a dime-stop right beside him. The driver's door flew open and David jumped out and ran to him.

"Let me on that thing, Enrique! Jump off! I can drive it!" David commanded as he ran toward Enrique. Enrique put the machine in neutral and got off, but when David jumped in the driver's seat and began moving, Enrique quickly mounted the small passenger seat and grabbed the passenger-hold bars.

"Shit!" David yelled in response to Enrique's action, but there was no more time to waste. David sped into the desert like a demon.

When Enrique had taken the pistol from his attacker, he had shoved it into the back waist of his pants. Now, bumping and jolting in his seat, he worried that it might fire; but he didn't dare take his hands from the bars. He was holding them with all his might just to stay on the vehicle. He squinted against the wind to attempt a look forward from around the side of David to see if he could see the two four-wheelers that they were pursuing. He only saw darkness and silhouettes of land shapes.

He knew that David was pissed that he had jumped on.

Maybe my weight slows us down! he realized, suddenly horrified by his rash decision.

But he did bring something that David might need. So he yelled into his ear, "I have a pistol!"

He didn't fire weapons, but he knew that David had done this throughout his career with the CIA. He was an excellent shot.

"Shit!" David said again, and then, "Ok, Enrique! But this is messed up, man!"

It was one of David's favorite sayings. Enrique knew that he was already forgiven. David was a man who adapted and made decisions in micro-seconds.

All of it had happened so fast. He had felt such relief to see David arrive at the very moment when he didn't feel adequate to the task of following the Zeta. He hadn't had a clue what he would do in the event that he would catch up to the two men. But when David had rushed up to him, in the lights of the Corvette he had seen the ferocity in David's eyes. David would know what to do. David had that maturity of experience for which Enrique yearned. Enrique wanted his eyes to be like David's.

Of course I jumped on the back of the four-wheeler! Enrique thought. *Every time I hitch myself to David, I ride into history!*

He ran up to the female paramedic standing at the rear of the ambulance, near its open doors. Ana, Raymundo, Jupiter, and his mother had sprung behind him from the SUV that Ana had driven. With all the police cars and vehicles filling the street, the closest that Ana had been able to maneuver was about a block's distance away from the house on Fortunada Avenue. But they were close enough for them to see the paramedics loading a stretcher with a woman who had long dark hair. This time Corvette knew who she was.

Corvette had sprinted to the ambulance almost as fast as a Z. He saw that its rear doors were still open.

"I'm riding to the hospital with her!" Corvette shouted. "That's my wife, Valentina!"

"You're her husband?" the woman asked him uncertainly. She looked at the absence of a wedding ring on his finger. "I don't think so!" she told him.

"Yes, he is!" Raymundo affirmed, arriving short of breath. "They just don't wear wedding rings for work purposes!"

"It's true!" Ana now announced, joining them. "It's important that he rides with her!"

"I'm telling you the truth! Please let me on!" Corvette said, sounding desperate. "Tell her that her husband has come all the way from Monterrey. We were supposed to go dancing again! Tell her!"

"Come on, Melissa, we've got to go!" a male voice shouted from the ambulance.

But Melissa had been staring at Corvette. She said, "You're Corvette Nightfire!" Then she lowered her voice to whisper, "What are you doing here?"

From the ambulance they all heard the weak but distinctly insistent voice of Valentina call out, "Let him on! He's mine! I need him!"

Corvette began bobbing up and down like an impatient child.

Melissa couldn't contain a trace of a grin while shaking her head. But it wasn't a negative shake of the head.

"Okay, get in there, Mr. Husband. Hurry! We have to go!"

David James
The Desert outside Las Vegas
Tuesday Night

He knew what he was driving. It was a Polaris 500cc Touring model with two seats. It had a top speed of about seventy miles per hour, but less in the desert. The desert terrain outside Las Vegas didn't require all-terrain-vehicles with large ground clearances in its wheels. The ride was jolting and more dangerous at night, but he knew that they were going fast enough, even with two passengers. This model had a strong power plant. He just didn't know what the other two were riding.

Plus, he didn't see a trace of them. From his car, he had watched the direction that they went when he saw them shoot across Fortunada Avenue and barrel into the desert. His route behind them was eastward. The lights of the city had blotted out the stars, but a half-moon hung high in the eastern sky. He had the headlight on but saw only desert in its narrow beam. He knew that somehow the Zeta and the other man were ahead riding without lights on.

What he was looking for was the same thing that they would be looking for:

The plane.

He was about to become discouraged when he thought that he heard the droning sounds of the four-wheelers a little to the southeast. He made a slight course correction. After about three or four minutes, the sounds became a bit louder, and then...he could no longer hear them!

Shit! he thought.

He pressed on, nevertheless. A minute later he began to hear one motor, and it sounded much closer than before. He heard also a new sound: the start-up of a single-engine plane. Moments later, like dark ghost figures, the sources of the noises came into view. Enrique saw them at the same time. "David, look!" he shouted.

The apparitions were silhouettes recognizable in their shapes. He saw the distinctive form of the Cessna 206 slowly taxiing to the left. It had no lights on, just the glow of the cockpit instruments, and, so far, it wasn't picking up speed. Straight ahead was a stationary four-wheeler. It was rider-less. But traveling at high speed away from them and more to the southeast was the other four-wheeler.

"David! The Zeta's getting away!" Enrique shouted in his ear.

David turned in the direction of the Cessna. Someone took a shot at them.

"Give me the pistol!" David commanded. Enrique risked taking a hand off the hold-bar to retrieve it from the back of his waist. He thrust it to David, who then held the pistol in his right hand while continuing to throttle the vehicle. He saw the big fat tires that the Cessna required for bush, mountain, and desert landings to stabilize it on uneven terrain. He just had to get close enough to shoot out those tires...

They were gaining rapidly on the plane. It continued to taxi slowly in a straight line.

Are they waiting for me to get closer for a gunfight? David wondered.

He maneuvered to the rear of the aircraft so that it would be more difficult for the men in the plane to fire at them. It also gave him opportunity to shoot the rear tires if he could get close enough.

He was getting closer quickly.

And that's when he realized his mistake.

No, no, no, no, no! he screamed in his mind.

Except that he hadn't done this in his mind. He had shouted out loud and Enrique had heard him.

"What's wrong?" Enrique demanded, with undisguised anxiety over David's outburst.

David fired two shots and blew out the rear tires of the Cessna. The aircraft fell back on its tail and convulsed along the sand a few moments before the engine cut off, choked by the sand dust. David wheeled the Polaris in a tight circle and full-throttled in the direction of the escaping four wheeler.

"David, what's going on? Why are you turning?"

"Fuck, Enrique," David shouted. "There's no one on the plane!"

"I don't understand! Someone on it took a shot at us!"

David was pushing the four-wheeler to its limit of speed in the sandy terrain. The bumping and jolting would leave them bruised for days.

"Someone shot at us, but not from the plane. The shooter was probably lying beside that ATV that wasn't moving! Can you hear it now?" he yelled.

David had begun hearing the sound of a single four-wheeler. The other one that they had seen before they had chased the plane was long gone.

Enrique affirmed that he heard one four wheeler.

"They set the plane in motion so we would follow it! That's why it drifted slowly in a straight line and never picked up speed. The Zeta and the pilot are on that first ATV we saw. I'm guessing that they're going to another pick-up place for the Zeta," David shouted in explanation. "We're following the other guy, and I can tell you, he's leading us away from the Zeta. He fucking got away, Enrique!"

"Oh my God, no, no!" Enrique cried, upset now like his friend. He pointed ahead, in the direction of the four-wheeler noise. "Then let's catch that puta and make him talk!"

But both of them knew that they weren't going to catch the man. They rode for several minutes until they could no longer hear the other motor.

David pulled to a stop in the middle of the nighttime desert expanse. He shut off the engine, and both dismounted and stood silently, nursing their injuries of body and soul. It was a while later, it didn't matter how long, when Enrique remembered something. It made him draw a long sigh, and when David looked at him, Enrique beat gently on his chest a couple of times and shared his reminder with David:

"We got Valentina back," he said softly. "I can't imagine the enormity of our loss if she were gone."

"God," David whispered. He closed his eyes, and his body suddenly shuddered from the release of his anger into the cold desert sky. He gave himself a couple of minutes to settle. He walked over to Enrique and put his arm around his friend's shoulder and gave him a quick squeeze of appreciation.

My life is rich with people who soothe me, he thought.

"Let's go home, Enrique," David said. "Let's go check on Valentina and our new friend, Corvette. Now there's an hombre with balls."

They both looked around as if trying to figure out which direction to go. They looked at the lights of Las Vegas in the distance, and then they looked at each other and broke out laughing.

David pointed and said, "I guess we go that way."

"I'll follow you," Enrique answered, and he climbed onto the passenger seat.

"Hmm. You're making jokes more often, Enrique. This is a good thing. But you should get off and let me get on first. It's easier for me that way."

Enrique chuckled and dismounted and got back on behind David. Before David started the engine, he said, "I don't really like Las Vegas so much. San Antonio is a nice place. I would like to see more of it. Perhaps I can come visit you there sometimes."

David knew that Enrique couldn't see him smiling. "Sure," he said. "Ana and I'll be pretty busy for a while. That's always the way with us. But when we can't do it, I'm sure Paula would love to show you a bit of the city."

"Dios, I wish she wasn't so young."

The engine roared. David's smile vanished as he thought of the Zeta. The Zeta still hadn't seen his eyes.

But he will, David promised himself.

Epilogue

Corvette Nightfire

In the ambulance, when Valentina lost consciousness a second time, Corvette had a panic attack and became short of breath. There had been too much stress. He thought that he had lost this woman when he lost to the Legend, and in the ambulance he worried that her head injury from the Zeta's shot was going to do her in after all.

He needn't have worried. Valentina recovered consciousness in the emergency room. It turned out that she had a slight bruising to the brain which gave her a temporary limp in her right leg but no damage to her ability to recall. She remembered every detail committed to her memory about the Zeta's activities, the house, the weapons, the ledger book, the vehicles, the cartel men who came and went, the communications gadgets, the visit to Ignacio, the celebration of the murder of El Asesino, and myriad other things. This information, which she was able to provide to the DEA, the FBI, and the police, led to several apprehensions and arrests of mid-level cartel figures whom Valentina could identify from her time in The Oasis and in the Zeta's house in Las Vegas.

Corvette played tournaments mainly in Texas while Valentina took a leave of absence from the DEA to sell her events planning business to the staff who so competently managed it. She also wanted the time to recover from what she herself regarded as psychological trauma with the Zeta. During this time, Corvette was able to come to Monterrey to be with her frequently. He took her dancing to heal her. Valentina's limp disappeared when he held her close. He kissed her neck when they danced, and with every kiss he heard her sorrows being carried away by her sighs and soft moans. In time she became in his arms as light as air and as carefree as joy.

He had his own demons to purge too. Valentina saw this in him. "We're both wounded warriors, honey," she told him one night.

"Yes, I thought I lost you when I lost the tournament," Corvette replied to her. "I dropped through the floor into the pit of hell at that moment. I couldn't believe that I lost after praying so hard! I even prayed to St. Rogelio."

"But you didn't lose!" Valentina responded. "Here I am alive, and I adore you! Corvette, you came to Monterrey for me! You came even when you couldn't speak Spanish. Then you played your heart out for my life and beat out seven other players. You did all this for me! You found purpose, Corvette, and made new friends. Your prayers were answered in ways you didn't expect. To me, you're the most amazing man of my life!"

Her words gave Corvette a boost, but restlessness stalked him. He puzzled over the unpredictable ups and downs of his emotions. Then one night when he was talking to Valentina, he saw Rogelio in his mind, and words burst from him in a swell of feelings:

"I want to finish what my dad tried to do! I want to give him peace. And me! I need to find my grandparents or whatever remains of their lives. I understand the half-British part of me, but I look Mexican. Where does that part come from? Am I indigenous? What ancestral DNA is at work in my life? I want to know! Once, Enrique introduced me to a Tarahumara Indian named Diego who had become a Z in Monterrey. Diego told me that my name, Nightfire, is a name that could live among his people. He had heard of a tribal family that used a similar name. Diego's people are scattered throughout the Copper Canyon in Chihuahua. Some of the Tarahumara are there because they reject the encroachment of civilization. My mum told me that she believed my grandparents sometimes were fugitives, not only from the law, but also from the cartels. They left my dad in Texas in a hurry and never came back for him. He looked for them. He never found them, but he came to believe that they might have returned to the place where they came from: among the Tarahumara in Chihuahua. Lately I can't stop thinking about this. It feels like my father wants me to go there."

"Then let's go find them," Valentina said without hesitation. "A good way to get into those mountains and the canyon is by train. I've done that as a tourist twice. I'll go with you! I have the time right now, and I have some money from selling the business."

Corvette was taken by surprise. "Hon, there could be arduous hiking. Your leg is still recovering."

"Then going there will help me heal faster," she said with determination on her face. "Look, I'm already walking with less limp. My legs are strong. My right one just hurts a bit at times."

The timing of the decision to go couldn't have been better. Corvette found out through Enrique that Diego had returned to his homeland after being frustrated that he couldn't find work that made him happy in Monterrey. Diego had a different world view than most of the people who lived in Monterrey. He had grown up close to nature in canyons quite dissimilar to the concrete canyons of the high rises in Monterrey. Even in the city of four million people, Diego had come to feel isolated and misunderstood. He decided to return to the cliffs and stony paths of the mountains in the area he knew as home. The only person in Monterrey who had seemed to love him was Enrique. Diego left him an e-mail address so that they could keep in touch.

When Enrique wrote Diego to tell him that Corvette and Valentina were coming to search for Corvette's ancestry, Diego responded with an enthusiastic volunteering to assist. He would meet them in Divisadero, an important rail stop in that part of the Sierra Madre Occidental Mountains. Valentina was familiar with the place from her previous visits to the mountains and canyons as a tourist.

It was mid-January when Corvette and Valentina met Diego there. His Spanish had improved enough that Valentina was able easily to understand him and translate for Corvette. They left

414

Divisadero and started the journey to find Corvette's grandparents immediately.

Many of the Tarahumara retreated into the depths of the canyons in the winters where it was much warmer than in the mountains. Diego led them deep along paths that had been trodden by his people for centuries. They camped overnight in rocky shelters of ledges or caves. The steep descent was at times painful for Corvette after a long hike. He worried, therefore, about Valentina's leg and endurance. She would be quiet long periods, but she insisted that she was okay. She was wide-eyed at the beauty around them.

Whenever they encountered people, Diego made inquiries whether they knew anyone using the name "Fuego de Noche." No one did, but Diego recalled meeting an old man who lived "in this deep place," and that once the man had mentioned this name to him. He was taking Corvette and Valentina there in the hope that the man would still be around.

Eventually they came to the place where Diego had last seen the old man who might know the people who called themselves Fuego de Noche. It was a tent encampment at the bottom of the canyon rim. The community swelled in population during the winter from about fifty people to around four hundred. The year-round residents lived in caves and in homes made under rock ledges where stones had been added to make walls. This encampment was about 40 kilometers from a little village known as Urique on the maps.

Diego found an ancient woman and inquired about the old man.

"He has died," she reported. Diego explained this in Spanish to Valentina, and then he went into a long conversation with the woman in their native tongue. Eventually the old woman beckoned them to follow her, and she led them a short distance outside the encampment to a cave dwelling. She pointed to another "anciano" sitting at a fire by the entrance of the cave, which was apparently the doorway to his home. Then she left.

Diego opened conversation with this elderly man, occasionally pointing to Corvette and gesturing to explain Corvette's presence. Then Diego rose and brought the old man to stand in front of Corvette. As Diego spoke, the old man traced his fingers around Corvette's eyes and peered deeply. Corvette assumed that the man had visual difficulties, but he remembered that once Diego had told him that he had the eyes of the Tarahumara. Finally, the old man nodded as if he had satisfied himself about something, and he ambled into the cave.

Diego's smile was that of victory. He explained to Valentina, "This man is the brother of the man who used a name that means "fire-of-night." He says that his brother and his wife had disappeared for many years into the States, into Texas. His brother told them that country deported them to Chihuahua because it suspected them of bringing drugs into the United States. The brother didn't come back here to the Tarahumara until years after his wife died. The brother told him that, no, they didn't transport drugs, but that they ran stolen cars between Mexico and the USA for one of the Mexican cartels. When they came to Mexico, they left their baby with a gringo couple in Texas because they were certain that they would be tracked and killed by the cartel. This was because they had been skimming some of the money from the car sales. They had done this out of financial desperation. The cartels didn't pay them well and often tried to cheat them because they were Indians. They hid from the cartel many years in different towns in Mexico when they could find labor. When the wife died, the brother came here."

"Where did that name come from?" Corvette asked.

Diego's smile grew bigger. "This man's brother had a favorite car. He stole it and hid it in Mexico just before the USA did the deportation. It was a very fast one that he sometimes took out on country roads at night. He claimed that fire sometimes shot from behind the car. The old man has a box that he's getting for us. It has some of his brother's things."

416

The old man returned with a beat-up cigar box and motioned for everyone to sit on the ground. He peered deeply into Corvette's eyes again and then handed Corvette the box. Suddenly Corvette could feel himself trembling. He tried to steady his hands as he raised the lid. Inside were a bunch of old keys, some quarters and dimes from the USA, odd things like whistles and tie clasps, some silver bracelets and rings, a black-beaded rosary, a folded piece of paper, and five crinkled black-and-white Polaroid photographs that were turned upside down.

The first one was a picture of a very pretty young Indian girl leaning against a wooden cattle fence in a flat agricultural area that might have been Texas. A crease in the photograph marred her face, but she obviously was a beauty.

Valentina moved next to Corvette and held onto his right arm. "I think you're looking at your grandmother, Corvette!" she whispered.

The next picture showed a couple in the same location. In this photograph the woman looked a few years older. She was leaning against a man dressed in dungarees and a light-colored short-sleeve shirt with faint vertical stripes.

Valentina gasped, and Corvette said, "Oh my God!"

The man in the picture was a dead ringer for Corvette. He had a mustache, but his dark hair was long and nearly shoulder length like Corvette's. Even Diego, who was observing over their shoulders, said something equivalent to, "Wow!"

"You look like your grandfather!" Valentina exclaimed.

What came next was almost equally a shock. Two of the pictures were of a car. The third photograph was taken through the windshield of the car. It showed a thin metal plate with an inscription of numbers and letters: a car vehicle identification number.

The grandson of the couple in the photographs, Corvette Fuego de Noche, stared at the car pictures a long time, looking at the curves and slant of the two-seater coupe and, especially, at its rear window which was bisected in the middle by a strip of car body that flowed from the roof to the car's rear. Corvette was looking at the model of vehicle that Chevrolet made only one year, in 1963.

"This is a 1963 Corvette Sting Ray," he explained to Valentina. "Most people call it the split-window-coupe. It's widely regarded as one of the most beautiful sports cars ever designed. I can't believe this! My grandfather had a Corvette!"

The old man, Corvette's great-uncle, began speaking again, saying something to Diego. Diego then translated for Valentina so the information could be passed along to Corvette:

"The car was red," Valentina explained. "When your grandfather died, his brother went to the place where the car was hidden and sold it. That paper in the box has the information on it about who bought the car back then. As you can see, having paper like this would be a big deal, Corvette. The Tarahumara who live in the mountains usually don't own things. So your great-uncle took pains to save this information in case anyone ever should need it. He says that since your grandfather died, he expected that one day your father would be the one who would show up."

Corvette was afraid that if he spoke, his voice would crack from emotion. Valentina brushed a tear from his cheek with her hand.

"This is all so amazing," Corvette said after a few minutes. "I want to find this car! My dad always loved Corvettes. I want to find this car. It should have been his inheritance. I really hope I can do this. I want to get it for him." He sat with his emotions a few moments more, and then he kissed Valentina warmly. He rose and went to the old man and helped him stand. Corvette towered over the shrunken gentleman, but he stooped low and pulled the man into a hug. "Uncle," he addressed him. Diego translated, but the old man already understood. He smiled and nodded happily.

Before they left Chihuahau two days later, they bid farewell to Diego at the train station in Divisadero. Corvette had been mulling something in his mind since he had spent this time with Diego. In a long conversation with him about some unusual

418

personal habits that Diego had, Corvette had discovered a unique mathematical talent that Diego possessed. He wanted to discuss this with the higher-ups of The Z Foundation. Corvette knew that he would have their ear. He had made a big impact on David, Ana, and Enrique when he had played in the poker tournament for Valentina's life. After he had collected his winnings from it and had paid taxes, he received four million dollars. He gave his mum the money to pay off his father's gambling debts; then he gave The Z Foundation a million dollars. He pledged that he would continue to help The Z Foundation financially from then on.

So he said to Diego, "Diego, I have something to discuss with Enrique and David James when we get back to Monterrey. It's regarding you. I think there's very meaningful work that you can do to help either David or The Z Foundation. It should pay well and challenge you in ways that will make you a happy person. Okay with you for me to talk with them about these things and then get back to you, perhaps by e-mail?"

Diego waited for Valentina's translation, and then he replied, "Of course! I'm still a seeker!"

The Sting Ray had been sold by Corvette's great uncle in 1974. Corvette spent a couple of months of research tracking the vehicle identification number, following leads, making phone calls, and sending e-mails to trace the car, which had passed through several owners through the years. The end result was to discover that the Corvette currently was in the hands of a Chevrolet car-dealer in Monterrey! The dealer had been the personal owner of the vehicle for the past seven years.

It required several meetings to convince him, but the dealer finally relented in the face of Corvette's story of family history and the symbolic meaning of the car returning to its rightful place. He sold the car to Corvette.

Enrique went wild when he saw it. The dealer had restored the Sting Ray to its original condition. It had power steering, power brakes, power windows, and even air-conditioning. "I think we should drive it to San Antonio and surprise David," he suggested. "He has a new red Stingray. He should see its heritage."

"Like I've seen mine," Corvette replied. "Yeah, let's take it up there. I have a tournament in that area the weekend after next. When we're about to go into San Antonio, I'll open it up on the road for my dad. He'll finally be home."

David Wilson James

The thirsty Stingray gulped high-octane fuel desperately because of what David demanded: a back-pressed-against-the-seat charge through the dark Texas desert. In the driver's seat, David felt the spit and gastric juices churning up a war inside his body. He felt as hot as his car's engine. He thrust the Corvette past his comfortable cruising speed of one-five-zero, a speed that was a walk in the park for the Corvette. In the past, he had wondered about the safe limits for man and car on a Texas highway. Tonight he didn't care about feeling safe. It was one of those nights since the Zeta got away that David couldn't sleep. He managed okay in the daytime. He was making progress with his computer models that helped find cartel money-laundering centers. In the sunshine he smiled and maintained calm. He was professional and efficient at work. He helped Ana's kids with their homework projects, and he seemed to balance work and play. But at night the obsession to find the Zeta came out of its black hole to eat David alive.

The Texas troopers had become accustomed to his after-midnight runs. They allowed him slack because he picked a straight stretch of highway when no one else was there. They knew David and what he did: They knew that he fought the bad guys from Mexico and the United States and that he did it with the Zs in very creative ways. They knew that he had close friends in high places, like the President of the United States, and that he slept with a woman who briefly had been Interim President of Mexico. She was now his wife. The troopers respected him, so they gave him the pass to burn the fuel of his Corvette and the sludge of his dark previous life with these fiery runs through the night.

David owned one of the first-made seventh-generation Corvettes. The Sting Ray was back, but unlike that of the second generation in the nineteen-sixties, its moniker was one word: Stingray. His was Torch Red, but no one could see its color in the midnight blackness of the Texas wilderness. To the troopers, the Corvette missile streaking past them was a sound and a light trail. They clocked him for amusement. A new recruit had gone after David once, and when David was done, he had pulled up behind him to give him his ticket. But something unfathomable in David's eyes, some purity of resolve, impressed the young trooper that David was a man of fierce commitment to secret crusades for the good. He let David off with an admonishment to "be careful out there." He didn't understand why he did it, but he felt right in his heart for letting the incident pass. He told other troopers about this, and they nodded their understanding.

Before, David sped to appease the memory-demons of his previous life. But on this particular night, the rage of speed was a protest of his lost battle: The Zeta had escaped him.

The Zeta had taken the money of The Z Foundation. Almost all of it. He had killed people to do it. Instead of killing Ana, instead of killing David, he had fired his AK-47 into the hopes and dreams of the Zs. He had wanted murder of spirit. But now David knew that things would be different. The Zeta would come specifically for him and Ana.

Nothing about his life had been normal or logical, David realized. He had found out that life did not have to be logical. It only had to have purpose.

David zipped through five of the seven gears and held. The car was hungry for the run. David saw one-eighty-six. He began a howl that started deep-throated but ascended into soprano-baying, in synch with the muscular acceleration of the Corvette. He saw one-ninety-six. Maintaining the car in fifth gear, David wailed the final notes of his madness-prayer as long as he could.

He could hear how he sounded: mournful; in stark contrast to what he suddenly felt, which was joyous! The reason was that the Stingray somehow was crying with him to God! Soon the rabid roar of the car's engine drowned his last dry notes. He smashed into the wall of breathlessness. His inhale came so violently that the shoulder harness locked against his heaving chest. His eyes filled with tears. He had seen two hundred and two! He was exhilarated! He knew that victory next time wouldn't elude him. He would find the Zeta!

I know, God. It's personal. With the cartels, it's always personal. But you forgive me!

He braked the car through a whistling deceleration. When the Stingray was almost stopped, he turned it perpendicular to the highway and pointed it to the east, a symbolic gesture. A distant thunderstorm shot thunderbolts like fire across the sky. Valentina had told him that she thought the Zeta was going to the Deep South. He stared in that direction.

He had the resources of a nation at his disposal.

He had an army: Ana, Enrique, and the Zs.

He had allies with special talents: Corvette and Valentina, and now Diego with the unique math skills that Corvette had discovered.

And he had an enemy: the Zeta.

He smelled him in New Orleans. He would find him there and show him his eyes. The Zeta would see in them a life filled with purpose.

The Zeta, Z-30

He wasn't accustomed to waiting for anyone. He was already leery because he had been in one city too long. It reminded him of the mistake that he had made in Las Vegas. He should have left there sooner. Valentina had robbed him of a little of his sense. He was enraged with her. She had chosen Corvette after all. It had been a bad night when he had barely escaped with David James nipping at his heels. Now he suspected that the man was on the road that would lead to the entrance to El Camino Oscuro (The Dark Road).

But he shouldn't be able to figure out how to open its gate, he thought, *unless Ignacio somehow passed him clues. Even then, it should be impossible.*

The thought of this made him antsy. He really needed to leave this city. Besides, in February, New Orleans was just uncomfortable: either rain-chilled, or humid, cloudy and windy.

He looked out on Jackson Square to see if El Ruso was approaching. He was worried a bit because he didn't know that much about Russian culture, and he liked to know everything that influenced a man. The Russian was powerful. He had been an early land-grabber in the territory of the Deep Web. He was experienced there, and the Zeta was still a novice. The Zeta wasn't naïve. He knew that the Russian was only coming to the table because he had what the Russian wanted: access to the plazas, business lines, and laundering centers of the Americas. Both he and El Ruso wanted to migrate these to the Deep Web. Both of them had organizational challenges and competitors. Both of them had allies and enemies. These were constantly shifting, the Zeta realized.

But I do have some enemies who are constant, and David James and Ana Valdez are their leaders, he reminded himself. *The next time, I won't be fooled by them. I need to remove them from my list of worries. Now! Immediately! I'll have enough problems figuring out how to work with a man such as the Russian.*

A successful alliance between the Zeta and the Russian would connect the now-patchwork El Camino Oscuro of the West to the bloody digital-asphalt sections of the Eastern Way. They could build across the entire planet a private digital highway that would facilitate indiscoverable illegal transactions. Such a global autobahn in the Deep would require international standards and a common language of numbers. There was much work to be done.

From his window table in the café, the Zeta began to see Slavic-looking men scattered among his own bodyguards in the square. El Ruso was coming.

Corvette Nightfire

On the Thursday of their trip to San Antonio, it wasn't until after sunset before they finally got through the back-up of cars trying to pass through the border to Laredo. It was fully dark on Interstate 35 by the time that they were halfway between Laredo and their destination. Forty miles from San Antonio they reached a long flat stretch where there were no other headlights of vehicles on the road.

Enrique looked at Corvette. "Are you ready to see what she can do?"

"Oh yeah!" Corvette growled. He had been thinking of his father. "This one is for you, Rogelio!"

He downshifted from fourth gear to third, letting the car slow a bit, but the revs in third said "Feed me!" The car was ready. He pushed the accelerator and shifted up to fourth gear at eighty miles per hour. The old car did fine breaking through one-hundred-twenty miles per hour and beyond. Suddenly Corvette saw a spark of light in his rearview mirror.

"Dios!" Enrique shouted. "Was that a flame coming from the tailpipe?"

Corvette removed his foot from the accelerator and looked nervously in the mirror.

"I don't know," he said. He didn't want the car to be on fire.

424

But he did think that a flame had shot from the tailpipe.

When he looked again in the mirror, he saw in the far distance the flashing lights of a Texas state trooper racing up behind them.

"Oh-oh," Corvette announced.

Enrique turned and looked through the split rear glass. He began to laugh.

"David will be proud of you," he said. "The two of you are definitely cut from the same mold."

Corvette sighed. He slowed and began to pull over so that the trooper could gain on them.

While they waited, Corvette looked at his friend and said, "I'm happy now, Enrique. I like playing poker, but I'll play a little less. I want to help you, Diego, David, and Ana with the work ahead: That of the numbers. I'm good with those, you know. And I'll show up sometimes where Valentina has assignments. It's magic when we dance together. In fact, I want a lifetime of that."

Enrique smiled. "There will be a lifetime of work ahead for you if you want it, Corvette. Evil never dies. A lot of good people need our help."

The trooper arrived and requested Corvette's license and registration. He then walked around the car and looked it over. Returning to the window, he asked, "Where's the fire, son?"

Corvette gave a sheepish smile and responded, "Officer, you wouldn't believe me if I told you."

The trooper nodded. "You're probably right. When you've been on the job as long as I have, you've heard just about everything. But your car is beautiful, and there aren't many of these. It has a place in history. You need to take care of it."

"Yes, sir, I will," Corvette replied, not knowing how to explain that he was speeding into San Antonio for his father. Enrique was quiet too. The silence became awkward.

"I could charge you with reckless driving, you know," the trooper finally said, "but for some reason, I don't know why, I'm inclined to give you a break. You think you can obey speed limits from now on?"

Corvette nodded.

"Be careful out there," cautioned the trooper, handing him a citation for speeding.

As the policeman walked away, Corvette watched him in the mirror. For a moment, Corvette thought that he looked like St. Rogelio.

The End

About The Authors

Daniel Wetta grew up in Richmond, Virginia. He loved to imagine adventures, write short stories, and pretty much embellish everything in his ordinary life, especially to get laughs. He ended up graduating from The College of William and Mary with a B.A. in History. Later he became a Certified Public Accountant after completing the accounting curriculum in the Graduate School of Business at Virginia Commonwealth University. While serving as CFO and CEO of a Virginia hospital, Mr. Wetta obtained his Master's in Business Administration from the University of Dallas. He currently resides in Williamsburg, Virginia, where live his wife, Judy; two married daughters, Keira and April; five grandchildren; and his father, Daniel Sr., a lifetime artist.

Contact http://danielwetta.com/contact-information/

E-mail: cursillo86@gmail.com

Robert Selfe, a retired career educator, also grew up in Richmond, Virginia. He graduated from the University of South Florida with a degree in Mass Communications/English Education. He worked at several schools and spent his last thirty years teaching English at Ridgewood High School in New Port Richey, Florida. Mr. Selfe served as Editor for *The Z Redemption* by Daniel Wetta and as Editor and story contributor to *Corvette Nightfire*. He wrote sections of the novel in *Corvette Nightfire* that featured the poker hands and play at the World Series of Poker. Mr. Selfe's family in Florida includes his wife, Carolyn, and their son, Michael.

E-mail: robertselfe@gmail.com

www.ingramcontent.com/pod-product-compliance
Lightning Source LLC
Chambersburg PA
CBHW071637260626
47170CB00001B/142